THE WORLD'S MOST SUCCESSFUL NOVELIST!

Since the publication of his first novel, *Never Love a Stranger,* he has consistently topped the bestseller lists with such titles as *The Pirate, The Carpetbaggers, The Adventurers,* and *A Stone for Danny Fisher.* It is estimated that more than 25,000 people around the world buy a Robbins novel every day.

Translated into 32 languages, his books have sold over 150,000,000 copies to date, and with the phenomenal success of his latest bestsellers, *The Lonely Lady* and *Dreams Die First,* he is well on the way to his second hundred million.

"HAROLD ROBBINS IS A MASTER OF SEXPLOITATION!"
—*Playboy*

HAROLD ROBBINS

The Betsy

A KANGAROO BOOK
PUBLISHED BY POCKET BOOKS NEW YORK

POCKET BOOKS, a Simon & Schuster division of
GULF & WESTERN CORPORATION
1230 Avenue of the Americas, New York, N.Y. 10020

Copyright © 1971 by Harold Robbins

Published by arrangement with Simon & Schuster, Inc.
Library of Congress Catalog Card Number: 74-169136

ISBN: 0-671-81885-6

First Pocket Books printing July, 1972

15th printing

Trademarks registered in the United States and other countries.

Printed in the U.S.A.

This Book Is Dedicated
With Love
To My Wife,
GRACE
for whom the name—
and the word—
were created.

The Betsy

Book One
1969

I WAS sitting up in bed, sipping hot coffee, when the nurse came into the room. The English girl with the big tits. She got busy right away with the drapes at the window, pulling them back so that more daylight spilled into the room.

"Good morning, Mr. Perino," she said.

"Good morning, Sister," I answered.

"Today is the big day, isn't it?" She smiled.

"Yeah."

"Dr. Hans will be here any minute," she said.

Suddenly I had to pee. I swung my feet off the bed. She took the coffee cup from my hand. I went into the john. I didn't bother closing the door. After one month here nothing was private any more.

The water burst from me with a reassuring force. When I finished I turned to the sink to wash my hands. The white bandages covering my face stared back at me from the mirror. I wondered what I looked like beneath them. I would find out soon enough. Then a funny thought crossed my mind:

If my ass itched would I scratch my face?

She had a hypo waiting when I came back into the room. I stopped. "What's that for?"

1

"Dr. Hans ordered it. A mild tranquilizer. He likes his patients relaxed when the bandages come off."

"I'm calm."

"I know," she said. "But let's do it anyway. It will make him feel better. Give me your arm."

She was very good. There was only the faintest ping when she hit me. She led me to the chair near the window. "Now, sit down and let me make you nice and comfy."

I sat and she wrapped the light blanket around my legs and fluffed a pillow behind my head. "Now, rest a bit," she said, going to the door, "and we'll be back in a little while."

I nodded and she went out. I turned to the window. The sun poured down on the summer snow topping the Alps. A man walked by, dressed in Tyrolean shorts. A crazy thought jumped through my head.

"Do you yodel, Angelo?"

"Of course I yodel, Angelo," I answered myself. "Don't all Italians yodel?"

I dozed.

I was eight years old when I first met him. It was 1939 in a little park where my nurse often took me to play. I was pedaling the miniature racing car my grandfather had given me for my birthday. He had it especially made in Italy for me. With the leather straps over the hood, electric headlamps that worked, it was an exact replica of the Type 59 Bugatti that set the record at Brooklands in 1936, even down to the oval Bugatti insignia on the radiator.

I was pedaling madly down the path when I saw them in front of me. The tall nurse pushing the man in the wheelchair. I slowed down and honked my horn.

The nurse looked back over her shoulder and moved her chair slightly toward the right side of the path.

I swung left and began to pass her, but by then there was a slight incline and, pedal as hard as I could, all I could manage was to keep even with them.

The man in the wheelchair spoke first. "That's quite a machine you got there, son."

I looked over at him, still pedaling as hard as I could.

I was told not to talk to strangers, but this one looked all right. "It's not a machine," I said. "It's a Bugatti."

"I can see that," the man said.

"The fastest car on the road," I said.

"No pickup," he said.

I was still pedaling with all my might but now I was beginning to run out of breath. "We're on a hill."

"That's what I mean," he said. "They're all right on the flat but give them a little hill and they have nothing in reserve."

I didn't answer. I had to save all my breath to keep pedaling.

"There's a bench just ahead of us," he said. "Pull off the road and let's have a look at your machine. Maybe there's something we can do about it."

I was only too glad to do what he told me. I was out of breath. I managed to pull up to the bench before him. The nurse turned the wheelchair alongside. I started to get out.

Gianno, who always came with us when the nurse and I went to the park, came running up. "You okay, Angelo?"

I nodded.

Gianno looked at the man in the wheelchair. They didn't speak but something seemed to pass between them and Gianno smiled. "Sure," he said.

The man leaned over the side of the wheelchair and looked into the car. He reached down and lifted the seat, exposing the gear and chain.

"Do you want to look under the hood?" I asked.

"I don't think so," he said, letting the seat drop back into place.

"Are you a mechanic?" I asked.

There was a startled expression on his face when he looked at me. It was gone swiftly. "I guess you can call me that," he said. "Anyway that's what I used to be."

"Can you do something about it?" I asked.

"I think so." He looked up at his nurse. "Could I have my notebook, Miss Hamilton?"

Silently she gave him a plain, hard-covered notebook much like the kind I carried to school. He took a pen from his pocket, and, looking down at the Bugatti, began to sketch swiftly.

I walked around the chair and looked at the pad. It looked like a strange combination of wheels and chains and lines. "What's that?" I asked.

"Variable gears." He saw the blank expression on my face. "It doesn't matter," he added. "It will work, you'll see."

He finished the drawing and gave the book back to his nurse. "What's your name?"

"Angelo."

"Well, Angelo, if you'll meet me here about this time the day after tomorrow, I'll have a surprise for you."

I looked over at Gianno. He nodded silently. "I can do that, sir," I said.

"Fine." He turned to his nurse. "Home now, Miss Hamilton. We have work to do."

I was early. But so was he. He smiled when he saw me. "Good morning, Angelo."

"Good morning, sir," I said. "Good morning, Miss Hamilton."

She sniffed. "Good morning." I had the feeling she didn't like me.

I turned back to him. "You said you would have a surprise for me?"

"Patience, young man. It's coming."

I followed his gaze. Two men dressed in white coveralls were carrying a large wooden crate up the path, followed by another man carrying a tool box.

"Over here," my friend in the wheelchair called. They put the crate down in front of him. "Everything ready?" he asked the man with the tool box.

"As you ordered, sir," the man replied. "I just took the liberty of allowing ten-millimeter leeway on the axle placement in case we had to make adjustments."

My friend laughed. "Still don't trust my eye, do you, Duncan?"

"No point taking chances, Mr. Hardeman," Duncan replied. "Now where is the car we're to work on?"

"Right here," I said, pushing it out in front of them.

Duncan looked down at it. "A fine lookin' automobile."

"It's a Bugatti," I said. "My grandfather had it made specially for me in Italy."

"Eyetalians do fine coachwork," Duncan said. "But they know nothing about engineering." He turned to the other two men. "Okay, boys, go to work."

For the first time I saw the lettering on the back of their coveralls. *BETHLEHEM MOTORS*. They worked swiftly with practiced efficiency. Two bolts unfastened the sides and top of the crate from the bottom which then became a workbench as they placed my car on top of it.

The two mechanics got busy. I looked down at the ground where the opened crate revealed a rectangular steel frame filled with gears, chains, and wheels. "What's that?" I asked.

"A new chassis," my friend replied. "It was much simpler to build the whole thing in the shop with everything in it than to pull yours apart."

I didn't speak. By that time the two men had lifted the body of my car from its chassis and were going to work on the wheels. A few minutes later they had the new chassis on the crate and were mounting my wheels to it, and in less than ten minutes they had the body of the Bugatti mounted on the new chassis. They stepped back.

Mr. Duncan walked over to it and looked inside. He fiddled around a bit, pushing first one thing, then another. After a moment he stepped back. "Seems okay to me, sir," he said.

My friend grinned. "Did you need the ten millimeters?"

"No, sir," Duncan said. He nodded to the two men.

They lifted the car to the ground. I looked at it, then at my friend.

"Go ahead, Angelo, get in."

I climbed into the car as he wheeled his chair alongside me. "There are several new things I want to show you before you drive off," he said. "See that gear lever coming up near your right hand?"

"Yes, sir."

"Put your hand on it." I did as I was told. "It moves

forward and back and when it's in the center it can move sideways and then forward again. Try it."

I moved it forward and back, then to the center and sideways forward. I looked up at the wheelchair. Something of what he had done suddenly began to make sense to me.

He picked it up from my eyes. "Do you know what that's for, Angelo?"

"Yes, sir," I said. "High, low and reverse."

"Good boy. Now there's one other thing I did. I put coaster brakes on your rear wheels. You slow down or stop merely by reversing the push on the pedals, just like you do on a bicycle. Understand?"

I nodded.

"All right," he said. "Try it out. But be careful. It's going to be a lot faster than it was before."

"Yes, sir," I said.

Cautiously I went down the hill, getting the feel of it and trying the brakes. Each time I came off the brakes it went a little faster, then I would hit the brakes again and slow down. At the bottom of the hill I turned around on the path by reversing, then going forward. I came up the hill almost as easily as going down. I stopped in front of them. "It's great!"

I got out of the car and walked up to my friend. "Thank you very much." I held out my hand.

He took it and we shook. "You're very welcome, Angelo." He smiled. "Just you be careful. You have a very fast car there."

"I'll be okay," I said. "I'm going to be a race-car driver when I grow up."

The men had been busy putting all the old bits and pieces into the crate. They started down the path and Mr. Duncan came over to us.

He held a sheet of paper toward my friend. "Sorry to bother you, sir, but I'll need your signature on this."

My friend took it. "What is it?"

"A new system L.H. Two put in. It's a work order. He also wanted me to ask ye what department to charge it to."

My friend grinned almost like I would. "Experimental car."

Duncan laughed. "Yes, sir."

My friend signed the paper and Duncan turned away. I called him back. "Thank you, Mr. Duncan."

He looked down at me dourly. "Ye're welcome, lad. But don't ye forget, ye might be drivin' a Bugatti but ye're powered by Bethlehem Motors, thanks to Mr. Hardeman there."

"I won't forget," I said. I watched him hurry down the path toward the other men, then turned back to my friend. "Mr. Hardeman, is that your name?"

He nodded.

"You're very nice," I said.

"Some people don't think so."

"I wouldn't pay any attention to them," I said. "Lots of people feel that way about my grandfather, but he's nice and I like him."

He was silent.

His nurse's voice came from behind me. "It's time for us to be going, Mr. Hardeman."

"In a moment, Miss Hamilton," he said. "How old are you, Angelo?"

"Eight."

"I have a grandson just two years older than you. He's ten."

"Maybe I can play with him sometime. I would let him drive my car."

"I don't think so," said Mr. Hardeman. "He's away at school."

I heard the nurse's voice again. "It's getting late, Mr. Hardeman."

He made a face.

"Nurses are always like that, Mr. Hardeman," I said. "Mine is always after me for one thing or another."

"I guess so."

"They tell me I won't have a nurse next year when I grow up. Why do you have one?"

"I can't walk," he said. "I need someone to help me get around."

"Did you have an accident?"

He shook his head. "I was sick."

"When will you be better?"

"I'll never walk again," he said.

I was silent for a moment. "How do you know? My daddy says that miracles happen every day. And my daddy should know. He's a doctor." I had an idea. "Maybe he could come and see you. He's a very good doctor."

"I'm sure he is, Angelo," Mr. Hardeman said gently. "But I've had enough of doctors for a while." He gestured to the nurse. "Besides, I'm leaving for Florida on the weekend and I won't be back for a long time." He held out his hand. "Good-bye, Angelo."

I held onto his hand, not wanting to let go. Everybody I liked had to go away. First Grandpa, now Mr. Hardeman. "Will I see you when you come back?"

He nodded.

I still held onto his hand. "I'll be in the park every Sunday at this time and I'll look for you."

"The first Sunday I'm back, I'll be here," he said.

I let go of his hand. "That's a promise."

I watched the nurse push him down the path until they were out of sight, then I got back into my car. It wasn't until almost twenty years later that I found out exactly how much trouble L.H. One had gone to in order to have the surprise for me.

I was in Duncan's office in Design Engineering getting a rundown on the car I was to be testing the next day when suddenly the old engineer turned to me.

"Remember that Bugatti L.H. One had us fix up for you when you were a kid?"

"How could I forget?" I replied.

It was true enough. From that moment on it was nothing but automobiles for me. Nothing else had a chance.

"Did you ever wonder how much it cost?"

"Not really."

"I have the original work order that he signed. I kept it as a souvenir." He unlocked the center drawer of his desk, took it out and gave it to me. "Do ye know he pulled the whole office of Design Engineering and Fabrication off the line and had them working on your car for twenty-four straight hours?"

"I didn't know," I said. I looked down at the paper in my hand. "Experimental Chassis," read the charge slip. "Ordered by L.H. I. $11,347.51."

I felt a light touch on my shoulder and opened my eyes. It was the English nurse. "Dr. Hans is here."

I turned the chair around. He was standing there, his spectacles shining and, as usual, his six flunkies behind him.

"Good morning, Mr. Perino," he said. "How do you feel this morning? Any pains?"

"No, Doctor. It only hurts when I laugh."

He refused to smile. He gestured to the nurse and she pushed over a table on which there were shining steel instruments. "Now we shall see how good we were," he said in his usual half whisper.

I stared down at the table in fascination. I felt almost hypnotized by the gleaming instruments. I watched him pick up a short-bladed curette. This was it.

How many men in their lifetimes have a chance to get a new face?

=== **Chapter Two**

IT ALL BEGAN in May after the Indianapolis 500. My beast burned out on the forty-second lap and I pulled in. I didn't have to see the look on the pit boss's face to know I'd had it. I left the track without even waiting around for the finish.

It wasn't until I opened the door of my motel room that I realized that I had left Cindy back at the raceway. I had forgotten all about her.

I opened the small refrigerator and broke out some ice cubes and poured some Canadian whiskey over them. Sipping the drink slowly, I went into the bathroom and turned on the hot water in the tub, then went back into the room and switched on the radio. I searched the dials for the race reports. TV was blacked out within a fifty-mile radius.

The announcer's voice came on. "It's Andretti and Gurney, one and two on the eighty-fourth lap. A real battle of the giants, folks——" I switched it off. It had been like that from the very start of the race.

I finished the drink, put the glass down on the refrigerator top and went back into the bathroom. I turned on the cold water and plugged in the portable Jacuzzi whirlpool pump and watched the clouds of steam leap from the churning water while I stripped down. The bathroom was filled with steam by the time I eased myself into the hot water.

I leaned my head back against the tub and let the churning water push away at the aches and pains in my bones. I tightened up my gut and closed my eyes. It happened again. Like it always happened every time I closed my eyes for the past five years.

I saw the first lick of the flames coming up from the engine against the windshield. I down-shifted into the curve and fought the wheel. The high wall came up in front of my face and we hit at one hundred and thirty-seven miles per hour. The beast went up on its nose and hung there for a moment while I stared into the roaring stands, then the flames reached up and we went over the wall into them. The sick sweet smell of my burning flesh and scorched hair came into my nostrils. In the distance I could hear myself screaming.

I opened my eyes and it was gone. I was back in the tub with the Jacuzzi singing its soothing song. Slowly I closed my eyes again.

This time it was all right. I floated in the water.

The telephone began to ring. Modern motels have everything. I reached across the john and took the telephone from the wall.

"Mr. Perino?" the long-lines operator singsonged.

"Yeah."

"Mr. Loren Hardeman calling. Just one moment, please."

I heard the click and he came on. "Angelo, you all right?" There was a genuine concern in his voice.

"I'm okay, Number One. And you?"

"Good," he laughed. "I feel like a kid of eighty-five."

I laughed. He was ninety-one on his last birthday.

"What the hell is that noise?" he asked. "Sounds like you're going over Niagara Falls in a barrel. I can hardly hear you."

I reached over and cut the Jacuzzi. The roar faded. "That better?"

"Much," he said. "I've been watching television and saw you go into the pit. What happened?"

"Valves burned out."

"Where do you go next?"

"I don't know," I answered. "The only thing I've penciled in for sure is Watkins Glen. But that's not until the fall." I heard the outside door open and Cindy's footsteps come toward the bathroom. I looked up and she was standing in the doorway. "I thought maybe I'd go over to Europe for the summer and try the action there."

Her face was expressionless. She turned back and went into the other room.

"Don't do it," he said. "It's not worth it. You'll get yourself killed."

I heard the refrigerator door slam and the clink of ice in the glasses. She came back with two Canadians on the rocks. I took one from her hand and she put the cover down on the john and sat there. She sipped her drink.

"I won't get killed," I said.

His voice was flat. "Quit now. You haven't got it any more."

"I've just had a run of bad luck."

"Don't give me that crap," he said. "I watched you on TV. I remember when you wouldn't give up a turn to God. On that last lap before you went in you left a hole big enough for Coxey's Army to drive through."

I was silent. I took a pull at my drink.

His voice softened. "Look, it's not so bad. You had

some pretty good years. In '63 you were the number-two driver in the world. You would have been number one in '64 if you hadn't climbed that wall at Sebring and been laid up for a year."

I knew just what he was talking about. And I had the nightmares to prove it.

"I think five years is enough time for you to give yourself to find out you haven't got it any more."

"What do you think I should do?" I asked sarcastically. "Join the 'Wide World of Sports' as a commentator?"

A touch of asperity came into his voice. "Don't get fresh with me, young man. The trouble with you is that you never grew up. I should never have souped up that kiddie car for you. You won't stop playing with it."

"I'm sorry." I had no right to let out on him the frustration I felt toward myself.

"I'm in Palm Beach," he said. "I want you to come down here and spend a few days with me."

"What for?"

"I don't know." From the way he sounded I knew he was lying in his teeth. Or maybe they weren't his teeth at all. "We'll just talk."

I thought for a moment. "Okay."

"Good," he said. "You coming alone? I have to let the housekeeper know."

I looked across at Cindy. "I don't know yet."

He chuckled. "If she's pretty, bring her. There's little enough to look at down here besides the sea and the sand."

He clicked off and Cindy took the phone from my hand and put it back on the wall. I got up and she gave me a towel. She took my drink and walked into the other room.

I dried myself and, wrapping the towel around my waist, followed her. My drink was on the table and she was on the floor doing things with her four-track tape recorder. I took another pull at the drink and watched.

She was placing the small reels in containers and marking the boxes. She was a motor-sound buff. Something about the roar of an engine turned her on. Some girls like vibrators, all she needed was noise. Put her in the car seat next to you and gun the motor, then place your hand on her cunt and you came away with a cupful of honey.

"Get any good sound?" I asked.

"Some." She didn't look back at me. "Is it over?"

"Why? Just because I forgot to pick you up?"

She turned around. "That's not what I'm asking," she said without expression. "Fearless says the talk around the track is that you're quitting."

Fearless Peerless was one of the backup drivers on J.C.'s team. He worked mostly on the dirt tracks trying to move his way into the big time. I tried to keep the edge of jealousy out of my voice. "Fearless bring you home?"

"Yes."

"You got eyes for him?"

"He's got eyes for me." It was fact. He wasn't the only one and I knew it. She was something special.

I felt the heat in my balls. "Set up the player."

She stared at me for a moment, then silently put the player on a small table at the foot of the bed. Expertly she set up the four speakers, two on each side of the bed, and plugged in the lead wires. She glanced at me.

"Put on the big tape. The one you made at Daytona last year."

She took the reel from her case and threaded it into the machine. She turned to look at me.

By now my hard-on had distended the towel around my waist into a tent. "Get out of your clothes."

She stripped and stretched out on the bed, her eyes watching me. She still hadn't said a word.

I reached over and switched on the player. The lead tape hissed and then the crowd noises filtered through. Suddenly there was an explosion of sound as the engines roared. The race had begun.

I stepped onto the bed and stood over her. Her lips were parted and she seemed to be scarcely breathing as the pink of her tongue parted her white teeth. She was all honey-brown and gold except for the narrow white band around her small full breasts and the triangle of her hips and legs. The coral pink of her nipples popped open and

up at me and the soft down between her legs began to
glisten with tiny diamonds.

I moved up on the bed and pushed my feet under her
armpits until her shoulders rested on that them. Then I pulled
off the towel.

My hard slapped up against my belly. I stood there over
her face and she stared up at me. I didn't move.

Suddenly she whimpered and reached up and grabbed
my cock. She pulled me down into her mouth, gobbling
and making noises deep in her throat. I sank to my knees
over her face, moving with the writhing and thrusting of
her hips behind me.

I felt her tongue licking at my balls and then move
under me, searching out the secrets of my anus. And all
the while she held the knob of my cock in one hand, moving it like a gearshift to position me.

Her whisper was muffled. "Let me get on top of you."

I rolled over to my side, then on my back. Still holding
my cock she clambered over me, then slowly lowered herself onto it. It was like dipping into a tub of boiling oil.

"Oh, God," she moaned, rocking herself slowly back and
forth on me, rubbing her clitoris against my pubic ridge.

The roar of the racing engines began to travel from
speaker to speaker around the bed, filling the room with an
explosive violence of sound, and she moved with it, climaxing anew at each cycle around the track. I could feel the
fuel of her excitement dripping down my testicles and
under me.

She began to half moan and scream with the frenzy of
her passion. Wildly she shook her head from side to side,
spilling her long hair into a constant fan. She began slamming into me, harder and harder. I smashed back against
her.

"Good," she muttered. "That's so good."

I held my arms straight out from my sides, behind her.
As she came back toward me I slapped her viciously, one
hand on each buttock. She jammed into me and came
back. I slapped her again and kept it up to the rhythm of
her movements.

She began to climb the walls, her moans became shrieks

of pain and ecstasy. The roar of the engines as they came toward the finish line began to mount, almost drowning her out.

Suddenly Carl Yarborough crossed the finish line in his Sixty-eight Merc at 143.251 miles per hour and she created her final orgasm, drowning me in the flood of her juices.

She hung there balanced on my cock for a moment, her eyes glazed and far away, then slowly, she crumpled and slid from me.

She lay quietly, her breathing slowing down to normal, her eyes open, looking into mine. "It was wild," she whispered.

I just looked at her.

She put her hand down on my cock. Her eyes opened slightly in surprise. She began to stroke it gently. "It's still hard," she whispered. "You're fantastic."

I still didn't speak. There was no point in telling her I hadn't made it.

She moved down and kissed me and took me in her mouth. After a moment she raised her head. "You're all covered with me."

I nodded.

She kissed my knob and tried to part its tip with her tongue. She turned her face and, holding my cock against her cheek, spoke softly. "Where will I ever find another man like you?"

I put my hand in her hair and turned her face up to me. "Are you going with Fearless?" I asked.

"Answer my question first," she said. "Are you quitting?"

I didn't hesitate. "Yes."

She did hesitate. I'll say that much for her. "Then I'm going with Fearless."

And it was over. Just like that.

THE SOGGY HEAT at the West Palm Beach airport came right through my shirt by the time I got to the Hertz counter. I sprang my freebie card and pushed it at the girl.

She looked at the card before she looked at me. Then her expression changed. "*The* Angelo Perino?" she asked respectfully.

I nodded.

"I watched you on TV the other day. I'm sorry your car burned out."

"One of those things," I said.

"I was just a kid when my father took my brother and me to Sebring that time you went over the wall. I cried. I said prayers for you all week until I read that you would be okay."

She had that Hertz look. All-American girl. "How old were you?" I asked.

"Sixteen."

I looked at her again. She was all orange-and-sun-country tan and over statutory age by now. "I owe you something for those prayers," I said. "Maybe we can make dinner."

"I have a date tonight," she said. "But I can break it."

"No, keep it," I said quickly. "I don't want to mess up your plans. We'll do it tomorrow night."

"Okay," she said. She wrote something on a slip of paper and pushed it at me. "That's my name and phone number. You can get me here before five and there after five."

I glanced at it. I might have guessed. Even her name was orange-and-sun country. "Okay, Melissa," I said. "I'll call you. Now what about a car?"

"We have a Shelby GT Mustang and a Mach One."

I laughed. "I'm not racing. Do you have something with the top down? I want the sun on my face."

She checked her list. "How about an LTD convertible?"

"Great."

She began to fill out the form. "Where are you staying?"

"The Hardeman place."

"How long will you need the car?"

"A few days. I don't know."

"I'll leave it open." She looked embarrassed. "Could I have your driver's license? It's for the form."

I laughed and pushed it toward her. She copied down the number and gave it back to me. She picked up the phone and spoke into it. "LTD convertible, Jack," she said. "And give it super service. It's for a VIP." She put down the phone. "Give us about ten minutes."

"Take your time, Melissa," I said.

Another customer came up and I walked over to the curb and lit a cigarette. I took off my jacket and threw it over my arm. It was hot.

I turned and looked back at the girl. I liked the way she moved. The way her breasts pushed against the tight-fitting uniform. There was more to look at down here than the old man thought. The trouble was that he couldn't get out to the right places.

After all, when you rent Hertz, you don't just rent a car. You rent a company.

I pulled up in front of the electrified iron gates and pressed the signal button on the side of the driveway. While I waited for a voice to answer I read the signs on the gate.

PRIVATE PROPERTY.
NO TRESPASSING.
DANGER! GUARD DOGS PATROLLING!
SURVIVORS WILL BE PROSECUTED.

I laughed. Somehow it didn't seem very convincing. But I changed my mind real quick. By the time I had finished reading the signs, there were two giant Belgian shepherds standing just inside the gate, their tails wagging deceptively at me.

The voice came from the speaker box over the signal button. "Who's calling?"

"Mr. Perino."

There was a moment's pause. "You're expected, Mr. Perino. Drive through the gates. Do not get out of the car to close them, they shut automatically. Do not, I repeat, do not get out of the car until you reach the front of the house and do not let your arm hang out alongside the car door."

The voice clicked off and the gates began to roll back. The dogs stood just inside, waiting for me. I started the car slowly and they went to one side to let me pass and then began to run silently beside the car as I went up the driveway.

Every once in a while I would look out at them and they would look back at me and I just kept on driving. I went around a curve and, hidden behind the trees, was the front of the house. A man and a woman were standing on the steps. I stopped the car.

The man put a sonic whistle to his lips and blew it. I didn't hear a thing but the dogs did. They froze and watched me get out of the car.

"Please stand there a moment and let them sniff you, Mr. Perino," the man said. "They'll recognize you after that and won't bother you."

I stood still as he raised the sonic whistle to his lips again. The dogs came running over to me, their tails wagging. They sniffed around at my shoes and then at my hands. After a moment, they left me and went over to the car. In less than a minute they had squirted over every tire and had run happily off.

The man came toward me. "I'm Donald. Let me get your bags, sir."

"There's only one," I said. "In the back seat." I turned toward the house.

The woman smiled at me. She seemed in her fifties, her gray-black hair pulled severely back behind her face and very little makeup. She wore a simply tailored black dress. "I'm Mrs. Craddock. Mr. Hardeman's secretary."

"How'd you do," I said.

"Mr. Hardeman apologizes for not greeting you but it's the hour for his afternoon nap. He asks if you will meet him in the library for a drink at five o'clock. Dinner is promptly at six thirty. We eat early here because Mr. Hardeman retires at nine."

"That's okay with me."

"Donald will show you to your room," she said, leading me into the house. "And you can freshen up. If you should care for a swim, there's a pool on the ocean side and a choice of swim trunks in the cabanas."

"Thank you. But I think I'll follow Number One's example. I'm a bit tired."

She nodded and moved off and I followed Donald up the staircase to my room. I went into the bathroom to wash my face and by the time I came out, my valise was unpacked, the bed turned down, the curtains drawn and a pair of my pajamas were laid out.

I took the hint and got out of my clothes. In ten minutes I was asleep.

He was waiting in the library when I came down the stairs. He held out his hand. "Angelo."

I took it. His grip was firm. "Number One."

He smiled. His voice was reproving. "I don't know whether I really like that. Makes me sound like an old Mafia chief."

"Nothing like it," I laughed. "If the stories I heard about my grandfather are half true, he was a Mafia chief and I never heard anyone call him Number One."

"Come over to the window and let me look at you."

I followed his wheelchair over to the large French windows that led onto the terrace overlooking the ocean and turned to face him. He peered up into my face. "You're not pretty, that's for sure."

"I didn't say I was," I answered.

"We're going to have to do something about those burn scars if you're coming to work for me," he said. "We can't have you going around frightening children."

"Wait a minute," I said. "Who said I was going to work for you?"

He peered up at me shrewdly. "You're here, aren't you? Or did you think I asked you down just to pass the time of day?"

I didn't answer.

"I'm too old," he continued. "I have plans. And I haven't that much time left to waste." He rolled his chair back into the room. "Fix yourself a drink and then sit down," he said. "I get a crick in my neck looking up at you."

I went to the sideboard and poured myself a Crown Royal on the rocks. He watched me hungrily as I sat down and tasted the drink.

"Damn!" he said. "I sure wish I could have one." Then he laughed. "I remember the time, back in 1903 or 1904, Charlie Sorensen had just given me a job over at the Ford Company building on the Model K and Mr. Ford came around because he made it a point to interview each new man personally at that time.

" 'Do you drink?' he asked.

" 'Yes,' I answered.

" 'Do you smoke?'

" 'Yes.'

"Mr. Ford was silent. He just stared at me. After a while I got to feel uncomfortable and had to say something. 'But I don't run around with women, Mr. Ford,' I blurted out. 'I'm married.'

"He stared at me for another moment, then turned on his heel and walked away without saying a word. Ten minutes later Charlie came down and fired me. That same morning he had hired me.

"I guess he saw the expression on my face. I was stunned. With a wife and a kid on the way, I guess he felt sorry for me.

" 'Go over to the Dodge Brothers and tell them I sent you,' he said. 'They'll give you a job.' He started to turn away and then turned back. 'You know, Hardeman,' he said, 'Mr. Ford has no vices. Absolutely none.'

"But he was wrong. Mr. Ford had the one unforgivable vice. He was intolerant."

I took another pull at my drink. I didn't speak.

His eyes fixed on mine. "I want you to come to work for me."

"Doing what?" I asked. "I wouldn't be happy test-driving any more."

"I didn't say anything about that," he said. "I have other plans. Big plans." His voice dropped to a confidential whisper. "I want to build a new car!"

I think my mouth fell open. "You what?"

"You heard me!" he snapped. "A new car. Brand-new from top to bottom. Like nothing ever built before."

"Have you talked to anyone about this?" I asked. "To L.H. Three?"

"I don't have to talk to anyone about it," he said testily. "I still vote eighty percent of the company stock." He pushed his chair closer to me. "Especially not my own grandson."

"And what do you expect me to do?"

"Get me out of this goddamn chair," he said. "I expect you to be my legs!"

Chapter Four

HE WAS still talking when we went in to dinner. We sat at a small table and the meal was simple. Salad, lamb chops and a vegetable, wine for me, a glass of milk for him. The wine was good, a '51 Mouton Rothschild, and so was the milk. Walker Gordon whole.

"The target date is the New York Automobile Show in the spring of '72. That gives us three years."

I looked at him.

He laughed. "I know what you're thinking. I'm ninety-one. Don't worry. I'm going to live to be a hundred."

"It's not going to be easy," I said.

"Nothing ever is," he said. "But I made it this far."

I laughed. "That's not what I'm talking about. I'm con-

vinced you'll live to one hundred and fifty. I'm talking
about a new car."

"I've been thinking about it for a long time," he said.
"For thirty years I've let them pin me to this chair. And
it's all wrong. I never should have let them do it.

"Before the war we had almost fifteen percent of the
market. Now we have two percent. Even the lousy little
Volkswagen sells more cars here than we do. And that's
not all of it. The Japanese are coming. They'll wipe us all
out. The little bastards are going to clean up the world.
They'll underprice and outsell all the rest of us put together.

"This year and next, the American companies will be
coming out with their sub-compacts. It won't do them any
good. Sure they'll sell cars. But they won't be stealing sales
away from the foreigners, they'll be stealing sales away
from themselves and reducing their over-all price-per-unit
volume.

"The only answer is a completely new car. Built in a
new fashion. On a completely automated, electronic production line. I remember when Ford came out with his
Model T. It set the world on fire. For only one reason.
Ford had a better idea. But it was the only idea they ever
had. Since then they've been flying tail to General Motors'
kite. And so has the rest of the industry. Even us."

"It's a pretty large order."

"It can be done," he said. "I don't like coming in out of
the money. I'm a winner. I've always been a winner."

"I read the annual reports," I said. "Bethlehem makes
money. They always make money."

"But not on automobiles," he retorted. "They account
for only thirty percent of our gross. The appliance division
supplies fifty-seven percent and the rest comes from manufacturing parts for the other companies. It's their way of
making sure we stay in the business. They're afraid of
antitrust and monopoly. Right now over seventy percent
of our production space is used for that and not automobiles."

"I didn't know," I said.

"Very few people do. It all began during the war. Ford,

GM, and Chrysler got all the big jobs. L.H. Two concentrated on the other areas. When the war was over, they were ready to go back into big production; we weren't. But we were equipped to go into the appliance field and, I must say, he did a fantastic job. It nets us better than forty million a year. But I don't give a damn. It's not automobiles."

I leaned back in my chair and looked at him. "What about Number Three?"

"He's a good boy," Number One answered. "But all he's interested in is profits. He doesn't care where it comes from, television sets, refrigerators, or cars. It's all the same. Sometimes I think he would have taken us out of the auto business a long time ago, but he doesn't want to upset me."

"How are you going to tell him?"

"I'm not," he said. "Not until we're set up."

"You'll never keep it a secret," I said. "Not in our business. They'll pick it up the minute I go to work."

He smiled. "Not if we tell them something else."

"Like what?"

"Everybody knows what you are. A race-car driver. They don't know what I do. That you're a graduate of MIT in automotive engineering and design. Or that years ago John Duncan wanted to put you on to take over the department when he retired.

"We'll give you a title, vice-president, special projects, then we'll let on that we're going in for factory-sponsored race teams and cars. That should be enough smoke."

Donald came into the room. "It's time, Mr. Hardeman."

Number One looked at his watch, then back at me. "We'll talk some more at breakfast," he said.

I got to my feet. "Right, Number One."

"Good night," he said.

I watched Donald roll the chair out of the room, then sat down again. I lit a cigarette and looked at my watch. It was eight thirty and I was wide awake. That afternoon nap blew it. On a hunch I called the girl from Hertz.

A man's voice answered. "Is Melissa in?" I asked.

His voice had a father's defensive edge. "Who's calling?"

"Angelo Perino."

He sounded impressed. "I'll call her, Mr. Perino." He turned away from the phone and I heard him yell. "Melissa! Mr. Perino's on the phone!" His voice came back to me. "Melissa told me you were in town, Mr. Perino. I hope we get a chance to meet. I'm a real admiruh of yours."

"I hope so," I said. "Thank you."

I heard the telephone change hands. She had enough southern tease in her voice to clog the lines. "Mr. Perino, this is a surprise."

"I had a hunch," I said. "What happened to your date?"

"I canceled him," she said. "He's really a bore."

"Want out?" I asked.

"That would be lovely," she said, and I knew that her father was still somewhere nearby.

"Where can we meet?"

"Do you know Palm Beach?"

"Not really. I know how to get from the airport to here. But that's about all."

"Then maybe I'd better come over there and get you," she said.

"Good idea," I said. "How long will it take you?"

"About a half hour okay?"

"Good enough," I said.

When I put down the phone, Donald was standing a respectable distance away. "Is there anything I can get you, sir?"

"Do you have any brandy?"

"Of course, sir." There was reproach in his voice. "Will you have it in the library?"

I nodded and he followed me into the library. He poured the brandy into a snifter and, swirling it gently, gave it to me.

"Thank you, Donald." Then I remembered the dogs. "Someone's coming to pick me up in about half an hour; can you do something about the dogs?"

"I'll take care of it, sir. Will you be needing your car?"

"I don't think so."

He took a key from his pocket and held it toward me.

"This will work the gate and the front door. Just leave it on the card table in the entrance foyer when you return."

"Thank you, Donald."

"Not at all, sir," he said and left the room.

I sank into one of the old-fashioned leather chairs and sipped at the brandy until I heard the roar of her car coming up the driveway. I went outside just as she came to a stop. Of course she had the Mach One.

I went down the steps and opened the car door. "That was quick."

"Super service." She smiled. "Want to drive?"

I shook my head and slid into the passenger seat. "No. I'm happy." I leaned across and kissed her cheek, then sat back and fastened my seat belt.

"Nervous?"

"Nope. Just habit."

"What would you like to do?"

I looked at her. "Let's go someplace and fuck."

Her voice was filled with honeysuckle reproach. "Why, Mr. Perino!"

"All right, if you're going to be so formal about it, what would you like to do?"

"I know a lovely romantic place on the beach where we could drink and talk and dance."

"Good enough for me."

"That's better, Angelo," she smiled.

I smiled right back at her. "Then we'll go someplace and fuck."

She put the car into gear and we went down the driveway like we were going down the line at a Grand Prix. Why was it every time I got into a car someone had to prove to me how fast they could drive? I closed my eyes and prayed.

I WOKE UP to the ringing of the telephone. I groaned at the pounding in my head. That lovely romantic place she took me to last night wasn't exactly. The drinks were watered, you couldn't talk for the screaming acid rock and the dance floor was more crowded than the Edsel Ford Freeway at rush hour.

"Mr. Hardeman would like to speak with you, sir," Donald's voice came from the receiver.

"I'll be right down."

"The young Mr. Hardeman," he said quickly. "He's calling from Detroit."

Suddenly I was wide awake. And Number One thought there were secrets. I wondered who filed the report, Donald or the secretary. "Put him on."

"Mr. Perino?" It was a girl's voice.

"Yes."

"Just a moment for Mr. Hardeman."

I glanced at my watch. Eight thirty. Detroit was an hour earlier and he was already in the office.

"Angelo." His voice was friendly. "It's been a long time."

"It sure has," I said.

"I'm so pleased that you're down there visiting Grandfather. Number One was always very fond of you."

"I'm fond of him," I said.

"Sometimes I think he spends too much time alone down there." Concern came into his voice. "How does he look to you?"

"Feisty as ever," I said. "I don't think he's changed in the thirty years I've known him."

"Good. I'm glad to hear you say that. We get all sorts of wild stories back here."

"Like what?"

"You know. The usual thing. Old-age things."

"You've got nothing to worry about," I said. "He's all there."

"I'm relieved," he said. "I've been meaning to get down there but you know how it is. The pressures never let up."

"I understand."

"There's talk about you retiring from racing," he said.

"That's what Number One is trying to talk me into."

"Listen to him," he said. "And if you should make up your mind, come up and talk to me. There's always a place here for you."

I smiled to myself. Very effectively, he let me know who was in charge. "Thank you," I said.

"Not at all. Mission accomplished. Good-bye."

"Good-bye." I put down the telephone and reached for a cigarette. There was a knock at the door. "Come in," I called.

The door opened and Number One came rolling in, followed by Donald bearing a tray. Donald set the tray on the bed and took the cover from it. There was orange juice, toast and coffee.

"How would you like your eggs, sir?" he asked.

"Nothing else, thank you," I said. "This will do just fine."

He left the room and Number One rolled his chair over to the bed. I picked up the coffee and took a swallow. It helped.

"Well?" he asked.

"Good coffee," I said.

"I know it's good coffee," he said irascibly. "What did my grandson have to say?"

I took another swallow of the coffee. "He said he was glad I was down here and he told me to come and see about a job if I were serious about giving up driving."

"What else did he say?"

"He said you were alone down here too much and wanted to know how you were."

"What did you tell him?"

"I told him you were nuts," I said. "You had some crazy idea about building a new car."

He started to get angry, then suddenly he began to laugh. I laughed with him and we were like two kids playing a joke on the teacher.

"I almost wish you had," he said. "I would have loved to see the expression on his face."

"He would have shit," I said.

Number One stopped smiling. "What do you think?"

"About what?"

"Me." He spoke slowly, cautiously, almost as if he were reluctant to get an answer. "Is what I want to do the crazy dream of an old man?"

I looked at him. "If it is, the whole world is crazy. And so is our business. A better car has to be everybody's dream."

"Last night I thought a great deal about what you said. It won't be easy."

I didn't answer. Just drank more of my coffee.

"It will take a lot of money. GM will have at least three hundred million dollars in their new sub-compact; Ford will be a lot less because they're just redesigning their British car for the American market and will import the engines from Britain and Germany. And still it should cost them close to two hundred million." He looked at me. "I figure that's the least we would need."

"Has Bethlehem got that kind of money?" I asked.

"Even if they had," he answered, "I'd never be able to get my grandson to go along with me. And he has the board of directors in his pocket."

We were silent for a long time. I poured myself more coffee.

He sighed heavily. "Maybe we better just forget about it. Maybe it is just the dream of a crazy old man."

He seemed to be shrinking into himself before my eyes. I think it wasn't until that moment that I realized how committed I really had been.

"There is a way," I said.

He looked at me.

"It won't be pleasant and they'll fight you every step of the way."

"I've done that all my life," he said.

"It will mean getting out of Detroit."

"I don't understand," he said.

"Spin-off. Sell the appliance company. You said it nets forty million a year. You could get at least ten times earnings for that. Four hundred million. With your eighty percent of the stock alone, that's three hundred and twenty million."

"I vote eighty percent," he said. "But I own only forty-one percent, thirty-nine percent belongs to the Hardeman Foundation."

"Forty-one percent is a hundred and sixty-four million. It shouldn't be that hard to get the rest of it. Then you move the automobile division."

"Where?"

"California. Washington State. They're loaded with big aerospace assembly facilities that are going to turn to instant shit with the cutbacks that are coming in the next few years. It won't take much to make them into automobile assembly lines. They have the space and the trained labor pool right there."

He looked at me. "It might work."

"I know damn well it will," I said confidently.

"Who would buy the appliance company?"

"I know a lot of companies that would grab at it, but you'd wind up with very little money and a lot of paper," I said. "There's only one way to do it. Sell it to the public. And, maybe, at the same time, sell a little bit of the car company and get the rest of the money we need."

"That means going to Wall Street," he said.

I nodded.

"I never trusted them," he said suspiciously. "They want too much say in what you do."

"That's where the money is," I said.

"I don't know how to deal with them," he said. "We don't speak the same language."

"That's what you got me for. I'll translate for you."

He stared at me for a long moment. Then, slowly, he began to smile. "I don't know what I'm so worried about," he said. "I started out poor. And no matter how it comes out, I had to be poor a lot longer at the beginning than I will be at the end." He turned his chair and rolled it toward the door. I got out of bed and opened it for him.

He looked up at me. "I wonder how my grandson knew you were here."

"I don't know," I answered. "You have a large staff."

"That girl you went out with last night. Where did she come from?"

"Hertz-Rent-a-Girl."

"You're crazier than I am," he said, and rolled his chair out into the hall.

== **Chapter Six**

THE PLANE put me down in Detroit at six o'clock in the evening and I was home by seven o'clock. Gianno opened the door and, in a moment, enfolded me in a bear hug.

"Signora! Signora!" he shouted, forgetting his English. *"Dottore!* Angelo is here!"

My mother came flying down the stairs. She was crying before she reached the halfway landing. I ran up the steps to her and put my arms around her. "Mamma."

"Angelo Angelo! Are you all right?" Her voice was anxious.

"I'm fine, Mamma. Absolutely fine."

"I saw the smoke coming from your car," she said.

"It was nothing."

"You sure?"

"Sure." I kissed her. "You're as beautiful as ever."

"Angelo, you say such silly things. How can a woman of sixty be beautiful?" She was beginning to smile.

I laughed. "Sixty-one. And still beautiful. After all, I should know. A boy's best friend is his mother."

"Stop teasing, Angelo," she said. "Someday you will find a girl who is really beautiful."

"Never. They don't make girls like you no more."

"Angelo." My father's voice came from the doorway to the study off the foyer.

I turned to look at him. The gray hair over his slim patrician face was the only thing that had changed about him since I was a boy. I ran down the steps.

He stood there very quietly, his hand outstretched. I pushed it aside and hugged him. "Papa!"

He hugged me back and we kissed. There were tears in his eyes, too. "How have you been, Angelo?"

"Fine, Papa, just fine." I looked into his eyes. He seemed tired. "You've been working too hard."

"Not really," he said. "I've been cutting down since my attack."

"You should," I said. "Whoever heard of a Grosse Pointe doctor going out all hours of the night?"

"I don't do that any more. I have a young assistant who makes my night calls."

We were silent for a moment. I knew what he was thinking.

I should have been that assistant. It had always been his dream that I would follow in his footsteps and come into his practice. But that was not the way it was. My head was someplace else. He never mentioned his disappointment, but I knew it was there.

"You should have let us know you were coming, Angelo," my mother said reproachfully. "We would have had a special dinner."

"You mean you have nothing to eat in the house?" I laughed.

"There's always something," she said.

At the dinner table I told them the news. Gianno had just put down the coffee. Espresso. Hot, thick, and heavy. I put two spoons of sugar into it and sipped. I looked at them.

"I'm giving up driving," I said.

There was complete silence for a moment, then my mother began to cry.

"What are you crying about?" I asked. "I thought you'd be happy about it. You always wanted me to give it up."

"That's why I'm crying."

My father was more practical. "What are you going to do?"

"I'm going to work for Bethlehem Motors. Number One wants me to be vice-president in charge of special projects."

"What does that mean?" my mother asked.

"You know," I said. "Handle problems. Things like that."

"Does that mean you'll stay here in Detroit?" she asked.

"Some of the time," I answered. "My job will keep me on the move."

"I'll have your room redecorated," she said.

"Not so fast, Mamma," my father cut in. "Maybe Angelo wants a place of his own. He's not a boy any more."

"Do you, Angelo?" my mother asked.

I couldn't stand the look in her eyes. "What do I need my own place for, when my home is here?"

"I'll get in touch with the painter tomorrow," she said. "You tell me what colors you like, Angelo."

"You pick the colors, Mamma." I turned to my father. "I want to get my face fixed. I'll be meeting a lot of people and I don't want to have to worry about it. I remember once you told me about a doctor who was the best in the world at it."

My father nodded. "Ernest Hans. He's in Switzerland."

"That's the one. Do you think he can do anything?"

My father looked at me. "It will not be easy. But if anyone can do it, he can."

I knew what he meant. It wasn't only the nose, which had been broken a few times, or even the left cheekbone, which had been flattened and crushed. It was the white patch of burn scars on my cheek and forehead. "Can you make the arrangements for me?"

"When do you want to go?" he asked.

"As soon as he will take me."

Two days later I was on the plane to Geneva.

Dr. Hans lifted the last gauze pack from my cheek and placed it on the tray. He leaned forward and peered closely at my face. "Turn your head from one side to the other."

I did as I was told. First to the right. Then left.

"Smile," he said.

I smiled. My face felt tight.

He nodded. "Not bad. We weren't too bad after all."

"Congratulations."

"Thank you," he said quite seriously. He rose from the chair opposite me in which he had been sitting. "You'll have to remain here about another week until the redness disappears. It's nothing to be disturbed about. Quite normal. I had to plane the old skin remaining on your face so that it would come in new with the grafted skin."

I nodded. After four operations in ten weeks another week more or less didn't matter.

He started to leave and then turned back. "By the way," he added, almost as an afterthought, "you can look at yourself in the mirror if you want to."

"I will," I said. "Thank you." But I didn't make a move to get out of my chair. Oddly enough, I wasn't in a hurry to look at myself.

He stood there for a moment and then, when he saw I was not getting out of the chair, he nodded and left the room followed by his six flunkies.

I sat there watching the English nurse cleaning the surgical tray and placing the bandages into a waste container. She didn't make a big thing out of looking at me, but I did notice that she kept glancing at me out of the corners of her eyes.

I caught her hand the next time she walked in front of me and turned her toward me. "What do you think, Sister?" I asked. "Is it that bad?"

"Not at all, Mr. Perino," she said quickly. "It's just that I never saw you before your accidents. I did see you when you came in. The transformation is quite remarkable. You have an interesting face, almost handsome I would say."

I laughed. "I was never handsome."

"See for yourself," she said.

I got out of the chair and went into the bathroom. There was a mirror over the sink. I looked into it.

In a moment I knew how it felt to be Dorian Gray and

never grow old. It was almost the same face that I had at
twenty-five. Almost. But there were subtle differences.

The nose was thinner, more aquiline. The doctor had
taken the original Italian out of it. The cheekbones were
slightly higher, making my face thinner and longer, my jaw
more square. The ridges of proud flesh that had puffed up
under my eyebrows after they had been split were gone, as
were the white burn scars, and my skin was all pink and
new and shining like a baby's. Only the eyes seemed wrong
in that face.

They were old eyes. They were thirty-eight-year-old
eyes. They hadn't changed. They hadn't been made younger to match the rest of the face. They still held the pain
and the glare of the sun and the lights of a thousand different roadways.

In the mirror I could see the nurse standing in the doorway behind me. I turned toward her and held out my
hand. "Sister."

She came toward me quickly. There was concern in her
voice. "Are you all right, Mr. Perino?"

"Would you be kind enough to kiss me?"

She looked into my eyes for a moment, then nodded.
She came toward me and, taking my face in her hands,
turned it down to her. She kissed me.

First, on the forehead, then on each cheekbone, then on
each cheek, and finally, on the mouth. I felt the kindness
and gentleness flowing from her. I lifted my face from
her.

There were tears standing in the corners of her eyes and
her lips were trembling. "Did I make it better, Mr. Perino?" she asked gently.

"Yes, Sister," I said. "Thank you."

She really did make it better.

Chapter Seven

"IT WILL be expensive," Loren Hardeman III said heavily.

I sat across the desk and looked at him. He was two years older than I, but he seemed much older. Maybe it was the office.

It was old-fashioned in heavy dark wood paneling, the chairs and couches were in black leather, the racing and automobile prints on the wall were ancient and faded. But it was *The Office*. It had been his grandfather's, then his father's, and now it was his. It was the office of the man who ran Bethlehem Motors.

He had the look of a man who was running toward weight but was fighting it. He had the ponderousness of a young man on whose shoulders responsibility had climbed at a very early age. Neither his eyes nor his smile had any real fun in them. Maybe he never had a chance.

He had been twenty-one, elected executive vice-president of Bethlehem Motors the year he had married the right girl, Alicia Grinwold, daughter of Mr. and Mrs. Randall Grinwold of Grosse Pointe, Southampton, and Palm Beach. Mr. Grinwold was then vice-president of the procurement division of General Motors.

Everything followed in order. Alicia was delivered of their daughter; Number Two died; he was elected president in his father's place; Bethlehem Motors was awarded the largest parts contract ever given by GM to a competitive contractor; and he celebrated his twenty-third birthday.

That was seventeen years ago and the Detroit papers were proud of their third generation. Many articles were written about their two bright young men, Henry Ford II and Loren Hardeman III. They had come forth like knights in their shining automobile chromed steel to do battle for their four-wheeled liege.

"Very expensive," Loren added into the heavy silence of the office.

I didn't answer. I took a cigarette and lit it. The smoke curled upward in the still air.

He pressed a switch on his desk intercom. "Ask Bancroft and Weyman to come down if they're free," he said.

He wasn't about to make it easy for me. John Bancroft wouldn't be any problem. He was Sales and my plan could do him nothing but good. But Dan Weyman was another matter. He was Finances and anything that might cost money was anathema to him. It didn't matter whether there was any value in it or not. He would only part with the money under duress.

They came into the office and went through the usual good-to-see-you-again bullshit. Then they arranged themselves on chairs and looked expectantly at their master.

Loren didn't waste words. "Grandfather wants to put us into racing. He's suggested that Angelo spearhead the project."

They waited for a reading. Loren didn't disappoint them.

"I don't know whether the time for that hasn't really passed. With safety and ecology becoming an increasing pressure factor, I think the emphasis on power will diminish. And then there's the cost factor. It's way up there now. Ford has already announced their pullout. Chevy cut back. Dodge is still in but only until their contracted commitments are used up. I thought I'd get you fellows down and skull it around."

Bancroft was the first to speak. His booming salesman's voice echoed in the room. "Can't see where it would hurt. We could use some excitement. The dealers are all bitching that we haven't any glamour." His voice suddenly faded as he realized that he might be on the wrong track.

Dan Weyman took it up smoothly. "There are two sides to the problem. No doubt about it that a good effort on the raceway could help us. But we have to weigh its cost against its benefits." He looked at me. "What do you estimate?"

"The least we should field is three cars," I said. "Formula Three. We couldn't make it in One or Two. We haven't a standard car that could meet the competition, so we would have to go to prototype. I figure with personnel and design and engineering, about a hundred thousand a car. That would be for the first three, after that they would cost progressively less."

Weyman nodded. "Right now we're selling a little over two hundred thousand cars annually and we're losing about a hundred and forty dollars per unit. You would be adding about a dollar and a half per unit to that loss." He looked at Bancroft. "That means you would have to sell at least thirty thousand more cars just to keep the unit loss at present levels. Do you think you could do it?"

Bancroft was so hungry for the sales you could almost feel him taste it. "I think we have a chance." Then he added the qualifying Detroit constant, "Providing the economy doesn't go to hell."

I looked at Weyman. "How many units do you have to sell to break even?"

"Three hundred thousand," he said quickly. "That's a fifty percent increase over our present rate. Once past that, we break into the profit column."

"That should be easy," I said, slipping him the needle. "Volkswagen sells more than that."

"Volks doesn't field a full line," he said. "We have to cover the whole American market to meet the competition."

I didn't answer. We all knew that was a crock of shit. The only reason for a full line was to protect their own parts division.

Loren had been silent while we were talking. Now he spoke. From his tone I knew his mind had been made up. "I think we'll take a shot at it. I have a lot of respect for my grandfather. Besides it won't make a big difference whether we lose a dollar more per unit or not at this stage of the game. And, who knows, with Ford and GM out of it, we might even pick up a few trophies."

He got to his feet. "Dan, you take care of the details. Get Angelo set up in an office and see to it that he gets whatever assistance he needs." He looked at me. "Angelo, you report to Dan on costs, and to me on everything else."

"Thank you, Loren," I said, and the meeting was over.

We walked down the corridor. "How's Number One?" Bancroft asked.

"Just fine," I answered.

"There's been a lot of talk around that he's slipping. Old-age things, you know."

"If he is, then we're all in trouble," I said. "He's as sharp as he ever was."

"I'm glad to hear that," Bancroft said. I could tell that he meant it. "He was a real automobile man."

"He still is."

"My office is right here," Dan said. "Come on in and we'll get the details over with."

I arranged to have lunch with Bancroft early in the following week and went into Dan's office. It was simple, efficient and modern, as befit the financial vice-president.

Dan walked around his desk and sat down. I seated myself opposite. "If my memory serves me right, you worked for us before," he said.

I nodded. He knew damn well that I did.

He picked up his phone and asked for my personnel file. He ran a tight ship. The file was on his desk within two minutes, even though the date of my last employment there was over eleven years ago. He opened it and looked at it. There was surprise in his voice. "Do you know that you still have a balance in our paid-up pension fund?"

I didn't know it but I nodded anyway. "I didn't exactly need the money," I said. "And it was as safe a place as any to leave it."

"Have you discussed your compensation?" he asked.

"We never got around to it."

"I'll take it up with Loren," he said. "Do you have any suggestions?"

"None at all. Whatever he says is okay with me."

"Have you discussed a title?"

"Number One suggested, 'vice-president, special projects.' "

"I'll have to clear that with Loren," he said.

I nodded my understanding.

He stared down at my file for a few moments, then closed it and looked up at me. "I guess that's all I need." He got to his feet. "Let's go over to Design and Engineering and see if we can find a nice office for you."

"Don't worry too much about it," I said. "I don't plan to be spending much time in it."

Chapter Eight

THE FRUSTRATIONS began to pile up. I didn't need a Seeing Eye dog to sense that the word was out on me. I got all the cooperation I asked for, but everything took twice as long. Six weeks later I was still in my office trying to get Engineering to spring three Sundancer engines for me. The Sundancer was the top of their line.

Finally I picked up the phone and called Number One. "I'm boxed in," I said.

He chuckled. "You're in there with real pros, son. They make those kiddie-car drivers you've played around with look like rank amateurs."

I had to laugh. He was so right.

"What are you going to do?" he asked.

"I just wanted your permission to play it my way."

"Go right ahead. That's what I got you for."

My next call was to Weyman. "I'm leaving for the Coast tomorrow."

He sounded puzzled. "But the engines haven't come through yet."

"I can't wait for them. If I don't begin to set my pit crew and drivers now for next year, we may have cars but that's all."

"What about the modifications?" he asked.

"Carradine in Engineering has them all worked out. He'll begin the moment he gets the engines."

"And the shell?"

"Design is already working on it. I've approved the plans and they tell me that they're waiting approval from Cost." That was a shot at him.

"They haven't crossed my desk yet," he said defensively.

"They'll get there," I said.

"How long will you be gone?"

"Two, maybe three weeks," I said. "I'll check in with you the minute I get back."

I put down the telephone and waited. In exactly two minutes it rang. It was Loren III. It was also the first time I had spoken with him since the day I came in. He was always in meetings and too busy to call back.

"I've been meaning to call you," he said. "But I've been locked up. How's it going?"

"Can't complain. With a little luck we should field our first racer in the spring."

"That's good." There was a pause. "By the way, I'm having some people over for dinner tonight and Alicia thought it might be nice if you could join us."

"That would be lovely," I said. "What time?"

"Cocktails at seven, dinner at eight thirty. Black tie."

"Haven't got one."

"Dark suit then. Alicia likes to dress up the table."

Carradine at Engineering was the next call. His voice was excited. "What did you do to them? I just got word that we'll have the engines tomorrow. They're pulling them off the line for us."

"When you get them, go to work," I said. "I'm leaving for California and I'll check in with you from there at the end of the week."

The next call was from Design. "We just got the approval back from Cost, but they cut us by twenty percent."

"Build them anyway."

Joe Huff's voice was puzzled. "You know better than that, Angelo. We can't build that design for twenty percent less."

"Did you ever hear of going over budget? You build it. I'll take the responsibility."

I left the office early, feeling better than I had in weeks.

The smokescreen was up and working. Now I could get on with the real thing.

I was the first to arrive. The Hardeman house was only four blocks away. The butler ushered me into the living room and put a drink in my hand. I had just begun to sit down when a tall girl appeared in the doorway.

"Hullo," she said. "Am I early?"

I got back to my feet. "Not for me."

She laughed and came into the room. Her laugh had a warm, throaty undersound. She held out her hand. "I'm Roberta Ayres, Alicia's houseguest."

"Angelo Perino."

She let her hand rest in mine for a moment. "The racer?" Her voice was puzzled.

"Not any more," I said.

"But—" Then she remembered her hand and took it away.

I smiled. I was getting used to it. "I had my face put back together."

"Forgive me," she said quickly. "I hadn't meant to be rude. But I have seen you drive. Many times."

"That's all right," I said.

The butler came into the room. "And what will be your pleasure, Lady Ayres?"

The name rang bells. Her husband was a very good amateur driver who bought the farm coming out of an apex at Nurburgring a few years back.

"Very dry martini, straight up," she said.

"Forgive me," I said. "I should have recognized the name. Your husband was a very fine driver, Lady Ayres."

"It's kind of you to say so. But John's big trouble was that he was never as good a driver as he thought he was."

"Who is?" I asked.

She laughed and the butler placed the drink in her hand. She held it up. "To fast cars."

"Good enough," I said. We drank.

"What are you doing now?

"Putting Bethlehem into racing."

"That should be interesting," she said politely.

"It is."

She looked at me curiously. "You don't talk very much, do you?"

I smiled. "It depends."

"See what I mean," she laughed. "You answer most of my questions with two words."

"I haven't noticed." Then I began to laugh. "That was three words."

Loren came in while we were still laughing. "I see you two have already met."

"We're old friends by now," she said.

A strange expression fleeted through his eyes. It was gone before I could record it. He bent over and kissed her cheek. "You look lovely tonight, Bobbie."

"Thank you, Loren." Her hand brushed his lightly. "I must say you look very mod."

"Like it?" He smiled with pleasure. "I had it made at that London tailor you told me about."

"Absolutely smashing," she said.

Then it all come together. Maybe there was hope for Loren yet. At least it proved there were other things on his mind beside business.

Alicia came down and I went over and kissed her cheek. "Hey, there," I said.

"Hey, there," she said and we both laughed.

Loren and Lady Ayres were looking at us.

"Private joke," I said.

"Angelo and I went to high school together," Alicia explained. "And that's how he used to call everybody. I told him that I wouldn't answer unless he called me by name."

"And then how did he call you?" Lady Ayres asked.

"Hey, Alicia," she replied. We all laughed. "It seems like such a long time ago now."

"You haven't changed that much, Alicia," I said.

She smiled. "You don't have to flatter me, Angelo. My daughter is seventeen."

The other guests began to arrive, and it turned into a typically intimate Grosse Pointe dinner for ten. Young-leaders-of-Detroit-society type.

The conversation was typical also. Taxes. Government

interference in production. The new pressure of safety and ecology, and its apostle, Ralph Nader, came in for his share of damnation.

"We don't decry the need," Loren said. "But we do object to the way in which we are cast as villains. The public forgets very conveniently that they wanted greater horsepower and speed. We only responded to that demand. Even now, with all the hue and cry, give them the choice of a hot car and a slower, more ecologically considerate one in the same price range, they'll choose the hot one every time."

"What's going to happen?" someone asked.

"More government regulations," Loren answered. "More problems for us. The costs will be tremendous and if we can't pass them on to the consumer, we could be pushed out of the automobile business."

But he didn't seem very concerned about that, and the conversation turned to the generation gap and drug abuse in the schools. Then everyone had a chance to tell their favorite stories about their children.

I couldn't contribute much to that, so I spent most of my time nodding and listening. Once when I glanced down the table at Lady Ayres, I caught her watching, a glint of secret amusement in her eyes. She was a very aware lady.

I didn't realize just how aware she was until she stopped next to my seat on the plane the next day. I had requested the lounge so I could spread my papers out on the table and work on the way. I got to my feet. "Why, Lady Ayres, what a pleasant surprise!"

That same glint of amusement that I had seen in her eyes the night before reappeared. "Is it really, Mr. Perino?" she asked, putting herself in the seat next to me. "Then why did you make such a point of telling me exactly what flight you would be on?"

I laughed. "Lady or no, I figured there's only so much of that anyone could take. You had to be human." I reached behind her seat and took the reserve card off and gave it to her.

She read her name on it and looked up at me. "You're pretty sure of yourself, aren't you, Mr. Perino?"

"It's time you called me Angelo."

"Angelo," she said softly, trying it on her tongue. "Angelo. It's a lovely name."

I reached for her hand. "Downhill all the way," I said.

The doors clanged shut and the plane began to roll away from the gate. A few minutes later we taxied down the runway and took off.

She looked out the window at Detroit for a moment, then back at me. "It's like getting out of jail," she said. "How can anyone live in that fucking, boring city?"

Chapter Nine

THERE WAS a Telex waiting for me at the Fairmont Hotel when I stepped up to the registration desk. It was from Loren.

> UNDERSTAND LADY AYRES ON YOUR FLIGHT TO SAN FRANCISCO. WOULD APPRECIATE ANY COURTESIES AND ASSISTANCE YOU CAN EXTEND TO HER. REGARDS.
>
> L.H. III.

I smiled wryly and gave it to her, then turned back to the desk and signed in.

The room clerk looked at the signature, then at the room chart. "We have your suite ready, Mr. Perino. It's in the new tower."

"Thank you," I said.

He signaled a bellboy. "Would you show Mr. and Mrs. Perino to 2112, please." He smiled at me. "Have a pleasant stay, Mr. Perino."

We followed the bellboy down the long corridor to the Tower elevators. She still held the Telex in her hand as we boarded. Silently she gave it back to me.

She didn't speak until we were alone in the room. "How do you think he knew?"

"The Detroit gestapo," I said. "Every motor company has one. They don't like secrets."

"I resent it," she said. "It's none of their affair where I go or what I do."

"You should be flattered. That sort of treatment is usually reserved only for people important to the business."

"What has that to do with me?"

"Come off it, Bobbie. I saw the way Loren looked at you. He's interested."

"All American men are interested. Young blond widow and all that rot. Why should he be any different?"

"Because he's Loren Hardeman Three, that's why. And kings are supposed to be above that sort of thing."

"Only American kings," she said. "We British know better."

I went over to the desk and pulled out a telegraph form. The bellboy came in with the luggage while I was writing. He put the valises in the bedroom. I signaled him to wait until I finished.

"Take a look at that," I said, handing the form to her. She looked down at it.

HARDEMAN III, BETHMO, DETROIT.
INSTRUCTIONS RECEIVED. EVERYTHING UNDER CONTROL. REGARDS.

PERINO.

She was smiling when she returned it to me. I gave it to the bellboy with his tip. He closed the door behind him.

The telephone rang just as he left. I picked it up. It was Arnold Zicker, otherwise known as the merger shark. He was responsible for more corporate mergers and acquisitions than perhaps any man in the United States.

"I've got Tony Rourke standing by for dinner," he said. "Eight thirty okay?"

"Eight thirty okay," I said. "Where?"

"Make it the hotel," he said. "It'll be easier." He was also one of the cheapest men in the world. If we ate at the hotel, it was only natural I should put it on my bill.

"Okay," I said. I put down the phone and looked up at her. "Dinner all right at eight thirty?"

She nodded. "Perfect. Do you have anything special to do until then?"

"No."

"Then let's go to bed and fuck," she said. "You don't think I flew all the way out here just to have dinner?"

It was beautiful. Really beautiful. I think both of us were surprised, then a bit shaken by the deep emotional impact.

We clung together after the passion had been spent. I didn't want to leave her. I felt her trembling. Her flesh was my flesh.

"Hey, man," I said, still trying to understand it. "What happened?"

Her arms tightened around my neck, holding my cheek close to her. "The stars fell in," she whispered.

I was silent.

"I needed you," she said. "You don't know how much."

I put my finger on her lips. "You talk too much."

She nipped my finger. "Women always do," she said. "It's because they never know what to say afterwards."

I put my face down on her shoulder.

She turned her head to look at me. "Somehow I knew it would be like this with us."

"Don't get sloppy," I said. "It's not British."

"What do I have to say to make you realize that it isn't always like this?" she asked, almost angry.

I smiled at her. "What makes you think I don't know? I'm still inside you, aren't I? Usually, by now I'm out of bed, washing my cock."

"I'll wash it for you," she said. "With my juices. I'll drown it."

Just then the telephone rang. I reached across her and picked it up. It was Loren.

"I just got your wire," he said.

"Good."

"Everything okay? Where is she?"

"Right here. I'll let you speak with her." I put the phone in her hand.

"I'm fine, Loren," she said. "No, really, everything is all right. . . . It was lovely, but I'd imposed long enough. . . . Yes, thank you. . . . I'll stay on the Coast for a few weeks and then maybe I'll go over the pole back to London. . . . I'll call you before I do. . . . We're just about to leave for dinner. . . . Give my love to Alicia. . . . Good-bye."

She put the phone back on the cradle, then pushed me off her. I rolled over on my back and she sat up and looked down at me. "You really are quite a bastard," she said.

Then we both began to laugh.

They were seated at the bar when we came into the cocktail lounge. Their eyes snapped open when they saw her. No one wears a micro-mini quite like an English girl. Her legs never stopped.

Arnold slid to his feet from the bar stool. "Tony Rourke, Angelo Perino."

Rourke was a big black Irishman with a squinting driver's face. I liked him right away. We shook hands.

I introduced her and they made room for her. All conversation halted for a moment as she climbed up on the bar stool. It was something to watch. Then we ordered drinks.

I allowed exactly five minutes for the usual pleasantries, then pushed right in. I looked at Rourke. "Arnold tells me that you might have the setup I'm interested in."

"We just might," he answered cautiously.

"It is right," Arnold came on enthusiastically. "Eighteen thousand acres of prime industrial site, two thousand of it with hangar construction that could fit right into your purposes, the rest can be developed as you need it. It also includes almost a mile of waterfront and railroad tracks coming right into it."

I ignored him. He was selling. "I don't understand," I said to Rourke. "Why are you looking for out?"

"Honest?"

I nodded.

"No tomorrows," he said.

I was silent.

"The handwriting is on the wall," he said. "With the cutbacks in defense coming up, we'll be the first to go."

"What makes you think that?" I asked. "They'll still need helicopters." That was their principal line.

"Nowhere near as many," he said. "We're fine as long as the big boys are busy with other projects. Boeing with their seven-forty-sevens; Lockheed's ten-eleven; the SST which will never pass Congress. It will be easy enough to move it away from us and give it to them. And they'll have to do it, there's more to protect there than with us. More personnel, more capital."

"What about commercial application for your planes?"

"Forget it. That market's already sewn up. Besides our helicopter just isn't adaptable. It was designed as a fighting machine." He took another sip of his drink. "We're already on notice that we won't be renewed for next year."

"I appreciate that," I said, looking into his eyes. "You're being very honest."

He smiled. "That's what you asked for, that's what you got. Besides I didn't tell you anything you wouldn't find out for yourself when you checked around."

"Thanks anyway," I said. "You saved a lot of time and bullshit. Do you have all the plans and information with you?"

"Right here," he said, pointing to an attaché case resting on the floor near his feet.

"Good," I said. "Let's go in to dinner and then we can go upstairs and look them over."

It was after three o'clock in the morning when they finally left the suite. "I have a plane at the airport to bring you out to the plant whenever you're ready," Rourke said.

"Thank you. You'll hear from me tomorrow."

John Duncan was due in on a morning flight. He had retired from Bethlehem four years ago when he was sixty. He was the only other man that Number One took into his confidence.

"John Duncan is to me what Charlie Sorensen was to Henry Ford," he had said. "There's nothing he can't do in Production."

"But he's retired," I had said.

"He'll come back," Number One said confidently. "If I know John he has to be bored out of his mind working alone on that gas turbine engine of his out in the garage back of his house."

And Number One had been right. All John Duncan wanted to know was when we were going to start.

The door closed behind them. I walked back into the room and fixed myself a drink. I pushed a pile of papers aside and sank onto the couch.

"They're gone?" Her voice came from the doorway to the bedroom.

I looked up. She was wearing a kaftan of polished cotton that clung to all the promises beneath. I nodded.

"I fell asleep," she said. "But I kept hearing the drone of your voices. What time is it?"

I looked at my watch. "Three twenty."

"You must be fagged."

She made herself a gin and tonic and sat in the lounge chair opposite me. She tasted the drink. "It doesn't make sense," she said. "You don't need all that just to build racing cars, do you?"

I shook my head.

"You're onto something else, aren't you?"

I nodded.

She hesitated. "Does Loren know what you're about?"

"No."

She was silent for a moment while she sipped at her drink. "Aren't you worried?" she asked finally.

"About what?"

"About me," she said. "That I might say something to him?"

"No."

"Why not? You don't know anything about me."

"I know enough," I said. I got to my feet and added some Canadian to my drink, then turned back to her. "Besides happening to be one of the great cunts of the world, I also happen to think that you're a very honorable lady."

She was very still, then she moistened her lips with her tongue. "I love you," she said.

"I know that too," I said. And grinned.

She threw her drink at me and we went to bed. It was still beautiful.

====================== **Chapter Ten**

SHE CAME UP behind me while I was shaving. I heard her over the hum of the electric razor. "You screamed in your sleep last night," she said. "You sat up in bed and covered your face with your hands and screamed."

I looked into the mirror at her. "I'm sorry."

"At first I didn't know what to do," she said. "Then I took you in my arms and you went back to sleep."

"I don't remember," I said, putting down the razor. But that wasn't true. The dream never left me. Asleep or awake. I splashed some aftershave on my face.

"What is it, Angelo?" she asked. "Is that why your eyes don't smile?"

"I died," I said. "The lucky ones stay dead when they've bought it. I didn't."

Abruptly her face disappeared from the mirror. Too late, I remembered about her husband. I followed her into the bedroom. She was standing at the window looking out at San Francisco. I put my arms around her and turned her toward me.

"I didn't mean that the way it sounded," I said.

She placed her head against my chest. I could feel the moistness of her cheek against me. "Yes, you did," she said in a soft voice. "You meant exactly what you said. And the terrible thing is that I understand it and can do nothing about it."

"You're doing fine," I said. "You're beautiful."

Suddenly she was angry. She pulled away from me. "What's the matter with you people?" she cried. "John was the same way. Can't anyone, anything ever reach you? Don't you have room for anything else inside you beside that crazy wish to destroy yourselves against some stupid wall?"

"Okay," I said.

"Okay, what?" she snapped.

"I've already done that," I said. "So what else is new?"

She stared at me for a moment, then, her anger dissolving, came back into my arms. I could feel her body trembling against me. "I'm sorry, Angelo," she whispered. "I had no right to——"

I put a finger over her lips. "You have every right," I said. "As long as you care enough."

The Fan jet Falcon sat out on the airstrip among the 747's and 707's awaiting takeoff clearance like a sparrow among a covey of eagles. The pilot turned his head back to us. "We won't be long. We're number four on the line."

I looked across the seat at John Duncan. His face was grim and tight. He didn't like flying at all and when he saw this plane, he almost called a taxi.

I looked across him and smiled at Bobbie. "Comfortable, John?"

He didn't smile. Small talk wasn't going to make him like it any better. He didn't say anything until we were positioned on the runway awaiting takeoff, then he looked over at me. "If it's all right with you, Angelo," he said, "I'll come back by train."

I laughed aloud. The years hadn't changed him. Maybe his hair had gone a little thinner, but his hands and eyes were still quick and sure. He still looked the same man to me who fixed my car in the park over thirty years ago.

The plane set down on the factory airstrip. Tony Rourke was waiting for us. I introduced them.

He looked at us. "I've taken the liberty of booking you into a hotel near here," he said. "I figure you'll need at least two days to go over the plant completely."

Two days turned out to be an understatement. We were there almost a week. And without John Duncan I would have been completely over my head. I began to understand why Number One had such faith in him. There wasn't anything that escaped his attention. Even to the depth of the channel in the river leading to our docks in case we should ever want to bring in bigger freighters.

At the end of the week I sat with him in the hotel room with the plant blueprints in front of us. Bobbie put out drinks in front of us and went back into the bedroom. "What do you think?" I asked.

"It could do," he said. "The main assembly plant would have to be enlarged considerably for maximum production-line efficiency, but there's no reason why that can't be done. There's space enough. The pre-assembly buildings are positioned well and we wouldn't have to build more than eighty thousand square feet more and it would be perfect. There's only one thing bothering me."

"What's that?"

"Steel," he said. "I don't know the West Coast mills. They might not have the capacity to supply us, and if it had to be shipped from the East we'd be broke before we started. I'd be happier if we had our own mill. That was where GM and Ford consistently wiped us out. They were turning out cars while we waited for steel."

"We'll look into it," I said. "Anything else?"

He shook his head. "Nothing I can think of at the moment."

"Do you have any idea of what it would cost to convert the plant?"

"Without any idea of the kind of car we're going to be building? No."

"I understand Ford put up a new plant to build their new compact. Do you knew how much they're putting into it?"

"I hear a hundred million dollars."

"Would we need that much?"

"Maybe," he said. "I would like to put a cost engineering team on it. I don't like guesswork."

"How long would that take?"

"Three, four months."

"Too long," I said. "If we decide to go for this plant we

have to make up our minds now. I can't keep them on the string that long."

"That's up to you," he said. He began to smile. "You remind me of Number One. He never could wait for the figures either."

"Do you think it's worth the six million Rourke's asking for it?"

"Did you have it appraised?"

"Yes," I answered. "Twice. One appraisal says ten million, the other, nine million six."

"What's Rourke planning to do with it when his contract is completed?"

"Sell it."

"He'll never find a buyer for the whole thing. He'll have to parcel it out. It will take him forever." He thought for a moment. "Depends on how hungry he is."

"I don't know," I said. "He should be in good shape."

"I've been wandering around the plant," he said. "I've developed a lot of respect for him. He'd make a hell of a production man in the auto business if he were interested."

"What are you saying?" I asked.

"Why don't you try him that way?" he suggested shrewdly. "Two years with me and he'd be the best man in the business. And I'm not getting any younger."

My appointment was for three o'clock. I walked into his office. I liked its look. No frills. It was a working office. From its windows he could see out on the plant.

He waved me to a chair. "Would you like a drink?"

"No thanks," I said.

He lit a cigarette. "What do you think?"

"I think I could give you a long list of reasons why I'm not going to buy your plant," I said. "But I don't think it's important, do you?"

He was silent for a moment. Then he nodded. "I agree with you. The reasons aren't important." He dragged on his cigarette. "In a way I'm kind of relieved. I practically built this place with my own two hands. It's only right I should stick with it. A captain should go down with his own ship."

"No," I said. "That's a romantic crock. Any smart captain finds himself another ship."

"Where do I go?" he asked. "Back to work for Bell? Sikorsky? Forget it. I've been on my own too long. Besides the helicopter's going nowhere. It's too specialized."

"Ever think about automobiles?" I asked. "They're all over the place."

"You got to be joking!" he said. "What the hell do I know about automobiles?"

"There's not that much difference between building cars and planes," I said. "Only with cars, you build a lot more of them."

He fell silent.

"John Duncan says that in two years he can make you into the best man in the business," I said. "And if you know that canny Scot the way I do, you wouldn't take him lightly. If he thinks you can cut it, you can. That's all there is to it."

"But what do I do with this?" he asked, waving a hand at the windows.

"Sell it."

"Who to? It would take me five years to get rid of this in bits and pieces."

"I don't mean the plant," I said. "Sell your company."

"Who'd buy it? A company that's ready to go out of business? By the time the assets were liquidated, they'd be lucky if there was a million dollars left."

"That's exactly the figure I had in mind," I said. "Providing you agree to come to work for us on a seven-year contract."

He began to laugh and stuck out his hand. "You know, I think I'm going to enjoy working with you."

I took his hand. "What makes you think that?"

"Because you're such a prick," he said.

"What are you complaining about?" I laughed. "I just made a millionaire out of you."

"Who's complaining?" he asked. He took a bottle from his lower drawer. "What's the next step?"

I watched him pour the drinks. "John Duncan is already

on his way back to Detroit to put together a survey cost engineering team. He'll be back here within a week."

"Fair enough," he said, passing me a drink. "Now that you own the company, how about some operating cash? You have about two hundred thousand due the banks at the end of the month."

"I've already sent your balance sheets to our accountants with instructions to move in and get things organized."

"You seem to have thought of everything except one thing," he said. "What do you want me to do while all this is going on?"

"You're going out to buy us a steel mill," I said. "One big enough to give us enough steel for at least two hundred and fifty thousand cars our first production year and close enough so that it doesn't bankrupt us getting the steel here." I tasted the drink. "And one other thing. Better lay in a stock of Canadian whiskey. You're in the automobile business now."

═══════════════════════════════ **Chapter Eleven**

ARNOLD CAME storming into my suite at the Fairmont with blood in his eyes. "You screwed me out of a nine-hundred-thousand-dollar commission," he screamed. "You went behind my back and made your own deal!"

I smiled at him. "Cool it or you'll wind up with a coronary."

"I'll take you into court!" he shouted. "I'll sue you for every penny you've got!"

"Why don't you do just that," I said. "I'd love to get you on the witness stand and have you tell the world in your own words how you tried to stiff me for six million dollars when you knew the company was practically bankrupt."

He stared at me. "You wouldn't do that?" His voice was shocked.

"Why not? You've been getting away with murder so long you think it's your own special privilege. I don't think it would be too difficult to get the SEC and Congress to launch an investigation into how much money you fleeced out of publicly held corporations and their stockholders."

He was silent for a moment. His voice came down two octaves. "What do you expect me to do? Settle for a lousy fifteen percent commission on a million dollars?"

"Nope."

"I knew you'd see it my way. It just wouldn't be fair."

"Right," I said.

"What do you think is fair?" he asked.

"Five percent," I said.

He went purple and speechless. After a while he found his voice. "That's chickenshit. I don't cross the street for that kind of money. I might as well take nothing."

"That's even better," I said.

"I don't do business like that," he said. "I have a reputation to consider."

I laughed. "That's okay with me too. But I was only beginning. There were other things I thought we might work together on, but if that's the way you want it—"

He didn't give me a chance to finish. "I didn't say I wouldn't take it. After all, there are more important things than money. Like relationships, for one."

"You're absolutely right, Arnold."

"I'm glad that's settled," he said. "Do I send the statement to Weyman at Bethlehem for payment?"

"No," I said. "Send it to me, care of Detroit National Bank."

"Why you?" he asked. "Aren't you acting for Bethlehem?"

I shook my head. "Whatever gave you that idea? I'm on my own in this one. The only thing I have to do for Bethlehem is field a race team."

He thought that over. I could see that he didn't believe me. "Okay," he said, "I'll go along with the game. Now what else did you have in mind?"

"I want a West Coast steel mill," I said. "Get in touch

with Tony Rourke. He's coming to work for me and he'll fill you in on the requirements."

I put in a call to Number One the moment Arnold left. "Where've you been?" his voice came over the long-distance line with a faint wheeze. "I haven't heard from you all week."

I brought him up to date.

"You move fast," he said finally when I had finished.

"I picked up a tow," I said.

"Have you heard anything from Detroit yet?" he asked.

"Not a word," I said. "But I don't expect that to last very long. Arnold Zicker just left here. He seemed to think I was acting for Bethlehem. I straightened him out. I told him I was acting on my own."

"Do you think he believed you?"

"No. That's why I expect some flap. He's going to do a little checking around in Detroit for himself. He can't stand not being on the inside."

"How are you handling the finances?" Number One asked.

"Out of my own trust account," I said. "You weren't the only rich grandfather in Grosse Pointe."

He laughed. "That's not very good business on your part. What if I don't come up with the money?"

"I'll take my chances. My grandfather said you were the best credit risk in Detroit. You were the only man who paid his bootlegger as if he were legitimate."

"You shamed me into it," he laughed. "How much are you in for?"

"About two million so far," I answered. "A million for the acquisition and about a million for operating expenses over the next few months."

"Will you take a million in cash and a million in BMC stock warrants?"

"Done," I said.

"It will be in your bank in the morning," he said. "Where do you go next?"

"Riverside, California," I answered, "to line up some drivers, then to New York. I have a date there with Len Forman about underwriting."

He was silent for a moment. "Forget Riverside. I think we've gone too far now to worry about a cover. Better get on to New York directly. I want to have as much preparation as possible before they catch up to us."

"Okay," I said. "But I think I ought to call Loren then and let him know that I'm quitting. I don't mind playing games, but I don't like outright cheating. I did say I would field a racing team."

"You'll do nothing of the kind!" His voice was sharp. "Leave Loren to me. Besides, you don't think he believed your story even for a minute, do you?"

I didn't answer.

"You keep your mouth shut and go to New York," he said.

"Okay. He may be your grandson, but I still don't like it."

"I'm not looking for your approval," he snapped. "Just do your job!"

The telephone went dead in my hand and I put it down. I made myself a drink and went into the bedroom.

She was lying on the bed, leafing through a magazine. She looked up. "Meeting over?"

I nodded.

"Everything all right?"

"Yeah." I took a sip. The whiskey tasted good. "There's been a change of plans."

"Oh?"

"We're not going to Riverside."

"I'm not sorry," she said. "I couldn't care less if I never saw another raceway."

"We're going to New York."

"When?"

"If we pack now, we can make the red-eye leaving at ten forty-five and we'll be in New York in the morning."

"And if we don't make the red-eye?"

"We leave in the morning. But then I lose a whole day."

"Is that important?"

"Could be."

"Then we'll make it," she said, getting out of bed.

I watched her slip out of her robe and walk nude to the

closet and reach for a dress. "Aah, the hell with it," I said. "Get back into bed."

I couldn't think of anything more stupid than spending the night on a plane.

Chapter Twelve

I HAD to say one thing for her. Lady or no, she ate like a stevedore. I watched her demolish her breakfast: juice, dollar-size pancakes with eggs and sausages, toast, marmalade and tea. And all the time I kept pouring coffee into myself to bring myself up to the day.

"You Americans eat such enormous breakfasts," she said between mouthfuls. "Lovely."

I nodded. We certainly did, I thought as I poured myself a fourth cup of coffee. The phone rang and I picked it up.

"Mr. Carroll at the front desk," the voice identified itself. "Sorry to disturb you, Mr. Perino."

"Quite all right, Mr. Carroll."

His voice lowered. "I have a long-distance call for Lady Ayres. It's from Detroit and I thought perhaps it might be wise if I got your permission before we put it through."

I covered the mouthpiece with my hand. "Who in Detroit knows you're staying here?"

"The only one I told was Loren," she answered.

Since her name hadn't appeared on the hotel register, it meant that security was on the ball. I spoke into the phone. "Mr. Carroll, you're a gentleman of intelligence and discretion. Put the call through."

"Thank you, Mr. Perino." I could tell he was pleased because his voice held that man-to-man feeling. "If you'll hang up, I'll instruct the operator."

I put down the telephone and pushed it toward her. A moment later it rang.

"Hello," she said. There was a faint crackle in the re-

ceiver. "Why, Loren, how nice of you to call. . . . No, it's
not too early, I was just having breakfast."

His voice echoed faintly on the phone. She listened for a
moment, then covering the mouthpiece, whispered to me.
"He said he was coming out to Palm Springs for a long
weekend of sun and golf and wants me to join him."

I smiled. Loren had balls after all. I wondered if he just
discovered them. "Tell him you were leaving for Hawaii
today."

She nodded. "What rotten luck, Loren. I would have
loved to see you but I've made plans to leave for Hawaii.
I've never been there, you know, and I've always been so
curious about the place."

His voice echoed again in the phone. Again she covered
the mouthpiece. "He said that's even better. He knows
some marvelous places on the outer islands. What do I do
now?"

I thought for a moment. It wasn't the worst thing in the
world. At least it would keep him out of Detroit, and the
longer he stayed away, the better our chances were to get
set. I grinned at her. "I guess you're going to Hawaii."

She spoke a few moments more into the phone, then put
it down. She reached for a cigarette silently. I held the light
for her. She dragged the smoke deeply into her, her eyes
never leaving mine. Finally she let the smoke out. "I don't
know whether I like it."

"Why not?" I asked. "It's not every day a girl gets a
chance to go to Hawaii."

"That's not what I'm talking about and you know it,"
she snapped. "It's your attitude. You dispose of me as if I
were some whore you picked up."

I smiled at her. "It seems to me that I read somewhere
of an Englishman who once said that's the only way to
treat a lady."

She didn't smile. "You really don't care anything at all
about me."

"Don't say that. I would not love thee half as much, my
darling, if I did not love honor more."

"Stop quoting at me," she said, annoyed. "What has
honor got to do with it?"

"It seems a very honorable thing for me to do," I said. "To sacrifice myself for a friend. Noblesse oblige. After all, I do owe him something. If it weren't for him we would never have met."

She met my eyes levelly. "You want him out of the way, don't you?"

"Yes," I said simply.

"What if he falls in love with me?"

"That's his problem."

"What if I fall in love with him?"

"Then it's your problem."

"You're a real shit," she said. I started to get up. "Wait a minute. Where are you going?" she asked.

"Get dressed," I answered. "I have a plane to catch at ten o'clock."

"You're not going anywhere, just yet," she said firmly. "I'm not meeting him at the airport until seven this evening. Now that you know he'll be out of the way, you can afford another day."

"What for?" I asked.

She looked up at me. "Because I'm going to fuck you into the ground. Fuck you until there's no juice left in your balls, no marrow in your bones. So much that you'll be lucky if you can raise a hard for a month."

I laughed and sank back into the chair. I reached for the phone.

"Who are you calling?" she asked suspiciously.

"Room service," I said. I had the sudden feeling I would need a large breakfast.

I went out to the airport with her even though my plane did not leave until two hours later. I checked my bags onto my flight, then went with her to the waiting area for the United flight from Detroit. We got there about fifteen minutes before the flight was due.

"We've got time for a quick drink," I said, and led her to the nearest bar.

The waitress put our drinks in front of us and walked away. I raised my glass. "Cheers."

She barely tasted her martini.

I looked at her. She had been silent all the way out. "Chin up," I said. "It's not so bad."

In the dim lights I could barely see her eyes under the wide brim of her soft felt hat. "I'm worried about you," she said.

"I'll be okay."

"You sure?"

"Sure."

She raised the glass to her lips, then put it down without tasting it. "Will I see you again?"

I nodded.

"When?"

"When you get back."

"Where will I find you?"

"I'll be around. I'll find you."

The mechanical voice came from the speakers built into the ceiling. "United Airlines, Flight 271 from Detroit, now arriving at Gate 72."

"That's you," I said. I finished my drink and we got to our feet. She hadn't touched hers.

We left the dark and walked into the million-watt fluorescents of the terminal. I stood there. "Have a fun vacation," I said.

She looked up into my face. Her voice was soft. "Don't get caught up in the dicing, there are other ways to get yourself killed besides climbing the wall."

"I won't," I said. I bent and kissed her lightly on the lips. "Good-bye."

I barely felt her lips move beneath mine. "Good-bye."

She made it as far as three steps away, then abruptly flung herself back into my arms. Her mouth crushed hungrily against mine. "Don't let me go, Angelo!" she cried. "I love you."

For a moment I almost heard the music, but the roll of drums was louder. "I'm not letting go," I said and gently took her arms from around my neck and placed them at her side.

She didn't say another word. This time she made it all the way. I stood looking there after her until she reached the gate.

The passengers were already coming through. He was among the first off the plane. He was a big man and he towered above the others with his gray Detroit felt snap brim.

A smile split his face when he saw her. He hurried toward her, removing his hat with one hand and holding out the other. Almost formally they shook hands, then awkwardly he bent and kissed her cheek.

I turned and got onto the electric walkway leading to the main terminal section and my flight. I looked back only once.

They were on the way into the bar we had just left. He had one hand on her arm as if he were supporting a basket of eggs, looking down into her face and talking.

The million fluorescent watts began to burn my eyes and I stopped looking. I couldn't wait until I reached the end of the walkway, then I headed for the nearest bar.

I had two hours before my flight and by the time I boarded, I was smashed. Not smashed outside, rolling and drunk, but smashed inside, bleak and empty.

I sank into my seat and fastened the belt. I leaned back and closed my eyes.

"Are you comfortable, sir?" the stewardess asked. "Is there anything I can do for you?"

I opened my eyes and looked into her professionally smiling face. "Yes," I said. "Give me a double Canadian on the rocks as soon as we take off and a pair of eye shades. Then don't disturb me for anything. No hors d'oeuvres, no dinner, no movie, no nothing. I want to sleep all the way to New York."

"Yes, sir," she said.

But it didn't work. Neither the whiskey nor the eye shades. Though I kept them on and my eyes closed for the whole of the flight, I didn't sleep.

All I could hear was the sound of her voice in my ear, all I could see was the expression on her face when she left me.

I was glad when the plane finally touched down in New York and I could open my eyes. The whole damn thing was too heavy.

IT WAS three days later; we sat on the lawn overlooking the swimming pool and the private beach with its white sand going down to the water. A faint early September wind rustled in the palm fronds over our heads. I closed my eyes and turned my face to the sun.

"Winter is coming," Number One said.

"It's still warm," I said.

"Not to me. Each year I've been thinking of going farther and farther south. Maybe to Nassau or the Virgins. As I grow older my bones seem to signal the oncoming cold."

I turned my head to look at him. He was sitting in his chair, his legs wrapped in the perennial blanket, his eyes looking out toward the sea. "What is it like to grow old, Number One?" I asked.

He didn't take his eyes from the white-capped water. "I hate it," he said, without giving his words any special emphasis. "Mostly because it's such a bore. Everything seems to be passing you by, you find out that you're not as important as you thought you were. The world moves on and after a while you become absorbed in the only game left to play. One stupid ambition: 12:01 A.M."

"12:01 A.M.?" I asked. "What's that?"

"Tomorrow morning," he said, turning to look at me. "The survival game. Only you don't know why you're playing it. Tomorrow is nothing but today all over again. Only more so."

"If that's it, why are you starting all this?"

"Because just once again before I die, I want something to matter more to me than 12:01 A.M." He turned to look again at the ocean. "I suppose I didn't think much about what was happening to me until last year when Elizabeth came down and spent a few days. Do you know her?"

Elizabeth was Loren's daughter. "We've never met."

"She was sixteen then," he said. "And, suddenly, she turned back the clock for me. Betsy, last summer, was the exact age that her great-grandmother was when we met. Time plays funny tricks on people, it jumps generations to recreate itself. For those few days I was young."

I didn't speak.

"I would get up early in the morning and look out from my window at her swimming in the pool. One morning, it was so beautiful that she dropped her swimsuit at the side of the pool and dove into the water. I watched her until the sheer youth and exuberance of her brought tears to my eyes. And then I realized what had happened to me. Too many years had gone by and I had not cared enough about anything to cry for it.

"My world had become my body. My body, my shell, my prison in which I served out my time. And that was very wrong. Because a prison is something you should try to get out of. I was doing exactly the opposite. My only concern was to find ways and means to spend more and more time in it. At exactly that moment I knew what I had to do.

"Take off my clothes and jump once more into the pool. For over thirty years I sat in this chair thinking I was alive when I was really dead. But I wasn't about to stay dead. There was still something for me to do, something I could do. Build a car for Betsy as I had built a car for her great-grandmother.

"When she came up from the pool and we sat at the breakfast table, I told her what I would do. She jumped up and threw her arms around me. And do you know what she said?"

I shook my head.

" 'Great-Grandfather, that would be the grooviest thing that anyone could ever do for me!' "

He was silent. "After she had gone, I called Loren. He thought it was a beautiful sentiment. But not very practical. Economically, our profit structure had stabilized; building a new car could possibly disturb that. Physically, we didn't have the space; over seventy percent was committed to other forms of manufacture. But I did get him to promise to look into it."

"Did he?"

"I don't know. If he did, I never heard from him. After a while I realized that if I wanted it done I would have to find someone else to do it for me. That's how I came to you."

"Why me?"

"Because automobiles are your life as much as they are mine. I knew that ever since that day in the park and I knew it would be just a matter of time before you stopped playing with toys and got to the core of what you're about. I knew I was right the moment I heard your voice on the phone after the Indy."

"Okay, you got me," I smiled. "But there's still Loren."

A puzzled look came over his face. "I don't understand that at all. I know Loren's not stupid. He should have found out what we're up to, long before now. But not a word from him."

"Loren has other things on his mind," I said.

"Like what? One thing Loren never does is take his eyes off the business."

"This time he did."

"Don't be so damned mysterious," he snapped. "If you know something I don't, tell me."

"Loren has romance on his mind," I said. "Right now he's in Hawaii."

"How do you know that?" he asked sharply. "I've called his home and the office. Nobody knows where he is."

I laughed. "I practically did everything but put the girl on the plane with him." Briefly I told him the story and at its finish he began to smile.

"Good," he said. "I was beginning to wonder if he was human. Maybe there's some hope for him yet."

I got to my feet. "I think I'll take a look inside and see how the boys are coming along with their figures."

I left him sitting there, looking out at the ocean, and walked back up to the house and into the library. Despite the opened windows there were always layers of blue cigarette smoke hanging in the air over the table around which the accountants were gathered. At one end of the table sat Len Forman, a senior partner of Danville, Reynolds, and Firestone, representing the combined underwriters, and at the other end of the table, Arthur Roberts, a prominent New York corporate attorney, who had been retained as our counsel. The thing I liked about Artie is that he wasn't afraid of a fight and we all knew, going in, that this was not going to be a waltz.

"Where are we?" I asked.

"Almost finished," Artie said. "I think we can begin talking now."

"I'll get Number One," I said.

"Don't do that," Artie said quickly. "We'll come with you. After three days locked up in this room a little fresh air can't hurt."

"I still have a few things to clean up," Len said. "You go ahead, I'll catch up."

We went back down to the pool. Number One was still looking out at the ocean. He turned his head when he heard our footsteps. He came right to the point. "What do you think, Mr. Roberts? Can we do it?"

"It can be done, Mr. Hardeman," Artie said. "But I think we should examine the various ways to accomplish our ends."

"Explain," Number One said succinctly. "But remember to keep it simple. I'm a mechanic, not a lawyer or an accountant."

"I'll try," Artie said with a smile. He knew as well as I that Number One had thought it all out long before any of us got into the act. "There are several ways to go. One, take the whole company public. I believe this can be accomplished without serious tax disadvantages. Two, splitting the appliance and manufacturing division away from the main body of the corporation and either selling them or going public with them. Three, the reverse of two, splitting away the automobile division and going public with it. Because of its profitless structure, I think this would be the least attractive."

"Do you think we could raise the kind of capital we require?" Number One asked.

"I see no reason why we can't," Artie said. "Regardless of the plan we adopt." He turned to Forman, who had come up just as the question had been asked. "What do you think, Len?"

Forman nodded. "No problem. It should be the most marketable issue to hit the street since Ford went public."

"Which plan do you recommend?"

"The first plan," Artie said quickly. "Take the whole company public."

"Do you agree?" Number One turned to Forman.

"Absolutely," he nodded. "That would be the most attractive."

"Is that your reason also?" Number One asked Artie.

"Not really," Artie said. "I just can't see why you have to relinquish your equity in the more profitable areas of your company in order to do what you want. I think if we follow the Ford formula, you can have your cake and eat it too."

Number One turned away and looked out at the sea again. He was silent for a long while, then he took a deep breath and turned back to me. "When do you think my grandson will be back in Detroit?"

"Sometime during the coming week."

"I think we should go up there and see him," he said. "Maybe I've been wrong about him all along. I think he should have a chance to make up his own mind."

"That's fair enough," I said.

"I'll have Mrs. Craddock call his office and arrange a meeting at my home in Grosse Pointe, Wednesday evening." He began to move his chair toward the house. Donald appeared mysteriously and began to push him. Number One looked at us. "Come, gentlemen, let me buy you a drink."

We fell into step alongside the chair. Forman asked, "Have you thought of the kind of car you're planning to build, Mr. Hardeman?"

Number One laughed. "One that will run, I hope."

Forman was polite. "I mean its design."

"We're just beginning now," said Number One. "Automobile design is a very complicated art. An art. That's ex-

actly what it is. Modern, functional art. A primary collage
of our technocratic society. That's what it is, gentlemen.
The Model T of Henry Ford does not belong in the Smith-
sonian. A more proper place for it would be in the Metro-
politan Museum of Art."

"Have you selected a name for the car as yet, Mr.
Hardeman?" Artie asked. "I understand that names are
very important."

"They are. And I have." He looked at me and smiled
a private smile. "The Betsy. That's what we'll call it. The
Betsy."

Chapter Fourteen

I DROPPED Artie and Len at the airport so they could make
the late afternoon plane to New York and when i came out
of the terminal, Hertz-Rent-A-Girl was standing next to
my car. "I'm shuah disappointed in you, Angelo," she said
in her honey-and-orange voice. "Heah you've been in town
foh three days now and you haven't called me."

"Sorry, Melissa. But I've been busy."

She pouted. "And I thought you were interested."

"I am, Melissa," I said. "I am."

"Then how about tonight? That is, if youah not busy."

"Tonight is fine," I said. "But no more places like the
last time. It took me three days to get my hearing back.
Don't you know a nice quiet motel where we could just be
together?"

She came on with the "Mr. Perino" shit again. "Mr.
Perino, this is a small town and a girl has to be careful of
her reputation. Maybe we could just go for a long, quiet
drive."

I remembered the way she drove and shook my head.
"No thanks. Besides I'm too old for backseat fucking." I
walked around the convertible and slid in behind the wheel.
I turned the key in the starter. "Be seeing you, Melissa."

"No, Angelo," she said. "Wait a minute." Her voice lowered as she leaned across the car door, giving me a good look at the two ripe Sunkists pushing against her blouse. "I'll have to make arrangements," she whispered. "I'll tell my folks I'm going to spend the night with a girl friend who has a small cottage just north of town. She's away and she left the key with me."

"Now you're making sense."

She had the Mach One again when she came to pick me up. She got out of the car when I came down the steps. "You drive."

"Okay." I got behind the wheel. I clipped my seat belt and looked at her. She fastened her belt. We went down the driveway.

"Turn right," she said. "There's a package store about a half mile up."

I swung the car into the road and, keeping it in low gear, revved the motor to an almost roaring red line on the tach. I hit the brake hard and slammed to a stop in front of the package store. I looked over at her.

Her eyes were half closed and her mouth open as she sucked in air. Her legs were open too. I reached over and put my hand under her dress. Her pantyhose were soaked. She was a born pit popsie. She shivered.

"What are you drinking?" I asked.

She closed her knees on my hand. "Champagne," she said. "French champagne. Make sure it's good and cold."

"Okay. Give me back my hand and I'll go get it."

I came back with three bottles of Cordon Rouge. I showed them to her. "This okay?"

She nodded. I got into the car and we pulled out onto the road. "You do drive a car, don't you," she said in a hushed voice.

"I do." I put my foot down on the accelerator. I knew just what she wanted. Lucky for me, there weren't any cops on the road. I think we made the seven miles to the cottage in under six minutes.

The cottage was one of many exactly like it on a small road a half mile off the highway. I pulled into the driveway she pointed out to me and stopped under the carport. I switched off the motor and looked at her.

Her eyes were shining. "You blew my mind."

I didn't speak.

"Remember that time you were passing three cars and that car came up the road at us?"

I nodded.

"I looked at the speedometer. You were doing one-twenty. When you cut back into the lane I came so hard I half peed. After that I couldn't stop coming for almost a minute."

"I hope you have some left," I said.

She laughed. "Never dry," she said, and got out of the car. She reached behind her seat and lifted out a small flight bag. I grabbed the champagne and followed her into the house.

She went through the whole house closing the blinds and pulling the drapes before she would let me turn on a light. "My girl friend is always complaining about nosy neighbors," she explained.

"It's nice to know somebody cares," I said.

She opened the flight bag. "I have to hang up my dress for tomorrow so it won't be wrinkled." She put the dress in the closet and came back. "Do you smoke?"

"Sometimes."

"Good," she said. "I've got some great grass." She took out a small cellophane bag and a package of Zig Zag papers and put them on the table. "Do you like poppers?"

"They're fun."

"A wholesale drug salesman gives me a can of them every time he comes through. These are fresh. I just got them today."

"How lucky can I get?" I reached for her but she slipped away from me.

"Don't be in such a rush," she said. "You open a bottle of champagne while I grab a quick shower. I feel all icky."

I looked at her. If she came just half as much as she said she did, she had to be solid glue by now. "Okay," I said.

She took a paper bag out of the flight bag and gave it to

me. It was ice cold. I looked at her questioningly. "Steaks," she explained. "If we get hungry later."

I laughed and patted her on the ass. "Go take your shower."

She thought of everything.

Hertz-Rent-A-Girl was climbing up the wall. Two sticks and a popper as she hit her first orgasm and she was on a trip that had no return. I had my head down between her legs and she was pulling at my hair, trying to stuff my face into her. She was right about one thing. She was never dry.

Suddenly she pushed me away. "You won't think I'm awful?" she asked.

I shook my head.

"I want you to come in my mouth," she said.

"Do I get a fuck first?"

"Yes," she said, "but I still want you to come in my mouth."

I rolled her over and went into her from behind. She reached underneath her and grabbed my balls and squeezed. "Oh, God!" she said. "They're so full and heavy."

I felt it starting to come up. So did she. She got away from me and spun around grabbing me in her mouth. The sperm started spilling and she sucked, making gobbling noises and squeezing and milking my testicles until long after they were empty. I lay there spent and exhausted.

"That was great," she said. "You taste like heavy sweet cream."

She was still holding me, playing with me. "Do you have to take a pee?" she asked.

"Now that you mention it, I do." I started out of the bed.

She followed me into the bathroom. "Let me hold it for you."

I looked at her. "Be my guest."

She stood behind me and aimed it at the bowl, but it was awkward and splashed over the seat.

"Just what I thought," I said. "Women don't know anything about taking a piss."

"Let me try," she said and climbed into the bathtub next to the toilet bowl. Then she held it. This time her aim was true.

I looked at her face. There was an expression of rapt concentration there that I had never seen before. A fascination that was almost childish. She turned her face up to me. Almost as if she were in a spell she put her free hand in the path of the stream. Abruptly she turned it to her.

I stopped in surprise.

She pulled angrily at my cock. "Don't stop!" she cried. "It's beautiful. Bathe me in it."

"Different strokes for different folks," I said. If that was what she wanted, who was I to say no?

It was a wild, crazy night. On top of everything else she turned out to be a screamer. Which only made a liar out of her girl friend. If the neighbors really had been nosy, they would have called the cops.

It was seven in the morning when she dropped me in front of the house. She put out her hand almost formally. "Thank you, Angelo," she said. "It was the most beautiful and romantic evening of my life."

I couldn't help but agree with her. She drove off. I went up the steps and into the house. Donald met me at the door.

"A Lady Ayres tried to reach you several times last evening," he said. "She left a call-back number. She says it's very important."

"Where's she calling from?" I asked.

"New York," he answered. "Shall I try to get her for you?"

"Please," I said. I followed him into the library. There was a pot of coffee on the table. I filled a cup while I waited. A moment later, he signaled. I picked up the telephone near me. "Hello."

"Angelo." Her voice was very tight. "I've got to see you. . . . Right away."

"What are you doing in New York?" I asked. "I thought—"

"Alicia knows about Loren and me going away," she said. "The office was trying to find him and they made the mistake of telling her."

"Why did the office want him?"

"It had something to do with you. He didn't say very much. But he was very angry and he said you might wind up in jail. Then Alicia called and he told her everything."

"The damn fool."

"He's not very sophisticated," she said. "It's a matter of honor with him. Now he wants to marry me."

"Where is he?"

"In Detroit. I must see you. Can I come down there?"

"No. I'll come up to New York. Where are you staying?"

"The Waldorf," she said.

"I'll be up this afternoon."

Her voice sounded relieved. "I love you, Angelo."

" 'Bye, darling," I said. Number One was in the doorway.

"Who was that?" he asked.

"The girl I told you about," I said. "The shit hit the fan. Loren is on to us."

"I know that," Number One said testily. "I've already spoken to him. But something else happened."

"Yes," I said. "Alicia nailed him with the girl. He wants a divorce."

"Oh, Jesus!" Number One said. "That boy will never grow up."

Chapter Fifteen

"I DON'T KNOW what the hell I'm doing here," she said, pacing up and down the large living room of the Bethlehem Motors suite in the Waldorf Towers. "Everything happened so fast."

I sat in the chair looking up at her. I took a sip of my drink without speaking.

" 'Go to the company suite in the Waldorf,' he said, 'and wait there until you hear from me. Just don't worry.' " She stopped pacing and looked down at me. "It wasn't until I got on the plane to New York that I thought about what he said. There was nothing to worry about. Nothing had happened between us."

I still didn't speak.

"You don't believe me, do you?" she demanded.

"Of course I believe you."

"You don't sound as if you do."

"Come over here," I said.

She crossed the room and stood in front of me. I leaned forward in the chair and kissed her right on the crotch, then looked up at her. "Now do you believe that I believe you?"

A half smile came to her mouth. "That's a very complicated question. You're crazy."

"Uh-huh," I said. "Now calm down and tell me exactly what happened. What might be nothing to you, might be something very different to him. Remember, we're talking about a very square guy."

"That's true," she said. "There is a boyish naïveté about him which, at first, I thought was a put-on. But it wasn't. That's the way he really is."

"Did you share the same suite?"

"No," she said. "Our suites were next to each other."

"Connecting door?"

"Yes. But he never came through the door without knocking first, even if it was always open. He never kissed me good night without first asking my permission. And he never once mentioned that he was in love with me until after he had spoken to Alicia."

"He must have shown something."

"Of course he did," she said. "There were all the signs. The fresh flowers every day, the way he looked at me with big round eyes, the constant accidental touching of my hand, you know what I mean. I thought it was charming, but I didn't take it seriously. Who could? It was all so Victorian."

"If everything was so proper, how did Alicia get on to you?"

"Because everything was too damn proper," she said. "That's what was so stupid about the whole thing. Alicia's call came through while we were having a drink in my suite. If we had been sharing the same suite, I never would have picked up the phone. This way I thought nothing of it. She recognized my voice instantly."

"Was this before or after he spoke to his office?"

"Before. Actually that's what she was calling him about. To find out whether he wanted her to let the office know where to reach him."

"Oh, baby," I said. "That isn't being square, that's being stupid. It takes a special talent for a man to let his wife know where he's going to be, especially if he's going away with another woman. He was looking to get caught."

"Do you really think that?"

"What else is there to think?" I looked at her. "I knew he was interested in you that first night we met at dinner at their house. Alicia isn't blind. I'm sure she saw it too."

She thought for a moment. "Of course. That had to be it. How could I be so stupid?"

I smiled at her. "You just take it for granted that men fall at your feet."

"But why didn't he say something to me?"

"Maybe he was afraid that you would reject him," I said. "Who the hell knows?"

"What should I do?" she asked. "I don't need all this *merde*."

A signal bell began to ring in the back of my head. Why the sudden change in language? She hadn't hesitated using the English before. "What shit?" I asked.

"You know," she said. For the first time she was vague. "All this. His divorce next year."

"Next year?"

"Yes. He didn't want to get a divorce before Elizabeth's debut next September. He doesn't want anything to spoil it for her."

"He seems to have thought it all out very thoroughly," I said. "And he wants you to wait?"

She nodded.

I felt the gears begin to mesh. Slowly I let the clutch out. "Okay, Bobbie, playtime is over," I said. "Let's get down to the nitty gritty. How long have you been after him?"

She stared at me for a moment. "You have a nasty mind."

"It takes practice," I said. "Truth time. How long?"

She hesitated. "Two years."

"What took you so long? Why didn't you just grab him by the cock?"

"It would have frightened him off," she said. "I had to do the lady bit."

"You're probably right."

"You're not angry with me?"

"Why should I be? I've only known you a few weeks." I reached for a cigarette. "I can't see where you have a problem. You got what you went after."

She looked into my eyes. "I didn't figure on falling in love with you."

"What difference should that make?"

"I don't want to lose you."

"You won't," I smiled. "I don't mind a little bit of adultery. If even adds some fun."

"You could ask me to marry you, you bastard," she said. "Just to be polite."

"No way," I grinned. "You just might take me up on it. And then where would we both be? No place either of us wanted."

"Then what do I do? Wait here for him?"

"No, that would be a mistake." I said. "You have to keep him coming after you. Don't give him the feeling he has you locked away for his own convenience. You get on the plane to London tonight."

"You're probably right," she said thoughtfully. "What do I tell him?"

"Be noble. Tell him you're leaving the country because you don't want to cause embarrassment for him, you respect him too much to allow that to happen. That should instill the proper guilt feelings in him."

She stared at me. "Last chance," she said. "Since you won't ask me, I'll ask you. Will you marry me?"

"No."

The tears suddenly came to her eyes. I held out my arms to her and she came into them. "I knew this would happen," she wept. "I tried to tell you in the San Francisco airport. Why did you let me go?"

"I had no choice. We both had already made our commitments."

Her voice was muffled against my chest. "Take me to bed. Please."

None of it made any sense at all. Everything had changed but nothing had changed. It was still beautiful.

We went directly from bed to the airport. I put her on her plane to London, then caught the last flight of the evening to Detroit.

We sat in the study of the Hardeman mansion in Grosse Pointe around a small, oddly shaped, ancient wooden table whose surface bore the burns of many meetings like this. There were four of us: Loren, Dan Weyman, Number One, and myself.

They had been silent while Number One carefully explained his plans to them. Now he had finished and we waited for their response. It was not long in coming.

"I'm sorry, Grandfather," Loren said. "We just can't permit it. The risk is too great. We can't afford to gamble the future of our company on just one car."

Number One snorted. "How do you think this company was built? Just on that idea. The future of one car."

"Times are different now," Loren said. "The economy is different. Diversification has proven the savior of our company."

"I'm not doubting the value of the other divisions," Number One said. "But I don't agree that it is the savior of our company. I believe it has almost cost us our company. Our automobile business is almost gone. The tail is now wagging the dog."

"Conditions have changed in the thirty years since you were running the company," Loren said stubbornly. "The last new American cars on the market were the Henry J. and the Edsel. And look what happened to them. Kaiser went out of the business and the Edsel almost broke Ford."

"Kaiser would have made it had he kept on, but he wasn't an automobile man," Number One said. "The Edsel didn't stop Ford. They're bigger than they ever were. Next year they're all coming out with sub-compacts. Do you think they would do that if they thought they were going to lose money?"

"They have to," Loren said. "They have to meet the foreign competition. We don't have to. We're satisfied where we are."

"You may be, but I'm not," said Number One. "I don't like being second cousin in a business where we used to be part of the main family." He looked at me, then back at Loren. "If that's your attitude, I can't see any reason we stay in the automobile business."

"It may very well be that next year we won't be in it," Loren said flatly. "We can't afford it any more."

"We'll go out of the auto business over my dead body," Number One said in a cold voice.

Loren was silent. He didn't look well. There were blue circles under his eyes and his face was pouchy and drawn from lack of rest. For a moment I felt sorry for him. He had to be catching hell from all sides. At home as well as the office. His next words dispelled my pity.

He stared right at his grandfather and spoke in an equally cold voice. It was almost as if they were the only two in the room. "At a special meeting of the board of directors held yesterday, three motions were passed.

"One, the immediate dismissal of Angelo Perino as vice-president of the company.

"Two, the institution of criminal proceedings against Mr. Perino for committing the corporation to certain expenditures without due and proper authorization.

"Three, to petition the courts of the State of Michigan to appoint a receiver for your stock in the corporation until such time as it could be determined that you are fully capable and responsible for your actions."

Number One was silent. His eyes never left Loren's face. He sighed. "Is that the way you want to play it?"

Loren nodded. He got to his feet. "Come, Dan. The meeting is over."

"Not quite." Number One's voice was calm. He pushed a sheet of paper across the table at Loren. "Read that."

Loren glanced at it. His face went pale and even more drawn than it had been. "You can't do that!"

"I've already done it," Number One said. "All proper and legal. You can even see the seal of the Corporation Counsel of the State of Michigan, attesting to it. Acting as major stockholder and voting trustee of eighty percent of the company, I have the right to dismiss any or all of the directors of the corporation with or without cause. And that's what I did. That board meeting you had yesterday did you no good. They've all been fired since Monday."

Loren stood there.

"You better sit down, son," Number One said gently.

Loren didn't move.

Number One's voice was still gentle. "You have two choices. You can quit or you can stay. Your father and I didn't always see eye to eye with each other, but we stayed together."

Slowly Loren sat down. He still didn't speak.

Number One nodded. "That's better," he said. "Now we can get down to the real business of this meeting. Building a new car. I promised your daughter I would build her a new car and by God, I'm going to keep that promise!"

I looked across the table at Loren. I would have felt better had he talked. Then I met his eyes and I knew I had been right.

Whatever else Number One thought, the war had just begun.

Book Two
1970

================================ **Chapter One**

HE AWOKE, as usual, a few minutes before the alarm went off. He lay there in bed, his eyes watching the softly illuminated numbers on the digital clock radio move inexorably toward the time it would turn on the music. As usual, he pressed the cut-off button just before the sound switched on: 6 A.M.

Silently he swung out of bed, his feet finding the slippers on the floor; picking up his robe he made his way, silent still, to the bathroom. He closed the door behind him before turning on the light so that he would not awaken his wife. He reached for the cigarettes on the shelf under the mirror, lit one and sat down on the toilet seat. Three cigarettes later nothing had happened and he was debating lighting a fourth, when he heard his wife's voice through the door.

"Dan?"

"Yes." he answered.

"How is it?"

"Nothing," he grumbled, getting to his feet and tying his pajama pants back around him. He opened the door. "That doctor doesn't know what the hell he's talking about."

"He does," she replied, reaching for the phone and

81

pressing the intercom button. "Mamie, we're awake." She
turned to him. "You're too tense. You have to relax."

"I'm relaxed," he said. "My own tensions have nothing
to do with it. I'm just constipated, that's all. I've always
been constipated. Ever since I was a kid. But then they
didn't have fancy doctors who treated you with psycho-
analysis; they gave you a laxative and pointed you at the
nearest toilet."

"Don't get vulgar," she said.

"I'm not vulgar. All I want to do is move my bowels.
Where's the Ex-Lax?"

"I threw it out. Eating Ex-Lax every day is the worst
thing you could do. It prevents you from functioning
naturally."

"Get some," he snapped. "I don't function naturally and
after twenty-one years of marriage you might as well recognize that fact." He went back into the bathroom, slamming
the door behind him.

Mamie came into the bedroom carrying the breakfast
tray. She placed it carefully on the bed across Jane
Weyman's legs. "Good mornin', Miz Weyman," she said, a
bright smile on her dark face. She glanced toward the
closed bathroom door. "How's Mistuh Weyman this
mornin'?"

Jane shrugged her shoulders. She uncovered the napkin
over the toast. "The same."

"That po' man," Mamie said sympathetically. "I do wish
he would let me fix him some grits in the mornin'. They's
nothin' like grits to get the machinery workin'."

"You know him," Jane said, spreading jam lavishly on
her toast. "All he'll do is drink coffee."

"That does nothin' but make his stomach sour," Mamie
said. She started for the door. "You-all tell him, I said
grits'll straighten him out."

She closed the door as the telephone began to ring. Jane
picked it up. "Hello," she said, annoyed. Her voice changed
quickly. "No, Loren, it's quite all right. I'm awake and
having breakfast. I'll call Dan."

She didn't have to; he had opened the door and looked
out at her with a face half-lathered. "Who is it?"

"Loren," she said, her hand over the mouthpiece. "Why is he calling so early?"

He didn't answer. He crossed the room and took the phone from her hand. The lather came off on the earpiece as he held it up. "Good morning, Loren." He wiped the phone with his free hand. "How was your flight in?"

Loren's voice was quiet. "Good. But I got in three hours late. I was wondering if you could come over for breakfast and fill me in before the meeting this morning?"

"Be there in twenty minutes," Dan said. He put down the telephone. "Loren wants me to join him for breakfast," he said to Jane. "There's a board meeting this morning and he wants me to bring him up to date."

"If he stayed home and paid attention to business instead of running around Europe after his English whore," Jane said, "maybe he wouldn't have to bother you at six o'clock in the morning."

"You better stop talking like that," Dan said. "Someday you're going to have to accept her as Mrs. Hardeman. Then what are you going to do?"

"Exactly what I'm doing now," Jane said. "I'll ignore her. Poor Alicia. After all she's been through."

"Poor Alicia," Dan mimicked. "Poor Alicia is going to get a six-million-dollar settlement for her pains. I don't feel sorry for her."

"I do," Jane said. "There isn't enough money in the world to compensate her for what she's going through."

"At least I won't have to show up in a tuxedo for dinner any more," he said, going back to the bathroom. He finished his shave quickly, came out and began to dress. "Turn on the radio and get the morning traffic report."

Jane reached over and pressed the button. Heavy rock music flooded the room. She lowered the volume. "Sometimes I think you never should have left Ford when Mac went to Washington. At least there nobody bothered you early in the morning and your constipation wasn't as bad."

He didn't answer. He was busy tucking his shirt into his trousers. The zipper caught on the shirttail. "Damn!" he muttered, struggling to loosen it.

"Who knows?" she asked. "You might have been president there by now."

"Not a chance. I was never a favorite of Arjay's. He kept me too far down on the pecking order. Besides, he didn't make it. Ford goes for automobile men. That's why Knudsen's there now."

"You'll never be president here either," she said. "Despite Loren's promises. Especially now that the Mafia has moved in."

"Jane, you have a big mouth." he said. "How many times do I have to tell you that Perino has no connection with the Mafia?"

"It's common knowledge that his grandfather was tied up with them," she said. "My grandfather used to sell him the trucks that brought the whiskey down from Canada."

"Your grandfather was also one of his best customers, too," Dan said. "The way he used to drink I'm willing to bet that Old Perino never had to pay a nickel in cash for those trucks. Besides, that has nothing to do with Angelo."

"You're defending him," she said accusingly. "And he's the man who became executive vice-president instead of you."

"I'm not defending him, Jane," he said wearily. "And he's exec VP of the auto division only, not the whole company. I'm still the senior vice-president."

"He doesn't report to you like all the others, does he?"

"No. He's responsible directly to the board of directors. He doesn't even report to Loren."

"That horrid old man," she said. "It's all his fault. Why didn't he stay in Florida like he was supposed to?"

He began to reply but held his tongue as the traffic report came on the radio. "This is WJR and the six-thirty traffic report." The disc jockey's voice was as staccato and harsh as the music had been. "Traffic on all expressways running light to moderate in all directions except for a slight tie-up on the Industrial Expressway around River Rouge where the normal shift traffic is slowing things up. US Ten, Woodward Avenue, clear into downtown Detroit, no traffic."

"Turn it off," he said.

She pressed the button and the voice dropped out of the room. "What's going to happen?" she asked. "There're rumors all over town that the old man's going to make Perino president of the company."

"That's possible. But not likely just yet. Perino still has to prove himself. Especially now that there are plans to go public. Even the old man knows that. Meanwhile Loren and I still run the only end of the business that's making a profit and we're doing better all the time."

He finished knotting his tie and slipped into his jacket. "I'll be leaving. See you tonight." He bent over the bed and kissed her cheek.

"Try to be home before eight o'clock," she said. "We have roast beef and I don't like it burned to a cinder."

He nodded and went to the door. Before he went out, he looked back at her. "Don't forget to get some Ex-Lax," he said. "I think three days is long enough to wait for psychology to work."

She waited until she heard his car leave the driveway, then she took the tray from the bed and placed it on the floor. She picked up the telephone and pressed the intercom.

Mamie answered. "Yes'm."

"I'm going back to sleep for a little bit," she said. "Wake me at nine. I don't want to be late for my tennis lesson."

She put down the telephone and turned off the light. She smiled slightly as she leaned back on the pillow. The new tennis pro down at the club was delicious. The way his lean body pressed against her from behind as he held her arm to straighten her forehand gave her the shivers.

The quiet hum of the 275-horsepower engine under the hood of the conservative all-black Sundancer reassured him as he turned out of his driveway onto the small road leading him to US 10. He looked both ways as he approached the highway. No traffic. He swung onto the road heading for downtown Detroit. He would follow Woodward Avenue to the Edsel Ford Freeway, then out to Grosse Pointe. With a bit of luck the whole trip shouldn't take him more than twenty minutes. The Sundancer responded to his pressure on the accelerator with a satisfying surge of power.

Loren was waiting for him in the breakfast room. "Sorry to be late," he apologized.

"That's all right," Loren said. "Gave me a chance to catch up on what's been happening around town." He gestured to a pile of back copies of the *Automotive News* on the floor next to him.

"Nothing much," Dan said. "Everything's pointing to the sub-compacts coming out in the fall. They're watching the Gremlin, but they don't really expect any action until the Pinto and the Vega are available."

He studied Loren. Loren looked well. There had been a time a few short months ago when Loren had looked as if he were going through a wringer. But apparently that had passed. Now he seemed to be a man who was waiting patiently for the things he knew would happen. He sat down.

"I have some good news," Loren said. "I've closed the deal in West Germany."

"Congratulations!" Dan smiled.

"They'll be ready to begin manufacturing immediately. The whole line. Refrigerators, ranges, television. It opens the whole common market for us on a competitive basis."

"That will mean an additional net profit to us of better than two million dollars this year," Dan said enthusiastically. "In three years we should be able to bring that up to fifteen million."

Loren nodded. "It means you will have to go over there next month to fine-print it. I also promised them a complete engineering team to train their own personnel."

"No problem," Dan said. He rubbed his hands together. "That will make good news for the board meeting this afternoon. So far, all they've been getting is approvals for appropriations. The money is beginning to fly out like a moon probe."

"The board doesn't seem to be concerned about it," Loren said.

Dan nodded. He knew what Loren meant. The new directors representing the banking and underwriting houses who had given them the advance funding went along with every suggestion Number One made.

"Strange," Loren continued in an almost puzzled voice, "here we make the money but all they care about is a new car, which at best is a risky gamble. Do you know, even in Europe, that was what most of them wanted to talk about. The new car. It seems they all want to get into that."

"What do you say to them?" Dan asked.

"I look mysterious and tell them I will talk to them at the right time. It would look damn silly if I were to tell them the truth. That I really don't know any more than they do." He paused for a moment. "By the way, what is happening?"

"He's completed the modifications on the three racing cars," Dan said. "But that was weeks ago. I haven't heard anything since."

"And the new car?"

"Not a word," Dan said. "Maybe we'll hear something at today's meeting. We're being asked to approve the removal of the auto design and engineering department to the Coast."

"When does he want to do that?"

"Next month. He says the new plant will be ready for them at that time."

"Will my grandfather be at the meeting?"

"He's expected. He always shows up when there's something on the new car."

A voice from the doorway interrupted them. "May I come in, Daddy?"

Loren looked up. His face, which had been serious, relaxed. "Of course, Betsy."

She came into the room and leaned over her father's chair and kissed his cheek. "Did you have a good trip?"

Loren noded. She turned to Dan. "Good morning, Mr. Weyman."

She turned back to her father without waiting for Dan's reply. There was a curiously reproachful tone in her voice. "You didn't tell me we're coming out with a Sundancer Super Sport."

Loren was puzzled. "A what?"

"A supercar. You know, a hot one."

Loren looked at Dan. They didn't speak.

"You don't have to go all mysterious on me," she said. "After all, I'm in the family. I never would have said anything to anyone."

The two men still didn't speak.

Betsy reached across the table and poured a cup of coffee. She started back for the door, the cup in her hand. "Okay, don't say anything if you don't want to. But I saw one on Woodward Avenue last night. And you know what, Daddy?"

Loren shook his head.

She smiled proudly. "It ran the wheels off everything in sight!"

Chapter Two

LOREN LOOKED DOWN at the report. "Are you sure about these figures?"

Bancroft nodded his head vigorously. "Cost accounting checked them out. Dan says we can't miss. I have firm orders for three thousand cars. That's two million net profit for us first crack out of the box. The dealers are panting for it."

"Word gets around quickly in this business," Loren said.

"The car's been on Woodward Avenue every night for the past three weeks. By now every dragger in the country is anxious to get his hands on one."

"What does Angelo say?"

"He says he didn't build them for the market. They're test cars. Nothing else." Bancroft took a deep breath. "But, Jesus, it's the first time in ten years that the dealers are calling us instead of me begging them. Even Mr. Sparks at Super Car Mart in Chicago called me. He's willing to put them on the lot with ninety miles run on them so he doesn't blow his Dodge franchise. That's how hot the car is."

"I'd like to see one," Loren said. "All I've seen is the designs so far."

"That's easy," Bancroft said. "One's at the test track right now on its way to fifty thousand miles."

Loren got to his feet. "Let's go." He pressed the button down on his intercom. "Call Dan Weyman," he told his secretary, "and tell him we're all going out to the test track."

It was a gray day with high clouds and occasional gusty bursts of wind and rain. The test track was out past the Willow Run Airport, southwest of the city, and it took them forty-five minutes to get there on the Industrial Expressway. They came off the highway and drove five minutes up a winding back road, finally coming to a stop in front of a wire cyclone fence behind which a tightly cropped cypress hedge obscured everything beyond it.

The security guard came out of his little booth in front of the gate. Another security guard watched them curiously from his booth inside.

Loren looked at him as he approached their car. He wasn't wearing the conventional gray uniform of their security force. Instead he wore the dark blue and Sam Browne belt of the Burns agency. "Gentlemen?" he asked in a pleasant voice.

Bancroft rolled down his window and leaned out from the driver's seat. "I'm Mr. Bancroft. This is Mr. Hardeman and Mr. Weyman."

The guard nodded politely. "How do you do, gentlemen?" He didn't move.

Bancroft looked at him irritably. "Well, don't just stand there, man. Let us in."

The guard stared back at him unperturbed. "Do you have a pass?"

Bancroft jumped over his usually low boiling point. "What the hell do we need a pass for?" he shouted. "Mr. Hardeman is the president of the company and we're vice-presidents!"

"I'm sorry, gentlemen," the guard said in an unruffled

voice. "I don't care if you're God, Jesus Christ and Moses, you don't get in here without a pass signed by either Mr. Perino or Mr. Duncan. That's my orders." He started back toward his booth.

Loren got out of the car. "Guard," he called.

The guard turned back to him. "Yes, sir?"

"Are either Mr. Perino or Mr. Duncan here?"

The guard nodded. "Mr. Duncan is."

"Would you be kind enough to call him and tell him that we're out here and would like to come in?" Loren's voice was pleasant but in the tone of command.

The guard studied him for a moment, then nodded. Without speaking he went back into the booth and picked up a phone. He spoke into it and then put it down. He didn't come out of the booth again, just stood there watching them through the glass window.

Loren reached for a cigarette and lit it. Bancroft and Dan came out of the car and stood there with him. "How come we're using Burns out here instead of our own security people?" he asked Dan.

"Angelo doesn't trust them," Dan replied. "He said he remembered when he was testing the air-cooled six-cylinder for us that Chevy had the plans almost before we did."

"Angelo doesn't trust anybody outside of engineers, mechanics and drivers," Bancroft added. He looked up. "Where the hell is Duncan?"

He walked over to the booth. "Did you speak to him?" he asked the guard.

"No, sir," the guard replied. "He was in the car with the driver. But they said they would get the message to him."

"Oh, Jesus!" Bancroft pulled a cigar from his pocket, stuck it in his mouth and, chewing it without lighting it, walked back to them.

It began to drizzle and they got into the car and sat there silently. Ten minutes passed before a car came down the road inside the gate and John Duncan got out. He signaled to the inside guard and the gate swung open. He walked over to their car.

"I'm sorry about the delay," he apologized. "But we didn't expect you."

"Quite all right, John," Loren said. "I've heard so much about the car, I decided at the last minute to run out and see it."

Duncan smiled. "I'm glad you could come. Follow me."

They followed him down the road to the driving grounds. He pulled his car into a parking slot and they stopped beside him. They got out.

"We'll go down to the garage," he said. "We can keep dry there."

They followed him through the slight drizzle to the garage, located just inside the driving oval. A few men were sitting at a table, playing cards, and a girl was curled up on a couch reading a paperback book.

"The men are mechanics," Duncan explained. "The girl is one of our test drivers."

Bancroft eyed the girl appreciatively. "I knew Angelo would find a better way to do things."

Duncan's voice was flat. "Women do fifty percent of the driving and very few cars are bought without their approval. Angelo's idea is to get their point of view."

"That girl makes points of her own," Bancroft said.

"She's a first-rate driver," Duncan replied.

"Where's the car?" Loren asked.

Duncan walked over to the electronic tracker and pressed a button. The tape-activated lights flashed on. "Just going through checkpoint three at the far end of the test track." He pressed another button. Numbers began to flash on the reading screen. "It's going through the tight turn at seventy-one point six two seven mph." The numbers began to drop rapidly. "It's down to fifty-two, now forty-seven point two three eight going into the corkscrew."

He turned to them. "Watch the screen. When it comes out of there into the straight, it should get up to one-sixty by the time it passes here."

They watched the reading screen in fascination. Suddenly the numbers began to jump up rapidly. In a matter of seconds it seemed that they had gone over 140 and were still climbing. In the distance they could begin to hear the faint roar of the engine.

The engine roar grew louder and they moved toward the

garage door better to see outside. In the distance the white headlight beams sparkled through the drizzle. Almost before they realized it, the beams turned into white blinding glare and the car flew by them, trailing the light like a wraithlike gray shadow, and disappeared down the track.

"A hundred and sixty-eight point seven one five," Duncan's voice came from the tracker.

"How fast will it go?" Loren asked, walking back to him.

"We've had it up to one-ninety-one," Duncan said. "But the track is wet and I told them not to take it over one-sixty-five."

"How many miles have you logged?"

"Thirty-eight thousand. At forty we pull it in, service it and send it out again."

"Is the engine holding up?" Loren asked.

"Real good. Only normal changes despite the fact we have it souped up. Better than I thought. All the sensor readings are solid."

"I'd like to see the car," said Loren.

"I'll call it in," Duncan said. He pressed another button on the panel. A yellow light on a turret outside the garage glowed into life and began to whirl, throwing golden shadows into the windows. He leaned over the microphone built into the panel. "Duncan to Peerless, Duncan to Peerless. Over."

There was a slight rasp of static. "Peerless to Duncan. I read you. Over."

"Cool her off and bring her in. Over."

"Anything wrong?" The driver's voice seemed annoyed. "It looks good out here. Over."

"Nothing wrong," Duncan said. "Just bring her in. Over and out."

"Roger. Over and out." There was a click and the speaker went off.

Duncan hit another button and the tracking screen went to black. He walked toward the garage door. They followed him just as the car went by. It was already slowing down. "He'll come in on the next lap," Duncan explained.

Loren gestured to the tracking console. "I didn't know we had one of those."

"It's Angelo's idea," Duncan said. "He got it from watching the space launch and had it built for us by Rourke's people on the Coast. It turned out to be so good that we're building them now for GM, Ford and Chrysler, and we have orders coming in from all over the world."

The car pulled in just as the rain stopped. They walked out toward it.

Loren studied the car. It was the standard two-door Sundancer hardtop. There was no doubt about that. But there were subtle differences. The hood sloped slightly down toward the headlights and the almost square rear window had been softened and rounded, molding gently down to the spoiler mounted over the trunk, giving the car a definite European look.

The driver got out. He moved stiffly in his fireproof coveralls, flipping the chin-strap of his crash helmet open as he came toward them. "Okay," he said belligerently. "What did I do wrong?"

"Nothing," Duncan said. "Mr. Hardeman here just wanted to look at it."

The driver let out a sigh of relief. He pulled a pack of cigarettes from his pocket. "Mind if I grab a cup of coffee then?"

Duncan shook his head. The driver walked into the garage.

Loren looked into the car. The dash was cluttered with all kinds of instrumentation. He looked back at Duncan. "What did you do to the car?"

Duncan moved up next to him. "The special instruments you see there all have built-in sensors which transmit readings to our control panel. We've put two four-barreled wide-scoop Webers, a new manifold and opened up the bore on the cylinders which gives us an eleven-to-one compression ratio and puts out up to three hundred and forty horse. The body is fiber glass draped on a steel wire net suspended from front and rear roll bars to a tubular chassis on an impact-absorbing suspension principle."

"Exactly what does that mean?" Loren asked.

"The harder you hit, the more it resists the impact," Duncan replied. "The same principle as the suspension bridge, the more weight, the stronger it holds. Combines safety with lightness and economy. This car weighs six hundred and seventy pounds less than the standard Sundancer with the same equipment, and the body shell costs forty percent less to fabricate." Duncan took out a cigarette and lit it. "Of course the car would be lighter still but we had to beef up the axle and the driveshaft to take the power."

"How does it ride?" Loren asked.

Duncan looked at him. "Why don't you take a spin around the track and see for yourself?"

Loren looked around the table. The board meeting was almost over and it had gone quietly, in almost routine fashion. There had been a great deal of satisfaction expressed over the West German deal and he felt bathed in a glow of commendation. Even Number One, sitting in his wheelchair at the foot of the table, had been thoroughly impressed.

The last item on the agenda was now before the board. Approval to move Design and Engineering to the Coast. Loren turned the page.

"Gentlemen," he said. "You all have item number twenty-one on the table before you, and before we move on that item, I would like to say a few words."

He waited for their silent assent before continuing. "First, I think the directors should commend Mr. Perino for a fantastic job done with the experimental cars. As you already know, he has converted three standard Sundancer hardtops into high-performance machines. What you may not know, because he has not mentioned it, perhaps due to his own modesty, is that he has come up with one of the most exciting cars Bethlehem has ever had the good fortune to produce. And I know whereof I speak, gentlemen, for this morning I had the pleasure to ride in one. My congratulations to Mr. Perino."

"Thank you, Mr. Hardeman," Angelo's voice was polite but noncommittal.

Loren waited for the murmur that spread around the table to die down. "Perhaps none of us present realized the potential of this car. Oddly enough it came to my attention this morning through my young daughter, who saw one of the cars dragging on Woodward Avenue the other night and in her words, it 'ran the wheels off everything in sight!' "

He waited again for the pleased murmur to die away. "The other bit of interesting news comes from Mr. Bancroft. He informs me that he is besieged by dealers who want to take immediate shipment on the car, that he already has firm orders for three thousand, which incidentally brings us two million dollars in additional net profits, and he feels that he can without effort sell ten thousand of this particular model in the current model year."

There was a general smiling air around the table. Loren followed through. "Therefore I propose that we add to the agenda, together with the item on the table, approval from this board to begin immediate production on the Sundancer SS and take advantage of this particularly high interest."

There was an almost immediate nodding of heads. "Just a minute, gentlemen." Angelo's voice was still noncommittal. "I do not think we should market these cars."

The directors looked puzzled. One of them, president of a Detroit bank, questioned him. "Why not, Mr. Perino? I know that the supercar market has been a very lucrative one for Dodge, Chevy and American Motors."

Angelo looked at him without expression. "There are several reasons. One, the test car, as is, cannot be marketed because it exceeds emission levels. Conforming to these levels would result in a considerable loss of power so that performance would not reach the heights of the test car."

Weyman spoke up. "Would the car fall below what we commonly understand are supercar standards?"

"There are no standards for supercars, Mr. Weyman," Angelo said dryly. "In answer to your question, I say yes and no. Yes, it will have higher performance than the standard Sundancer; no, it will not match the performance of the hemi and the Mopar." He looked down the table at Loren. "But even that is not the important consideration. We are about to undertake to build a new car. A car that will put us back solidly into the automobile industry. A

specialized car, a supercar, no matter how attractive it may
be, is not the answer to the main issue. The market is a
limited one and my own personal feeling is that it will
shrink rapidly due to the solid restraints of ecological
measures being brought into law. For the sake of a few
dollars in profit, gentlemen, I do not think we ought to risk
the goodwill of an aware future market that we are target-
ing.

"I, perhaps more than anyone here, enjoy a hot car. But
that's not the business we're in. We're about to build a car
for the masses, not for the speed afficionados. I think at the
present time, seeking a hot-car image is wrong. That is
something that should have been done seven years ago.
Today it is out of date."

The banker spoke up again. He looked over at Number
One. "Could you give us your opinion on the matter, Mr.
Hardeman?"

Number One's face was unreadable. He had been doo-
dling on a pad while Loren and Angelo were speaking. Now
he looked up. "I think we should build the car," he said
quietly.

The vote of the board of directors was sixteen for the
proposal, one against. The meeting was concluded several
minutes after that, and they began to leave the room in
groups.

Angelo had just finished returning his papers to the file
when Number One called him. He looked up. "Yes, sir?"

"Wait a moment," the old man said.

Angelo nodded silently.

At last they were alone in the room. Number One
pushed his chair toward Angelo. "You know that I agreed
with you, didn't you?"

"That's what I thought," Angelo said.

"I owe you an explanation why I voted against you," the
old man said.

"You don't owe me anything. You're the boss."

"There was a time," the old man's voice was almost re-
flective, "that people used to say I had destroyed Loren's
father by countermanding every decision he made. That
eventually I was the cause of his death."

Angelo was silent. He had heard the stories.

The old man looked up into Angelo's face. "I couldn't let that story begin all over again, could I?"

Angelo let out a deep breath. "I guess you couldn't."

But later, when he got back to his office, he wondered whether Number One had been telling him the truth.

Chapter Three

HE WOKE with a start. The faint sounds of the orchestra playing in the grand ballroom downstairs floated in through the open windows on the warm June night wind. He sat up in bed, grunting involuntarily as a sudden sharp pain stabbed through his temples. "Jesus!" he exclaimed, almost aloud to himself. "It can't be the booze, I didn't drink that much. Besides Perino told me it was the real stuff."

He got off the bed and padded in his bare feet into the bathroom. The marble of the floor was cold and he went back for his slippers. He turned on the water and splashed it on his face. The headache began to ease and he stared at himself in the mirror. Bit by bit the day came back to him.

It had begun with the wedding at St. Stephen's at noon and then moved to the lawn reception at Hardeman Manor from two o'clock until five. Then everyone began to leave. But it wasn't over yet. They were merely going home to rest and change their clothes. The grand wedding ball was to begin at eight o'clock that evening.

He remembered going upstairs and taking off his jacket. But that was all. He did not remember undressing, but apparently he had, for he was in his pajamas and an entirely new wardrobe was laid out for him. He rubbed his chin reflectively. Another shave couldn't hurt.

He took the shaving mug with the engraved golden picture of the first Sundancer automobile he had built back in 1911 and began to stir the shaving brush in the cup, bringing up a full white lather. Slowly he applied the lather to his face and then massaged it into his skin with strong, firm fingers. Afterwards another layer of hot lather over the first and then he took the ivory-handled straight razor from its case and began to strop it gently against the leather strap hanging from the wall beside the mirror. A few moments later he was ready for his shave.

He began under his chin. Short, gentle strokes up from the neck. He smiled to himself. The razor was perfect. Carefully then he came down from his sideburns toward the chin, then sideways across his upper lip toward his cheek. He ran his fingers over his face. Smooth.

As carefully as he had stropped the razor, he rinsed it and dried it and placed it back in its case. Then he stepped into the shower and turned the water on full force. First hot, then cold, until he was completely awake and tingling. He stepped out of the shower and pulled a rough towel around him and began to rub vigorously. The tingling of his flesh warmed him.

He began to think of Loren Junior and his new bride. Now he remembered that they, too, had gone upstairs to change and he began to wonder if they had waited. Then he thought of his son, the studious, quiet, gentle boy so unlike himself that at times he wondered how he could have a son like that. Of course Junior would wait. But his bride. That was another matter.

She was a Mormon. And he knew about the Mormons. They thought nothing of sharing a husband with several other women and the only times they quarreled was when one of them missed their turn in bed. They didn't like to be done out of their share.

Not that he blamed them. He didn't like being done out of his either. Especially since Elizabeth had always been such a delicate woman, and even more so after Loren's birth. He knew he was a big man and he tried to be gentle with her, but she was so small that he knew he hurt her, even if she bit her lips to keep from crying out when he entered her. He could see the pain in her eyes.

Good thing in a way, that Junior wasn't as large as he was, though he didn't think it would matter with Junior's wife, Sally. She was a solidly built girl even if she was

skinny in the modern flapper sense. She still had a big bust
and wide hips no matter how much she dieted to get into
size. She probably could take all Junior had to give her and
then some. He hoped that Junior would be enough of a
man for her. Then he felt the heat swelling into his loins
and he laughed aloud. He had to be a dirty old man thinking thoughts like that about his son's wife. But then, he
wasn't that old. He was forty-seven this twentieth day of
June, 1925.

He threw the towel carelessly on the floor and walked
into the bedroom. He pulled a union suit from a drawer
and stepped into it, his fingers buttoning up the front as
soon as his arms went through the sleeves. A pair of black
silk sox were folded neatly over the tops of his black
patent-leather shoes. He slipped into them and locked the
garters tight and reached for the freshly starched dress shirt
resting across one of the two wooden valets next to his
closet.

The linen rustled sharply as he put on the shirt. He
walked over to the dresser and picked up the diamond
studs and began to fasten them into the shirt front. He
slipped the matching cufflinks into the sleeves and picked
up the gold collar stud. This was not easy. In less than a
moment, he was red in the face and the collar was crushed.
Angrily he threw it away and took another from the
drawer. Holding it in his hand, he walked into Elizabeth's
room.

He stopped in the doorway. His wife was not there.
Only the young dressmaker who had come from Paris to
make the gowns for this occasion.

She was kneeling, her back to him, on the floor in front
of the dressmaker's form and placing some pins in the fold
of a skirt. She had been humming quietly to herself as she
worked. Suddenly she became aware of him and the humming stopped. She looked back without getting to her feet,
then rose swiftly, raising her eyes to his face.

Her eyes were dark blue, almost purple in tone against
her white skin surrounded by heavy black hair drawn
tightly in a chignon behind her head. He stared at her as if
it were the first time he saw her. They were deep limpid

eyes and a hidden light seemed to be lurking in their depths.

After a moment, he found his voice. It sounded harsh and strange to his own ears. "Where's Mrs. Hardeman?"

Her eyes dropped. "Downstairs, Monsieur." Her voice was low and with the faintest hint of accent. "She is greeting the guests."

"What time is it?"

"Almost nine o'clock, Monsieur."

"Damn!" he swore. "Why didn't someone wake me?"

"I think Madame tried," she said, raising her eyes again. "But you would not, how you say it, awaken up?"

He started back to his room, his fingers fumbling with the collar stud. Suddenly he turned back to her. "I can't fasten this damn thing."

"Perhaps I can be of help, Monsieur," she said, coming toward him.

He placed the studs in her outstretched palm. She reached up toward his collar. "You are tall, Monsieur. You will have to bend a little."

He leaned toward her. For a moment her eyes looked into his, then turned away. Her fingers were light and sure as she pressed the stud into the back of the collar. She then tried to match the front of the collar to the shirt. It didn't work.

She looked closely at the collar and then laughed. "No wonder you could not place the stud," she said. "You have made the buttons in the wrong buttonhole."

He felt the shirt. She was right. He had matched the buttons and the studs one buttonhole short. "I'm sorry," he muttered, his fingers clumsily trying to unfasten them.

"Let me, Monsieur," she said. The faint scent of her perfume came to him as her fingers flew down his shirt front rearranging the buttons.

He felt the sudden strong surge of heat in his loins as her fingers came down to the bottom buttons. He felt his face begin to redden. He could tell that she was aware of what was happening to him, though she gave no sign. He felt he had to say something. "What's your name?" he asked awkwardly.

"Roxanne, Monsieur," she answered, not looking up. She was at the third button from the bottom of the shirt and moving down to the second.

He felt the pressure growing stronger against his union suit. A quick downward glance revealed his deepest fears. The swelling against his underwear was unmistakable. He bent his hips back away from her hand, trying to keep himself away from her. The position was awkward and also hopeless. By the time her fingers reached the last button, his phallus was swollen and beating against his shirt.

She stopped suddenly and looked up into his face. She did not raise her hands, her eyes were very wide. Her mouth opened slightly as if she caught her breath, but she did not speak.

He stared down into her eyes. After a moment, he spoke. "How much?"

Her eyes did not waver. "I would like to stay here and open a small shop, Monsieur. There is nothing for me in Paris."

"You've got it," he said in a harsh voice.

She seemed to nod slightly and slowly sank to her knees before him. Gently her fingers opened his union suit and he sprang out at her like an angry lion from its cage. Carefully she peeled back his foreskin, exposing his red and angry glans, and took him in both hands, one behind the other as if she were grasping a baseball bat. She stared at it in wonder. *"C'est formidable. Un vrai canon."*

He laughed deep in his chest. He did not know the meaning of her words, but he did recognize the tone. It was not the only time he had heard it in a woman's voice when she first saw him. "You're French, aren't you?" he asked.

She nodded.

"Well, then, French it."

She opened her mouth wide and placed it on him. He felt the tiny sharpness of her teeth on his raw glans and in his excitement dug his hands deep into the chignon in her hair and jammed himself into her mouth.

She began to choke and cough. He held her for a moment and then let her pull away. She looked at him, no

longer quite sure of herself, her breath rasping in her
throat.

"Take off your dress," he said.

Her eyes fell from his face and fixed on his thrusting
phallus. She did not move.

"Take off your dress!" he said harshly. "Or I'll tear it
off!"

She moved slowly, almost as if hypnotized, without
taking her eyes from his phallus. The dress fell from her
shoulders revealing round, heavy breasts with bursting
plum-colored nipples. Almost sluggishly she began to rise
from it.

He tugged angrily at his shirt. The studs and buttons
tore, flying wildly around the room. He threw the shirt
away and pulled off his union suit. Naked, he looked even
more an animal than before. Shoulders, chest and belly
covered with hair out of which sprang the massive erection.

She felt a weakness in her knees as she poised to take off
her stockings, and she would have fallen if he suddenly
had not put out a hand to steady her. His touch was hot
against her arm and she felt the fire running into her and
the wetness begin to pour from her.

He placed his hands under her armpits and raised her
naked out of her shoes and held her high in the air over
him. He laughed, the exultation deep inside him.

She almost fainted looking down at him. Slowly he began to lower her on him. Her legs came up, circling his
waist, as he began to enter her. Her breath caught in her
throat. It was as if a giant of white-hot steel were pen-
etrating her vitals. She began to moan as it opened her and
climbed higher into her body, past her womb, past her
stomach, under her heart, up into her throat. She was panting now, like a bitch in heat. But there was no other way
she could breathe. She clung to him in sudden weakness.

As if she were weightless, he crossed the room with her
wrapped around him. He stopped at the side of his wife's
bed and with one hand flung the satin covers to the floor.
He stood there for a moment, then suddenly threw her
from him onto the bed.

She stared up at him in shock, her legs still open and

drawn back, her knees almost at her belly. She felt empty, almost hollow, as if he had withdrawn all her insides with himself.

Then he was poised over her, like a giant animal blocking out the light until all she could see was him. His hands reached and grasped each of her heavy breasts as if he wanted to tear them from her body. She moaned in pain and writhed, her pelvis suddenly arching and thrusting toward him. Then he entered her again.

"Mon Dieu!" she cried, the tears springing into her eyes. *"Mon Dieu!"* She began to climax almost before he was fully inside her. Then she couldn't stop them, one coming rapidly after the other as he slammed into her with the force of the giant body press she had seen working in his factory on a tour just the day before. Somehow she became confused, the man and the machine they were one and the same and the strength was something else she had never known before. And finally, when orgasm after orgasm had racked her body into a searing sheet of flame and she could bear no more, she cried out to him in French.

"Take your pleasure with me! Take your pleasure with me! Quick, before I die!"

A roar came from deep inside his throat and his hands tightened on her breasts. She half screamed and her hands grabbed into the hair of his chest. Then all his weight seemed to fall in on her, crushing the breath from her body, and she felt the hot onrushing gusher of his semen turning her insides into viscous, flowing lava. She discovered herself climaxing again.

"C'est pas possible!" she murmured against his ear as he lay quietly now across her. She closed her eyes as she felt him growing soft and smaller. She began to smile inside herself. The woman always was the victor. The man was only the stronger for the moment.

He got to his feet. "I've got to dress," he said. "Before someone downstairs comes looking for me."

"Yes," she said. "I will help you."

But what neither of them knew was that they had been seen. By the newly wedded bride who had thought it would

be great fun if she were to be the one who could awaken
her father-in-law and get him to come downstairs to his
own party.

== **Chapter Four**

SALLY HARDEMAN shut the door quietly behind her and
stepped out into the hallway. Suddenly her legs were too
weak to support her and she leaned back against the door,
trying to control their trembling. She took a deep breath,
fumbling in her tiny evening purse for a cigarette. She lit
it and sucked the smoke deeply into her lungs. It didn't
matter now whether anyone saw her smoking. Somehow
that wasn't very important any more. Not after what she
had seen.

It was true. The stories she had heard. They were all
true. Now she believed them all. Even the one her closest
girl friend had told her about how at a very formal dinner
in Hardeman Manor one night, she had felt a hand sliding
up her back beneath her loose evening blouse. Almost before she had become aware of the touch, her brassiere had
been unfastened and the hand came around, fondling and
cupping her naked breast.

She almost shrieked aloud and turned angrily toward the
man sitting next to her before she remembered who he was.
Loren Hardeman. He wasn't even looking at her, his face
turned away, talking to the woman on his left.

Only his right arm was there, behind her chair and
under her blouse. She looked around the table. Everyone
seemed engrossed in his own conversation. Even Mrs.
Hardeman almost diagonally across the table from her was
talking to her neighbor. It was with a feeling of shock that
she realized no one seemed to notice the slightly billowing
movement of her blouse as his hand circled and fondled
the breast beneath.

"What did you do?" Sally had asked.

Her girl friend had looked at her with a curiously wise expression. "Nothing," she had answered flatly. "If no one saw what was happening or, at least, pretended not to, who was I to make a fuss? After all, it was Loren Hardeman." And then she giggled. "Then when I looked around the table and thought how stupid they all were not to see what was happening, I began to enjoy it."

"You didn't!" Sally breathed.

"Yes," the girl had answered. "There was something about his touch that was very exciting."

"Then what did you do?" Sally had asked.

Her girl friend had smiled. "After dinner was over I went to the bathroom and hooked up my brassiere."

That was all there was to that story, but there were others. Now Sally could believe them all. She dragged again on the cigarette but her legs still refused to stop trembling. She hoped no one would come into the hallway and see her like this.

She had knocked softly on the door when she had come upstairs. "Daddy Hardeman," she called softly.

There was no answer.

She knocked and called again, then thinking he was still asleep, she tried the door. It swung open silently and she went inside. "Daddy Hardeman," she called softly again before she saw that the bed was empty and noticed the light coming through the bathroom door.

She had turned to leave when a reflection in the large mirror over the bureau on the far wall transfixed her. In the mirror she could see through the open door into her mother-in-law's bedroom and silhouetted in it were two naked figures.

Her father-in-law was holding a naked girl in the air above him. He began to laugh and the sound seemed to rumble in the room as he lowered the girl onto him. The girl cried once and began to moan as he disappeared into her.

It wasn't until he began to walk across the room, the girl still with her legs wrapped around his waist, and disappeared from the mirror that Sally found herself able to move. There was a creak from the protesting bedsprings, then a cry almost of pain, and the mirror was empty. Quickly Sally slipped out of the bedroom.

The cigarette was half finished and she felt self-control coming back. She began to feel anger rising inside her. Almost as if she had suffered a strange kind of personal violation, an ache began to spread through her loins with a warm, pulsing pain. He wasn't like a man at all, he was an animal not only in the way he looked, all covered with hair with swollen giant parts, but also in his brutal manner, careless of all sensitivities.

She began to feel better. Her anger had helped. How fortunate she was that Loren was nothing like his father. Kind, considerate, and gentle. Even today, when they had gone upstairs to their first bedroom together to rest for the ball this evening.

She had not known what to expect. But all he did was to kiss her softly and tell her to lie down on the bed and rest until it would be time to get ready. Then he lay down beside her and closed his eyes. In a moment, the soft sound of his breathing told her he was asleep. She could not fall asleep at once; she lay there watching his quiet face and after a while she, too, slept.

She dropped the cigarette into a tall urn standing in the hall and started for the staircase, when the door to her father-in-law's bedroom opened and he stood there.

"Sally," he said, his voice calm as if nothing had happened. "Why aren't you at the party? After all, it is in your honor."

She felt her face begin to flush. "Actually," she said, "I was just on my way to get you. The guests were beginning to wonder where you were."

He looked at her silently for a moment, then he smiled. "How thoughtful of you," he said, taking her arm. "Then let's not disappoint them, shall we?"

Her legs began to tremble again at his touch and she stumbled slightly as they turned toward the steps. He paused and looked at her. "You're shaking. Are you all right?"

Again that curious, warm, pulsing pain inside her. Somehow she couldn't bring herself to meet his direct gaze. "I'm okay." She managed to laugh. "After all, it's not every day that is a girl's wedding day."

Elizabeth, looking up, saw them coming down the grand stairway. Loren's red hair was just beginning to pepper with gray but his face was as strong and as young as the day they had met. She felt a twinge inside as she saw Sally's blond head turn toward Loren. Loren and she used to be like that. At first it seemed as if they were always laughing.

But that changed as soon as they had arrived in Detroit. Back in Bethlehem Loren had always been fun, never serious, had a joke and a good word for everyone. Then he got into the automobile business and everything changed.

There were the early jobs at Peerless and Maxwell, then Ford, which was over almost before it had begun, and finally with the Dodge Brothers, where Junior had been born in 1901, Loren's first year there. He had remained with the Dodges for almost nine years until they had a falling-out. The trouble was that Loren wanted to build a better car which would sell for slightly more than the standard medium-priced car of the time and the Dodge Brothers weren't at all interested. They were still angry at Ford and all they wanted to do was to compete with him.

In vain Loren had argued with them. The Model T was unassailable. There was nothing that could be built that could compete with it in its time. He correctly predicted that the Model T, which first came on the market in 1908, would sweep the country. And he had been right. In less than two years Ford was producing almost fifty percent of the cars in America, and Loren left the Dodge Brothers.

There was a market for a good medium-priced car, however, and Loren drew a tight bead on it. In 1911 the first Sundancer appeared on the streets of Detroit. And from that point on, none of the medium-priced cars could come anywhere near it in popularity. Not the Buick, nor the Leland, nor the Oldsmobile. They weren't even in the same league, and almost overnight, it seemed, Bethlehem Motors had become a big business and Loren had lost the gift of laughter.

But tonight he was smiling and there was something in

his face that made him seem young again. The orchestra broke into a waltz and Loren held out his arms. Sally swept into them and they began to dance.

Tears filled Elizabeth's eyes. He looked so young, so strong, so vital that if one did not know, they would think that he, not his son, was the bridegroom. Junior came up to the couple on the floor and with a bow, Loren relinquished Sally to her husband. He turned and came toward her.

He kissed her cheek. "It's a beautiful party, Mother."

She looked into his face. "How do you feel, Father?"

He smiled ruefully. "A little bit hung over, I think. I'll have to learn to handle bootleg a little better."

The butler came up to them. His voice lowered discreetly. "Everything is ready, sir."

Loren nodded. He turned to Elizabeth. "Is it all right to do it now, Mother?"

She nodded and he took her arm and led her out into the middle of the ballroom floor. He held up both hands and the music came to a stop.

"Ladies and gentlemen." His voice boomed into every corner of the large ballroom. "As you all know, this is a very special occasion for Mother and myself. It isn't every day that our son finds himself a bride, especially such a beautiful one."

A ripple of laughter and a scattering of applause went through the room. "Loren and Sally," he called. "Come out here on the floor where the folks can get a good look at you."

Junior was smiling and she was blushing as they took up their places beside his parents. Junior stood next to his father, slim and straight and as tall, but without the bigness of the older man.

"This is Detroit," Loren said in his large voice. "And what better gift to give a newlywed couple than a brand-new car? That's the Detroit way of doing things, isn't it?"

An answering roar of approval came from the guests. Loren smiled and held up his hand for silence. He turned to his son. "So, Loren, here is the surprise we have for you and your bride—a brand-new car. New from front bumper to rear, from top to the very bottom of the tires. Your very

own car. We're calling it the Loren Two, and next year it
will be on sale in every Bethlehem dealer's across the
country."

The orchestra broke into a popular Sousa march as the
French doors to the garden opened. There was the quiet
sound of a powerful motor and the automobile came into
the ballroom. The crowd parted and the chauffeur carefully drove it to the center of the ballroom floor and came
to a halt in front of the Hardemans.

A murmur of approval came from the crowd and they
began to press forward to get a closer look at the new car.
They were Detroiters and to them there was nothing more
important. And this car was important. There was no doubt
about that. The burgundy-red-and-black sedan was easily
one of the most important cars ever to be seen in this
automobile-conscious city.

They stopped, suddenly aware that the rear passenger
compartment behind the chauffeur was completely filled
with what seemed thousands of sheets of green-and-gold-
colored paper. Loren held up his hand and they all looked
at him.

"I suppose you're all wondering what that is in the back
of the car?" He didn't wait for their reply. Instead he
walked over to the door of the car and opened it. The
sheets of paper spilled out as if propelled. He picked up
one sheet and held it over his head toward the crowd. His
voice boomed over the sudden silence.

"Each one of these pieces of paper represents one share
of stock in the Bethlehem Motor Company and there are
a hundred thousand of them in this car. Each one of them
made out to my son, Loren Hardeman, Jr. These hundred
thousand shares are equal to ten percent of my company
and my accountants tell me that they are worth somewhere
between twenty-five and thirty million dollars."

He turned to his son. "And that, Loren, is just a small
token of the love and affection your mother and I have for
you."

Junior stood there for a moment, his face pale. He tried
to speak but no words came. Silently he gripped his father's
hand, then turned to his mother and kissed her.

At the same moment, Loren bent and kissed his daughter-in-law. A startled look came into her eyes and she felt the trembling suddenly return to her legs. She put a hand on his arm to steady herself, then turned to kiss her mother-in-law.

The guests went wild with approval and began to surround them with congratulations and good wishes. It was pandemonium.

At the back of the ballroom a reporter for the *Detroit Free Press* was busy scribbling his notes. The headline the next day was both a question and a statement.

AND WHEN HENRY GAVE EDSEL A MILLION IN GOLD FOR A WEDDING PRESENT, HE THOUGHT THAT WAS SOMETHING?

=== **Chapter Five**

THE FAINT SOUNDS of "Three O'Clock in the Morning" came from the ballroom into the library of the Hardeman Manor where a bar had been set up for the men who wanted to have a real drink, away from the dance floor. Only champagne was served at the ball.

Loren was standing at the bar, one foot on the rail, the whiskey in his hand. His face was flushed and perspiring as he stood in the small circle of men. "The sedan is the car of the future," he said. "You mark my words. In the next ten or fifteen years the open touring car as we know it will be gone. People have got to be tired of freezing in the winter, getting soaked in the rain, and cooking in the sun. Someday they'll even have air-conditioners in cars the same way they're beginning to have heaters now."

"It won't seem like driving then," one of the men said.

"So what?" Loren retorted. "The idea is to get there in comfort. That's what it's going to be all about. The smoother the ride, the more customers for the car. Wait

until the Loren Two gets on the market next year, you'll
see I know what I'm talking about."

The same man said doubtfully, "Seventeen hundred dollars is a lot of money."

"They'll pay it," Loren said confidently. "The American
public knows what it wants. They'll pay a little more for
quality anytime."

"Did you make a bid for the Dodge Brothers?" another
man asked.

Loren shook his head. "It's not for me. I'm not about
to go up against Ford and Chevy. I'm strictly middle
range."

"I heard GM offered a hundred and forty-six million,"
the first man said.

"They're damn fools," said Loren.

"You mean the offer is too much?"

Loren shook his head. "Too little. They won't get it. I
know a Wall Street house has come up with a higher bid."
He turned around to the two men standing behind him.
"Hey, Walter," he said to the taller man. "You're the one
that ought to buy the Dodges. It could fill a hole in your
line and then you could give GM a real run for their
money."

Walter Chrysler smiled. "I looked into it. But I'm not
ready yet. I've still got my hands filled with the Maxwell.
Maybe in a few years."

"Once Wall Street gets their hands into something, it'll
be too late. You know how those boys operate."

Chrysler smiled again. "I can wait, Loren. Wall Street
may be able to sell stocks and bonds, but running an automobile company is another game altogether. They'll find
that out. By then, I might be ready."

A butler threw open the two massive doors of the
library which had insulated them against the rest of the
house, and the sounds of the affair ending came into the
room. Quickly the men finished their drinks and left to
claim their wives and make their departures, and soon
Loren was standing alone in the room except for the bartender. He had just poured himself another drink when
Junior and Sally entered.

He held up his glass. "To the bride and groom." He swallowed the whiskey neat. "It was a great party," he said. "A great party."

Junior laughed. "That it was, Father."

Loren looked at him. "Where's your mother?"

"She went upstairs," Junior said quickly. "She asked us to find you and tell you. She was very tired."

Loren didn't speak. He signaled for another drink. The bartender refilled his glass. "Join me in a drink," he said.

"No, thank you, Father," said Junior. "I think we'll be going up too. It's been a long day."

Loren chuckled knowingly. "You kids can't wait, eh? I would've thought you'd already grabbed one during the matinee this afternoon."

A quick vision of the naked, hairy body she had seen in the mirror flashed through Sally's mind. Her voice was indignant. "Daddy Hardeman! How can you say something like that?"

Loren laughed genially. "I'm not that old that I don't know what's on the minds of you youngsters." He put his hands on her shoulders and spun her around and sent her toward the door with a slap on the behind. "You go upstairs and get ready for your husband. I want to talk with him for a minute. I promise I won't keep him long."

She left the library, her nose in the air. Loren looked after her appreciatively, then turned to his son. "That's a fine hunk of woman you got there, Junior," he said. "I hope you know it."

"I know it, Father," Junior said quietly.

Loren clapped him on the shoulder. "C'mon, have a drink."

Junior hesitated a moment. "I'll have a brandy," he said to the bartender.

"Brandy!" Loren roared. "What kind of a sissy drink is that? Have a real drink. Bartender, give him a whiskey."

The drink was placed in front of Junior. "What did you want to talk to me about, Father?"

"Mother tells me you and Sally are thinking of buying a house out in Ann Arbor," Loren said.

Junior nodded. "We like it out there."

"What's wrong with Grosse Pointe?" Loren asked. "I can get the Sanders' place. Or if you don't like that, any place else you choose."

"Sally and I like the country, Father," Junior replied. "We thought we'd get a place with some room and land for a few horses, things like that."

"Horses!" Loren exploded. "What the hell do you want with horses? We're in the automobile business!"

"Sally and I like to ride," Junior's voice became slightly defensive. "I don't think anyone can criticize us for that."

"No one is," Loren said quickly. "But Ann Arbor, that's way the hell out. You'll have nobody to talk to on the weekends. There are no automobile people out there. How about Bloomfield Hills? At least there are people there that you know."

"That's just it, Father," Junior explained stubbornly. "We want to be by ourselves."

Loren drank his whiskey and got another. "Listen to me, son," he said heavily. "Beginning the first of the year, you're the executive vice-president of this company, in a couple of years, you'll be president. I don't want to be working forever and I think your mother and I are entitled to some time off. When you have that kind of responsibility you got to be where people can get to you real quick. You can't live off somewhere in the wilderness where people can't find you."

"Ann Arbor isn't the wilderness," Junior answered. "It's only a little more than an hour away."

Loren was silent for a moment. He looked around the room. "You know, son, if it weren't for your mother, I wouldn't even live here. Maybe someday I'll put up an office building out at the plant and the top floor of it will be an apartment."

Junior smiled. "That's one way of keeping on top of things."

Loren looked at him and then laughed. "Okay, son, you do what you want. But mark my words, in a little while you'll be looking for a place back here."

"Maybe, Father. We'll see."

His father shoved him on the shoulder. "Okay, Loren,

get on upstairs. It's not a good thing to keep a bride waiting on her wedding night."

Junior nodded and started to turn away, then he stopped and turned back. "Father."

"Yes, Loren?"

The young man smiled. Loren felt something tug inside him, he saw his wife in that smile. Almost the same gentleness. "Thank you, Father, thank you. For everything."

"Go on, go on," Loren said gruffly. "Your bride is waiting." Then he turned to the bar so that his son would not see the sudden wetness in his eyes.

"Good night, Father."

"Good night, son." He listened to the footsteps recede and when they were gone he finished his drink. Junior's was still on the bar, untouched. He looked at it for a moment, then took out his massive gold pocket watch and opened it. The picture of Elizabeth and Junior taken so many years ago looked back up at him. It was 4 A.M. He sighed.

He closed the watch and put it back in his pocket. He left the library slowly and wandered through the house to the ballroom. It seemed strangely silent and empty now that all the people had gone and there were only a few scattered servants tending to the final chores of the night.

He went to the French doors leading to the garden. The Loren II was standing out there on the terrace, dark and beautiful in the pale moonlight. Slowly he walked over to it and around it. It was sheer beauty, no matter from what angle you looked at it.

He opened the driver's door and got in. He sank comfortably into the cushions and put his hands on the steering wheel. Even without the motor running, it felt alive and strong to him. He wondered whether Junior felt the same things about the car that he did.

But even as he wondered, he already knew the answer. Junior did not. For Junior it was not the car itself, it was merely the business he happened to be born into. Maybe someday Junior would feel as he did. Junior had never built a car with his own hands. That could be the reason.

He leaned forward and rested his head on his arms on

the steering wheel and closed his eyes. A peculiar weariness came over him.

"Loren," he whispered half to himself. "Couldn't you see? It wasn't the stock certificates, it wasn't the money. It was the car. That's what I wanted to give you. That's why I called it the Loren Two."

He fell asleep.

Sally was naked beneath the sheets in the dark bedroom when he came back from the bathroom. He stood next to the bed, looking down at her while he buttoned the top button of his pajamas.

"Sally," he whispered.

"Yes, Loren."

He knelt beside the bed, his face level with her own. "I love you, Sally."

She turned and put her arms around his neck. "I love you."

He kissed her gently. "I will always love you."

She closed her eyes, her arms tightening around him, drawing him up to her. They kissed again.

He raised his head. "I know you must be very tired—"

She placed a finger over his lips, then drew his head down to her breast, letting him feel the nakedness of her. His breath drew in sharply and his mouth closed on her nipple. She felt the heat begin to run through her and she closed her eyes.

A vision of a naked, giant, hairy body jumped onto the screen of her lids and she climaxed even before her husband was inside her.

It was at that moment that she knew her father-in-law had taken possession of her body and had come between them on their wedding night.

She fought her way up through the field of pain and opened her eyes. Her vision blurred, then cleared as she focused on the face of the doctor, leaning over her. As he straightened up, she saw the nurse behind him, and Loren.

Loren looked tired, as if he had been awake all night. The doctor stepped back and Loren came forward. He seemed so tall standing there beside the bed. So tall and so strong.

She tried to smile. "Loren."

His voice was gentle. "Yes, Elizabeth."

"It didn't turn out to be much of a vacation, did it?" she whispered.

He reached for her hand. "We can always have a vacation. When you're well again."

She made no reply. There would be no more vacations. Not for her. But she didn't have to say it. He knew that as well as she.

"Have you heard from the children?" she asked.

"I spoke to Junior on the telephone. He wanted to come down here. But I told him not to. Sally's due any day now."

"Good," she whispered. "He should be with his wife. Especially after they waited so long for the first baby."

"They didn't wait so long."

"They've been married almost four years," she said. "I was beginning to feel I would never be a grandmother."

"What's so important about being a grandparent?" he asked. "I don't feel like a grandfather."

She smiled. He didn't look like a grandfather. At fifty-one he was still a young man. Big and broad and virile. Bursting with the forces of life.

She turned her eyes toward the window. Outside the bright Florida sunshine fell from a clear blue sky and the breeze ruffled through the gently swaying palm trees. "Is it beautiful outside?" she asked.

"Yes," he answered. "It's a lovely day."

Her eyes were still on the window. "I love it here. I don't want to go back to Detroit, Loren."

"There's no hurry," he said. "First, you get well—"

She turned to look up at him, her eyes were steady on him. "You know what I mean, Loren. Afterwards. I want to stay here."

He was silent.

She pressed his hand. "I'm sorry, Loren."

His voice was husky. "There's nothing to be sorry about."

"Yes, there is," she said quickly. There was so much she had to say that she could never tell him until now. But now it was all clear. The triumphs, the failures, the laughter, the pain. There was so much they had shared together and so much more they might have shared that they had not. Now she could see it all. "I was never enough of a woman for you," she whispered. "Not that I didn't want to be. But I couldn't. You knew that, didn't you? That I wanted to be."

"You're talking like a ninny," he said gruffly. "You've always been a good wife, the only wife I ever wanted."

"Loren, I know I've been a good wife." She smiled, almost reprovingly. "But that's not what I was talking about."

He was silent.

"I wanted you to know I never blamed you for the others. I knew what it was that you needed and in a curious sort of way was glad for you that you could have it. My only regret was that I, who wanted to give you everything, couldn't find it in myself to give you that."

"You gave me more than any woman ever gave a man, more than any woman ever gave me," he said earnestly. "You never failed me. Maybe it was I who failed you. But I love you. I have always loved you. You believe that, don't you, Elizabeth?"

She looked into his eyes for a long moment, then she nodded slightly. "And I have always loved you, Loren," she whispered. "From the moment I walked into your little bicycle shop in Bethlehem all that time ago."

Their hands tightened and memory flowed alive and present between them.

It had been a warm summer Sunday in Bethlehem; the great steel mills had banked their furnaces on Saturday night and only the faintest wisps of gray smoke came from the chimneys. The sun shone bright and high as Elizabeth walked her bicycle out the side door of her house to meet her girl friend.

The basket attached to the handlebars was filled with goodies for the picnic they had planned. She hadn't told her mother but there were also going to be two young men. Her mother was very strict about those things. Before she would let Elizabeth see any man, he had to come to the house first for an inspection, and by the time that was over, he had been made to feel so uncomfortable that she rarely ever saw him again. Now she knew better. The young men were to meet them at the edge of town where there would be no chance of her parents seeing them.

Her girl friend had been waiting, the basket on the handlebars of her bicycle also packed tightly. They started off, the wide brims of their hats flapping in the breeze, pulling against the ribbons tied under their chins.

They chattered as they rode along the quiet streets. It was early in the morning and there wasn't much traffic about. The carriages would be out later when it was time for church services. Then the streets would be filled and difficult to pass as each driver would try to urge his horse to step smartly.

The trouble came two blocks from her house when they turned off the cobblestoned street onto a dirt road. Elizabeth didn't see the deep wagon rut on the side of the street and over she went, the picnic goodies spilling over the ground beside her.

"Are you hurt?" her girl friend asked, coming to a stop.

Elizabeth shook her head. "No." She got to her feet and

began to brush off her dress. It wasn't too bad. "Help me pick up."

She began to place the food back into the wire basket when she saw the front wheel of the bicycle. "Oh, no!" she groaned in dismay.

The wheel was bent out of shape. There was no way the bike could move. "What do we do now?" she asked. It was Sunday and all the repair shops would be closed. "That's the end of the picnic for me," she said. "I might as well go home."

Her girl friend said quickly, "I know where you can get it fixed." She picked up the last of the wrapped sandwiches. "My cousin just rented an old barn back of his house to a young man who repairs bicycles. He's there all the time. Even on Sundays. He's working on some kind of an invention."

Twenty minutes later they were at the barn back of the house. The door was open as they came up. Inside they heard a man singing in a loud, untuneful voice. The song was mixed with the clanging of a hammer against metal. They knocked on the open barn door. Apparently they weren't heard because the singing and the banging went on uninterrupted.

"Hello," Elizabeth called. "Is there anyone in there?"

The singing stopped and so did the hammering. After a moment a voice came out of the dark interior. "Nope. Only some field mice."

"Do the field mice know how to fix a bicycle?" Elizabeth called back.

There was a silence, then a young man appeared out of the darkness. He was tall and broad and covered with a light red-gold hair down to his waist which was bare. He stood there squinting at them in the bright sunlight. Then he smiled. It was a warm smile filled with a very masculine knowledge. "What can I do for you, ladies?"

"First you can put on a shirt," Elizabeth said. "Then when you're properly dressed, you can fix my wheel."

Loren looked down at the bicycle for a moment, then back up at her. He stood there silently, just staring at her.

Elizabeth felt the color begin to flow into her face.

"Don't be all day about it!" she said sharply. "Can't you see we're going on a picnic?"

He nodded, almost as if to himself, and disappeared into the barn. A moment later the tuneless singing and hammering began again.

Five minutes later after waiting in vain for the young man to reappear, she went to the barn door and peered in. At the back of the barn there was a forge with an open fire and the young man stood in front of it, swinging a hammer against a piece of metal on an anvil. "Young man!" she called.

The hammer stopped in mid-air. He turned. "Yes, ma'am?"

"Are you going to fix my bicycle?" she asked.

The answer came promptly. "No, ma'am."

"Why not?"

"Because you haven't told me who you're going to picnic with."

"You have a nerve!" she snapped. "What business is it of yours who I picnic with?"

He put the hammer carefully down on a bench and walked toward her. "I think the man you're going to marry has every right to know who you're going to picnic with."

She looked up into his face and there was something in his expression that turned her legs to water. She put a hand on the door to steady herself. "You?" she said breathlessly. "That's silly, I don't even know your name."

"Loren Hardeman, ma'am," he smiled. "What's yours?"

"Elizabeth Frazer," she said. Somehow the saying of her name seemed to strengthen her. "Now, will you fix my bicycle?"

"No, Elizabeth," he said quietly. "What kind of a man would I be if I fixed your bicycle so that my girl could go off and picnic with another man?"

"But I'm not your girl!" she protested.

"Then you soon will be," he said calmly. He reached out and took her hand.

She felt the weakness come back into her. "But, my parents," she said in a confused voice. "You don't—they don't—know you."

He didn't answer. Just held onto her hand and looked down at her.

Her eyes fell. "Mr. Hardeman," she said in a small voice, looking down at the floor, "now will you please fix my bike?"

He still didn't answer.

She didn't look up. Her voice grew even smaller. "I apologize for being rude to you when you came out, Mr. Hardeman."

"Loren," he said. "You might as well get used to the name. I'm not the old-fashioned kind who holds to the idea of wives calling their husbands 'mister.' "

She looked up at him. Suddenly she smiled. "Loren," she said tentatively as if trying its sound on her tongue.

"That's better," he smiled back. He let go of her hand. "Now you wait right there."

He started toward the rear of the barn. "Where are you going?" she called after him.

"To wash up and put on a clean shirt," he said. "After all, a man should look his best when he goes to meet his future in-laws."

"Now?" she asked in an incredulous voice. "Right now?"

"Of course," he called back over his shoulder. "I'm not the type of man who believes in long engagements."

But he still had to wait almost two years before they were married. That wasn't until May of 1900 because her parents wouldn't let her marry before she was eighteen years old. And during the time they waited he built his first automobile.

It wasn't really an automobile. It was more of a quadricycle, with its strange bicycle wheels and tires and spindly frame. It ran well enough to get itself banned from the main streets in Bethlehem for causing a disturbance, but not well enough to satisfy him.

There was more he had to learn and he knew it. And only one place to get that knowledge. Detroit. There were more automobile builders there than anywhere else in the United States. Henry Ford. Ransom E. Olds. Billy Durant. Charles Nash. Walter Chrysler. Henry Leland. The Dodge Brothers. These men were his heroes and his gods. And it

was to sit at their feet and to learn that, one week after
their marriage, he and his already pregnant but unknowing
bride moved to Detroit.

The memory was still warm within him. He glanced out
the window at the sun and the swaying palms. "It was a
day like this," he said. "It was a beautiful Sunday."

"Yes," she whispered. "I'm grateful for that. It was the
first of many beautiful Sundays we had together."

"We haven't seen the last of them," he said, turning to
look down at her. "Just you get well and—" His voice
suddenly broke. "Elizabeth!"

There were to be no more beautiful Sundays for her.

Chapter Seven

JUNIOR'S VOICE was unemotional, the figures rattling from
his tongue as if he were a tabulating machine. "The 1928
report looks good," he said. "The Sundancer passenger
cars, all models, went over four hundred and twenty thousand units, eighty percent top of the line, mostly sedans.
Accessories and extras were sold for over sixty percent of
the units. The truck division also had a substantial increase,
up twenty-one percent over the previous year, accounting
for forty-one thousand units. The only line which did not
show an increase was the Loren Two. There we had
trouble holding our own and if it weren't for the liberaliza-
tion of the consumer credit terms and our own guarantees
to the dealers we would have fallen back. As it is, we held
even with thirty-four thousand units. It's the only division
in which we're losing money. By the time the car is passed
on to the consumer, we're dropping almost four hundred
and ten dollars per unit."

Loren picked up a heavy Havana cigar from his desk
and toyed with it. Slowly he clipped the end from it, then
sniffed it gently. It smelled good. He lit a match and

toasted the end of it carefully, then put it in his mouth and held the fire to it. After a moment, he blew out a gust of blue smoke which curled like a cloud over his head as it rose to the ceiling.

He pushed the box toward his son. "Have a cigar."

Junior shook his head.

Loren took another deep puff and let the smoke out. "There are only two things that will ever get a man to wear perfume," he said. "One is if they make it smell like a fine Havana, the other is if they make it smell like pussy."

Junior didn't smile. "The dealers don't like the Loren Two either. Their big complaint is that there's no service business on the car after they sell it."

Loren looked at him shrewdly. "You mean they're bitching because the car's too good."

"I didn't say that," Junior said. "But maybe that's it. Most cars require oil changes every thousand miles, the Loren Two only once every four thousand miles. The same goes for brake adjustments. The Loren's the only car on the road right now with self-adjusting brakes."

"Are you suggesting we bring down the quality of the car?" his father asked.

"I'm not suggesting anything," Junior said. "I'm just calling it to your attention because I think we ought to do something about it. We're dropping almost fourteen million a year on it."

Loren studied the fine gray ash on the end of his Havana. "That's the best car I ever built," he said. "Pound for dollar it's the best car on the road today."

"Nobody is going to dispute that fact," Junior said calmly. "But what we're talking about is money. People shop price, not quality. Give them a big average-quality car at an average price or a medium-size high-quality car at the same price and they'll pick the big one every time. Buick, Olds, Chrysler, and Hudson are proving that every day. They're walking away from us."

Loren looked down at his cigar again. "What do you suggest?"

"The market in electrical refrigerators and ranges is growing every day," Junior said. "I have a chance to buy a small company that's turning out a very commercial line and is in trouble. They need capital for expansion and can't get it. I figured out that I can move them into the Loren plant and we'd wind up making a lot of money."

"Nothing will ever replace the icebox," Loren said. "Did you ever smell anything that comes out of those electric refrigerators?"

"That was years ago," Junior said. "Now it's different. General Electric, Nash, General Motors, even, they all are in it. It's the coming thing."

"And what about the Loren Two?" his father asked.

Junior looked at him. "We'll drop it. We're licked and we might as well admit it."

Loren put the cigar carefully into a tray on the desk. He rose from the chair and walked over to the window of his office. Everywhere he looked there was activity.

Down at the far end of the plant, a train was beginning to move out slowly, trailing flatbed cars filled with automobiles. On the river side of the plant, a cargo ship was unloading coal to stoke the furnaces of the refining mill near the docks. The long, almost tunnel-like assembly plants were humming with activity as the raw materials went in one end and came out as automobiles at the other. And over it all hung the heavy gray pall of the smoke called industry.

"No," he said finally, without turning around. "We keep building the Loren Two. We'll find a way to make it go. I can't believe that in the middle of the greatest prosperity this country has ever known a quality car won't sell. Remember what the President said—two cars in every garage, two chickens in every pot. And Mr. Hoover knows what he's talking about. It's up to us to make sure that in this year of our Lord, 1929, one of those two cars in every garage will be ours."

Junior was silent for a moment. "Then we'll have to do something about getting the cost down. At the present rate, the more we sell, the more we lose."

Loren turned from the window. "We'll get on that right away. You tell that young man, what's his name, in production-engineering, to come up and see me. I like his spirit."

"You mean John Duncan?"

"That's the one," Loren said. "I hired him away from Charlie Sorenson at Ford. We'll turn him loose on the Loren production line. Let's see what he can come up with."

"Bannigan will be angry," Junior said.

Bannigan was the chief production engineer and head of the department. "Too bad," said Loren. "We pay off on work, not temper."

"He might quit," Junior said. "He's got that offer from Chrysler."

"Good," Loren said. "In that case don't give him a choice. Tell him to take the offer."

"What if he doesn't?"

"You're president of the company now, fire him anyway," Loren said. "I'm sick and tired of listening to him tell me why it can't be done. I want someone who will do it."

"Okay," Junior said. "Is that all?"

"Yes," Loren answered. The tone of his voice changed. "How's my grandson?"

Junior smiled his first smile of the meeting. "Growing. You ought to see him. He's almost eleven pounds now and only two and a half months old. We think he's going to be big like you."

Loren returned the smile. "Sounds great. Maybe I'll take a run out there one morning."

"You do that," Junior said. "Sally will be glad to see you too."

"How is she?"

"Fine. She's got her figure back but she keeps complaining she's too heavy."

"Don't give her a chance to get set," Loren laughed. "Have another real quick. And make it a girl this time. I think it would be nice to name her after your mother."

"I don't know. Sally had a pretty rough time with this one."

"She's all right, isn't she?" Loren asked quickly. "Nothing wrong with her?"

"She's perfect," Junior replied.

"Then pay no attention to her, son. Women always have to have something to bitch about. You just do your job and you'll find soon enough that she'll have no complaints."

"We'll see." Junior was noncommittal. He started to leave. His father called him back. "Yes?"

"That icebox company you were talking about. You really think it's a good deal?"

"I do."

"Then buy it."

Junior looked at him. "But where will we put it? I was figuring on the Loren building."

"Come over here," Loren said. He walked to the window and opened it. The roar of the factory came flooding into the room. He leaned out the window and pointed. "How about there?"

Junior stuck his head out the window and looked. "But that's the old warehouse."

Loren nodded. "It's also a hundred and ten thousand square feet of production space that ain't doing nothing but gathering dust and rust."

"It's also where we store parts and replacements," said Junior.

"Get rid of it," Loren said. "Why the hell did we establish regional parts depots all over the country if we're going to keep that junk in our own backyard?" He walked back to his desk and picked up his cigar. He smelled it with obvious satisfaction. "Ship it all out to the depots and tell them what a great favor we're doing them. Instead of the usual ten days or tenth of the month, they won't have to pay us for ninety days."

"That's not fair, Father, and you know it. They'll never sell at least fifty percent of that stuff."

Loren relit the cigar and puffed on it. "Who said anything about being fair? Shove it to them just like they shove it to us when they get the chance. One thing you better learn and learn real good. There's no such thing as an honest car dealer. They're the direct descendants of the old horse thieves. And they'll steal from anybody who gives them the opportunity. You, me, their customers, even their mothers. You didn't hear them weeping when they hit us for the extra two hundred dollars a car on the Loren Two when they knew we were losing over two hundred a unit at that time. Oh, no, they promised to pass it on to the customer. But you and I know better. They kept it for themselves. So don't go feeling sorry for them. Save your sympathy for where it counts. For us."

Junior was quiet for a moment. "Somehow I can't believe that. Not all of them can be that bad."

Loren laughed. "Did you ever meet a poor automobile dealer?"

Junior didn't answer.

"Tell you what, I'll make you an offer," Loren said. "You take a lamp and go like Diogenes to look for one honest car dealer. Just one, no more. And when you find him, you bring him here to me and I will give you all the rest of my stock in this here company and quit the business!"

"Will there be anything else, Mr. Hardeman?" his secretary asked.

Junior shook his head wearily. "I think that should do it, Miss Fisher."

He watched her gather up the papers and leave the office. The door closed silently and respectfully behind her. He leaned back in his chair and closed his eyes. It seemed that the details never ended. It was always a surprise to him how much his father knew about what was taking place in the business without seeming to exert any effort. He had to exhaust himself just to keep up with the tiny day-to-day affairs, much less the over-all management of the company.

Right now, he could use an administrative vice-president just to keep the organization moving smoothly. But his father was against it.

"The only way to run a business is to run it yourself," he had said when Junior asked for permission to hire an assistant. "That way everyone knows who is the boss. I did it that way all my life and it worked."

It didn't make any difference how much Junior explained that times were changing and the demands were greater.

His father's final word on the subject was that he hadn't made him president of the company so that he could shirk his responsibilities. That he was not about to go off and leave his business in the hands of strangers. And that the only reason he felt secure in leaving for Europe in May for the first vacation he had ever taken in his life was because his son was in charge.

Junior had listened with a certain kind of inner skepticism. He had heard those tales before. He would believe them when his father got on the boat. He took out his watch and looked at it.

It was nine forty-five. He reached for the telephone. His secretary answered.

"Would you get Mrs. Hardeman for me?"

There was a buzz on the line and a moment later Sally answered. "Hello."

"Hello, darling," he said. "I'm sorry, I didn't realize it was so late. I hope you didn't wait dinner for me."

Her voice was cool. "When I didn't hear from you by eight, I figured you were tied up and had something."

"Good," he said. "How's the baby?"

"Fine."

"Look, it's late," he said. "And I don't feel up to that hour's drive home tonight. Especially when I have a seven o'clock appointment back here tomorrow morning. Do you mind if I stay down at the club?"

There was the barest hesitation in her voice. "No. Not if you're that tired."

"I'll make it home early tomorrow night," he promised.

"Okay," she said. "You get a good night's rest."

"You, too. Good night, darling."

A click told him she had gone off the line. Slowly he put the telephone down. She was angry. He knew that. It was the second time this week he had stayed in town. His father had been right. It had been a big mistake moving all the way out to Ann Arbor. This weekend he would have a long talk with Sally about moving to Grosse Pointe.

He picked up the phone again. "Call the club," he told his secretary. "Tell them I'll be in and to have Samuel wait for me. I'll want a massage before I turn in."

He began to feel better almost before putting down the phone. That was the ticket. A very light dinner, then a hot, relaxed bath. Afterwards he would climb into bed nude and Samuel would come in with his mixture of soothing oils and alcohol. The tensions would leave him almost at the first laying on of his hands and languor would overcome him. He would be fast asleep by the time the masseur left. A deep, safe, dreamless sleep.

Sally put down the telephone and walked back into the living room. Loren looked up at her from the couch. "Is there anything wrong?"

She shook her head. "That was Junior. He's staying at the club tonight. He's too tired for the drive home."

"Did you tell him I was here?"

"No," she said. "It wouldn't have made any difference." She picked up another glass from the cocktail table in front of him. "Let me fix you a fresh drink."

"Fix one for yourself while you're at it," Loren said. "You look like you can use it."

"I can't have any," she said. "Not till I finish weaning the baby." She handed him his glass. "Now you just relax and make yourself comfortable while I give your grandson his ten o'clock feeding. I won't be long."

Loren got to his feet. "I'll come with you."

She gave him a curious look but didn't answer. He followed her up the steps to the nursery. A tiny night bulb glowed in a corner of the room, casting a faint yellow light behind the crib.

They walked silently and looked down at the baby. He was asleep, his eyes tightly shut. She reached in and picked him up. He began to cry almost immediately.

"He's hungry," she whispered, crossing swiftly to a chair and sitting in it. She was in the shadows, her back to the light. He heard the soft rustle of her clothing, then abruptly the cries ceased and instead there was a faint smacking sound as the baby fed.

She looked up at him. His eyes glowed like an animal's in the reflected yellow light. There was a strangely intense expression on his face. "I can't see," he said.

Slowly she turned in the chair until she and the baby were bathed in the soft glow. She heard his footsteps and when she looked up, he was standing over them.

"My God!" he said in a hushed voice. "That's beautiful!"

A warm wetness rushed through her and she was suddenly angry. "You might try telling that to your son."

He didn't speak. Instead he placed his hand on her bare shoulder and pressed her reassuringly.

Startled, she looked up into his face for a moment, then turned and kissed his hand. The tears ran into her eyes and spilled down her cheeks onto his hand. She leaned her face against him. "I'm sorry, Daddy Hardeman," she whispered.

His free hand stroked her hair gently. "That's all right, child," he said softly. "I understand."

"Do you?" she whispered, almost savagely. "He's not you. He's cold, he keeps everything inside himself, locked up where nobody can reach him." She looked up at him. "I'm not like that at all. I—"

He placed a silencing finger on her lips. "I said I understand."

She looked at him without speaking. She felt the strength of him flowing out and enveloping her and she knew he felt all the things that she did. "Is it so wrong?" she asked.

He shook his head.

"I saw you with that woman on my wedding night," she said.

"I know you did," he answered. "I saw it in your eyes."

"Then what makes that right and this wrong?"

Again he shook his head slowly. "The time. This is not the time." He looked down at the suckling child. "You've got more important things to do."

The old unreasoning anger came up in her. Why did he always have to be sure of himself, so right? "I'm a fool," she said bitterly. "A damned stupid fool."

"No, you're not," he said with a smile. "You're just a normal healthy young woman whose husband deserves a swift kick in the ass for neglecting his homework." He started for the door. "And maybe I'm just the man to do it."

"No," she said. "You keep out of it. There's only one thing I want from you."

"What is that?" he asked.

She rose from the chair and placed the baby back in the crib. Carefully she arranged the covers around the sleeping child and turned to him. She walked toward him, her fingers fastening the buttons on her blouse. She stopped in front of him and looked up. "You tell me when it is the time."

The muscles of his face seemed to reshape themselves into planed angular lines. She could see a pulse beating in his temple. His hands shot out suddenly and took her breasts. She felt the milk from them seep through her blouse into his palms.

His voice was angry. "You bitch! You couldn't wait, could you?"

"No," she said almost calmly. She put her hands on him and felt his bursting strength. Her insides seemed to turn into a hot boiling liquid. Her legs gave way and she sagged against him. "My bedroom's through that other door," she managed to gasp.

He picked her up and carried her through into the other room. With one hand he closed the door silently behind him and carried her over to the bed. She tumbled into it and stared up at him as he began to undress. She reached across the bed and turned on the small night table lamp.

He was almost naked now. "What are you waiting for?" he asked savagely. "Take off your dress!"

She shook her head without speaking, never taking her eyes from him as his union suit dropped to the floor and he stepped toward her. Then she looked up into his face. "You tear it off me," she said. "The way you did that girl's."

In a moment the dress was torn into shreds and he was on his knees before her. He held her legs back and apart and lowered himself into her.

She shoved her half-clenched fist into her open mouth to keep herself from screaming. "Oh, God! Oh, God!" She was seized by paroxysm after paroxysm of climax and spending. She shut her eyes tightly and this time she was the girl she saw in the mirror.

Chapter Eight

SHE AWOKE a few minutes before the baby's two o'clock feeding. Loren was sleeping on his stomach, one arm thrown across the pillow, shielding his eyes from the night lamp, his long legs stretched down the length of the bed, his feet awkwardly reaching past the edge. This close he didn't seem to be as hairy as she had thought, his body covered instead with a fine, soft, red-gold fur through which the whiteness of his skin gleamed.

Carefully, so as not to awaken him, she moved from the bed. The moving made her suddenly aware of her own body. Every cell of her was filled to the bursting, alive, rich, and completed. "So this is what it is like," she thought in wonder.

Silently, she slipped into a robe and went into the baby's room, shutting the door behind her. She stood over the crib, looking at the sleeping baby. For the first time, it all made sense to her. He was not a baby any more. He was a man child and some day he would be large and strong and fill a woman just as she had been filled.

Her breasts began to ache and she touched them, then went to the dresser and took the already prepared warm bottle from its thermos container. She tested the temperature of the formula against the back of her hand. It was just right. She took the baby from the crib, sat in the chair, and gave him the rubber nipple.

He took one suck and spit it out. He cried protestingly. "Shh," she whispered softly, pushing the nipple back into his mouth. "You have to get used to it sometime."

He seemed to understand because he began to suck hungrily at it. She bent and kissed his suddenly sweating face.

"Man child," she whispered. She had never felt her love for him as strongly as she did at this moment.

She heard the door open behind her and when she looked up, Loren was standing over them. He was naked and tawny in the yellow light and the strong male smell of him was pungent in her nostrils.

"How come the bottle?" he asked after a moment.

"You left nothing for him," she replied simply.

He didn't answer.

"It's all right," she added. "He's in the middle of being weaned anyway."

He nodded without speaking and then went back into the other room. She looked down at the baby. The bottle was half empty, it was time to burp him.

When she came back into the bedroom, he was sitting on the edge of the bed smoking a cigarette. He looked at her inquiringly as she closed the door behind her. "He went right back to sleep," she said.

"It's a great life," he smiled. "Nothing to do but eat and sleep." He got to his feet. "Time for me to go."

"No."

He looked at her. "We've been crazy enough," he said after a moment. "The thing for me to do is get out of here and make sure it never happens again."

"I want you to stay."

"You're crazier than I am."

"No, I'm not," she said steadily. "Do you think I could let you go now that you taught me what it is like to really be a woman? What it is like to really be loved?"

"Fucked, you mean," he said flatly. "They're not the same things."

"Maybe to you they're not," she answered. "But they are to me. I love you."

"One good fuck and you're in love?" he asked sarcastically.

"Isn't that enough of a reason?" she returned. "I might have gone my whole life and never known how much I could feel."

He was silent.

"Look," she said quickly, the words tumbling from her

lips almost one on top of the other. "I know that after tonight it will be over. That it will never happen again. But it's not tomorrow yet, it's still tonight and I don't want to lose a moment of it."

He felt the stirring in his loins and knew from the expression in her eyes that she was aware of it. He felt a sudden anger with his self-betrayal. "We can't stay in this room," he said harshly. "The servants—"

"You stay in Loren's room," she said. "Through the connecting door."

He began to pick up his clothing. "What will you tell them?"

"The truth," she smiled. "That it was too late for you to drive home. After all, what can they say, you're still my father-in-law, aren't you?" She looked up at him. "One thing bothers me. I don't know what to call you. Daddy Hardeman seems ridiculous now."

"Try Loren," he suggested. "That shouldn't be too difficult." He followed her into the other room. "How long have you had separate bedrooms?" he asked.

"Always," she answered. She reached for the clothing over his arm. "Let me hang these for you, or they won't be fit to wear in the morning."

He watched her drape the suit neatly over the wooden valet. "I thought you had the same bedroom."

"Never," she replied. "Loren said that he was a poor sleeper. Besides, you and Mother had separate bedrooms."

"Only after she became sick," he said. "We slept in the same room for the first twenty years of our marriage."

"I didn't know that," she said, taking his shirt and placing it on a hanger.

"You're both too young to have separate rooms," he said. He looked at her shrewdly. "I know there's nothing the matter with you. What's wrong with Loren?"

"I don't know," she said, her eyes meeting his. "He's different. He's not like you."

"What do you mean, different?"

"He just doesn't seem to demand very much from me." She hesitated a moment. "Now that I think about it, the only time we ever make love is when I seem to suggest it.

Even on our wedding night, I wanted him so badly that I lay naked in the bed waiting for him, and he asked if I was too tired."

"He was never a very strong boy," he said awkwardly. "Sort of delicate. His mother used to worry a great deal about him. I thought she worried too much at times. But that was the way she was. He was her only child and she knew that she would never have another."

"I would like to give you a child," she said.

"You already did. A grandchild."

She shook her head. "More than that. One of your own. You're a man who should have had many children."

"It's too late for that now."

"Is it, Loren?" she asked, walking toward him. "Is it too late?"

He looked down into her face without answering.

"You never kissed me," she said.

He placed his hands under her shoulders and lifted her toward him. She felt his thumbs digging into her armpits, his strong fingers pressing into her back, crushing her breasts against him. His mouth came down hard against her lips. The hot liquid fire began to soak her loins.

She tore her mouth from him and laid her head on his chest. She closed her eyes and her lips brushed against his shoulder and he could hardly hear her soft whisper. "Oh, God, I hope this night never ends."

He held her very still and very tightly. Because the one thing both of them knew was that morning was just a few hours away.

"More coffee, Mr. Hardeman?"

Loren nodded. He looked across the breakfast table at Sally and waited until the impassive butler had filled the cup and left the room. "You didn't eat your breakfast."

"I'm not really hungry," she said. "Besides I still have ten pounds to lose until I'm back to where I was before the baby was born."

He picked up his cup and sipped the strong black coffee. He thought of the way she looked at six o'clock that morning.

He awoke when she had slipped from the bed to give
the baby his morning feeding but he deliberately kept his
eyes closed so that she would think he was still asleep. He
felt her standing there at the side of the bed, looking down
at him. After a moment, she moved away and he peeked
at her through slitted lids.

She was nude and in the gray light of the early morning
he could see the faint blue and purple bruises of his passion on her fair skin. She seemed to wander about the
room almost aimlessly and without purpose. She paused
before the dresser and suddenly there were two of her,
back and front, one in the mirror. But she didn't look at
herself. Instead she picked up his heavy pocket watch and
looked at it for a moment, then put it down and took up
the gold cufflinks made in the shape of the first Sundancer
he had built. These she looked at for a long time. After
she had put them down, she turned and looked back at
him in the bed. He shut his eyes quickly.

He heard her moving around the room again, then the
closing of the door behind her and, after a moment, the
faint sound of running water coming through the walls
from her bathroom. He rolled over on his back and opened
his eyes.

He was in his son's bed, in his son's room, and the smell
of his son's wife was still on the pillow beside him. His
eyes wandered around the room. Everything in it reflected
Junior's love of antique furniture. The dresser and mirror,
the chairs, even the delicate Duncan Phyfe desk that sat
in the bay of the window. All were his son's.

A peculiar sorrow seemed to weigh him down. Elizabeth had said so many times that his life had been a suc-
cession of failures when it came to his son. That he never
really allowed for the differences between them and that
try as he might, he could not reshape Junior in his own
image.

He closed his eyes wearily. If those were failures, what
was this? Another failure? Or betrayal? Or even worse, a
final usurpation of his son's life and place? He drifted into
a fitful sleep.

When he opened his eyes again it was after eight o'clock

and she was standing next to the bed. She was wearing a simple dress and her face was scrubbed, without makeup, her eyes clear and her hair pulled back behind her head in a neat bun.

"Junior's calling you from the office," she said in a flat voice.

He swung his feet off the bed. "What time is it?"

"About eighty forty."

"How did he know I was here?"

"When you weren't at the meeting this morning, they tried your house. They were told that you had mentioned you might come over here last night but they didn't think of calling until they tried several other places first."

"What did you say to him?" he asked.

"I told him that we were up late and that I thought you should stay over instead of driving back."

"Okay," he said, getting to his feet. A stab of pain shot through his temples. "Could you get me some aspirin?" he asked, walking to the small desk and picking up the telephone. "Hello."

"Father?" Junior's voice was thin and metallic in the phone. "I'm sorry I didn't know you were there, I would have come home."

"That's all right," Loren said. "I made up my mind at the last minute."

She came back into the room with two aspirins and a tumbler of water. He gulped them down.

"Duncan's completed the plans for the revised assembly line for the Loren Two," Junior said. "We wanted to get your approval."

"How does it look?"

"It seems all right to me," Junior said. "We should be able to save about two hundred and ten dollars per unit by final assembly."

"Then okay it," he said abruptly.

"Without your seeing it?" There was surprise in Junior's voice.

"Yes. You might as well get used to taking the responsibility. You're the president of the company, you make the decisions."

"But—what are you going to do?" Junior was puzzled.

"I'm taking that vacation I promised myself," he heard himself saying. "I'm going to Europe for a year and I'm leaving tomorrow."

"I thought you weren't going until next month," Junior said.

Loren looked up at Sally. "I changed my mind."

She looked into his eyes for a moment, then silently left the room. He turned back to the telephone. "I'll go home and change clothes," he said to his son. "I'll see you later this afternoon." He sat down wearily in the spindly Duncan Phyfe chair behind the desk and waited for the aspirin to take his morning headache away.

Now she looked across the table as he put his coffee cup back on it. Her voice was controlled. "You're running away."

"Yup," he nodded.

"Do you think it will make anything different?"

"Maybe it won't. But five thousand miles can keep us out of a lot of trouble."

She didn't speak.

He looked at her steadily. "I have no regrets about what happened. But we were lucky. No one got hurt. This time. But I know myself. If I were to stay, I wouldn't be able to keep away from you. And eventually, that's got to destroy all the things and people we don't want to hurt."

She was motionless in her chair. "I love you."

He was silent for a long moment. "And I love you, I think." There was a note of pain in his voice. "But that doesn't matter now. It's much too late in the game. For both of us."

Chapter Nine

"YOU BITCH! You low, whoring bitch!" Junior's voice rose to a shrill scream. "Who was it?"

She stared in amazement at the sudden transformation in

him. It was as if his body had been taken over by a
virulent female spirit. For the first time, she noticed the
subdued effeminate characteristics of him. With the knowledge, her fear seemed to vanish. "Lower your voice," she
said quietly. "You'll disturb the baby."

His open hand slashed across her face and she went
over with the chair in which she had been seated. The pain
came like a red flash of fire a moment later as she stared
up at him.

He stood over her, his hand outstretched, ready to strike
again. "Who was it?"

She didn't move for a moment, then pushed the chair
away from her with her legs. Slowly she rose, the white
imprint of his palm clear on the redness of her cheek. She
backed away from him, until the dresser was against her.
He followed her, threateningly.

She placed her hands on the dresser top behind her without taking her eyes from his face. His hand started down.
She moved even more swiftly. He felt the sharp sting even
through the heavy cloth of his vest. She spoke only one
word. "Don't!"

His hand paused in mid-air and his eyes fell to his waist.
The silver handle of the long nail file gleamed in her hand.
His eyes went incredulously back to her face.

"You touch me again and I'll kill you," she said calmly.

He suddenly seemed to deflate, his hand fell to his side.
The tears sprang to his eyes.

"You go back there and sit down," she said. "Then we'll
talk."

As if in a daze, he stumbled back to the armchair in the
corner of her room and sat down. He put his hands over
his face and began to cry.

The burst of anger that had engulfed her evaporated as
quickly as it had come. Nothing was left inside her except
pity. He was not so much a man that he was not still a
child.

She put the nail file back on the dresser and walked
over to him. "I'll go away," she said. "You can get the
divorce."

He looked up at her through the open fingers covering his face. "That's easy for you," he half-sobbed. "But what about me? Everyone will know what happened and they'll all be laughing and talking behind my back."

"No one will know," she said. "I'll go so far away no word will ever come back to Detroit."

"I'm going to be sick!" he said suddenly. He got to his feet and ran to the bathroom.

Through the open door she heard him retching into the bowl. She followed him and saw him bent over the open toilet, heaving. His entire body shuddered and he seemed ready to fall. Quickly she moved in behind him and supported his forehead with her palm.

He sagged against her as he spasmodically heaved again. But he was already empty. Nothing came out. After a moment, he stopped shaking.

She reached across him and turned on the cold water in the sink. She took a washcloth and, after soaking it, applied it to his forehead. He began to straighten up. She rinsed the washcloth and wiped the traces of vomit from his mouth and chin.

"I made a mess," he said helplessly, looking down at the yellow and brown vomit splattered across the bottom of the upturned toilet seat and porcelain edges of the bowl.

"It's all right," she said soothingly. "I'll clean it up. You go inside and lie down."

He left the bathroom and she set about straightening up. When she came out a few minutes later, her room was empty, but the door leading to his bedroom was open.

He was lying on his back atop the covers of his bed, an arm thrown over his eyes. She walked over to him. "Are you all right?"

He didn't answer.

She turned and started back toward her room.

"Don't go," he said. "I feel faint. The room is spinning around."

She came back to the bed and looked down at him. His face beneath his arm was pale and sweating. "You need something in your stomach," she said. "I'll have them bring up some tea and milk for you."

She pulled the signal tassel on the wall. A moment later the butler was at the door. "Some weak tea and milk for Mr. Hardeman," she said.

"Yes, ma'am."

She closed the door and went back to the bed. "Let me help you out of your things. You'll be more comfortable."

Like a child, he let her undress him and help him into his pajamas, then stood there patiently while she turned down the covers. He got back into the bed and pulled the sheets up around him.

The butler came back with the tea and placed the bed tray over his legs and left. Junior sat up, pulling another pillow behind him. She filled the cup with the tea and hot milk, half and half. "Drink that. You'll feel better."

He sipped slowly at the steaming cup and the color began to return to his face. When the cup was empty, she refilled it.

She looked down at him. "Do you mind if I smoke?"

He shook his head silently and she went into her room and returned with a cigarette. "Feeling better?"

He nodded.

She took a deep drag. The acrid smoke tingled through her mouth and nostrils. "I'm sorry," she said. "I didn't want to hurt you."

He didn't answer.

"Actually I was going to go away and leave a note for you. I never wanted you to know about it. The doctor promised he wouldn't say anything to anyone."

"You forgot to tell him that you included your husband in that," he said. "I didn't know what he was talking about when I ran into him at the club and he congratulated me."

"It's out now," she said. "And that doesn't matter any more. I'll leave tomorrow and you can handle the divorce any way you like. I don't want anything."

"No!"

She stared at him.

"You're not leaving."

"But—"

"You're going to stay and have the baby," he interrupted her. "Just as if nothing happened."

She was silent.

"A scandal right now would break the company," he said. "We're just completing bank loans for fifty million dollars to retool for the new 1930 cars. Do you think any bank would give us that money if this got out? Not one. On top of that, my father would kill me if I let anything happen that would keep us from getting that money."

They sat in heavy silence for what seemed a long while. She ground out one cigarette and lit another. He watched her.

"Why didn't you do something about it?" he finally asked. "What took you so long?"

"I didn't find out about it until it was too late. Then no doctor would touch me. I was all mixed up with my periods after the baby was born."

"You won't tell me who the father is?"

She shook her head. "No."

"You don't have to tell me," he said. "I know who it is."

She didn't speak.

"It was him," he said.

He didn't have to mention his father by name for her to know who he meant. "You're crazy!" she said, hoping he wouldn't notice the sudden trembling of the hand that held the cigarette.

"I'm not as stupid as you seem to think," he said, a sudden effeminate craftiness appearing in his face. "He spent the night here and the next morning he suddenly decided to leave for Europe a month ahead of time."

She forced a laugh. "That doesn't mean anything."

"Maybe this does!" he said, getting out of bed. He crossed the room to the cabinet in which his sox and underwear were kept. He pulled open the bottom drawer and took something out and came back to her. He snapped his hand and the bedsheet billowed out on the floor in front of her. "Recognize this?"

She shook her head.

"You should," he said. "It was the sheet that was on

my bed that night. The night he stayed here. Do you know what those yellowish ringed stains are?"

She was silent.

"Semen stains," he said. "Any boy could recognize them. And I don't think he's the type to have wet dreams."

"That still doesn't prove anything," she said.

"Then how about this?" With his other hand he flung something at her.

It fell to her lap and she picked it up. It was the nursing brassiere she had been wearing that night. Now the torn and ripped pieces of it hung from her fingers. She hadn't even missed it.

"Where did you get it?" she asked.

"In the hamper in my bathroom," he said. "I had dropped a shirt in it with my cufflinks still in the sleeves and when I opened the door to get it, the sheet fell out and the brassiere was wrapped in it."

She was silent.

"He raped you, didn't he?" It was more a statement than a question the way he said it.

She didn't answer him.

"The sick, filthy old man!" he swore. "I don't know how my poor mother stood him all those years. He belongs in an institution. It's not the first time he's done something like this. He tore the clothes off you, didn't he?"

She looked down at the brassiere in her hand. "Yes," she half whispered.

"Then why didn't you do something?" he asked. "Why didn't you scream?"

She took a long, deep breath and looked up at him. Her voice was clear and steady. "Because I wanted him to."

His shoulders suddenly slumped and he seemed to shrink inwardly; before her eyes he seemed to grow twenty years older. His face turned gray and pale. He put out a hand and sat on the edge of his bed.

"He's hated me," he whispered as if he were talking to himself. "He's always hated me. From the moment I was born. Because I came between my mother and him. Ever since I was a child, he always took things away from me. Once I had a doll. He took it away and gave me a toy car. Then when I wouldn't play with it, he took the car away too."

He stretched out on the bed on his stomach, burying his face in the crook of his elbow and began to cry again. Her face began to throb with the ache. Wearily she got to her feet and started back to her room.

"Sally!"

She turned and looked back at him. He sat up in the bed, the tears streaking his cheeks. "You're not going to let him take you away from me too, are you?"

She stood there without answering.

"We'll forget it ever happened," he said quickly. "I'll be good to you, you'll see. I'll never say anything about it again."

He got out of the bed and fell to his knees and clasped his arms around her legs, burying his face against her thighs. "Please, Sally," he begged. "Don't leave me. I couldn't bear it if you left me."

She let her hand fall on his head and rest there. For a moment, she felt as if he were her child. And maybe that was the way it was supposed to be.

"Get up and go back to bed, Junior," she said gently. "I won't leave you." Then she turned, closing the door behind her.

On a day that came to be known as Black Friday in the economic history of the world, the New York stock market plummeted from the heights, throwing the nation and the world into the depths of an economic depression never known before.

Four months later in the middle of January, 1930, the doorbell rang in the suite at the Hotel George V in Paris where Loren was staying.

"Roxanne," he called from his bath. "See who it is."

A few minutes later she came into the bathroom. "A cable from America for you."

"Open it and read it. My hands are wet."

She tore open the pale blue envelope. Her voice was expressionless as she struggled with the English words.

LOREN HARDEMAN, SR.
   HOTEL GEORGE V
      PARIS, FRANCE

HAVE ORDERED PRODUCTION STOPPED AND DISCON-
TINUANCE OF LOREN TWO AT BANK'S INSISTENCE TO
REDUCE LOSSES DUE TO LACK OF SALES, STOP. OTHER
ECONOMIES IN WORK AND WILL KEEP YOU INFORMED
AS TO DECISIONS TAKEN. ALSO WISH TO INFORM YOU
THAT MY WIFE GAVE BIRTH TO A GIRL, ANNE ELIZ-
ABETH, YESTERDAY MORNING, AT EIGHT O'CLOCK.

                              LOREN HARDEMAN II

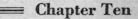 **Chapter Ten**

ANGELO LOOKED out the window as the plane settled into
its final approach pattern in a wide banking turn over the
Ford River Rouge plant. The giant industrial complex
sprawled like a hydra-headed monster beneath him, its
clouded breath rising toward the skies, its liquid wastes
pouring into the grayed cloudy waters of the Detroit
River, the multipatterned colors of the tiny cars parked
like clusters of ants in the lots between the buildings. The
no-smoke signal snapped on just as the late afternoon sun
brightened the glass windows and façade of the long Ford
Central Administration Building.

He snubbed his cigarette out in the tray and began to
place the papers on the table back into his case. Finished,
he pushed the table up into the seat and put the case on
the floor.

The stewardess came down the aisle. She looked down
at him. "Seat belt fastened?"

He nodded, holding up his hands so that she could see
it. She smiled and went on to the next row. He looked at
his wristwatch. Four thirty in the afternoon. Right on
schedule. He turned to the window again.

River Rouge was now behind the plane. For the first time he began to feel a tinge of admiration for the men who had conceived it. It had to be an almost impossible task. He knew that now. In the year since he had been working on the West Coast plant, one problem after the other had arisen until there were times when he thought he was going out of his mind. And that plant wasn't even ten percent of River Rouge.

But there were two things that made it all work and both were people. The knowledge, experience and wise counsel of John Duncan, and the driving, indefatigable energy and enthusiasm of Tony Rourke who became part of it all as if he were born into the automobile business. That, plus his inventive use and adaptation of the new technologies he had used in aerospace, brought them over the first and perhaps the most difficult hurdles.

The design and engineering division had been successfully transferred from Detroit and had been functional for over six months. The steel foundry they bought in Fontana was in the process of changeover to their production requirements, and the mill they had built at the plant would be ready for operation by the summer of next year. The casting division would be ready for work a few months later, and the final assembly line could be in operation as early as September, 1971, if need be. The labor pool was in the process of being analyzed, the requirement plans were being drawn and the thousand and one other details were being buttoned up. Now, all that was needed was a final decision on the kind of car to build. And that was the one problem on which no one seemed to be in agreement.

Perhaps it was because of the present state of the, industry itself. Over the past few years a storm had been brewing, and now the eye of the hurricane was upon them and the whole industry was searching frantically for a place of safety with no clearly defined shelters in view. In response to pressure, local and federal governments were imposing stringent regulations that would affect the performance and production of automobiles. Ecological and environmental factors were subjected to new controls and stricter standards. There was a five-year plan to which the industry had to conform to reduce gasoline engine emissions to certain acceptable levels by 1975. Other safety factors were being regulated to protect the driver and the passenger, even against their own mistakes. All in all, it was a direct refutation of the policy that had been the industry's privilege all these years. No longer were these decisions that concerned the public's safety and welfare to be left to their own tender mercies. Despite their cries of economic ruin and that the costs would have to be passed along to the consumer, the standards would have to be met or the cars would not be allowed on the road.

There was another side to the problem. And that seemed to be the changing taste of the American car buyer. It seemed only a few years ago that the little Volkswagen Beetle had only been a subject for puns and jokes. But that was twenty years back. Suddenly Detroit turned around and found the little bug was the fourth largest-selling car in America in 1969 and that for 1970 the industry had already conceded that it would knock Chrysler Motors' Plymouth out of the third place in sales it had held for many years. Then, to add to their woes, in 1967 another invasion began to take place, this one from the opposite side of the world. Japan. In just four years the Japanese had captured another giant section of the American market with their products. The Datsun, Toyota and the others were now a viable part of the American scene. Their rates of market growth and penetration were so rapid and so complete, and, even more remarkable, showed no sign of slowing up. For the first time it was not only Detroit that showed evidence of concern, also concerned was the Volkswagen company, who saw its own eminent position in the American market being threatened. Now Volkswagen, like the Ford Motor's famous Model T of many years ago, felt itself in danger of being bypassed in styling and improvements, and was casting about for a new car that would eventually replace the Beetle. But that was still in the future.

For now, the American companies had come forth with their version of the economy compact: the Vega, Pinto and Gremlin. Chrysler was still holding back from domestic

production but had two of its cars, which had been manu-
factured abroad, imported into the States and sold under
their own names: the Dodge Colt and the Plymouth
Cricket. But it was all stopgap and even Detroit was ready
to admit that.

The first reports on the sales of the American sub-compacts indicated that their market was drawn from their
own sales of larger cars and that the sales of the import
cars were not affected at all but continued to show an ap-
preciable rate of increase.

All of these factors, plus the additional investment and
costs added to the sales and manufacturing burden by gov-
ernmental edict, turned the industry's eyes inward upon
itself. Trim, cut, pare and prune as much as they would or
could, would not of itself supply the answer.

The answer itself would only come with a totally new
car, one that was born of the technology of demand, a new
car that would have built into it all the requirements of
both the government and the consumer. And that was the
one thing that Detroit was not yet ready to consider. For
that meant calling the old ballgame and beginning a new
one. And there were still too many fans in the old stadium.

The wheels of the plane touched the ground, jarring
Angelo from his reverie. He sat there quietly while they
taxied to the gate. They had to make the commitment. It
was the only choice they could make. And at tomorrow's
board meeting, he was going to put it on the line. The
Sundancer was yesterday's automobile. It had to go. If they
were going to build a new car, it would have to have the
total commitment of the corporation behind it. Any con-
tinuation of the Sundancer would be taken as a hedge and
would, in his opinion, lessen the chances of success for the
new car.

The plane rolled to a stop and he picked up his attaché
case and rose to his feet. But that was tomorrow and tonight there was another matter that was almost as important in the world of Detroit.

An event that had been heralded in the Detroit papers as
the great social affair of the year, the preparations for

which had been as religiously reported as the preparations for the inauguration of a President of the United States.

Elizabeth Hardeman's debut. She was eighteen years old. And ready to take her place in the world.

"You look very well, Grandfather," the Princess said.

Number One smiled. "I feel good, Anne. Better than I have in years."

"I'm glad," she said simply. She walked over to his wheelchair and kissed his cheek. "You know that, don't you?"

The faint scent of her perfume came to his nostrils. He reached out and patted her hand. "I know it," he said. "And you? Are you happy?"

She nodded thoughtfully. "As happy as I could be, I guess. I've long ago given up the childish dreams of what happiness should be. Now, I'm content. Igor is very good to me. He looks after me. You know what I mean."

He nodded. He thought he understood but never would be quite sure. The problem of being an heiress had destroyed the lives of many others. Being a rich girl had its own peculiar hazards. But she seemed to be one of the fortunate ones. It was difficult for him to realize that she was now forty years old, she was still a child in his mind. "Where is Igor?" he asked. "I haven't seen him."

"In the library downstairs with Loren," she said. "You know Igor. He loves the chance to talk business, man to man. And if there's a bottle of good whiskey around, that doesn't hurt either."

He smiled. "How is business in Europe?"

"Igor was concerned," she said. Igor had taken over the operation of Bethlehem Motors S.A., France, when they had been married, and much to the surprise of everyone had done a very creditable job of it. "You know how he loves cars. He hated it when auto sales fell off, even if the other divisions went well. Now he's all excited again. He couldn't wait to get to Loren and talk about the new car."

Number One said, "I'll have him invited to the board meeting tomorrow. I think he'll like that."

"Are you kidding?" Anne laughed. "He'll love it. That's what he always dreamed about. Being there when the big decisions are made. He'll be in paradise."

"Good."

"What time is it?" she asked.

He looked at his wristwatch. "Seven thirty."

"I'd better begin to dress."

"What's the rush? The party doesn't begin until ten."

"I'm not as young as I used to be," she smiled. "And looking like a princess takes a little longer."

"You always looked like a princess to me," he said.

"Do you remember, Grandfather? That's what you used to call me when I was a little girl. Princess. And Daddy used to get angry. He said it was un-American."

"Your father had some peculiar ideas," he said.

"Yes." She was thoughtful. "I always had the feeling that he didn't like either of us. I used to wonder about that."

"Does it matter?"

"Not now." She looked at him and smiled. "You know, I'm glad I came home. I'm glad you opened the Manor for this party. I've always heard how grand the parties were here."

"Some of them were pretty good."

"How long has it been, Grandfather?" she asked. "Since the last one?"

He thought for a moment. Time washed over him like the tide of the ocean. He closed his eyes and for a moment it was yesterday and then he opened them. "Forty-five years ago," he said slowly. "For your father and mother's wedding."

Chapter Eleven

IT WAS REALLY two parties, not one. The main ballroom was the formal affair. In that room one of Meyer Davis' society orchestras held forth with what Elizabeth's friends termed "music for the middle-aged."

The other party was in the giant game room of the pool house. This had been transformed into a discotheque, and music was electronically blasted forth by two alternating rock groups.

Both parties were jammed with people and even standing room was measured in centimeters. There had been nothing like it ever seen in Detroit. It was an Armageddon of sound and confusion.

The warm late September gardens were also thronged with people wandering back and forth between the two parties, anxious to see everything and be everywhere at the same time. It was almost midnight before the jam of automobiles that had backed all the way down the long driveway into the streets around the house was cleared and Angelo found himself entering the wide-flung great wooden doors.

The reception line had long since broken down; Loren, smashed even before the party began, was nowhere to be seen, and Betsy had adjourned to the discotheque with her friends. Only Alicia, slightly frazzled and the worse for wear, remained anywhere near the entrance.

For the third time, Angelo presented his invitation for inspection. The first two times had been at the driveway entrance and in front of the house. This time a butler in formal livery took it.

The gray-haired man turned to the room. "Mr. Angelo Perino," he announced in sepulchral tones that were completely lost in the clamor.

Angelo walked down the steps toward Alicia. He kissed her cheek. "You look lovely."

"I look terrible and you know it."

"Quite a party," he said, glancing around the room.

"Yes," she said. "But I wish we had never given it. Somehow it all seems such a waste. But Loren insisted."

"It looks like fun," Angelo said.

"I hope he's enjoying himself," she said sarcastically.

"Where's the deb?" he asked. "Shouldn't I congratulate her or something? I don't know exactly what you do at things like this."

For the first time that evening she laughed. "Angelo,

you're marvelous. You have to be the only honest person left in Detroit." She glanced around. "I don't see her anywhere. She must be out in the game room with her friends."

"I'll catch up to her," he said.

"Come," she said, taking his arm. "I'll find some pretty young thing for you to dance with."

"What's wrong with you?"

"Me?" There was a note of surprise in her voice. She hesitated. "I don't know. I should remain here. Someone should."

"Why?"

She stared at him for a moment, then nodded. "You know something? You're absolutely right. There's no reason at all why I should stay here."

He led her out to the dance floor and she came into his arms. She was slightly stiff at first. He moved her closer to him. "Relax," he smiled. "You're allowed to have fun at your own party."

She laughed again and they moved off to the music. She rested her head against his shoulder and after a moment, she looked up at him. "Thank you, Angelo."

"For what?"

"For making me feel I'm really here. I've had the strangest feeling all night that I wasn't."

"I don't understand."

"You know what's happening," she said. "Everyone does. It's an open secret that Loren is keeping that girl in the apartment on top of the administration building out at the plant and that I'm leaving for Reno the day after tomorrow. People have been looking at me with that, 'the queen is dead, long live the queen,' sort of look. It's been very strange. They're just not quite sure how friendly they should be."

"You're imagining things," he said. "You grew up here. These people have always been your friends. Married to Loren or not won't make any difference."

A sad look came into her eyes. "At one time I thought so. Now I'm not that sure."

The song ended and they stopped on the floor. A woman's voice came from behind them. "Alicia, darling! Where have you been hiding this perfectly ravishing man?"

They turned and Angelo saw the beautifully tailored couple standing next to them. The woman's face had a vaguely familiar look.

Alicia smiled. "Angelo Perino, my sister-in-law and her husband, the Prince and Princess Alekhine."

The princess held out her hand. Angelo took it. "Kiss it or shake it?" he smiled.

"You can do both," she laughed. "And the name is Anne. You went to school with my brother but we never met."

"My hard luck." He kissed her hand and turned to take the hand of her husband.

The prince was taller than Angelo, with thick gray-black hair and bright dark eyes set in a strong, tanned face. His grip was firm and direct. "You call me Igor," he said in a deep friendly voice. "And I have been looking forward to meeting you. There is much we have to talk about. I want you to tell me all about the new car."

"That can wait," Anne said. "Tomorrow is time enough for you men to talk business." The music began again. "Igor, you dance with Alicia," she commanded, taking Angelo's arm. "I want to learn all about the new man in Detroit."

She came into his arms with all the assurance of a woman who had been there many times before. He looked down at her. "You've been reading too many magazines," he said.

"Of course," she answered. "What else do you think Americans in Europe do with their time? They read magazines and that way they keep in touch. It makes them feel a part of things."

"They could come home," he said.

"Aren't you clever?" she smiled. "Changing the subject so quickly. But I won't be put off that easily. I saw the article in *Life*. The one about DeLorean at Chevy, Iacocca at Ford, and you. Is it true what they said about your grandfather? That he was the liquor dealer who supplied the liquor for my parents' wedding in this house?"

"Not true," he said. "He was never a liquor dealer, he was a bootlegger."

She began to laugh. "I think I'm going to like you. I'm beginning to understand what Grandfather sees in you."

At one o'clock in the morning the grand portieres were drawn back, revealing the sumptuous buffet and the gaily decorated dinner tables. Half an hour later, the dinner entertainment began.

The orchestra leader spoke into the microphone, but even with the amplification his words were lost in the greater bedlam coming from the tables. He turned and gestured to the wings of the small temporary stage. The girl who stepped in front of the microphone was recognized by everyone there. For years they had seen her face on television every week and for a long while she had even been the voice for one of the major automobiles. Now she opened her mouth to sing but no one could hear her or even cared to listen. They were too busy with their conversation and food.

Loren stood at the side of the stage, swaying slightly. He tried to hear her, but nothing. He moved closer to the stage until he was standing right beneath her. Still nothing. Suddenly he was angry.

He climbed up on the stage quickly and crossed to the microphone. The singer looked at him in bewilderment. He help up a hand and the orchestra stopped playing. He turned and looked out at his guests.

No one had even noticed what was happening on the stage. He bent down and picked up a spoon from a table in front of the stage and banged it on the edge of the microphone until he had caught their attention. Bit by bit the room began to quiet down.

He stared out at them, his face flushed and angry, his collar wrinkled and soft with his perspiration. "Now, listen to me, you slobs!" he shouted into the microphone which carried his slurred words into exaggerations that filled every corner of the two giant rooms. "I paid fifteen thousand dollars to bring this little lady all the way here from Hollywood to sing for you and you all better shut up and goddamn well listen!"

Suddenly, the room was silent, not even the sound of a fork or spoon could be heard. He turned to the singer and made an exaggerated courtly bow.

"It's all right, little lady," he said. "Now you can sing."

The orchestra began again, and as her soft voice began to fill the room, Loren turned and started from the stage. He stumbled slightly on the last step, but recovered his balance before he fell and weaved off toward the bar.

Angelo was standing at the bar as Loren came up to him. He put his hand out to steady him.

Loren shook his hand away. "I'm alri'." He turned to the bartender. "Scotch on the rocks." He looked at Angelo as if he had just seen him for the first time. "Ungrateful bastards!" he mumbled. "They don't appreciate anything you do for them."

Angelo didn't answer.

Loren picked up his drink and tasted it. "Good Scotch," he said. "You don't get the hangover you do from Canadian. You ought to try it sometime."

"I get hangovers from everything," Angelo smiled. "Even Coca-Cola."

"Ungrateful bastards!" Loren said again, looking out at the crowded rooms. He turned back to Angelo. "When did you get into town?"

"This afternoon."

"You didn't call me," he said.

"I did," Angelo replied. "But you had already left the office."

"I want to see you before the meeting tomorrow," said Loren. "We have some important things to talk about."

"I'm available."

"I'll call you," Loren said. He put his empty glass on the bar and started away. He turned back abruptly. "There won't be time tomorrow morning," he said. "You meet me here at the bar when the party is over. That'll be around three o'clock."

Angelo looked at him. "It's a pretty large evening. Sure it won't keep until the morning?"

"Think I do' know what I'm doing?" Loren asked belligerently.

Angelo smiled. "I know you don't," he said easily.

Loren's eyes narrowed and his face flushed even more. He stepped toward Angelo.

"Don't," Angelo said quietly. "It would be a shame to spoil your daughter's party."

Loren stood there for a moment, then he relaxed. He even smiled. "You're right," he admitted. "Thank you for keeping me from making a horse's ass of myself."

Angelo returned his smile. "That's what friends are for."

"Will you do me a favor?" Loren asked.

"Of course."

"Will you meet me at three fifteen and drive me back to the plant?" Loren asked. "I don't think I'm in any condition to drive myself."

"I'll be here," Angelo said.

He walked out through the giant French doors into the garden. The gaily colored lanterns hung along the paths swayed gently in the late night wind. He lit a cigarette and started down the path toward the pool house.

The heavy beat of the rock group grew louder as he approached the building. Through the large picture windows he could see into the discotheque. It was filled with wall-to-wall dancers who seemed oddly frozen in flashes of colored light.

He walked in through the open doorway and pushed his way to the bar. He ordered a drink and the bartender put it down in front of him. He picked it up and sipped it. His nostrils also picked up the acrid-sweet smell of marijuana. He looked around him. In the dark he could not tell who was smoking the grass or who was on tobacco. Cigarettes filled the room like fireflies.

"Do I know you?" The girl's voice came from behind him.

He turned around. She was young, there was no doubt about that, but then so were all the girls in this room. Her eyes were a pale blue and her long blond hair fell straight along her face to her shoulders. There was an oddly familiar look about her mouth and chin.

"I don't think so," he smiled. "But then, I don't know you, so that makes us kind of even."

"I'm Elizabeth Hardeman," she said imperiously.

"Of course," he said.

"What do you mean?" she asked.

"Who else could you be?" he smiled. "Is it proper to congratulate you, Miss Elizabeth?"

She stared at him. "You're making fun of me."

"I'm not really," he said quickly. "I just don't know what's the right thing to do in these circumstances."

"You're not putting me on?"

"Honest Injun," he said seriously.

She grinned suddenly. "Can I tell you the truth?"

He nodded.

"I really don't know what's proper either," she laughed.

"Then I'll let my congratulations stand," he said.

"Thank you." She snapped her fingers. "I never forget a face. You're the man who was driving the Sundancer SS the first time I saw it on Woodward Avenue one night last winter. You were with that girl with the big—. The one who looked like Miss Hurst Golden Shifter, I mean."

He laughed. "Guilty."

"Do you work for my father?" she asked. "Are you one of the test drivers?"

"In a kind of way," he admitted. "I guess you can put it like that."

A dismayed look suddenly crossed her face. "I know you," she said. "I saw your picture in *Life*. You're Angelo Perino."

"That's right," he smiled. "But I'd rather be listed as your unknown admirer."

"I'm sorry, Mr. Perino. I didn't mean to put my foot in my mouth."

"I'll forgive you if you give me this dance," he said.

She looked at the dance floor, then back at him. "Here?" she asked doubtfully. "Or back at the main house?"

"Here," he said, laughing and leading her onto the floor. "I'm not really as old as I look."

Chapter Twelve

THE MEYER DAVIS orchestra began playing "Three O'Clock in the Morning," and the sound of it filtered through the half sleep into Number One's bed. A vague memory stirred and he pushed himself upright, pulling the pillow behind him. He sat there thoughtfully for a moment, then pressed the button on the night table beside him.

A moment later Donald came into the room. As usual, he was dressed as if he had never gone to bed.

"Tell Roxanne I want to see her," Number One said.

"Roxanne?" Donald's voice was puzzled.

Number One looked at him. Then he remembered. Roxanne was gone. Many years ago. That was the trouble with memory. You never outlived it, only people.

"Get me dressed," he said. "I want to go downstairs."

"But the party is almost over, sir," Donald said respectfully.

"I don't care," Number One said, annoyed. "Get me dressed."

Twenty minutes later, Donald pushed the wheelchair out of the room and down the long corridor. Number One held up his hand as they came to the balcony overlooking the grand staircase leading to the entrance hall. Donald paused and they looked down.

The guests were still thronged around the door as they waited for the parking attendants to bring their cars. They were still talking brightly and seemed reluctant to leave.

"It must have been quite a party," Number One said.

"Yes, sir."

"About how many people do you think?"

"Between four-fifty and five hundred," Donald answered.

Number One looked down at the crowd silently. People never changed. They weren't very different than the people

who came to his parties all that many years ago. He looked
back at Donald. "I don't want to get caught in that
crowd," he said. "Take me to the library elevator."

Donald nodded and turned the wheelchair around and
they went back along the corridor. At the end of the corridor, they turned into another that led to the other wing of
the house. They stopped in front of the elevator door and
Donald pressed the call button. The clock on the wall
next to the elevator door told them it was ten minutes to
four.

The discotheque was silent, only the musicians were left,
disconnecting their electronic amplifiers and gathering their
instruments. Somehow, now that they were not playing
they seemed oddly awkward and their monosyllabic instructions to each other were strangely stilted and archai-
cally formal.

Angelo put his drink on the bar and looked at Elizabeth.
She seemed curiously pensive and into herself. "I guess
we're the last," he said.

She glanced around the darkened room. "I guess so."

"You're down," he said shrewdly.

She thought for a moment, then nodded.

"It's always like that after a big one," he said. "Somehow you gear up for it and while it's happening, everything's a ball. But the moment it's over—boom! You
crash."

"I could use a drink," she said.

He signaled the bartender.

"No," she said quickly. She looked at him. "What I
mean is—I would like a drag. Liquor doesn't turn me on.
I don't like the taste of it."

"All I have are cigarettes," he said.

"I'm cool," she said, opening her small evening purse,
taking out what looked like a package of cigarettes. She
opened the fliptop box and shook out a corktip filter cigarette. She placed the cigarette in her mouth.

He held the light for her. "That is cool," he said. "I've
never seen them like that."

"There's a dealer who brings them in from Canada. You

can get your favorite brand. Kent, Winston, L&M's, Marlboro, you name them." She dragged deeply and then
giggled. "Only you have to be careful sometimes you don't
pass them out by mistake."

He smiled.

She looked at him. "Do you turn on?"

"Sometimes," he said. "But not when I'm drinking. They
don't mix."

She dragged again on the cigarette. This time she held
the smoke in her lungs for a long while before she let it
out. She blew the smoke out toward the ceiling. "I'm beginning to feel better."

"Good."

She laughed. "Matter of fact, I'm a little high." She
looked at him. "But then I figure that I'm entitled to it. I
haven't had one drag all night, even though everyone else
was turning on."

"So I noticed," he said dryly.

She took one more pull on the cigarette then ground it
out in a tray on the bar and got to her feet. Her eyes were
smiling again. "Okay, Mr. Perino," she said. "I'm ready to
go back to the manor house and face my family." She
laughed humorlessly. "What's left of it, that is."

He took her arm and they walked out into the garden.
The hanging lanterns went out, plunging the paths into
darkness. She stopped abruptly and faced him.

"It really was a farce, wasn't it?"

He didn't answer.

"You know my mother's leaving for Reno tomorrow to
get a divorce, don't you?"

He nodded.

"Then why the hell did they have to put me through all
this?" she exploded. Suddenly she began to cry. The hard,
bitter sobs of a child.

He took a handkerchief from his pocket and gave it to
her. She dabbed at her eyes and stepped toward him, burying her face against his chest. "What were they trying to
prove?" she sniffled.

He held her lightly, almost impersonally. "Maybe they
didn't want to cheat you out of anything."

"They could have asked me," she said.

"The one thing I've learned about parents, Miss Elizabeth," he said quietly, "is—that they always ask when they shouldn't and that they never ask when they should."

Her sniffling stopped. She looked up at him. "Why do you call me Miss Elizabeth?"

In the night, his teeth flashed whitely. "Because it's your name. And I like the sound of it."

"But almost everyone calls me Betsy."

"I know," he said.

She touched her eyes with the handkerchief. "Do I look all right?"

"You look all right to me."

"I hope my eye makeup didn't run. I don't want anyone to know I've been crying."

"It didn't," he said.

"Good." She returned the handkerchief. "Thank you."

"Not at all," he said, putting it back in his pocket.

They walked along silently for a moment, hand in hand. Suddenly she stopped and looked up at him. "Do you believe in astrology?"

"I haven't made up my mind," he answered.

"I do," she said firmly. "I've just had my chart made up. You're Taurus, aren't you?"

"How did you know?" he smiled. He really wasn't. He was a Leo.

"You had to be!" she said excitedly. "It was all in my chart. I was due to meet an older man and he would be a Taurus and I would dig him very much."

He laughed aloud. "And do you?"

A mischievous smile came to her lips. "You wouldn't want me to make a liar out of my chart now, would you?"

"Miss Elizabeth," he smiled. "That's the very last thing in the world I would want to do."

Abruptly she put her hands on his face and, standing on her toes, kissed him. Then her mouth grew hot and opened and her body clung to him. His arms tightened around her, almost crushing the breath from her, then let her go as quickly as he had taken her.

He looked down, shocked at his own unexpected response to her. "Why did you do that?"

She smiled a secret smile and suddenly she was no longer a child. "Now you can stop calling me Miss Elizabeth," she said.

Number One came through the elevator doors into the library. A lonely barman was there cleaning away the remnants of the party. He looked up when he saw them.

"Don't put away the whiskey," Number One said.

"Yes, Mr. Hardeman." The barman picked up a bottle of Canadian and placed it on the bar.

Number One turned to Donald. "You find my grandchildren and bring them here. All of them. Betsy too."

Donald hesitated.

"Go on, do what I say!" Number One snapped.

Donald still hesitated. "You're not going to drink, are you, sir?"

"No, goddamnit!" Number One roared. "What kind of a fool do you think I am? You fetch them here!"

"Yes, sir."

Alicia was the first to enter the library. "I didn't know you were still awake, Grandfather."

"I couldn't sleep," he said. "Besides, I thought at least one time this evening we should all be together. Where's Loren?"

"I don't know," she said. "I haven't seen him for several hours."

"Donald will find him."

Igor and Anne were the next to come in. "Grandfather," Anne said, crossing the room to him.

He held up an interrupting hand. "I know," he said. "You didn't know I was still awake."

"Are you all right?"

"I never felt better," the old man said. He looked up as Elizabeth and Angelo appeared in the doorway. He gestured to her. "Come in, my child."

Betsy ran across the room to him. "Great-Grandfather! I didn't think we'd see you tonight!" There was a genuine pleasure in her voice.

He smiled at her. "I didn't want to miss seeing you, especially tonight."

"Great-Grandfather, you're lovely!" She kissed his cheek.

He saw Angelo begin to walk away. "Angelo!" he called after him. "Please join us."

Angelo hesitated.

"Please do, Angelo," Betsy said quickly. "I know Great-Grandfather feels as if you're one of the family."

Number One glanced at her, then at Angelo. He smiled. "That's an official invitation."

Angelo came into the room. Donald appeared in the doorway behind him. "I can't seem to find Mr. Loren anywhere, sir," he said.

"He should be around somewhere," Angelo said. "We arranged to meet here after the party. I'll help you look for him."

"No need to bother," Loren's voice came from the open terrace door. He came into the room. "You're half an hour late, Angelo," he said. "I told you we'd meet at three fifteen."

"I'm sorry," Angelo said. "I'm afraid I lost track of the time."

Loren shot him a hard glance, then turned to his grandfather. "Now that we're all here, Grandfather, what did you have in mind?"

Number One looked up at him. "I thought since this may be the last time we are all in this house together, it might be nice if we shared a final drink."

Loren nodded. "That's a nice sentimental gesture." He turned to Alicia. "I'll bet you never thought my grandfather was so fond of you that he would offer a farewell toast."

Number One's voice was suddenly icy. "Being my grandson doesn't excuse bad manners. I think you owe Alicia an apology."

"I owe her nothing!" Loren flashed. "She's already gotten all she's going to get from me."

The old man's voice became even colder. "I won't allow Hardeman women to be spoken to like that."

"In a few weeks she won't be one," Loren retorted.

"But right now she is still your wife," Number One snapped. "And, by God, you will treat her with respect or—"

"Or what, Grandfather?" Loren asked sarcastically. "You'll cut me out of your will?"

"No," the old man said quietly. "I can do better than that. I'll cut you out of my life."

There was a long silence in the room as they stared into each other's eyes. Loren's eyes dropped. "I apologize," he mumbled in a low voice.

"Barman." Number One turned his chair. "Give everyone a drink."

They were silent while the servant filled glasses and handed them around. Then they turned to Number One.

He held up his glass. "First—to the debutante. May she have many happy years."

He touched the liquor to his lips while they all drank, then he raised his glass again. "There's one other thing I have to tell you," he said.

"This is the last party that will ever be held in Hardeman Manor. When your grandmother and I built this house we had dreams that it would be filled with the laughter and the sound of our family. But it didn't quite work out that way. I guess neither of us ever thought that our children would go their own way and make their own lives. Maybe it was foolish of us to even dream of it, but now that the dreams are gone, I have no use for it.

"Tomorrow, Hardeman Manor will be closed. In the course of the next few weeks, certain personal things will be removed to Palm Beach and at the beginning of next month the State of Michigan will take it over to do with it what they will. That's why I wanted this last party to be held here. To just once more feel this house alive with people."

Number One looked around him. He held up his glass. "To Hardeman Manor, to my wife, to all my children, and to you."

He touched the glass to his lips, hesitated a moment, then threw the liquor down his throat. He coughed once, the tears coming to his eyes, then smiled. "Don't look so sad, children," he said gruffly. "It just shows you how far an old man will go to find an excuse to drink a shot of whiskey!"

Chapter Thirteen

DAN WEYMAN'S voice was dry and flat. "What you're doing, Angelo, is asking us to throw away our dirty water before we get clean. That doesn't seem good business to me."

"Then we go thirsty," Angelo said. "But I'm sure that we'll have what we need."

"Sure?" Weyman's voice was unchanged. "Between the new plant on the Coast and research, we have already invested over sixty million dollars and we haven't even got an idea of what our new car will be."

"Maybe," Angelo replied. "But we do know what it will not be. And that's a step in the right direction."

"It's a negative step," Dan said. "What we have to take before the board is something positive." He looked across the desk at Loren, who had been silent. "I, for one, can't go along with Angelo's idea to scrap the Sundancer for a car that nobody knows and may never be built. Half a loaf is better than none and in one year without a new car we may never get back into the market."

"According to the figures you gave me," Angelo said, "that half a loaf cost us almost forty-one million last year. If that's true, dumping the car will in one year pay for the original capital investment in the new plant."

"I pointed out that was an extraordinary loss," Dan said. "Almost half of it was due to the failure of Sundancer Super Sport to sell."

Angelo refrained from mentioning that he was the only member of the board who had been against the hot car, that he had correctly predicted the turning of the market.

"Let me just recap your recommendations so that I clearly understand them," Loren said. He placed his palms together judicially on the desk in front of him and studied them. "It is your recommendation that the Sundancer line be converted to a production line for the engine and transmission of the new car so as to create greater space on the Coast for final assembly. Is that correct?"

Angelo nodded.

"Have you taken into account the cost of shipment to the Coast of those items and then the reshipment of the same parts in completed cars back East to market? Wouldn't that be a wasteful additional cost?"

Angelo nodded again. "It might. Perhaps it would be better to ship shells for the eastern market back to Detroit for assembly here, if we can find room on the line for it. I don't know yet and I won't know until the car is designed and approved. Then we can refine manufacturing procedures."

"I fail to see the rush to disavow the Sundancer," Loren said.

Angelo looked at him. "Because it's yesterday's automobile and I want to establish a brand-new outlook. A point of view that reflects today's market in both attitudes and concerns."

"Have you spoken to Number One about this?" Loren asked.

"Not yet," Angelo said.

"Do you think he will like the idea of stopping production of the Sundancer?" Loren asked. "After all, it was the car that built this company."

"I don't think he will like it," Angelo answered.

"Then why don't you try to find a compromise, a middle ground, one that will be easier for him to accept?"

Angelo looked at him. "Because that's not what he asked me to do. He asked me to build a new car that would get this company back into its former position in this industry. That's what he asked me to do and that's what I'm doing to try to do. He didn't ask me to make him like it."

"I know my grandfather," Loren said. "And I suggest you better talk it over with him before the board meeting."

"I intend to do that." Angelo rose to his feet. "Thank you, gentlemen. See you later this afternoon."

They watched the door close behind him, then looked at each other.

"What do you think?" Dan asked. "Is he holding something back on us? Like maybe the design plans for the new car?"

"I don't know," Loren said thoughtfully. "I really don't know."

"He's talking awfully positive for a man who doesn't know what he's doing."

Loren looked at his friend. "Don't you make the same mistake that I did once."

"What do you mean?" Dan huffed.

"Once I thought he didn't know what he was doing and you saw what happened. In his own quiet Machiavellian manner, he almost destroyed us." He picked up a cigarette and lit it. "I'm not in the mood to give him another shot at me."

"Then what do we do?" Dan asked.

"We sit tight and wait," Loren said. "He's the man in motion, he has to prove himself. We don't have anything to prove. Our end of the business is paying the freight for all of us."

There was a message to call John Duncan at the Coast lying on his desk when he returned to his office. He picked up the telephone and held on while the operator put the call through.

The old Scot's voice came burring through the lines. "How was the party, laddie?"

"Fine," Angelo replied shortly. "But that's not what you called me about."

Duncan laughed. "What's happened to your sense of humor, Angelo?"

"Gone," Angelo snapped. "Along with eight missing hours of sleep. What's up?"

"I want your okay to do some work on my gas turbine engine."

"You finish the tests on the Japanese Wankel?"

"Not yet. But we already know it's good. Very good."

"Then maybe we can make a deal."

"Not a chance, laddie. One, they're planning to come on strong in the States next year; two, Ford's already wheeling and dealing for a share of Toyo Kogyo and they have the inside track. And with GM making their own deal with the Germans, we might as well forget it. They'll royalty us right out of the market."

Angelo was silent.

"I've been going over the turbine with Rourke," Duncan said. "And we'd like to try some experiments with titanium and steel castings. We have a feeling that we can get it to take the heat and stress as well as the nickel and carbon alloys. If it can, we may have a way to bring down the cost."

"Okay," Angelo said. "Try it." He reached for a cigarette. "Do you have the aerodynamics report on the designs yet?"

"No," Duncan said. "We have the models sideways in the wind tunnel to see what will give first but nothing's come through from them."

"Keep me posted," Angelo said.

"I will, laddie." Duncan hesitated a moment. "Tell me, how does Number One look to you?"

"Good."

"Have you spoken to him about the Sundancer yet?"

"No," Angelo replied. "I'm going to try to get to him before the meeting."

"Good luck, Angelo," Duncan said.

"Thank you. You too." Angelo put down the telephone. It rang again. He picked it up.

"Lady Ayres on the line," his secretary said.

He switched over. "Hello, Bobbie."

"You could have called me, Angelo." Her voice was faintly reproachful.

He laughed. "Stop putting me on. Mere vice-presidents don't call the boss's intended."

She laughed. "Now, you're putting me on. I thought I might invite you to lunch."

"I'd love to," he said. "But I have a hectic afternoon coming up. I thought I'd grab a sandwich at my desk."

"That's funny," she said. "That's exactly what Loren told me. Is that common among American executives? A sign of diligence or something?"

"I don't really know," he answered.

"Then come upstairs," she said. "I promise not to eat you."

"Wrong promise," he laughed.

"You come upstairs," she said, "and I'll promise to give you my latest American discovery for lunch."

"What's that?"

"A hero sandwich," she answered.

He laughed aloud. "I'll be right up. You certainly know the way to an Italian boy's heart."

"Take the last elevator on the bank," she said. "I'll clear the switch so that it comes up to the penthouse."

She was waiting at the door when he came off the elevator. The doors closed behind him and they stood there silently for a moment, just looking at each other.

"I'm only a bird in a gilded cage," she sang in a cracked voice. She tried to smile but she couldn't make it. Then she came into his arms and they stood there very quietly for a long time.

After a while she stepped back and looked up at him. "You've lost weight."

"A little."

"I've missed you."

He didn't speak.

"I've really missed you," she said.

He remained silent.

"You don't know what it's like, staying up here. There were times I thought I would go crazy."

"You could have left any time," he said. "You weren't chained here." He turned and pressed the call button for the elevator to return.

"Where are you going?"

"Back downstairs," he answered. "I was stupid to come up in the first place." The doors opened and he stepped into the elevator.

She placed a hand on the door to keep it from closing. "Stay."

He shook his head. "If I do, I might blow it for you. Do you really want that?"

She stared at him.

"Do you?" he repeated.

She let her hand fall from the door. He saw her turn and walk away as the doors rushed shut. Slowly, the elevator began its descent.

Number One sat quietly at the foot of the long directors' table. "Then we're all agreed, gentlemen," he said. "We'll approve production of the Sundancer until April of '71 and if Mr. Perino has completed satisfactory plans for the new car by that time, we will entertain a motion to convert."

He looked at Angelo. "Is that acceptable to you?"

"No, sir," Angelo said steadily. "But do I have a choice?"

"You don't," Number One said.

"Then there is just one further item I would like to call to the attention of the board," Angelo said. "I had set as a target for production and sales of the new car, five hundred thousand units in the first year. What you are doing is making that goal impossible to achieve by half, simply because it will take that much time to break down the old assembly line."

"We'll make a note of that in the minutes," Number One said. "In that case, with no further business to come before the board, I declare the meeting adjourned."

The door chimes finally made their way into his sleep. He opened his eyes and it took him a few moments to realize that he was in his suite at the Pontchartrain. He got out of bed and staggered through the living room to the door and opened it.

Betsy stood there. He couldn't tell which of them was the more surprised. "I'm sorry," she said. "I didn't think you'd be asleep so early."

"I was wiped out," he said groggily. "I've only had about four hours sleep in the last three days."

"I'm sorry."

"Don't apologize any more. You'll make me feel guilty. Come on in."

He led the way into the living room. "What time is it?" he asked.

"About ten thirty."

He pointed to the bar. "Help yourself to a drink while I get my robe." He padded off into the bedroom, his pajama trousers flapping around his legs.

When he came back she was drinking a Coke in a tall glass choked with ice cubes. He crossed to the bar and made himself a Canadian and water. He turned to look at her, taking a long sip of his drink. "Now, Miss Elizabeth," he said heavily, "what can I do for you?"

She looked at him for a moment, then her eyes fell. "I need a favor," she said. "A very important favor."

He took another pull at his drink. "Like what?"

Her eyes came up and met his gaze. "You'll think I'm being silly, or stoned, or something."

"No, I won't."

"Angelo," she said in a small voice.

"Yes?" he said, beginning to feel annoyed.

She hesitated a moment.

"Yes?" he repeated.

"My chart says it will work out okay."

"What will?"

"You know," she explained. "You, me. Taurus and Virgo."

"Oh, sure," he said, completely bewildered.

"Then it's all settled," she smiled. She put the glass down on the bar. "And we can go to bed." She placed her arms around his neck.

"Wait a minute!" he protested. "Don't I have anything to say about this?"

"Not really," she said. "It's all written in the stars."

"But I'm not a Taurus," he said. "I'm Leo!"

An expression of hurt came into her eyes. "What's the matter, Angelo?" she asked. "Don't you want to marry me?"

Book Three
1971

A HUSH fell over the small hearing room in the old wooden building that served as the county courthouse in the little town midway between Seattle and Spokane. Quietly, the coroner's jury filed into the room and took their seats on the wooden chairs that were placed near the table that served as the coroner's bench. The coroner, a tall man with a weatherbeaten face, ambled to his chair and sat down. He nodded to the bailiff.

The bailiff turned to the room. "The coroner's court is now in session to hear evidence into the cause of death of one Sylvester Peerless while driving a test car in the employ of Bethlehem Motors Company." He glanced down at a sheet of paper he held in his hand. "The court calls Miss Cindy Morris as witness."

Cindy turned in her chair and looked at Angelo. "I'm nervous. What do I tell them?"

Angelo reassured her. "Tell them the truth. You can never go wrong that way."

She got to her feet. An appreciative murmur went through the little room as she made her way to the witness chair, the form-fitting jump suit with the words *BETHLEHEM MOTORS* lettered across the back, left no one with the illusion that she wasn't a girl.

The bailiff administered the oath quickly and asked her name.

"Cindy Morris."

"Please sit down," he said and went back to his own chair.

She sat down as the county prosecutor got to his feet. Like all the men in this portion of the country, he was a tall man who gave the impression that he might have stepped out of a Marlboro Country advertisement. But the outdoorsy look did nothing to hide the keen intelligence of his gray eyes.

He stopped in front of her. His voice was soft with a deceptively gentle western twang. "How old are you, Miss Morris?"

"Twenty-four," she answered.

"Twenty-four, he repeated, nodding.

"Yes."

"You are an employee of Bethlehem Motors?"

"Yes."

"In what capacity?"

"Test driver and design consultant."

"Please explain your duties."

"I drive the cars and report to the design and engineering chief as to a woman's point of view about the cars."

"How long have you been thus employed by Bethlehem Motors?"

"About a year and a half."

"How many cars have you driven and tested in this time?"

"Approximately nineteen."

"Do you regard your work as dangerous?"

"Not really."

The district attorney looked at her. "That's a curious answer. What do you mean by it?"

"I feel much safer driving a car on a test track where every possible safety precaution is taken than I do driving in ordinary everyday traffic."

He was silent for a moment, then he nodded. "I see." He walked back to his table and picked up a sheet of paper. Holding it in his hand, he walked back to her.

"Were you acquainted with the deceased driver, Sylvester Peerless?"

"Yes."

"In what manner?"

"We were good friends."

The attorney looked down at the paper. "I have here a copy of the registration card at the Starlight Motel. It reads and I quote, 'Mr. and Mrs. Sylvester Peerless, Tarzana, California.' In brackets after that, 'Cindy Morris.' Were you ever married to Mr. Peerless?"

"No."

"Then how do you explain the registration?"

"I said we were good friends. We shared the room. I wasn't aware of how Fearless registered us."

The attorney smiled. "You mean to say you were roommates and that's all?"

Cindy smiled back at him, her nervousness disappearing completely. This kind of talk she understood. "I didn't say that, you did. If you are interested in whether Fearless and I ever had sexual relations, why don't you ask?"

"Did you?" the attorney shot back.

"From time to time," she said calmly. "When we felt like it."

The attorney stood there silently. Then he shrugged his shoulders and went back to his table. He put the sheet of paper back on it and turned to her. "Were you present at the test track the day the deceased met his death?"

"Yes."

"Was there anything unusual about the circumstances of that day?"

"Yes."

"What were they?"

"Fearless got himself killed."

A small ripple of laughter ran through the room. The attorney made a face and waited for it to pass. "Was there anything else?"

She thought for a moment. "I don't think so. That was unusual enough."

Again the ripple of laughter. Again the attorney waited

for it to pass. "I mean," he said, "was there anything unusual about the performance of the car he was testing?"

"I didn't think so," she answered. "I turned the car over
to him after my two-hour trick and it was behaving perfectly."

"Did he say anything to you that might have indicated
his concern over the performance of the automobile?"

"No."

"Did he say anything at all to you at that time?"

"Yes, he did."

"What did he say?"

"He made a remark. A joke. You know."

"I don't know," the attorney said.

"A private joke," she said uncomfortably. She glanced
around the room. "The kind of thing you don't say in
public."

"What did he say?" the attorney insisted.

Her face flushed and she looked down at the floor. She
spoke in a low voice. "He said he felt so horny he hoped
his cock wouldn't get caught in the steering wheel."

The lawyer's face reddened as a murmur ran through
the room. "Did you say anything to him?"

"Only what I usually say."

"What was that?"

"Drive carefully."

The lawyer was silent. "What did you mean by that?"

"Nothing," she answered. "I always say that whenever
someone gets behind the wheel of a car."

"You didn't mean that to indicate something special that
might be wrong with the particular car you were driving?"

"No," she replied. "I always say that."

"Did you see the accident happen?"

"No, I did not," she said. "I went back to the motel and
went to sleep."

The attorney looked at her for a moment, then walked
back to his desk. "I have no further questions."

The coroner leaned across his table. "Do you have any
ideas or opinions as to what might have caused the accident that resulted in Mr. Peerless' death?"

"No, sir, I do not," Cindy answered.

"I understand that the car was powered by a new kind of engine," the coroner said. "A gas turbine. I also understand that kind of engine could sometimes explode under certain conditions. Do you think something like that might have happened and caused the accident?"

Cindy looked at him thoughtfully. "It might have but I doubt it. That engine had over thirty thousand miles on it and if it was going to blow up, it would have done so long before then."

"But it might have?" the coroner persisted.

Cindy's voice was level. "I don't know. But isn't that the purpose of this court? To determine what happened?"

The coroner looked at her. His voice was cool. "We expect to do just that, young lady." He glanced at the jury. "Do you have any further questions?"

A murmur of no's came from the jurors and he turned back to Cindy. "That will be all, Miss Morris. Thank you. You may step down now."

The room was silent as Cindy walked back to her seat. She looked at Angelo. "Was I all right?"

He patted her hand. "You were fine."

"The son-of-a-bitch," she whispered. "He didn't have to ask me all those questions."

"You told the truth," Angelo said. "Don't worry."

The bailiff's voice came through the room. "Will Mr. John Duncan take the stand?"

The Scotsman got to his feet. He didn't look his sixty-five years as he walked firmly to the stand and took the oath.

"Your name, please?" the bailiff asked.

"John Angus Duncan," he replied and sat down.

The county prosecutor rose and walked toward him. "Would you please tell us your position with Bethlehem Motors?"

"Vice-president, engineering."

"How long have you held that position?"

"One and a half years."

"And before that?"

"I was for twenty years vice-president of automotive production at that company. At the age of sixty I retired.

Two years later I rejoined the company in this present capacity."

"Would you please define your present responsibilities?"

"I am in charge of the engineering part of the Project Betsy."

"What is Project Betsy?"

"It is the building and development of a new car presently being considered by the company."

"Can you elaborate on that?"

"No." The Scotsman was terse. "It would be disclosing confidential information privileged to my employer."

The county prosecutor glanced at his notes. "I understand that you hold certain patents in connection with a turbine engine. Is that true?"

"Yes," Duncan nodded. "I might point out that they are held jointly with my employer."

"Is that the engine used in the vehicle in which Mr. Peerless met his death?"

"A variation of that engine was used."

"Can you elaborate on that?"

"No." Duncan was firm. "For the same reason mentioned by me before and also that certain patents are currently pending and disclosure would give information to our competitors."

The county prosecutor went back to his table. "Were you present at the scene at the time Mr. Peerless met his death?" he asked.

"Yes, I was."

"Could you tell us about it?"

"Mr. Peerless entered curve number four at a speed of one hundred and seventy-one miles per hour despite our warnings to him and went off the track into the wall."

"You say he was warned. How was this done?"

"We are in constant radio communication with the driver of the car."

"You were able to judge the speed of the vehicle?"

"Yes. Our test cars are equipped with radio sensor devices which constantly send information back to a control computer which records the performance of every part of the automobile."

"Would it be possible for us to see this record?"

"No," Duncan replied. "For all the reasons I mentioned before."

"But your sensor devices indicated there was nothing mechanically wrong with the car?"

"The car was operating perfectly."

"Do you have a record of your warning to Mr. Peerless?"

"Yes. There is a tape of that communication."

"Is it possible for us to hear that?"

Duncan looked across the room at Angelo. Angelo turned to Roberts, sitting next to him. The attorney nodded.

"Yes," Duncan said. "I have a tape playback unit in my attaché case which I left on my seat and can play it for you right now."

The coroner leaned forward. "Would the bailiff please fetch Mr. Duncan's case?"

The bailiff brought the case to Duncan. The Scotsman opened it and took out a cassette playback unit. He looked questioningly at the coroner.

"It's all right, Mr. Duncan. You can place it on the table in front of me."

Duncan got up and set the small machine on the table. He pressed the button. A faint hum filled the room. He turned up the volume control. The hum grew louder.

"I don't hear any engine sound," the coroner said.

"There is very little," said Duncan. "This is a turbine engine and the noise level is negligible compared with the normal I.C. engine. The only background sounds you might hear are the wind and the tires."

A man's voice broke into the tape. "I read one seventy-five on the speedometer. Verify. Over."

Duncan's voice came on the tape. "One seven four point nine nine seven, verified. Better start taking her down. You're coming up on number four. Over."

For a moment there was nothing but the background hum on the tape, then Duncan's voice came on again. "We read you at one seven three point one two five. Bring it down. You're running out of time. Over."

Silence again, then Duncan's voice. This time there was

a note of urgency in it. "Duncan to Peerless. We read you at one seventy-one point zero five zero. Bring it down! This is an order! Over."

Silence. Duncan's voice, harsh and angry. "Are you crazy, Peerless? Bring it down before you get yourself killed! Over."

Peerless' voice came on. He laughed. "Don't be such an old fuddy-duddy. I can take her through."

Duncan's voice overrode him. "You've only got a four percent grade, you'll never make it!"

"You got no faith in your own machine, old man," Peerless laughed. "Leave it to Fearless Peerless. I know what I'm doing. I drive with the angels."

For a moment there was nothing but the faint whine, then the sound of a faint pop, then nothing. Complete silence.

There was a complete silence in the room as Duncan reached out and turned the machine off. He looked at the coroner.

The coroner cleared his throat. "Were you able to hear that?" he asked the jury.

The foreman stood up. "Yes."

The coroner turned to Duncan. "You mentioned a four percent grade on that turn. What did you estimate a safe speed for it? Maximum?"

"One hundred ten."

"Were there any warning signs posted to that effect?"

"Yes, sir. Every two hundred yards beginning two miles before the turn."

"Then you estimate that Mr. Peerless entered that turn at sixty miles per hour in excess of the maximum safe speed?"

"Yes, sir."

"Could you tell me at what point then the engine exploded?"

"The engine did not explode," Duncan said.

The county prosecutor cut in. "But previous witnesses testified that there was an explosion followed by a fire. How do you explain that, Mr. Duncan?"

The Scotsman turned to him. "The explosion did not

take place in the engine. It took place in the fuel tank ignited by an electrostatic spark as the tank cracked open."

"Then there could have possibly been a fault in the fuel tank?"

"There was no fault in the fuel tank. It was equipped and built with every safety precaution known to man. But there is nothing in our present technology that will enable us to build a tank that can resist an impact at one seventy miles an hour."

"How can you be sure that it was the fuel tank and not the engine?"

"Because we have the engine. It is smashed beyond repair but the engine itself is mostly in one piece. If it had exploded, it would have been scattered all over the place."

The county prosecutor nodded and went back to his seat. The coroner looked at the jury. "Do you have any further questions?"

The foreman stood up hesitantly. "I drive a car, Mr. Duncan. And because of the high power performance of your engine, I suppose you have to use a very high octane gasoline. Is that what was used?"

"No, sir," Duncan said. "That is one of the advantages of a turbine engine. It does not require high octane or leaded gasoline to achieve maximum efficiency."

"What kind of gasoline did you use then?" the foreman asked.

"We did not use gasoline."

"What did you use then?"

"Kerosene," Duncan replied.

"Thank you," the foreman nodded and sat down.

The coroner leaned across his bench. "Do you think, Mr. Duncan, that had you used gasoline instead of kerosene the explosion and the fire that followed it might have been prevented?"

"Not under the circumstances." Duncan was very sure of himself. "As a matter of fact, it would have been more susceptible to explosion and fire. The octane rating in gasoline is a measure of its combustibility, thus the higher the rating, the more combustible."

The coroner glanced around the room, then back at the

Scotsman. "It seems there are no further questions. Thank you, Mr. Duncan. You may step down."

The room was silent as the Scotsman returned to his chair. Angelo shook his hand and Cindy kissed the old man's cheek. "You were wonderful," she said.

The Scotsman flushed, pleased. "But I'm still angry," he whispered. "What I want to know is who put them up to this?"

"We'll find out," Angelo said calmly. "First let's see what happens next."

The coroner and the county prosecutor were conferring in whispers. After a moment the attorney returned to his seat and the coroner looked at the court.

"There will be no further witnesses called," he said. He turned to the jury. "You have heard the testimony of the doctors who performed the autopsy on the remains of Mr. Peerless as to the fact that his death was due directly to injuries received in the course of the collision and that the burns on his body were after his decease. You have also heard the testimony of other witnesses supplying information in connection with circumstances surrounding the death of Mr. Peerless. Do you have any further questions to ask pertaining to this matter?"

The foreman shook his head. "No."

The coroner nodded and continued. "You are then requested to reach a determination as to the cause and responsibility for Mr. Peerless' death. There are several such determinations available to you. Let me list some of them.

"One, in the event that you feel Mr. Peerless' death was the fault of anyone other than himself, you may so state. If you further feel that there was criminal negligence resulting in that fault, you may so state. You do not in either of the above cases need to name the person or persons responsible, though you may if you should so desire.

"Two, in the event that you feel Mr. Peerless' death was his own fault, you may so state. In that case you may state simply that the cause of death was due to driver error."

He paused and looked at the jury. They were silent. "Do you wish now to retire and consider your verdict?"

The foreman of the jury leaned over to his confreres.

For a moment there was a whispered conversation, then he rose to his feet. "No, sir."

The coroner looked at him. "Ladies and gentlemen of the jury, do you wish to render your determination?"

The foreman nodded. "Yes, sir."

"And that is?"

The small room was very silent as the foreman began to speak. "It is the unanimous conclusion of this jury that in the matter of the death of Mr. Sylvester Peerless, the cause of his death was his own fault, driver error and plain damn foolishness on his part."

A rustle of noise burst in the small room as reporters began to rush toward the door. The coroner's gavel banged on the table before him. His voice could hardly be heard over the bustle of sound.

"The determination of the jury has been heard and the coroner's inquest into the death of Sylvester Peerless is now closed."

Chapter Two

IN THE CORNER of the dimly lit cocktail bar of the Starlight Motel, a goateed black piano player made gentle drink-time noises which tinkled behind the hum of conversation in the crowded room. They sat jammed into a tiny booth against the far wall.

Artie Roberts looked across the table at Angelo. "What's my best connection to New York tomorrow morning? Spokane or Seattle?"

Angelo shrugged. "I think Seattle has more flights but Spokane is sixty miles nearer. Check it out with the front desk."

Artie got to his feet. "I'll do that now. Be right back."

Cindy picked up her drink and stared into it. "It's the death wish, that's what it is."

"What did you say?" Angelo asked.

She didn't look up from the glass. "I think that's what it is. You all really want to die, don't you?"

Angelo didn't answer.

"You know, I knew he was going to kill himself when he got in that car," she said, still staring into her glass. "That's why I went back to the motel instead of hanging around for him. I didn't want to be there when he did it."

"If that was the way you felt, why didn't you try to stop him?" Angelo asked.

"What for? If he wouldn't do it that day, he would another. I wasn't going to be around to stop him forever."

Angelo signaled for another round. She picked up her fresh drink and tasted it.

"I think I'll be moving on tomorrow," she said.

"What for? Got anything better to do?"

She shook her head. "No. But this isn't my bag. You know that. These cars don't make any noise."

"Someday all cars won't make noise," he said. "Then what'll you do?"

"By that time, I'll be too old to enjoy it anyway," she said.

"You're a good driver," said Angelo. "I know Duncan won't like to lose you. He says you have a good point of view."

"I like the old man. But I only took the job to go along with Fearless. He thought you were going into racing then."

"So did we," Angelo said. "But that's not where it's at any more. At least not in what we're trying to do."

"I know that," she said. She picked up her drink and looked at it. "When did you stop being crazy?"

"What do you mean?"

She looked at him. "You were like all the others once. Ready to buy it any time, any place, on any corner. Then, like all in one crazy day, it was over and you weren't the same man in the afternoon that you were in the morning. I knew that when I came and found you in the tub."

"We all have to grow up sometime," he said. "Maybe that was my time."

She was silent. She put her drink down with a kind of finality. "Maybe that's it. I don't want to grow up. Grown-

ups don't need me. They can manage very well by themselves. But guys like Fearless, like you used to be, need
someone to hold them together when they're not behind a
wheel. Someone who can make them feel a little bit alive
when they're not doing what they're about."

She rose. "I had them move me to another room."

"That's a good idea," he said.

"I have some new tapes you haven't heard. Maybe after
dinner you'll come over and we'll listen to them."

"We'll see. I'll give you a call about eight o'clock when
we're ready for dinner."

"Better make it closer to seven if you figure on getting
anything to eat," she said. "They roll it up early around
here."

"Okay." He watched her thread her way through the
crowded lounge and there was something very alone and
young and wistful in the way she moved.

The waiter appeared at his elbow. "There's a long-distance call for you, Mr. Perino."

He followed the waiter to a booth in the corner of the
room. He closed the door and the sounds faded into the
background.

"Mr. Perino?" the long-lines operator singsonged.

"Speaking."

Number One's voice came on. "You're a hard man to
find," he complained irascibly.

"No, I'm not," Angelo replied. "This is the only bar in
town."

"I just heard over the radio about the coroner's finding.
I thought you were going to call me."

"I figured it was too late back East by the time we got
out of court. But it worked out all right."

"We were lucky. It could have turned up a real stink,"
the old man said.

"I would still like to find out who put the finger on us,"
Angelo said. "I'm sure the coroner and local county prosecutor didn't dream this up by themselves."

"You sound more like your grandfather every day," said
Number One. "He was always convinced there was a plot
behind everything. That nothing happened by itself."

"Maybe he was right," Angelo said. "But you know as well as I that had we been caught off base, the publicity could have wiped out the whole project before we even got started. Doesn't it seem a little strange to you that the news and wire services had the story on the inquest even before we were served?"

"We're building a new car," Number One said. "That's big news. You might as well get used to it. They'll be watching you every minute."

"I know that already," Angelo said. "The photographers have been all over the place trying to get pictures of the car. They've even come over the proving grounds in helicopters with telescopic cameras."

"They get anything?"

"Not of our design. But they have plenty of photos of Vegas, Pintos and Gremlins. Maybe even a Maverick or Nova or two."

Number One chuckled. "That should annoy them. How many cars do you have on the road?"

"Thirty-one on the roads all over the West and Southwest. Eight on the proving grounds plus six without camouflage which we run only at night."

"You're doing all right. When do you think you'll be ready to freeze the design?"

"Seven, eight months. September or October," Angelo replied.

"We won't make the fall showings."

"That's right," Angelo said. "But I figure we can make the New York Automobile Show in the spring. It might even be to our advantage. All the other seventy-two's will be frozen, we can be the first out with a seventy-three."

"I like that," Number One said. His tone changed. "I have someone here who wants to talk to you."

Angelo heard the phone change hands. Betsy's voice came on the wire. It had a faint, breathless quality. "When are you going to let me come out and drive one of those cars?"

"When we're finished with our tests, Miss Elizabeth," he replied.

"You don't have to be so formal, Angelo," she said. "I

told Number One about the night I came to your hotel room."

He laughed. "I hope you also told him I drove you home."

"I told him that too and he wanted to know why."

"Could be you just turned eighteen," Angelo said.

"That's how old Great-Grandmother was when he married her. You better think it over. Girls like me don't stay available too long."

Angelo laughed. "Maybe it's just that I'm not the marrying kind, Miss Elizabeth."

"I'm going to Europe to visit my aunt after Daddy's wedding," she said. "You know about the men over there."

"I know about them," he smiled. "I hope you do."

"You still think I'm a child. Just because you went to school with my mother doesn't mean that I'm not old enough for you."

"I don't doubt that for a minute," he said. "But I'm the old-fashioned type. I think the man should do the asking."

"Okay," she said. "Ask me."

"Not just now," he laughed. "I've got a car to build." There was a knock on the door of the phone booth. A sheriff's deputy stood there. "Hold on a moment," he told her and opened the door.

"Mr. Perino?" the deputy asked politely.

"Yes?"

"This is for you." He handed Angelo an official-looking document.

It seemed to be a standard warrant form. His name, Duncan's and Bethlehem Motors Company were typed on the cover sheet. He opened the paper and looked at it. It was an injunction signed by a judge forbidding them to drive any of their test cars powered by a gas turbine engine on any road in the state of Washington. He looked up. The deputy was already halfway through the lounge. He turned back to the telephone. "Put Number One back on."

A note of concern came into her voice. "Is there anything wrong?"

"Plenty," he said sharply. "Put him on."

"What is it?" Number One's voice echoed in the phone.

"I was just served an injunction that orders us not to drive any of our cars on public roads in this state."

"What?" Number One was surprised. "How can they do such a thing?"

"I don't know how they can do it but they did," he said. He paused a moment while he fished for a cigarette with his free hand. "Now, tell me that no one's behind all this."

Number One was silent.

"Whoever it is has a lot of muscle going for him," Angelo said.

"What are you going to do?"

"Artie Roberts is still here," Angelo replied. "He was checking the next flight to New York. But he's not going to make it. He can fight this in the courts."

"That could take a lot of time," Number One said.

"If it was nothing but time I wouldn't be that worried," said Angelo. "If we don't get this injunction lifted, the Betsy may never get on the road."

Chapter Three

"ONLY THIRTY DAYS more and the divorce will be final," Loren III said.

Bobbie put down the empty martini glass. "By that time it won't matter. Another month here and I'll go out of my mind. I'm not used to being a prisoner."

"You're not a prisoner, darling," he said patiently. "You know the people here. Once we're married everything will change. We'll move out to the house and life will become normal."

"What makes you think that?" she asked sarcastically. "The few times we have gone out, Detroit has done a pretty good job of cutting me dead."

"Stupid women," he replied. "It will change. Believe me, I know it will."

"Fuck them!" she said angrily. "I don't need them or

their fucking approval." She rose from the couch. "I just have to get away from here for a while."

He looked up at her. "Where do you want to go?"

"I don't know. Anywhere. Just as long as it's away from here." She walked to the bar and poured herself another martini from the pitcher. She looked back at him. "I swear to God I'm becoming an alcoholic."

"I can't get away just now," he said.

"I know that." She walked over to the window and looked out. The factory lights gleamed in the dull black night, the tips of the chimneys belching rose-colored flames into the sky. "Look at that view," she said bitterly. "You know, for almost a year I've been looking out this window without ever seeing a tree or a bit of green. I think I've almost forgotten what they look like."

Loren got to his feet and came over to her. He put his arms around her and drew her to him. She rested her head on his shoulder. "I know it hasn't been easy," he said. "But we expected it."

"I'm sorry," she said. "I know it hasn't been easier for you. But at least you have your work to keep you busy. I have nothing to do but go out of my mind."

"Look," he said. "Give me a few days to clear things up here and then maybe we'll go out West and take a look at how they're doing with the test cars. It's time I went out there anyway."

"I'd love that. I have a feeling the new car will be great."

"I hope so," he said without enthusiasm.

She looked at him. "You're worried about it, aren't you?"

He nodded.

"Why? When everybody in the business is so excited about it?"

"They can afford to be," he said dourly. "It's not their money. If the car misses, it can take the whole company down with it." He walked back to the bar and picked up his drink. "If it hits, we'll do all right, but within a couple of years, GM and Ford will step in to take over the market, so in reality all we're doing is risking our capital for them."

He walked back to her. "I remember the year I was

made president of the company. Nineteen hundred and
fifty-three. The year the Kaiser-Frazer Company finally
gave up the ghost and went down the drain. They had a
good car but they couldn't beat the system. Between the
competition and the Korean War, which cut their sources
of supply, they got wiped out. I made up my mind then I
was not going to fight them. I would settle for whatever
share of the automobile market we could squeeze out and
concentrate on the other areas for profit. And I wasn't
wrong. There hasn't been a year since in which the company netted less than six million after taxes. Now, a ghost
from the past threatens to blow the whole company sky
high."

It was the longest speech she ever heard him make. She
stared at him thoughtfully. "Did you ever tell Number One
that?"

His voice was bitter. "There's no one alive that my
grandfather will listen to. Except maybe Angelo. And, even
then, only if Angelo tells him what he wants to hear."

"But what about you?" she asked. "Wouldn't you like to
build a new car? A car that everyone would want?"

He looked at her. "Of course I would. That's the dream
of every man in this business. But when I was a boy I
wanted to be the first man on the moon. That didn't happen either."

"Then why didn't you get out of the automobile business
altogether?"

"I should have. I know that now." He looked down into
the amber of his drink. "But I knew that if I did, my grandfather would die. That was the only reason for him to stay
alive, that was all he cared about."

She was silent for a moment, then put her drink down
and took his from his hand. She put it down beside her
own. "Come to bed," she said.

"The big problem with the turbine engine has been ac-
celeration response and lack of engine braking," Tony
Rourke said. "We think we finally licked it." He gestured
to the blueprints on Loren III's desk. "By adding a counter
rotor to the drive rotor which would be activated by a

stator vane deflecting the thrust pressure as the throttle is lessened, we create the artificial equal of normal I.C. engine braking. It also serves to hold the car from rolling when in gear and idling at normal speeds. And, conversely, it eliminates the response lag normally present in a turbine, so that speed for pickup and passing is always there."

Loren looked across the desk. "Has this been tested?"

"Thoroughly," Rourke said. "It's been in use on all the test cars since last December and so far has averaged approximately twenty thousand miles in use per car."

"It's expensive," Loren said. He looked at Weyman. "You have the figures?"

Weyman nodded. "It will add approximately one hundred and thirty-one dollars to the cost of each engine if we manufacture it here in quantities of two hundred thousand or more."

Rourke turned to him. "Does that include the savings resulting from the fact that we won't have to build an auxiliary power source to operate the accessories at idling speeds?"

Weyman nodded. "We took that into consideration," he answered in his precise accountant's voice. "The principal factor is labor costs here in Detroit. At the moment fine tolerances involved in manufacturing these rotors take the job out of the unskilled classification into that of skilled machinists."

"It can't be that bad," Rourke said. "Toyo Kogyo is building rotors and selling them in low-end cars."

"That's the edge the Japanese have on us," Weyman said. "Their labor is much more controlled."

"I could build them for less on the Coast," Rourke said. "I'm sure of that. But it doesn't make sense to build the rotors there, ship them here for incorporation into the engine then ship them all back for final car assembly."

"By the time you get through with all that you wouldn't be saving very much." Weyman spoke positively. "It wouldn't be worth it."

"What does the car cost out at now?" Loren asked.

"Nineteen hundred and fifty-one dollars before adding

the new rotors. They put us up to almost twenty-one hundred."

"It doesn't make sense," Rourke said. "I'm sure that the Gremlin doesn't cost American Motors much over seventeen hundred to manufacture."

"It costs less," Weyman said. "That's what they average from the dealer, including federal taxes. But that's stripped. They don't have to include power accessories and air-conditioning to use up available engine power. There's almost seven hundred dollars of extras that we have to have on our car which have to be included in the cost."

"At that rate the Betsy would have to retail at about twenty-five hundred dollars," Rourke said.

"Twenty-four ninety-nine is the figure Sales came up with," said Loren.

"Sounds high compared with the others. The Pinto at nineteen, the Vega at twenty-one, not to mention the imports. They'll kill us."

"Now you're getting an idea of what we're up against," Weyman said.

"It's not that bad," Loren put in. "With accessories and options you can add four hundred dollars to the average selling price of those cars. We're not that far off on a net basis."

Rourke looked at him. "Then you think we have a chance?"

Loren's gaze was steady. "Not the chance of a snowball in hell. Not the way the costs on this are climbing. It will take a miracle car to convince the public that paying more in this case is actually paying less. We're going to price ourselves right out of the low-end market and we'll be right back where we are now. The only difference will be that we'll be out some three hundred million dollars." He reached for a cigarette and lit it. "I'm afraid my grandfather is still living in the past, when Henry Ford showed the world how the American production line could bring down the cost per item. But since then the world has caught up and in the case of Japan and Germany has even surpassed us in new equipment and automation. And they have a fantastic advantage that we don't. German labor costs are sixty percent of ours and the Japanese maybe forty percent."

He blew out a cloud of smoke and ground the cigarette into the tray on his desk. "The way I see it, Angelo made one big mistake. He should have built his plant in Japan instead of on the Coast. It was the only way he could be cost competitive."

"Your grandfather wanted an American-built car," Rourke said.

"I know he did," Loren replied. "But that doesn't make it right. People don't care any more where a thing is built. Only if it is good and its price is right."

"I'd like a chance to go over those figures," said Rourke. "Maybe I could come up with something."

"I hope you can," Loren said. "We can use all the help we can get."

"I won't make any promises," Rourke said. "Your boys are pretty good."

"How are things going out there?" Loren asked.

"Okay, now," Rourke answered. "That injunction last week threw us. But after we showed them that Chrysler had gas turbines on the road since sixty-three and Ford and GM are bringing it out in trucks, it was lifted. Angelo still thinks someone is trying to throw a monkey wrench into the works."

Loren smiled. "It doesn't make sense. The other companies know we're doing them a favor by going so far out on the limb. They're not risking a penny of their own money and while we're doing that, they're minding the store and taking it in as usual."

"You got to admit that it seems like more than a coincidence. The inquest and the injunction right on top of it."

"Probably some hot local crusader trying to make a name for himself," Weyman said.

"If so, why hasn't he come to the surface yet?" Rourke asked. "I've been out there ten years now and have a lot of friends but no one seems to know just where it came from."

"Will you be talking to Angelo later?" Loren asked.

"Yes."

"Would you ask him to reserve a suite plus two extra

bedrooms for next Friday through Tuesday. I'm coming out there with my daughter and my fiancee."

Rourke looked at him curiously. He was about to mention that he had met the Lady Ayres but decided to keep his mouth shut. "I'll give him the message," he said. "But if you want to stay near the proving grounds, I don't think the Starlight Motel has any suites."

"We'll settle for three large rooms then," said Loren.

"I'll take care of it." Rourke got to his feet. He held out his hand. "Thank you for your time, Mr. Hardeman."

Loren took it. "You don't have to thank me. It may not seem like it at times but there is one thing I would like you to remember. We're all on the same team."

Rourke met his gaze. "I never doubted that for a moment, Mr Hardeman." He looked down at Weyman. "I'll be over in Production Estimating when you want me, Dan."

"Right." Dan sat in his chair and when the door closed behind Rourke, he spoke again. "What do you think, Loren?"

"I think Angelo picked himself a winner. Rourke's a good man."

"What I want to know is do you think they'll come up with who is behind their troubles out there?"

Loren looked at him steadily. "It all depends on how clever your man was in covering his tracks."

"He's supposed to be very good," Dan said. "At least for the money he cost us, he should have been."

"Then stop worrying about it," Loren said. He got to his feet. "I guess there's nothing we can do now to stop it. Just watch the Betsy drive us down the merry road to bankruptcy."

"You're still president of the company," Dan said. "There's something you can do if you want to."

Loren's voice went cold. For a moment he sounded like his grandfather. "Leave it alone."

Weyman got to his feet. He made a gesture with his hands. "As you say. You're the boss. Just remember one thing. Time's running out. In less than sixty days from now we're going to have to decide if we turn over the Sundancer plant to Angelo or not."

Loren stared at him. "Aren't you getting things just a little mixed up, Dan? The question isn't whether we turn the Sundancer plant over to Angelo. The question is, do we drop the Sundancer and go with the Betsy?"

"It's the same thing," Weyman said smoothly. "What I can't make you understand is that in the eyes of the industry and the public, the man who builds the car runs the company." He rose from his chair and walked toward the door. There he paused and looked back at Loren. "But the man they'll hold responsible for the losses will be the president of the company. And that's you."

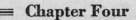 **Chapter Four**

THE INTERIOR of the giant hangarlike garage hummed with activity. Jump-suited mechanics in white with *BETHLE-HEM MOTORS* lettered in red across their backs swarmed in beelike clusters around various cars, each over a pit, the body shell raised on front jacks so that the engine and chassis of the car were completely exposed.

"Those are the chameleons," Angelo explained as he led them toward the rear of the garage.

"Chameleons?" Bobbie asked.

"Camouflaged cars," Angelo explained. "We use bodies of other companies' cars so that they can't get our design. It enables us to test the car on the road without attracting attention."

He paused in front of giant doors at the back of the hangar. A large sign was posted:

RESTRICTED PERSONNEL.
ALL OTHERS KEEP OUT!

He unpinned the plastic I.D. card from his lapel and inserted it into the slot of an electric lock. The doors began to whir open. He withdrew the card and they walked through, the doors automatically closing behind them. Behind the doors there was a large screening wall, so that no one outside could see into the back when the doors were opened. Angelo led them around the wall.

They came into a large open area in the center of the garage. In this room there were no cars to be seen; instead they were each kept in large, closed-in stalls around the sides of the room. An occasional mechanic would come out of one stall and enter another. An armed security guard came toward them.

He recognized Angelo and nodded. "Good afternoon, Mr. Perino."

Angelo gave him the I.D. card. He turned to the others. "Give him your I.D. cards. He will return them when you leave."

Loren unpinned the card and gave it to the guard. He looked carefully at Loren's photo on it, then at Loren. He nodded and collected the cards from Bobbie and Elizabeth and walked away.

Angelo explained. "The reason for the extra security in this room is because in here we keep our production design prototypes."

John Duncan came out of one of the stalls. He came toward them with a smile on his face. "Loren!" he said with obvious pleasure.

"John!" They shook hands. "You look fifteen years younger."

"I feel that way," the Scotsman said. "We're at it again. Doing what we should do."

"I'd like you to meet my fiancee, Roberta Ayres. Bobbie, this is John Duncan, whom I told you so much about."

The Scotsman's face gave no visible sign that they had met before as he took her hand. "A pleasure to meet you, Miss Ayres."

"My pleasure, Mr. Duncan," she said politely.

"And you know my daughter, Betsy?" Loren added.

Duncan smiled. "She's grown a little since I saw her last. How are you, Miss Hardeman?"

"Fine, thank you." She turned to Angelo. "Now can we see the car? I can't wait any longer."

Angelo looked at Duncan. "Can we get the Silver Sprite out here?"

The Scotsman nodded. "I think we might." He walked back toward one of the stalls.

"The Silver Sprite is a prototype high-performance sports car. We don't intend to put it on the market until after we establish our production line. We plan to use it for auto shows and maybe in a race or two if we can get it qualified." Angelo looked up. The doors to one of the stalls were opening.

The car appeared rolling toward them, being pushed by four men, while Duncan sat in the driver's seat, guiding the wheel. It came to a stop in the center of the hangar, the light from the bright fluorescents overhead shimmering on its silver aluminum body.

"It's beautiful!" Betsy caught her breath, the surprise echoing in her voice. "Oh, Angelo, it's just beautiful!"

"What did you expect? A funny car?"

"I don't know what I expected," she said. "I thought with all that talk about a popular car, it would turn out something like a Volks."

"With a name like the Betsy? Do you think either your father or your great-grandfather would let me get away with that?"

She turned to her father. "Did you see it?"

Loren shook his head. "I saw the clays, mockups and drawings. This is the first time I've seen the car." He looked at Angelo. "It's a great design."

"Thank you, Loren. I hoped you would like it."

They walked around the front of the car. The sloping hood led down to a contoured oval air scoop, larger at the top than the bottom, looking very much like the jet engine scoop of the 707. An additional air scoop rose from the engine cover with still another air scoop mounted under the nose. The total over-all effect was that the car seemed to be lunging toward you even when it was standing still.

"The scoops are all functional," Angelo explained. "The nose scoop directs all the air into the main combustion chamber, the hood scoop directs the air to the afterburner and the under scoop directs cool air between the heat wall and front interior panel, further insuring passenger compartment comfort from the very high combustion heat of the turbine."

Duncan got out of the car, leaving the door open. "Want to get behind the wheel?" he asked.

Elizabeth didn't wait for another invitation. She was in the car before the others had even walked around it. "When do I get to drive it?"

"Supposing I take you all out for a drive in it first?" Angelo said. "At the same time I can explain to you the few things you'll have to know in order to drive this baby. A turbine is a little different than a conventional I.C. engine."

"I'm ready," Betsy said.

"You'll have to wait until dark," said Angelo. "We don't take any of these models out during the day."

A public announcement system blared overhead. "Mr. Perino, telephone. Mr. Perino, telephone."

Angelo straightened. "You'll have to excuse me." He turned to Duncan. "Would you take over for me? I'll be back as soon as I can."

He heard the Scotsman's voice as he walked away. "The first thing you have to learn, lassie, is that you just don't put the key in the switch in this car and start it. A turbine doesn't work like that. There are two igniter switches and a starter generator switch that are activated electronically when you turn the key to position one. You will note that when you do, a red light appears on the dash in front of you. After about ten seconds, the red turns off and a yellow light comes on, then you turn the key to position two. This fires the turbine. In about five seconds, the yellow light should be replaced by a green light. That means your engine has reached idling speed and you can go. Since the turbine heat is so great, sometimes in firing up they overheat. In that case the green won't come on and the red light will come back, only this time it will be blinking. In that case, switch off and start all over. Just one thing. Nothing will start unless the car is in parking gear and the parking brake is on. Now, for important lesson number two—"

By this time Angelo had gone into the small office and the Scotsman's voice disappeared as he closed the door. The guard looked up from his desk.

"May I use the phone?" Angelo asked, picking it up. The guard nodded as the operator came on. "Mr. Perino here."

"Just a moment, Mr. Perino," the operator said quickly. "I have Mr. Rourke on your office line. I'll transfer him over."

"Is it worth a thousand dollars to find out the name of the man who put the county prosecutor up to getting an injunction against us? I have a friend in Olympia. He says he can get it for us."

"Pay it," Angelo said.

"Where will you be tonight?" Rourke asked. "I'll call you."

"I'll be at the Starlight." He put down the telephone and walked over to the observation window looking into the hangar.

Loren was behind the wheel now, Duncan was still talking and Bobbie and Elizabeth were standing next to him. From the window it almost seemed as if they were sisters.

The door opened. Cindy came in and stood at the window beside him. After a moment she reached over and took the cigarette from him and dragged on it, then passed it back.

"He's younger than I thought," she said. "His pictures make him look much older."

"Yeah."

"Which one is his daughter?"

"The one on the right."

She took the cigarette from him again and pulled on it, watching him. "She likes cars. More than her father."

He looked at her curiously. "What makes you say that?"

"I saw her reaction while they were rolling the car out. She was the only one of them who was really excited."

Angelo gave up on the return of his cigarette and lit another. He turned back to the window without speaking. Duncan had raised the hood and was now explaining the engine to them.

"Going to marry the girl?" Cindy's question was unexpected.

"They're getting married next week, I understand," he answered before he realized she wasn't asking about Loren and Bobbie. "You mean me?"

Cindy smiled. "There's been some talk."

"You ought to know better than that," he said. "I'm not the marrying kind."

"But she is," Cindy said. "And I can see enough of Number One in her to know that she generally gets what she wants."

"She's still a kid."

"She's as old as I was when I first went down to the track," Cindy said. "She's not as much of a kid as she plays at being."

Angelo didn't answer.

"What about the other one?" Cindy asked.

"What about her?"

"She's got eyes for you too. And I don't mean like a future mother-in-law."

"Forget it," Angelo said shortly. "She's a money player and she just took the big one."

"It won't keep her from trying to pick up a side bet here and there. She never looked at the car even once. All she kept watching was you."

Angelo turned and looked out the window. Bobbie was standing almost alone now as Loren and Betsy bent over the open hood of the car. She seemed to be waiting patiently for them to finish.

A note of surprise came into Cindy's voice. "You fucked her, didn't you?" Without waiting for him to answer. "That's what it's all about. I should have guessed."

Angelo didn't look at her. "Now you've really topped off."

"I'm not crazy," she said. She looked at him. "Don't forget, I've been there too. And it takes one to know one."

THE WHITE tensor lamp splashed down on the blueprint on the desk. Angelo stared at it. Space, the problem always was space. This time it was the trunk. Due to the oversize exhaust ducting necessary for the turbine, the trunk had less than half the space considered normal in the average American car and, with the spare tire inside, there was practically no room for luggage.

He moved the template idly across the blueprint. If there were only some way he could take the space from the engine compartment and move it to the trunk he could solve the problem. Even with all the power equipment there was room to spare under the hood because of the smaller size of the turbine engine.

He picked up the wheel and tire template and looked at it. Too bad they couldn't mount it on the side of the car as they did many years ago. That would solve the problem. He remembered the '29 Olds Viking his father had when he was still a child and the '31 Duesenberg of his grandfather. There was something to be said about the side-mounted wheels and tires. They did give the automobile a sporting flair. It was economics as much as design that probably finished it off. One spare wheel and tire cost less than two.

He placed the template on the drawing and moved it along the side drawing until it came to a stop alongside the front right fender under the hood. He stared at it. It could fit here with room to spare. But there were other problems.

Interstage heat in the turbine at normal operating driving temperatures averaged 800° centigrade. There wasn't a tire made that could withstand that temperature constantly. It needed insulation, venting and perhaps additional cooling. He made some notes on the comment sheet to have

Design and Engineering look into it and come up with its practicality and costs.

The telephone rang. "Hello."

The familiar British voice was in his car. "Angelo?"

"Yes, Bobbie?"

"What are you doing?"

"Working," he answered.

"Would you like to have a drink?"

He was surprised. "Where are you? I thought you went out to the test track with the others."

"I didn't feel up to it," she said.

"Anything wrong? You sound strange."

"No." She seemed vague. "I don't know. Anyway it's not important. I'm sorry I disturbed you."

The phone abruptly clicked off as she hung up. He stared at it a moment, then put it down. He thought about calling her back but decided against it and got up and made himself a drink instead.

The phone rang again as he was walking back to the desk, the ice tinkling in his glass. He picked it up. "Yes, Bob—"

Rourke's voice interrupted him. "Angelo, I have the name of the man. Mark Simpson. He's with an outfit called the Independent Automobile Safety Organization. IASO. They're out of Detroit. Know anything about them?"

"Not the outfit," Angelo answered. "But I heard something about the man—" The doorbell rang. "Hold on a minute, I have to get the door."

He put down the telephone and crossed the room. The doorbell rang again. He opened the door. Bobbie stood there.

She looked up at him. "Am I interrupting anything?"

"No." He shook his head. "Come in. I'm on the telephone."

He went back to the phone and picked it up while she closed the door behind her. "Help yourself to a drink."

"Tony," he said into the phone. "The guy's a hustler. He claims to be another Ralph Nader but that's a lot of crap. He publishes a weekly newsletter which supposedly gives out inside information on new cars. There's been talk around Detroit that he's on the take, but nobody seems to know from whom."

"Why would he go after us?" Tony asked.

"That's a good question," Angelo said. "As far as I know, he's never been near our place. Somebody there has got to be backing him."

"Well, I've done everything I could," Tony said. "Detroit's your town."

"I'll take care of it," Angelo said. "Thanks for the information."

He put down the telephone and looked across the room. Bobbie hadn't moved from the door. "You made it this far," he said. "You might as well come all the way in."

She walked toward him, her eyes taking in the piled-up papers on the desk and the file cabinets along the wall. "You really were working," she said.

"What did you think I was doing?"

She didn't answer. She crossed the room to the table on which the bottle of whiskey and ice rested. She poured some into a glass. "I didn't know you had one room fixed up as an office."

"I do a lot of work here," he said. "The days aren't always long enough."

"I don't want to disturb you."

"You said that before," he said pointedly.

"I know." She put her drink down on the table without touching it. "I'm sorry. I'll leave." She started back to the door.

"Why did you come down?" he asked.

She stopped and looked at him. "I was jealous. I thought you had a girl here. That was stupid of me, wasn't it?"

He didn't answer.

"I love you," she said. "I thought——"

His voice was harsh. "Don't think. We went all through that once before."

"I made a mistake," she said. "I thought I knew what I wanted. But it's not too late."

"It is too late. You're supposed to be married next week, remember?"

"I know that," she said. She walked back toward him slowly. She looked up into his eyes. "But there will be times. We can still see each other once in a while."

He didn't move. A pulse began to beat in his throat. "Now you're thinking with your cunt," he said. "I liked it better when you thought with your head."

She put her arms around his neck and pressed herself against him. "You tell me you don't want me," she whispered.

He stared into her eyes without moving.

"Tell me!" she repeated, a note of triumph in her voice. She dropped a hand to his trouser front. Quickly, she zipped open his fly and searched him out. "Tell me if you can while I hold your cock, hard and hot and juicing in my hand."

She began to go down on him and was almost on her knees when a knock came on the door and it swung open.

"Angelo! The car is fantastic!" Betsy's voice trailed off as she saw them.

They stared at her. Bobbie almost stumbled and fell as she got back to her feet. Angelo turned away for a moment, adjusting his pants. By the time he turned back to her, she was inside the room, her face suddenly very pale and very young.

"I know it's hard to understand," he began.

"Don't say anything. Please," she said in a thin small voice. She looked at Bobbie. "Daddy's on his way to your room to get you," she said, almost calmly. "You better go to the bar and tell him you were there waiting for him. Because he was going to bring you down here to have a drink to the new car."

Bobbie looked at her for a moment, then at Angelo. He nodded. She went silently past Betsy and out of the room. Her footsteps echoed down the corridor outside.

They stared at each other silently until the sound of the footsteps vanished. He picked up his drink from the desk behind him.

"I guess the stories I've heard about you are all true," she said. "You're not a very nice man, Mr. Perino."

He held the glass without drinking, his eyes steady on her face. He didn't speak.

"Don't think I did it for either of you," she said. "I did it for Daddy. He's very much in love with her. And it would break his heart. You see, he's not like you. He's really a very naïve man. Not hip at all."

Angelo still didn't say anything.

"You could have been honest with me," she began to sniffle. "You didn't have to go through that virtuous shit and how-important-it-was-that-we-get-to-know-each-other-first routine with me."

"It was the truth," he said.

"No it wasn't!" she cried bitterly. "And you'll never get me to believe you! Why didn't you just fuck me when I wanted you to?"

He didn't answer.

"Was it because you thought I didn't have enough experience for the great Angelo Perino?"

"Now you are talking like a child," he said.

She came toward him, her clenched fists pummeling at his chest. "I hate you, Mr. Perino! I hate you!"

He caught her wrists and held her still. She looked up into his face. Suddenly she slumped against him, weeping.

"I'm sorry, Miss Elizabeth," he said quietly. "Truly sorry."

"I feel like such a fool," she cried.

"Don't," he said.

"Leave me alone!" She pulled away from him. "You don't have to patronize me!"

"I'm not—"

"Good-bye, Mr. Perino," she said frostily.

He looked at her silently for a moment. "Good-bye, Miss Elizabeth."

She stared back at him, then began to cry again and, turning abruptly, ran out into the hall, almost stumbling over Number One's wheelchair in the corridor.

"Betsy!" Number One called.

She didn't turn back. "Not right now, Great-Grandfather," she shouted over her shoulder as she ran down the steps.

Number One pushed the wheelchair into the open doorway and looked at Angelo. "What the hell is going on here?" he asked irascibly. "When I get on the elevator downstairs, Loren's girl comes off it looking all upset; when I get up here, Betsy comes storming out of your door, crying like a baby."

Angelo stared at him. "Oh, Jesus!"

Number One looked at him and then began to smile. He pushed the wheelchair through and the door shut behind him. "You look like a man who's just been caught with his cock out."

Angelo swallowed his drink in a single gulp. "Aah, shit!"

Number One laughed aloud. The more things changed, the more they were the same. He could still remember the last time it happened to him.

And that was over thirty years ago.

Chapter Six

THE ENGINE of the big black 1933 Sundancer sedan bearing the license plates L H 1 purred quietly as the chauffeur turned the car off Woodward Avenue onto Factory Road, three and a half blocks before the plant gate. The sidewalks on both sides of the street were filled with men, standing patiently in the cold March drizzle.

"What's going on?" Loren asked from the back seat.

"I don't know, sir," the chauffeur replied. "I never seen nothin' like this before." He began to slow the car down. As they came nearer to the gate, the lines of men grew thicker, spilling over into the roadway.

"Turn on the radio," said Loren. "Maybe we'll get something on the news."

The familiar voice of H. V. Kaltenborn filled the car. "In closing, I would like to repeat to all Americans once again this morning the words President Roosevelt uttered in his Inaugural Address yesterday in Washington. 'The only thing we have to fear is fear itself.'

"They are well worth remembering. This is H. V. Kaltenborn signing off from New York."

Another voice came on. "This closes our morning newscast. The next news will be on at noon."

They were almost at the gate. "Turn it off," Loren said.

The car crawled up to the gate through the men thronged before it. The chauffeur blew the horn. The men looked back and slowly parted to let the car inch its way forward. Two men opened the gate so the car could go through, then closed it.

Loren rolled down his window. "What happened, Fred?"

The older guard looked at him. "We advertised in the papers for six machinists, Mr. Hardeman."

"Six machinists?" Loren looked back at the crowd. "But there must be at least a couple of hundred out there."

"More like a thousand by my reckoning, Mr. Hardeman."

"Did we hire them yet?"

"No, sir. The personnel office doesn't begin interviewing until nine o'clock."

Loren looked at his watch. It was a few minutes after seven. "That means they have to stand out there two more hours in this freezing rain."

"Yes, sir," the guard said. "A lot of them have been here all night since the evening papers came out yesterday."

Loren looked back at the crowd. Some of the men held newspapers over their heads to keep off the rain, others had their coats pulled up over their necks across the brims of their hats. Their faces were all the same pale gray of the morning.

He turned back to the guard. "Call the canteen and have them send a truck down here with hot coffee and doughnuts for them."

"I can't do that, sir," the guard said uncomfortably. "It's against the rules."

"What rules?" Loren was too surprised for the moment to get angry.

"From the personnel office," the guard said in a nervous voice. "They said if we start that we'll have a lineup of men every morning whether we need help or not, just to get themselves a free breakfast."

Loren stared at him without speaking for a moment. "Who made that rule?" he asked finally.

"I was told that it came from the president's office," the guard answered. He was very careful not to mention Junior by name.

"I see." Loren drew back into the car. "Drive on," he said. The chauffeur drove the car behind the administration building into the parking place beside Loren's private entrance. Loren got out of the car without waiting for him to open the door. The small elevator was in use so he went up the stairs to the second floor, then down the long corridor. He pushed open the door and walked past the startled secretaries into Junior's office.

Junior was just putting down the telephone. His voice was excited. "I was just speaking to Washington. There's talk that the President's going to call a bank holiday right away!"

Loren stared down at him. "Did you have breakfast?"

Junior was bewildered. "Didn't you hear what I said? The President's going to close the banks! Do you know what that means?"

"Did you have breakfast?" Loren repeated.

"Of course I had breakfast," Junior answered, annoyed. "What's that got to do with what I just said? If he closes the banks we're on the verge of anarchy, a revolution can break out the next day and the Communists will take over the country!"

"Bullshit!" Loren exploded. "Come over here to the window."

Junior got out of his chair and walked over. Loren pointed to the crowd of men beyond the gate. "See them?"

Junior nodded.

"Did you sign an order that the canteen was not allowed to give them coffee and doughnuts?"

"No. That would come out of Warren's office."

"If it came out of Joe Warren's office that means you approved it. He's your man."

"Father," Junior's voice was placating. "How many times do I have to tell you that Joe has nothing but our own best interests at heart? If it weren't for him, those kidnappers might have got their filthy hands on Anne and Loren Three And you have to admit that there have been no problems with labor since he took over.

"Sure, I approved the order but we're not the only one that has that rule. Half the companies in Detroit have adopted it. Bennett over at Ford says if we don't keep a firm hand on things, they'll take over."

"Who'll take over?" Loren's voice was sarcastic. "And what makes Bennett such an expert? He's nothing but an ex-sailor."

"Joe says that Bennett's the number one man at Ford. He says that Mr. Ford trusts him implicitly and keeps Edsel in there only for window dressing."

"Then the old man has reached his dotage. Edsel's got more brains than all of them." Loren said. "I want those men to have coffee and doughnuts."

"No, Father," Junior said stubbornly. "I'm afraid I'm going to have to overrule you on this one. Believe me, I know what I'm doing."

"You stupid little shit!" Loren stared at him. "If you like being president of this company, you'll call that prick Warren in here and see to it that those men out there have coffee and doughnuts."

Junior's face was pale. "No, Father."

Loren's voice went hard and cold. "Then I'll expect your resignation on my desk in ten minutes." He turned and started from the office.

"Father," Junior's voice turned him around. "I won't give it to you."

"Then you're fired!" he snapped.

"You can't do that either, Father." Junior's voice held a thin edge of bitter triumph. "Along with those notes you signed for the bank loans, you escrowed your voting stock into a trust voted by them until such time as the loans are repaid. And the bank is very satisfied with my management of the company."

Loren stared at him speechlessly.

"Unless you have thirty million dollars in cash to repay their loans, Father, you might as well get used to the idea that I'm the chief operating officer of this company."

Loren was still silent.

"If the idea doesn't appeal to you," Junior continued, "I would like to suggest that you might find it much more pleasant if you were to go back to Europe with your French whore."

"Is that all you have to say?" Loren asked.

"Not quite," Junior answered. He was very sure of himself now. "I hadn't intended to raise the issue this soon but since we're speaking frankly, we may as well face it.

"We've managed quite well the past three years while you've been away. Now that you've returned with a wild idea to rejuvenate the automobile business with a new low-priced car, I might as well inform you that the matter has been completely gone into by both the board of directors and the banks. There is unanimous agreement among them to reject your plan. They have no intention of committing another twenty million dollars to experimentation in this kind of market with industry sales peaking at about a million and a half cars this year. Now that we have the automobile division under control we plan to eliminate further losses on that end by going into subcontracting bodies for Ford. Bennett was kind enough to give us a contract for one hundred thousand units since they've been having problems with Briggs. For the first time in two years we'll be in the black and everybody likes it."

"You haven't changed, have you?" Loren said. "When you were a little boy you used to hide behind your mother's skirts, now you're hiding behind Harry Bennett."

"It's merely good business," said Junior. "We're guaranteed a profit without risking a penny of our own."

"You're also delivering your company into the hands of Bennett. Before long he will be able to dictate everything you want to do and all he will have to do to close you up is cut you off." Loren's voice was sober. "Even you have to see that. The only chance we have to stay alive is to stay independent."

Junior laughed. "I'm afraid you've lost touch with reality, Father. See those lines out there? I've been watching them grow for three years now. Do you think any of them can afford to buy our cars?"

Loren stared at him. "I'm sorry, Junior," he said reluctantly. He began to tug at his leather trouser belt. "I guess you're still a child and will have to be treated like one." The belt came free and, holding it in his hand, he started toward Junior.

Junior stared at him, horrified. "You wouldn't dare!"

Loren smiled. "Watch me." He raised his arm, the belt dangling from his hand.

"No!" It was almost a scream. Junior darted behind his desk, pressing a button on it. "You can't hit me! I'm president of the company!" He pushed the button frantically.

"You're still my son," Loren said coldly, moving behind the desk after him.

The door to the connecting office opened and Joe Warren came into the room. "Yes, Jun—?"

Junior darted behind him, holding Warren between himself and his father. "Joe! Don't let him hit me, Joe!" he almost shrieked. "He's gone crazy!"

Warren turned toward Loren. "Let's all calm down, Mr. Hardeman," he said. "I don't know what the trouble is but I'm sure we can settle it like reasonable men."

Something in his voice told Loren that he already knew exactly what the trouble was. He glanced down at Junior's desk. The intercom switch above Warren's name was open. He had been listening to every word said in the office. He looked back at Warren. His voice was ice cold. "Keep out of this, Warren. It's a family matter."

He started forward again, then stopped. A revolver suddenly appeared in Warren's hand. "Now, will you be reasonable?" Warren asked.

Loren looked into the man's eyes. They were glinting with a curious kind of triumph. He relaxed slightly. "You're not going to pull that trigger, Warren," he said quietly, moving toward him. "Or you'll spend the rest of your life regretting it."

Warren's eyes stared back at him balefully. "Don't push me, Mr. Hardeman. Just stop where you are!"

Loren's hand moved almost too quickly for the eye to follow. The looped belt caught Warren's wrist, pulling the gun from his hand, sending it clattering to the floor. Warren dove for the gun as Junior shrieked and ran into the other office.

Warren's fingers were just closing around the revolver when Loren's shoe came heavily down on his forearm. He screamed in sudden pain as the arm snapped like a matchstick. He stared up into Loren's face with a kind of frozen horror.

"This may teach you to keep out of family matters," Loren said calmly.

Warren saw Loren's shoe coming toward his head but there was nothing he could do to avoid it. The world exploded in a shattering fireworks of pain. Then blackness.

Loren looked down at the man lying at his feet. Warren's head was against the corner of Junior's desk, blood streaming from his nose and mouth. He turned and walked to the connecting door.

It was locked and bolted. He took a half step backward and kicked. The door flew open, half torn from its hinges, and he stepped through.

The other office was empty. The open door at the far end told Loren that Junior had fled. He went back into Junior's office.

Warren was moaning, trying to sit up. Loren crossed the room to the far door and opened it. The two secretaries, who had their ears pressed to the panel, almost fell into the room.

"Clean this mess up," Loren said emotionlessly and walked past them.

Chapter Seven

HE WALKED up the flight of stairs to his third-floor office and let himself into it through his private entrance. The room was dark in the poor gray light of the morning. He pressed a wall switch and the lamps around the room went on. He went behind his desk and pressed the intercom switch down. His secretary's voice came from it. "Yes, Mr. Hardeman?"

"I want two canteen trucks with coffee and doughnuts down at Gate Three right away."

"Yes, Mr. Hardeman."

"Then I want you to get Coburn and Edgerton up here."

"Yes, Mr. Hardeman."

He flicked up the switch and walked from the desk to the window. In the rain the men outside the gate were still huddled together like so many animals seeking shelter. He stood there for a moment watching them, then went back to his desk and sat down.

The pain began in his temples and started to throb. He groaned to himself. That was all he needed. Another migraine headache. Doctors were all stupid. There was nothing they could do about it, he had been told. Avoid excitement and take aspirin. He pressed the intercom switch down again. "Get me three aspirin tablets and a cup of hot black coffee."

"Immediately, Mr. Hardeman."

He leaned back in his chair. The aspirin should help and the doctor in Switzerland had told him that the caffeine in coffee made the aspirin work faster.

The door opened and a girl came in. She carried the sterling silver tray with the cup and saucer and coffee pot to his desk. Cream and sugar were in small silver servers. Next to them was a bottle of aspirin and a glass of water. She shook three aspirin out into her hand.

He looked up at her as he took the aspirin. "You're new here, aren't you?"

"Yes, Mr. Hardeman," she answered, giving him the glass of water.

He swallowed the aspirin with a gulp of water. "What's your name?" he asked, giving her the glass.

"Melanie Walker," she said. She picked up the coffee pot. "Black?"

"Yes. No sugar, no cream." He took the coffee and tasted it.

"Is it all right?"

"Fine. What happened to the girl who was here all last week?"

"Miss Harriman?"

"I never did get her name."

"She went back to her regular job in personnel."

"I see," he said, taking another sip of coffee. "What department are you from?"

"Personnel," she said.

He was silent for a moment. "Do you have a regular job there?"

"Yes, Mr. Hardeman. In the steno pool. We fill in whenever a regular girl is absent."

"What do they pay you for that?" he asked curiously.

"Twenty-two fifty a week."

He gave her the empty coffee cup. "Thank you."

"You're welcome, Mr. Hardeman." She picked up the tray and started for the door.

"Would you also ask Mr. Duncan to come and see me?" he called after her.

"Yes, sir."

He watched the door close behind her. Warren had it all organized. The steno pool was a perfect nucleus for an espionage system to check on what everyone was doing.

Duncan was the first to arrive. "Sit down, Scotty," Loren said. "I'm waiting for Coburn and Edgerton."

Duncan took a chair just as the other two men arrived. Loren waved them to their seats, then sat looking at them silently for a moment. He opened the cigarette box on his desk and took one out and lit it. The faint sound of an ambulance siren came from outside.

The silence grew uncomfortable. The three men glanced uneasily at one another, then back at him. Loren drew on his cigarette calmly.

The siren grew louder and then stopped abruptly. Loren walked over to the window. The ambulance was parked in front of the main building entrance and two white-coated men were hurrying inside with a stretcher.

He walked back to his desk and looked at them. "Okay," he said. "You tell me. What the hell is going on around here?"

"I don't know what you mean," Coburn said quickly.

"Don't give me any of your lawyer crap! You know damn well what I mean, Ted!"

They were silent.

"What the hell are you guys afraid of?" Loren asked. "You've all known me for years and you've never been afraid to open your mouths before. This isn't a prison."

"You don't understand, Mr. Hardeman," Edgerton said. He was a big man, almost as large as Loren, the last person in the world to look like the accountant he was.

"I know I don't, Walt," said Loren. "That's why I asked you to come up here."

There was a moment's silence while they again exchanged uncomfortable looks. Finally Coburn got out of his chair. He walked around Loren's desk and bent over the intercom. His fingers checked all the switches, making sure they were down.

"What are you worried about?" Loren asked. "No one can listen in."

Coburn didn't answer. Instead he bent down beside the desk and pulled the cable plug connecting the intercom to its socket from the floor. "There's no point taking any chances," he said, straightening up. He turned to Loren. "Now send your secretary out of the office on an errand."

"Why?" Loren asked. "She seems like a nice girl."

"She is a nice girl. Too nice," Coburn said. "But she's one of Joe Warren's girls."

Loren looked at him for a moment. Without a word, he went to the secretary's door and opened it.

The girl looked up at him. "Yes, Mr. Hardeman?"

"Go down to the canteen and have some coffee. I'll call you there when I want you back."

She met his gaze. "I can't do that, Mr. Hardeman. The rules are that I can't leave the desk without relief."

"I just changed the rules," he said.

"But the phones? There will be no one to answer them."

"I'll answer them," he said.

She sat there silently, not moving. "I'll lose my job," she said finally.

"You've already lost it," he said. "Your only chance to get it back depends on how fast you can get your ass out of here!"

She stared at him for a moment, then picked up her purse and went out the door.

Coburn's voice came from behind him. "Lock that door while I lock your private entrance."

Loren locked the outside door and walked back into his own office. He walked around his desk and sat down. "Now, I want some answers and I want them fast!"

"You want it fast, Mr. Hardeman?" Coburn said. "I'll give it to you in two words. Joe Warren. You can't get it any faster than that."

Loren got to his feet and walked to the window. Outside, the ambulance was still parked. The attendants came out of the building, carrying a man on the stretcher between them.

Loren gestured to the men in the room behind him. They came to the window. He pointed to the stretcher being loaded into the rear of the ambulance. "There goes your Joe Warren."

An attendant ran around the ambulance and got in behind the wheel. The siren began again as the ambulance started for the gate.

Loren walked back to his desk and sat down. "Now maybe we can get back to the business of building automobiles," he said.

"It's not going to be that easy," said Edgerton. "Between Warren and your son, they have the board of directors and the banks sewed up."

"Leave them to me," Loren said. "What we're here to talk about is building a low-priced car to compete with Ford and Chevy and Walter Chrysler's new Plymouth."

"We haven't got the money to retool," Edgerton said quickly. "That will take fifteen million dollars and the banks won't give it to us."

"How much have we got?"

"About one and a half million in cash and another three million in receivables."

"Could we discount the receivables?"

"For twenty percent."

Loren turned to Duncan who had been silent until now. "Can you get a new car on the line for four million dollars?"

Duncan shook his head. "Impossible."

"Nothing's impossible," Loren said. "Do we still have the jigs for the Loren Two?"

Duncan nodded.

"Supposing we cut two feet out of the car by going from four doors to two? Would that be an expensive retooling job?"

Duncan was thoughtful. "It shouldn't be. But there is another problem. We'd have to design a whole new engine for it."

"Why?" Loren asked. "Couldn't we make the small Sundancer ninety-horsepower fit?"

Duncan smiled suddenly. "I think we could. It would also reduce our inventory. We overproduced that engine by almost fifty thousand units last year."

"That's more like it," Loren said. "You get down to your office and start on it right away. Check your costs out with Walt. I want figures in two days." He turned to the lawyer. "Now I want some answers from you, Ted. Is there anything in the book that can keep me from doing this?"

Coburn thought for a moment. "Not if you're not challenged."

"And if I am?"

"There are only two people who can do it. Your son and, maybe, Warren. I'm not quite sure, but he is the executive vice-president and his powers might spill over into that area."

"What about the board and the bank?"

"They don't come into it until the next meeting. And that's almost a month away. Of course, your son can call a special meeting any time."

"I understand," Loren said.

"Just another word," Coburn said. "Make sure that you don't dictate any memos on your plans. All secretaries now have to make a blind copy of everything they type. It's Warren's way of knowing everything that goes on."

Loren looked at him. "Did my son know about that too?"

"I don't know," Coburn said carefully. "None of us can see him unless the appointment is arranged by Warren. I haven't seen him except at board meetings for more than a year now."

Loren turned to Edgerton. "How about you?"

"Much the same story."

He looked at the engineer. "How about you, Scotty?"

"The last time I spoke to him was the time he told me to stop production on the Loren Two. That was three years ago." The Scotsman's voice was caustic.

Loren was silent for a moment, then he got to his feet. "Okay," he said. "Go to work."

They got to their feet and started for the door. Loren's voice stopped them. He was smiling. "Can one of you fellows reconnect this damn thing?" he asked, pointing to the intercom. "I might have to use it for something legitimate."

THE TELEPHONE began to ring just as she came from the kitchen after talking to the cook about the children's lunch. She picked it up in the living room. "Hello."

A familiar voice echoed in her ear. "Sally?"

She sank into a nearby chair. "Yes."

"This is Loren."

"Yes, I know," she said. "How are you?"

"Fine," he answered. There was an awkward pause. "I wanted to come out and see you and the children but I've only been back a few days and I've been tied up."

"I understand," she said.

"Is Junior home?"

"No. Isn't he in the office?"

"No," he answered.

"He left early as usual," she said. "Maybe the car broke down on the road."

"No. He was in the office." There was the barest hesitation in his voice. "We had an argument and he left. I want to reach him. Do you have any idea where I might find him?"

"Sometimes he goes to the Athletic Club for a steam and rubdown."

"Thanks," he said. "I'll try there. Good-bye."

"Loren!" she said quickly.

"Yes?"

"Aren't we going to see you?" she asked. "Loren Three is a big boy already and you've never even seen your granddaughter." She had just caught her tongue in time to keep herself from saying daughter.

"I'll be out later this week," he said. He hesitated a moment. "Are you all right?"

"Yes," she said.

"If Junior should come in, tell him to call me."

"I will," she said.

"Good-bye."

"Loren, I still love you," she said quickly. But the click in the telephone told her he was off the line and hadn't heard her. Slowly she put the phone down and sat there. She could still feel the pounding of her heart and wondered if she would ever get over the way she felt about him.

The front door burst open and Junior came rushing in. Through the archway he saw her seated in the living room and came toward her.

Still filled with her own thoughts, she spoke to him. "Your father just called. He wants you to call him."

"He's crazy!"

For the first time she saw how distraught he was, his face pale and ashen. "What happened?"

"He tried to kill me! Joe Warren's in the hospital with a broken arm and possible skull fractures! He's crazy, I tell you!"

"Why?" she asked.

"All I told him was that he couldn't build a new car and he went crazy. He came after me. If it weren't for poor Joe, I might have been the one in the hospital, not him."

"It doesn't make sense," she said, bewildered. "There has to be a reason. He sounded perfectly calm on the phone just now."

He stared at her. His voice changed. "Go upstairs and pack. We're taking the children and going away for a while."

"Calm down," she said, rising. "Let me fix you a drink."

"I don't want a drink," he said sharply. "Just do as I tell you. We're going over the border to the summer cottage in Ontario."

She looked at him. "I'm not dragging the children anywhere," she said stubbornly. "Not until I know what we're running away from."

"You're on his side!" he shot accusingly.

"I'm on no one's side," she replied. "I've just got two small children that I'm not going to drag around like so many pieces of baggage, that's all."

"I've turned it all over to my attorneys," he said. "They told me to go away for a while. He can't take the company away from me."

"But how could he?" she asked. "It's not your company, it's his."

"Don't tell me whose company it is!" he almost shrieked. "I'm its chief executive officer."

She didn't speak.

"He's going to jail!" Junior snapped. "Joe signed an assault-and-battery complaint and right now the police are on their way out there to pick him up. I signed a deposition."

"Joe had to do something to get himself hurt," she said. "I don't believe your father would—"

"You don't believe!" he almost screamed. "You're in love with him!"

She didn't answer.

"Listen," he said earnestly. "All Joe did when Father came after me was to get between us. Even the gun Joe had didn't stop him!"

"Joe had a gun?" The amazement showed in her voice.

He was suddenly silent. Then he looked at her shrewdly. "What if he did?" he asked defensively. "He was only trying to protect me."

"Did you say that in your deposition?" she asked.

He didn't answer.

"Is that why your attorneys want you to go away? So that you don't have to answer questions?"

"What difference does it make?" he asked. "It's about time someone showed my father that he can't run the world."

"You were willing to let that cheap thug pull a gun on your father?" Her voice filled with a strange loathing. "You're really sick."

"You're jealous!" he screamed suddenly. "You were always jealous of my friendship with Joe from the moment I first met him! Because he's a real man, that's why."

"He's a cheap gangster who does nothing but terrorize and threaten people weaker than he is. And if you were a real man, you wouldn't need friends like that!"

He started toward her, raising his hand.

"Don't!" she said sharply, picking up the telephone. "If you're going anywhere, you better go upstairs and pack because I'm going to call your father right now and tell him you're here."

He stood there for a moment as she began to dial. Then he started for the door; suddenly, he stopped, bending almost in two, clutching at his stomach. "I'm going to be sick!" he said in a small, frightened voice.

She put down the telephone and went toward him. He began to retch, dry, hard, gasping breaths. She put an arm around his shoulders and he leaned weakly against her as she steered him into the guest washroom off the foyer. He began to vomit into the toilet bowl.

"You've got to help me," he said weakly, between gasps.

"I am helping you," she said quietly. "Can't you see that if I let you destroy your father you're destroying yourself? If you weren't his son, who do you think would even give a damn whether you lived or died?"

"I've got to get away," he said. He began to wring his hands. "I don't know how I'll manage if anything happens to Joe."

"You can go if you want to," she said calmly. "But if you do, you'll do it without me and the children. And when you come back, we won't be here."

Hardeman Manor seemed strangely dark and deserted as she drove up the long winding driveway to the front door. Even the light in the entranceway was off as she stopped the car under the stone-pillared car portals. She turned off the engine and got out.

The moonlight cast a pale shadow as she walked up the steps to the doorway. She pressed the bell. From deep within the house, she heard an answering sound. It echoed in the still night.

She waited quietly. After a moment when there was no answer, she pressed the doorbell again. Still no answer.

She pulled a cigarette from her purse and lit it. The match flared briefly in the dark, illuminating her face in the curtained glass window of the door. Then it went out, leaving only the glowing tip of the cigarette shining back at her.

She went down the steps again and looked up at the house. It was dark and quiet, not a light behind any of the front windows. Slowly she began to walk around to the side of the house, her high heels crunching and sinking into the gravel of the driveway. It was the only sound in the night.

She turned the corner of the building and saw the light glowing from a room on the second floor. She knew the room. The small sitting room next to Loren's bedroom where he would have his morning coffee while he read the papers and the mail.

She hesitated a moment, looking up at it. The light meant that he was home, but now that she knew it there was a peculiar reluctance to see him. Then she bent down quickly, scooped up a small handful of gravel and threw it up against the window. It rattled strangely in the night and fell with scraping sounds down the sides.

A moment later, the French windows opened and he stood there, silhouetted, the light of the room against his back. He stood there silently, looking down into the night.

From her angle he looked even taller and larger than she remembered and it was a moment before she realized that he could not see her because she was standing in the shadows. She felt her heart begin to pound inside her. "Oh, God!" she thought wildly, suddenly wanting to run and hide. "What will I ever say to him?"

His voice echoed in the night. "Who is it?"

Somehow the strength in the sound of him moved her out, where the pale moonlight shone on her face. Suddenly she giggled, a feeling of light-headed ridiculousness overcame her. "Romeo, oh Romeo," she called. "Wherefore art thou, Romeo?"

He was silent for a moment, looking at her, then he laughed. "Wait there, I'll be right down." He took a half step back, then vaulted over the low windowsill.

"Loren!" she screamed, as he hurtled down. He hit the

ground and sank half to his knees, his hands breaking his
fall. He was straightening up by the time she got to him.

He grinned at her, brushing his hands off against his
trousers like a small boy. "How's that for a Douglas Fair-
banks?"

She stood very still, looking up into his face. "You're
crazy! You might have been killed!"

His eyes went from her up to the window and then back
to her. A rueful tone came into his voice. "You know,
you're right." Then he laughed again. "But it was something I wanted to do ever since I built the house and I
never had the excuse." He began to rub his hands together.

"Here, let me see." She took his hands and looked at
them. They were scratched and dirty. "You're hurt," she
said.

"It's nothing." He took her by the arm and began to
walk her around to the front of the house. "Come on, let's
go inside."

"How?" she asked. "I rang the bell twice. No one answered."

"The servants aren't all back yet," he said. "And the
butler left after dinner."

They walked up the steps to the front door. "Then how
are we going to get in?" she asked.

"Easy," he said. He turned the knob and the door
swung open. "It isn't locked." He switched on the lights as
they went into the house.

"Let me see your hands again," she said.

He held them out toward her, palms up. Traces of
blood seeped through the scratches.

"You better wash them right away. And put something
on them so you don't get infected."

"Okay," he said. "I have some peroxide in my bathroom."

She followed him up the staircase into the bathroom.
She turned the faucet on in the sink and took the soap
from the tray. "Let me do that for you," she said.

He held his hands under the water and she washed
them gently. After a moment, she looked at them and, still

not satisfied, cleaned them again with a washcloth. "Where's the peroxide?"

He gestured to the medicine cabinet. She opened it and took out the bottle. "Hold your hands over the sink."

He held out his hands and she poured the peroxide over them. He winced and pulled them away. "That burns."

"Don't be a baby," she commanded. "Hold still." She emptied the bottle and the liquid bubbled and sizzled over his hands. She took a clean hand towel from the rack and patted his hands gently dry. "Now, isn't that better?"

He looked at her. "Yes."

She felt the color rising in her cheeks. Her eyes fell. "I had to see you," she said.

"Come," he said, "let's get a drink."

She followed him downstairs into the library. He opened a cabinet and took out a bottle of Canadian whiskey and two glasses. "I can get ice if you like."

She shook her head.

He poured the liquor into two small tumblers and gave one to her. "Cheers."

She tasted her drink and the whiskey burned its way down her throat. He swallowed his and refilled his glass. "Sit down," he said.

She sat down on the leather couch and awkwardly straightened her skirt over her knees as he pulled a chair opposite her. She looked at him. "Junior went to the cottage in Ontario," she said.

He didn't speak.

"I refused to go with him," she said.

He was still silent.

"I'm leaving him," she said.

He hesitated a moment. "What about the children?"

"I'm taking them with me."

"Where are you going?"

She stared at him. "I never thought about that." There was a note of surprise in her voice. "I'll think of someplace."

He emptied his glass and got up, walked back to the bar and refilled it. He turned and looked back at her. "I'm sorry," he said.

"It would have happened sooner or later."

He hesitated a moment. "I suppose so," he said, walking back toward her. "I just didn't want it to happen because of me."

"I know," she said. "But it wasn't that reason. I think I had that straightened out in my mind. But from the moment he met Joe Warren, it began to go from bad to worse."

He stared at her. "Joe Warren," he said bitterly. "Everywhere I turn I hear that name."

"Junior told me that Warren signed an assault complaint against you and the sheriff's office was going to pick you up."

"I know about that," he said. "But I have some pretty good friends downtown. They sat on it."

"I'm glad," she said. "But don't think that it's over. Joe is a real bastard and he won't give up. He's got Junior under his thumb."

He stared at her. "That's the one thing I don't understand. What the hell power has he got over Junior that makes him jump when he pulls the strings?"

"Don't you know?" she asked, her eyes meeting his steadily.

"No."

"Joe Warren is Junior's boyfriend," she said in a matter-of-fact voice.

A puzzled look crossed Loren's face. "His boyfriend?"

Suddenly the naïveté of this giant of a man, his blindness about his son, reached out and touched her. Her voice grew very gentle. "I thought you knew," she said. "It seems as if everyone else in Detroit knows it. Ever since the day they met in the steam room at the Athletic Club."

She could see the shock well up into his eyes as he looked at her. His hand began to tremble, spilling the whiskey over the sides of the glass. Slowly he put the glass down on a table next to him. She could see the gray winter of age etch its way into his face. Suddenly, he put his hands up to his face and hard, wracking sobs shook his body.

She was very still for a moment, then went over to him and knelt in front of his chair. She pulled his head down to her shoulder and held him tightly against her.

"I'm sorry," she said softly. "I'm so sorry."

Chapter Nine

IT WAS a few minutes after seven o'clock in the evening when Melanie Walker got off the streetcar and started the four-block walk to her house. It had turned cold during the day after the rain of the morning had stopped and now the night winds blew strongly through her thin coat. She pulled it tightly around her as she turned the corner and started down the street.

"You're late," her mother said as she came in the door. "We already ate. You'll have to make do with the left-overs."

"I don't care," Melanie said. "I'm not really hungry."

"We thought—" her mother began to say.

"Shut up!" her father yelled from his seat in front of the radio set in the corner of the kitchen. "Can't you see I'm listening to 'Amos and Andy'?"

She took off her coat and walked into the room. She hung it carefully on a hanger on the back of her door. Then she got out of her dress and slip and laid them neatly on the bed. She would iron out the wrinkles after dinner so that it would be crisp and neat for the morning. She slipped into a cotton housedress and, tying the sash around her waist, went back into the kitchen.

Her mother had laid out some cold cuts on a plate on the table together with some already browning lettuce and squashy sliced tomatoes next to a plate of bread and butter.

She looked at it. "Not liverwurst and bologna again?"

Her mother shook her head. "What did you expect? You should have been home in time for dinner."

"I had to work late," she said. "I was in Mr. Hardeman's office today."

"You should have called," her mother said.

"I didn't have time. Besides you know Mr. McManus doesn't like us to bother him too much."

McManus was their neighbor on the floor below. He was the only tenant in the house who had a telephone. He was a cop on the city police force. "We don't bother them that much," her mother said.

Her father erupted in a shout of laughter. Still chuckling he got out of his chair and walked over to the icebox and took out a bottle of home brew. With a practiced motion of his hand, he swept off the stopper and got the bottle in his mouth before the foam had a chance to spill over. He took a long pull, then held it down in front of his large stomach. "Those niggers are the funniest," he belched. "Especially that Kingfish. He talked Amos into buying a new car and now Amos can't make the first payment and he wants the dealer to take the car back and give him back his old flivver." He began to laugh again thinking about it. "Andy got into the act to straighten it all out and now the dealer has both cars and they have nothing."

Neither of the women laughed. He stared at them for a moment. "It's funny, see," he explained. "Amos bought a new car and—"

"If you think niggers are so funny then why are you so mad because they're moving in a few blocks from us?" her mother asked.

"That's different," he said. "Amos and Andy are good niggers. They know their place. They ain't trying to move into white neighborhoods. They stick with their own kind like they should."

The women didn't answer him; he looked over at Melanie who had just begun to butter a slice of bread. "How come you're so late?"

"I had to work late in Mr. Hardeman's office today," she said. She picked at a piece of liverwurst.

Her father grinned. "At least you don't have to worry about him trying to grab a feel of you when you walk past his desk."

"It wasn't that one, it was his father," she said. She chewed at the liverwurst. It tasted mealy and flavorless.

"You mean Number One?" her father asked, curiosity in his voice. "He's back?"

She nodded.

"Your boyfriend ain't going to like that."

She stared at him. "How many times do I have to tell you that Mr. Warren isn't my boyfriend? Just because I have dinner with him once in a while don't mean anything."

"Okay, okay," her father said placatingly. "So he ain't your boyfriend. He still ain't going to like it. He's got Number Two under his thumb. The old man is another story. Nobody pushes him around."

Melanie tried the bologna. It was no better. She pushed the plate away from her. "I'm not hungry," she told her mother. "Do you have a cup of coffee?"

"How about some eggs?" her mother asked.

She shook her head. "No. Just coffee." She looked at her father. "Did you go out for a job today?"

"What for?" her father answered. "There ain't nothin' around."

"There were openings for six machinists at our place today. Over eight hundred men showed up."

"You don't expect me to get on line with all them rednecks, Polacks and niggers, do you? Don't forget I was a foreman out at Chrysler."

"Right now, you ain't nothin'," her mother said. "You been out of work for almost three years. If it wasn't for Melanie's workin' we'd all been on the streets."

"You stay out of this!" her father snapped angrily. He turned back to Melanie. "Besides, didn't your boyfriend promise me the first openin' that came along?"

Melanie nodded.

"But that was for a foreman's job," her mother said. "None of the plants are hiring foremen. What are you going to do, wait around forever for one to come along?"

"I told you to stay out of it!" her father roared. "What do you want me to do? Come down in the world?"

"I just want you to get a job," her mother said stubbornly.

"I'll get a job," her father muttered. "Just as soon as we can get rid of all those foreigners and niggers that came pilin' up here after the war to grab the easy money."

"They ain't goin' away," her mother said. "The war's over fifteen years now an' they're still here."

"We'll get rid of them," her father said. "You wait and see. We'll show them that nobody can push real Americans around." A blast of music from the radio caught his ear. "That's the 'Fleischman Comedy Hour,' " he said, starting back to the radio. "Now you women talk real quiet. I don't want to miss any of it."

"Is there enough hot water for a bath?" Melanie asked. "I'm so tired, I think I could use one."

"Wait a minute, I'll see." Her mother walked to the corner of the kitchen and put her palm on the outside of the water tank. "No."

She knelt beside the water tank and turned on the gas heater at the same time, striking a match. Nothing happened. "The meter must have gone off again," she said. "Do you have a quarter?"

"I'll get one," Melanie said. She went into the bedroom and opened her purse. She took a coin from the small pile of change she kept in it and went back into the kitchen. "Here."

Her mother took the quarter and pulled a chair over to the sink, then climbed on it. She reached up and placed the coin in the slot in the meter and hit the meter two resounding slaps as the coin tinkled its way into it.

"You always do that," Melanie said.

"Makes the meter give you two extra hours of gas that way," her mother said smugly, getting down. She went back to the water heater. This time the gas went on.

She was just about to step into the tub when her mother knocked at the bathroom door. "There's a telephone call for you from Mr. Warren on McManus' phone downstairs."

"I'll be right there," she said, reaching for her housedress. She went down the flight of steps. The McManus door was ajar. She knocked on it before she went in. Mr. McManus was in front of the radio in much the same position as her father upstairs. Mrs. McManus came to the door.

"I'm sorry to bother you," Melanie said.

"That's all right," the woman answered.

Melanie went into the tiny hallway between the kitchen and the bedrooms. The phone was on a small table. She picked it up. "Hello."

"Melanie?" asked the familiar voice.

"Yes."

"I want to see you right away. I'm in St. Joseph's Hospital."

"I know," she said. The stories and rumors were all over the plant. "Are you all right?"

"I'm fine," he said. "But the stupid doctors won't let me out. They want to keep me for observation."

"Maybe you'd better rest," she said.

"I want to see you."

"I was just going to take a bath," she said. "Besides it will take me almost two hours to get there by trolley."

"I'll send a car for you," he said flatly. "You be downstairs in front of your door in half an hour." The phone went dead in her hand and she put it down.

She went back into the kitchen. "Thank you," she said to the little Irishwoman.

McManus turned from his radio and looked at her. Something in his policeman's eyes told her that he knew she was naked under the housedress. Unconsciously her hand pulled it closer over her chest. "Is your father workin' yet?" he asked.

"Not yet, Mr. McManus," she answered politely, moving toward the door.

"Times are bad," he said heavily. "No tellin' now what's goin' to happen."

She was almost out of the door. "Thank you for letting me use the phone, Mr. McManus."

"That's okay," he said. "As long as you don't abuse it like some people I know."

"Good night," she said, closing the door behind her. Half an hour later she came out of her room fully dressed.

Her mother looked at her in surprise. "Where are you going this time of the night? It's almost nine o'clock."

"I'm going to see Mr. Warren," she said. "He's in St. Joseph's Hospital."

Her father turned from the radio. "What happened to him?"

"He had an accident. He says it's nothing serious."

"It'll take you almost two hours to get there this time of the night," her mother said. "It's not safe for a girl to be out alone in this neighborhood now that the niggers are only a few blocks away."

"He's sending a car for me."

Her father got to his feet. "He must want to see you real bad. What for?"

"I don't know. But he is my boss. It's probably business."

Her father leered. "Monkey business, you mean." He turned to her mother. "I think maybe Mr. Warren has got something on for our little girl."

Her mother made a face. "Stop thinking with your dirty cracker mind. I know my Melanie. She's a good girl."

"I'll be back as soon as I can," Melanie said, slipping out the door.

Her father called after her as she went down the stairs. "Don't forget to remind him of the promise he made to your daddy!"

He was sitting up in bed, his right arm held out in front of him on a pulley sling, his head bandaged, and several large square patches on his right cheek. He didn't wait for her to speak as she came into the room.

"Personnel told me over the phone that they didn't receive the usual nightly batch of blind carbons from your office today."

"There weren't any," she replied. "Mr. Hardeman didn't dictate a single note."

"That's strange," he said. "He was in three days last week and spent all day writing memos."

"There were none today," she said. "There are stories all over the plant that Mr. Hardeman beat you up. What happened?"

"I tripped on a rug in the office and hit my head against the corner of a desk, that's all."

She looked at him without speaking. If it had happened in Number Two's office like they said, he should know better than to tell a story like that. Mr. Hardeman, Jr., did not have any rugs in his office.

"They didn't get your telephone call sheet either," he said.

"Mr. Hardeman came out at the end of the day and took it away from me. Besides he made all his outside calls on his private line. That doesn't cross my desk."

"What about his meetings? Who came to see him?"

"First thing in the morning, he called Mr. Coburn, Mr. Edgerton and Mr. Duncan."

"What did they talk about?"

"I don't know," she answered. "He sent me down to the canteen. When he called me back, they were gone."

"Who else came to see him?"

She thought for a moment. "In the morning, Mr. Williams of Sales and Mr. Conrad of Purchasing."

"What did they talk about?"

"I don't know."

"You were told to keep your intercom switch open whenever there was a meeting in his office so you could make notes!"

"I did," she said. "But nothing came through. He pulled the plug every time someone came into his office."

Warren was silent for a moment. "Anybody else come?"

"In the afternoon, no one from the plant."

"Anyone from outside?"

"Yes," she said. "A Mr. Frank Perino."

"I know what they talked about," Warren said. "Perino's his bootlegger. And Number One likes his whiskey."

"That wasn't it," she said. "Mr. Perino's son is a doctor and he wanted Mr. Hardeman to get him into a Detroit hospital. It seemed he was having trouble because of his background. Mr. Hardeman fixed it."

He was surprised. "How do you know about that?"

"Mr. Hardeman called me into his office for coffee and aspirin. I was there all the time with Mr. Perino." She hesitated a moment. "Mr. Hardeman takes a lot of aspirin. He must have had at least twelve tablets during the day."

"Okay," he said. "Just keep your eyes and ears open. Find out as much as you can and call me every night."

"I'll do that," she said. "How long do you expect to stay here?"

"The doctors say they'll let me out in a couple of days."

"I'm sorry you were hurt," she said.

He looked at her. "Do you know why I picked you to go into Number One's office?"

She shook her head.

"Because you're a big girl and he likes big women."

"I don't understand," she said.

"Don't be stupid," he snapped. "You know his reputation. Sooner or later, he'll make a pass at you."

"Then what do I do?"

"You pretend to go along with him," he said. "Gain his confidence. Then we'll have him."

"What if I don't go along with him?"

He stared at her. "There are other girls who would like that job."

Her eyes fell. She was silent.

He laughed. The tone in his voice changed. "You said you were going to take a bath. Did you have anything on when we talked on the phone?"

She didn't look up. The look on McManus' face flashed through her mind. "A housedress."

"Anything under it?" His voice was getting husky.

"No."

"Come closer to the bed."

She raised her head, looked at him, then at the man who had driven her here. He was standing, his back against the door, watching them impassively.

Warren caught her glance. "Don't mind Mike. He's my bodyguard. He really doesn't see anything."

She didn't move.

"I said come over here!"

Reluctantly she moved to the bed. He took her hand and put it on the sheet between his legs. "I got a hard-on just thinking about it," he said.

She was silent.

"Pull the sheet down."

She started to move the sheet. He winced in sudden pain. "Carefully, damn it!"

She moved the sheet down slowly until the bottom of his hospital gown revealed skinny, hairy legs. The front of the gown hung like a small tent over his erect phallus. "Push the gown up and jack me off," he said. "But be careful, don't shake the bed because that hurts my arm."

She raised the gown gently. His organ was full and erect, the red tip of his glans trying to push its way through his foreskin. Slowly she freed it and began to massage him. Soon her hands were wet and slippery with the fluid that came pouring from him.

"Oh, Jesus, that's good," he said, leaning his head back against the pillows, his eyes closed. "Put your other hand under my balls and squeeze them a little."

His testicles felt like small rocks in her hand. "Faster, faster."

She began to pump him rapidly; his mouth opened and his breathing seemed to keep time with her motion. "Now you really got it," he groaned.

A moment passed. "Take me in your mouth!" he said suddenly. "I'm going to come!"

She hesitated, glancing at the man standing against the door. His eyes looked blankly back at her. Then she felt Warren's hand in her hair, pulling her face down to him. Her mouth opened automatically.

He had already begun his orgasm by the time she reached him and the first hot drops of his viscous semen spat against her cheeks and then she got it in her mouth. She swallowed quickly to keep the frantic flow from choking her and after a moment it was over.

He leaned back against the pillow, his eyes closed. "You're almost as good a cocksucker as some of the little pansies I know."

She didn't answer.

He opened his eyes and looked at her, then at his body-guard. "What do you think, Mike? Is she as good as our little friend?"

"It don't look like it, Boss," the bodyguard replied. "He seems to like it more."

Warren laughed. "Maybe when we get out of here, I'll have you give her some lessons."

For the first time the bodyguard's voice was shocked. "You know I don't like girls!"

Warren laughed again. "I don't mean that. I mean show her how to really do it." He turned back to her, his voice going cold. "Get a washcloth and a towel and wipe me off."

She went into the small bathroom. In the mirror her cheeks were shining and wet with his milky fluid. She wiped her face and then went back into the room.

A few moments later, the sheets were straightened over him once again. "That's better. No point having the nurse know what's going on."

She didn't speak. This was what happened every time she went with him. Not once had they ever had sex together nor had he ever wanted it. Had she been a virgin, her hymen would have been intact if it were up to him.

"Give her five dollars and send her home in a cab," he said to the bodyguard.

Mike came toward her, a five-dollar bill in his hand. She took it from him and he walked back to the door. She turned to the bed.

"You call me here right after work tomorrow," he said.

"I will," she said. "Good night."

"Good night," he answered.

Mike stepped aside and opened the door to let her out. She heard the door close behind her as she walked down the long hospital corridor.

Once outside, she looked down at her hand. The five-dollar bill was still clutched in it. The clang of a streetcar approaching came to her ears. She looked at the bill again, then at the taxi line. Suddenly she began to run toward the corner to the trolley stop.

It might take her more than two hours to get home. But five dollars was more than a whole day's pay.

EDGERTON WALKED across the office. "I'm worried, Mr. Hardeman," he said. "This is the second payday the banks have been closed and we're getting a lot of complaints from the employees. The stores won't accept our checks."

"We're good for it," Loren said.

"It's not only us," Edgerton said. "It's the banks. Too many have already closed down for good. Now I hear talk that the men won't show up for work unless they get paid in cash."

"Pay them in cash then," said Loren.

"We haven't got it," Edgerton said flatly. "Our weekly payroll is over a hundred and forty thousand. Nobody keeps that much cash on hand."

"Get it then."

"Where? The banks are closed to us as well as to them."

Loren was thoughtful for a moment. "What does Personnel have to say about this?"

"Warren bucked it to me. He says it's the treasurer's job to provide the money for the payroll."

"Has he explained the situation to the employees?"

"He says he has."

"That's not what I asked. Has he?"

"I don't know. I heard that a group of men came in to talk to him about it and that he fired the whole bunch of them."

"Why?"

"He says they were troublemakers. All Wobblies trying to unionize the plant and that they were just using this as an excuse."

"What do you think?"

"I know some of those men. They're old-line employees. I don't think they are Wobblies."

"If they were would it make any difference? Wouldn't they still be entitled to their pay?"

"Yes," said Edgerton.

Loren flipped the switch on his intercom. Melanie's voice answered. "Yes, Mr. Hardeman."

"Ask Mr. Warren to come up here right away," he said, flipping off the switch.

A few minutes later, Joe Warren came into the office. His arm was still in a sling, his eyes wary.

"Warren, I hear we're having problems over the fact that employees can't cash their pay checks."

Warren began smoothly. "You have to recognize the fact, Mr. Hardeman, that during the past few years we have been infiltrated by the I.W.W., Communists and union organizers. It isn't our men stirring up the trouble. It's them."

"You mean to say our men can cash their checks?"

"No," Warren said. "But our men aren't complaining."

"How do you know?"

"I know the good ones and the bad ones," Warren said.

"And only the bad ones are complaining, is that it?" Loren asked sarcastically.

"Yes, Mr. Hardeman."

"Did you explain the situation to them?" Loren asked.

"There's nothing to explain," Warren answered. "Every other company in town is in the same boat. They all know that."

"But if they can't cash their checks and they can't get credit at the stores, how are they going to eat?" Loren asked.

"That's not our problem," Warren said. "We can't be expected to manage our employees' money. If they can't establish their own credit, it's unfortunate."

"If the stores won't accept our checks," Loren asked, "don't you think it's our credit that's being questioned, not theirs?"

Warren didn't answer.

"Have you taken any steps to assure the local merchants that Bethlehem Motors will back up their checks regardless of the bank upon which they were issued?"

"I didn't see where it was necessary," Warren answered.

Loren was silent. He studied the man sitting in front of him. Warren had a feral quality, even while sitting still. There was an air of cold ruthlessness about him that no amount of surface amenities could dispel.

"I don't see why you should concern yourself with such petty details, Mr. Hardeman," Warren said. "I can control the situation. Meanwhile we can use the circumstance to smoke out the bad employees in our plant and get rid of them."

Loren didn't speak.

"We've already rid ourselves of more than twenty troublemakers," Warren said. "And we have our eyes on more of them."

Loren was still silent.

Warren rose to his feet. "Just leave everything to me, Mr. Hardeman. I'll work it out, you'll see." He started for the door.

"Sit down, Warren!" Loren snapped. "I didn't give you permission to leave!"

Warren hesitated a moment, then returned to his seat. Carefully he rested his sling on the arm of the chair.

"I want you to send a letter out to every merchant and store in the area that Bethlehem Motors will guarantee every pay check issued by them regardless of the bank concerned."

Warren shook his head. "Can't do that, Mr. Hardeman. Such a letter has to be approved either by the president of the company or the board of directors."

"Then get the president to sign it," Loren said.

"I don't know where he is," Warren said blandly. "I haven't seen him for over two weeks. Have you?"

Loren stared at him. Warren knew damn well he hadn't seen his son since that day in the office. "Then prepare the letter, I'll sign it."

"You haven't the authority," Warren said calmly. "You cannot commit the company to that kind of loss in case the banks should fail."

"There's nothing in the company bylaws to prevent me from guaranteeing those checks personally, is there?"

"What you do personally is none of our concern," Warren said.

"Then prepare the letter that way for my signature," said Loren.

"If you like," Warren said. "Is there anything else?"

"Yes," Loren said. "Also inform the employees that the next payroll will be cash."

"I'll do that," Warren said. "But all hell will break loose if the money isn't there on payday."

"That will be my problem," Loren said. "You can go now."

They were silent until the door closed behind Warren, then Edgerton turned to Loren. "Where are you going to get the money?"

"I'll get it someplace," Loren said. He looked at the closed door. "What's the latest report from Duncan?"

"Everything will be set in a week. The new cars should be rolling off the line within the month."

"Good." Loren smiled with satisfaction. "That cuts Charlie Sorensen's new model changeover time at Ford exactly in half. Six weeks instead of ninety days." He took a cigarette from the box on his desk. "Do you think he knows anything about it?"

"With his spy system?" Edgerton asked, then answered his own question. "I'm sure that he does."

"But they've done nothing about it." Loren asked, "What do you think they're waiting for?"

"Actually, there's very little they can do at the moment. The bank closing played right into our hands in this case. The bankers are too busy with their own problems to pay attention to us. And the board meeting is still more than a week away."

Loren thought for a moment. "Get after Duncan and tell him I want the production line rolling within a week and I don't care how he does it. I want that car coming off the line before the board meeting."

"That means dumping the contract with Ford for car bodies," said Edgerton.

"Dump it then."

"Bennett will be sore. He'll sue."

"No, he won't," Loren said. "I'll straighten it out with Edsel and Charlie Sorensen." He was silent for a moment. "I wonder if there's any tieup between Bennett and Warren?"

"I know they're good friends," Edgerton said. "Warren just built a house on Grosse Pointe Isles next to Bennett."

Loren looked at him. "I understand all purchasing has been consolidated into Warren's department."

"It's not a bad idea," Edgerton said. "Central control. We get better prices than purchasing department by department."

"I'm not saying it's not," Loren said quickly. "I'm just wondering if a close look into purchasing won't be useful."

Edgerton smiled. "It can't hurt."

"Can you do it without him becoming aware of what's happening?"

"I think so," Edgerton said. "It's near the time for our annual audit. I'll just have the boys take an extra hard look at the purchasing contracts."

"You do that and keep me posted." Loren got to his feet.

Edgerton rose also. He looked at Loren. "Mr. Hardeman," he said tentatively.

"Yes, Walt?"

"I'm glad you're back," he said.

"Grandpa! Grandpa!" The children's voices greeted him at the door. He opened his arms and swept them up to him. He kissed Anne's cheek first, then Loren III.

"Were you a good boy today?" he asked his grandson.

"He was a very good boy," Anne said in her three-year-old voice. "He only hit me once today."

"Only once?" Loren pretended shock. He looked at the boy. "Why did you do that?"

"I deserved it," Anne said. "I hit him first."

"Remember the rules," he said sternly. "I said no more fights."

"We're trying to remember, Grandpa," the little boy said. "But sometimes we forget."

"Don't forget," he said.

"Piggyback! Piggyback!" Anne cried.

"Yes! Piggyback!" her brother echoed.

Loren put them down and got on his hands and knees. The children climbed on his back, Anne in front, her little hands digging into his hair, Loren III in the back, clutching his grandfather's belt.

"Pony Express!" the boy yelled, slapping Loren's behind with his hand.

"Faster! Faster!" Anne yelled happily.

Loren crawled rapidly into the library with them bouncing up and down on his back. He came to a stop in front of silk-clad legs in high-heeled shoes and looked up.

"Exactly what do you think you're doing down there?" Sally asked, trying to keep her voice stern.

"Look out," Loren said. "We're the Wells Fargo Pony Express." He set out at a rapid gallop around the room. He came to a stop again in front of Sally.

"All right, children," Sally said firmly. "That's enough. You're annoying your grandfather. It's time for your dinner."

"We want to play!" Loren III yelled.

"Your grandfather is tired. He had to work hard all day," Sally said, lifting him from Loren's back. Anne slid to the floor. "Now give Grandfather a kiss and go in to dinner."

"Can we play some more after dinner?" Anne asked.

"No. After dinner, you're both going to bed, but if you both eat all your dinner, Grandfather will come upstairs and tell you a bedtime story."

"Will you, Grandpa?" Loren III asked.

"You bet your sweet patootie," Loren said, getting to his feet.

The children picked it up. "You bet your sweet patootie!" they shouted, running from the room, their voices echoing back from the hall. "You bet your sweet patootie!"

Sally frowned. "That's a fine thing to teach the children," she said, trying to keep a straight face. "You're more of a child than they are."

He laughed. "It won't hurt them."

"I have ice and whiskey on the bar," she said. "Want me to fix you a drink?"

He nodded, watching her go to the bar. She came back to him, the whiskey amber and the ice tinkling in the glass. He took the drink from her. His eyes were on her face. "I always said a house needs a woman's touch."

She looked at him for a moment without speaking, then turned and went to the bar and made herself a drink. She came back to him. "I spoke to Junior today," she said without sitting down.

"Yes," he said in an expressionless voice.

"He wanted me to return home. He said he would come back if I did."

He sipped at his drink without speaking.

"I told him I was never coming back," she said.

"Then what did he say?"

"He got nasty and said all sorts of things."

"What sorts of things?"

"That he knew what we were doing and we didn't fool him or anyone else. That he had the evidence that we were sleeping together and he wouldn't hesitate to use it in court to take the children away from me."

Loren shook his head sadly.

"It's more than that," she said. "He hates so much he's blind."

Loren looked up at her. "What are you going to do?"

"I can't stay here," she said. "There's no point in dragging you into this mess. I was thinking of moving to England."

"Would you get a divorce first?"

"Yes," she said. "If he would agree, I could go to Reno."

"Then what would you do?"

"Go to England with the children. The schools are very good there. And at least they speak the same language."

After a moment, he put his glass down. "When did Junior say he would return?"

"Next week. He said something about having to be here for a board meeting."

That added up. It also provided the reason why Warren was lying low. They were going to let him dig his own grave. He got to his feet. "You don't have to go anywhere, you know that," he said. "You can stay right here in Hardeman Manor. The children are happy and I don't give a damn what he does."

She looked into his eyes. "The children have never been happier. You've played with them more in these two weeks than their father has since they were born. But it's not fair to you. You have enough problems as it is."

"Think about it," he said. "Don't make up your mind yet."

She nodded.

"I'm going upstairs to lie down a bit before dinner. Call me when it's ready."

"Headache again?"

He nodded.

"Want me to get you some aspirin?"

"No. I had enough of those today. I'll try to do without it. Maybe I'll feel better after a little rest."

She watched him leave the room and heard his footsteps on the staircase, then sank into a chair. She could feel the tears just behind her eyes. It wasn't fair. It just wasn't fair.

A thought suddenly came to her. She ran up the steps and into his room without knocking at the door.

He was just coming from the bathroom, his shirt already unbuttoned. He looked at her.

"I never thought of you," she said quickly. "Or of what you want."

He didn't speak.

"I'll go back with him if it will make things easier for you."

He took a deep breath, then held his arms open toward her. She came into them and laid her cheek against his broad chest.

"I don't want you to go anywhere but here," he said.

MELANIE'S VOICE through the intercom was hushed and impressed. "The White House calling, Mr. Hardeman."

Loren flipped the switch and picked up the telephone. "Hello."

A man's voice spoke. "Mr. Hardeman?"

"Speaking."

"Just a moment for the President of the United States." There was a click.

"Mr. Hardeman?" There was no mistaking that voice. He had heard it too many times on the radio.

"Yes, Mr. President."

"I regret very much that we have never met but I want you to know that I am personally very grateful for your contribution to the Democratic campaign fund."

"Thank you for being so kind, Mr. President."

"Now I have an important favor to ask of you, Mr. Hardeman, and I beg of you to consider it." The President came right to the point. "As you know, I consider the most important problem facing this country to be the Depression and the unemployment resulting from it, so I have placed before Congress a bill which I have entitled the National Recovery Act. Contained within this bill is the framework to rebuild and rehabilitate our industries through an adoption of mutual practices to be effected by self-help and government regulations."

"I've read about it, Mr. President," Loren said. The Detroit newspapers were already filled with it, denouncing it for the most part as an attempt to socialize and bring the automobile industry under government control.

"I'm sure you have, Mr. Hardeman." The President paused for a moment. "And I'm equally sure that you've read nothing good about it."

"I wouldn't say that, Mr. President. There are some practical proposals in it that merit further consideration."

244

"That brings us to my favor," the President said. "I would like you to come to Washington to help develop that section of the NRA that pertains to your industry. You, of course, will be working directly under General Hugh Johnson who has accepted the position of over-all responsibility. Since we regard the automobile industry as the keystone of our economy, you can see how important a contribution you can make to your country."

"I'm most flattered and honored, Mr. President," Loren said. "But I am certain there are others more worthy and more capable for that position."

"You're being modest, Mr. Hardeman," the President chuckled. "And that's not in keeping with what I've heard about you. But you are our first choice and I do hope you will give it every consideration."

"I will, Mr. President," said Loren. "But my own company is in serious trouble and I don't really know if I could leave it at this time."

"Mr. Hardeman," the President said, "the entire country is in serious trouble. I am sure that as a responsible citizen you cannot fail to see that unless the country recovers from its malaise, neither will your company." He paused for a moment. "I would appreciate your decision within the week, Mr. Hardeman, and I do hope that it will be favorable."

"I will let you know, Mr. President," Loren said.

"Good-bye, Mr. Hardeman."

"Good-bye, Mr. President." Loren put down the telephone. He reached for a cigarette and lit it. President Roosevelt didn't waste time. He promised to stir up some excitement and that was exactly what was happening.

The intercom buzzed again. He flipped the switch. "Yes, Miss Walker?"

"It's almost time for the board meeting, Mr. Hardeman."

"Thank you, Miss Walker. Will you bring in my folder?"

"Right away, sir."

A moment later she came into his office and placed the folder on his desk. Instead of leaving, as she usually did, she hesitated.

He looked up at her. "Yes, Miss Walker?"

She blushed. "Was that really President Roosevelt on the telephone?"

"It was." He nodded. He opened the folder and looked at it, then looked up. She was still standing there. "Yes, Miss Walker?"

"I voted for him," she said. "It was the very first time I voted."

"So did I," he smiled.

She smiled suddenly. "I like the sound of his voice on the radio. It's so warm and friendly. It seems like he's really talking to you."

It was the first time he had seen her smile. He looked at her. "You know, you're a very pretty girl, Miss Walker," he said. "You should smile more often."

She blushed again. "Thank you, Mr. Hardeman."

He watched her walk to the door. Odd that he had never really looked at her before. She was an attractive girl. The door closed behind her and he looked down at the file folder.

He deliberately arrived a few minutes late. The other board members were already in the room, clustered in small groups, deep in conversation. They fell silent as he entered. He wasted no time on the usual greetings. Instead he rapped his knuckles on the table.

"Will the board members kindly take their seats?" he asked.

Silently they took up their positions around the long rectangular table. Junior sat facing him at the foot of the table, Warren sat at Junior's right. There were eleven others at the table as it came toward him. Coburn and Edgerton were the only other company employees on the board. The rest consisted of representatives of the banks and insurance companies to whom they were in debt and several token members, officials of other noncompetitive corporations.

"The chair calls this meeting to order and will entertain a motion to suspend the reading of the minutes of the previous meeting, a copy of which is in the folder in front of you."

He waited. Coburn made the motion, Edgerton seconded it, and it was carried unanimously and quickly by the rest of the board. That done, he awaited a motion to place the current agenda before the board.

"Mr. Chairman!" Junior said.

"Yes, Mr. President," he said formally.

"I would like to place a motion to delay the consideration of the agenda in favor of other and more important business."

"The chair has no objections, Mr. President," he said. "Do I hear the motion seconded?"

"Second the motion," said Warren.

"The chair will abstain from the vote," he said. "The board will now vote on the motion placed before it by the president. All in favor say 'Aye.'"

There were eleven Ayes, the two Nays came from Edgerton and Coburn. He smiled. "The motion is carried." He took a cigarette from the box on the table before him, lit it and leaned back in his chair.

Junior was on his feet almost before Loren could let out his first breath of smoke. "I accuse the chairman of the board of overstepping his authority in the exercise of his duties and of other gross improprieties detrimental to the welfare of the company and I demand his resignation!"

There was a stony silence in the room. Loren smiled again. He put down the cigarette carefully. "The chair will be pleased to consider Mr. President's request if he puts it before the board properly as a motion." He paused for a moment but not long enough to give Junior a chance to speak again. "The chair will also be pleased to entertain a motion for the board to visit Assembly Plant Number Three before any other business."

Coburn came through on cue, Edgerton seconded. Curiosity swung the board in their favor. The only two votes against were Junior and Warren.

"The motion is carried." Loren got to his feet. "The meeting is adjourned to Assembly Plant Number Three. Follow me, gentlemen."

Duncan fell in step beside him as they came out of the administration building. "Walk slow," the Scotsman whispered out of the corner of his mouth. "The first car isn't due to reach the end of the assembly line for another ten minutes."

Loren nodded. Deliberately he led them the long way round. It was exactly nine minutes until they arrived at the end of the production line in Assembly Plant Number Three.

Loren turned to the board members. "I assume all you gentlemen know how to drive a car?"

They nodded.

"Good." Loren smiled. He looked down the production line. A car was coming toward them. "In case you gentlemen are wondering why I asked you to come down here, I want to show you the reason."

The car came through the final inspection shed and arrived, dark blue and shining before them. "Here is the first Baby Sundancer off the line. It will sell for under five hundred dollars and put us firmly in the low-car market with Ford, Chrysler, Plymouth and Chevrolet!"

He paused a moment. "Mr. John Duncan, our chief engineer and designer, will drive off in the first car to the freight yard where the car will be loaded on a train and begin its journey to the dealer. If each one of you will take a car as it comes off the line and follow Mr. Duncan, you will have an opportunity to judge for yourself how well the car performs and handles. A bus will be waiting there to bring you back to the administration building at the end of your drive."

Duncan got into the car and started the engine. He moved off slowly just as the second car arrived. This was a dark burgundy color.

Loren took one of the directors by the arm. "Go ahead, drive it."

The man got into the car and started it. After that there was no problem. The men couldn't wait their turn. They were like children with a new toy. One car after another took off until only Loren, Junior and Warren were left.

"You can't get away with this!" Junior snarled.

Loren smiled. "I already did, son." He took a pack of cigarettes from his pocket. "Let's face it. You already lost the fight. The minute those men got into the automobile."

Loren lit his cigarette. "My advice is that you jump into the next car off the line and drive down to the freight yard to accept the congratulations of the board. There's no one here will say anything to the contrary."

Junior hesitated. He looked at Warren.

"Better make up your mind," Loren said. "Here comes the next car. If you don't get into it, I will."

The car, a bright yellow, came to a stop. Without a word, Junior got into it and drove off.

The next car arrived, carbon black and shining. Warren looked questioningly at Loren. Loren hesitated a moment. "That's car number thirteen off the line," he finally said.

"I'm not superstitious," answered Warren.

Loren shrugged his shoulders. He watched Warren jump into the car and drive away eagerly. The car was about five hundred yards down the road when the explosion came.

The roar echoed around the plant, bringing men and women from their offices and production lines. A pall of dust hung in the air and when it settled, there was nothing to be seen of the automobile but twisted and tortured pieces of metal.

Loren turned and began walking toward the administration building as people ran past him. There were three white-suited jumper-clad mechanics, the blue letters B.M.C. across their backs, walking toward the gate in front of him.

The smallest of the three fell back and into step with Loren. They walked silently until they reached the door of the administration building. Then Loren turned and looked down at him. "I told him it was car number thirteen," he said. "But he said he wasn't superstitious."

The small man's dark brown eyes peered up at him from under heavy black brows. "A man without superstition is a man without a soul," he said.

Loren didn't speak for a moment. "I wonder what would have happened if I got into that car," he said finally.

There was a note of injury in the small man's voice. "My boys are very professional," he said. "You never would have been allowed to start that car."

Loren nodded. A flicker of a smile came into his eyes. "I apologize for even having the thought," he said. "Goodbye, Mr. Perino."

"Good-bye, Mr. Hardeman."

Loren stood there looking after the little man as he hurried after his two companions. He saw the security guard at the gate carefully turn his back so that he would not see the three men walking through.

The receptionist at the entrance desk to the administration building was just putting down the telephone as he came into the building. "Mr. Hardeman!" she exclaimed in an excited voice. "A car just blew up outside of Assembly Three!"

"I know," he said, walking to the elevator and pressing the button.

"I wonder who was in it," she said, as the elevator doors opened.

He walked into the elevator and pressed the button. "Some unlucky bastard."

Chapter Twelve

THE SNOW falling in soft white flakes partly laced the brightly lit great dome of the Capitol as she looked out of the window of the small house in Washington in which they had spent the last year and a half. It was after nine o'clock. Another late night.

She went back to the sofa in front of the blazing hearth. The leaping flames threw their warmth at her, lending a familiar, old comfort. So many nights she had waited for him in this chair, in front of this fire. Somehow there always was an emergency in Washington.

"Government by crisis," he had said one night when he

had come in particularly late. "It can't be much fun for you."

"I'm not complaining," she had said. And she had meant it. Detroit seemed far away and another world. A completely self-centered world whose horizons began with a front bumper and ended with the rear bumper. "I don't ever want to go back," she had added.

He had given her a curious look but didn't speak.

"The children like it too," she said. "Every day their nanny takes them to someplace new, someplace exciting and filled with history. Imagine how much they've learned since they've been here. It's like growing up with everything in the world happening in front of your eyes."

"It hasn't been lonely for you?" he asked. "Away from your friends?"

"What friends? Back in Detroit the only friends I had were the wives of men who either worked for Bethlehem or wanted to. I was more alone there than here. At least here when we go to a party we have more things to talk about than just automobiles."

The sound of the front door interrupted her thoughts. She rose from the sofa and walked toward the foyer. The butler had already taken Loren's snow-covered hat and coat and was hanging them in the closet when she reached him.

"I'm sorry I'm late," he said, kissing her cheek.

His lips were cold. "That's all right," she said quickly. "Come inside in front of the fire where you can warm up."

He sank wearily onto the sofa, stretching his hands out toward the fire. She looked down at him with concern. She had never seen him so tired before, his brows knitted with the headache he seemed to have constantly now. "Let me fix you a drink."

She went to the sideboard and made his drink quickly. When she came back, he had leaned his head against the sofa and closed his eyes. He felt her next to him. Silently he took the drink and sipped it. She sat down beside him without speaking.

He turned to her. "Well, it's over," he said in a tired voice.

She looked at him in bewilderment. "What do you mean?"

"You didn't hear the news?"

She shook her head. "I was reading a book. I didn't listen to the radio this evening."

"The Supreme Court ruled today that the NRA was unconstitutional."

"What does that mean?" she asked.

A half smile came to his lips. "For one thing it means I'm unemployed. Out of a job like a lot of other people." He sipped at his drink and smiled again. "I wonder how much severance pay a dollar-a-year man is entitled to."

"Maybe two dollars a year?" she suggested.

He laughed. "Anyhow, the President never did promise me that the job would be a steady one."

"Did you see him?"

"No. But I did see Hugh Johnson. The general was in rare form, swearing a blue streak, convinced the country would go to rack and ruin without him at the helm."

"What happens now?" she asked.

"I don't know," he said, shrugging his shoulders. "As near as I can make out, in the world of politics when you lose, you fold your tent and silently steal away in the night."

"It's so sudden, I still can't believe it," she said.

"You'd believe it if you saw clerks and secretaries loading up their briefcases with supplies and paper clips," he said.

"When did you find out?"

"This morning when the Supreme Court convened. It was instant pandemonium. Everybody running around in circles doing nothing except adding to the general confusion." He was suddenly angry. "Worst of all was the news from Detroit. They went crazy out there. They did everything except declare a holiday. The damn fools!"

He took a swallow of his drink. "What no one seemed to realize was that without the NRA they might as well turn around and hand the entire industry over to the Big Three. Nash, Studebaker, Willys, Hudson, Packard, they're all doomed. It will only be a matter of time before every independent auto manufacturer will be out of business."

"Surely they can see that," she said.

"They can't see their noses," he said sarcastically. "They think they can compete with Ford, GM and Chrysler now that controls are off. They don't stand a chance. The big companies will make it cheaper and sell it cheaper."

"Does that go for Bethlehem too?" she asked.

He looked at her. "Yes."

"Can anything be done about it?"

He nodded. "Concentrate on the low end of the medium-priced range. A car priced between the Chevy and the Pontiac. That should be the Sundancer market for at least the next ten years."

"What about the Baby Sundancer?" she asked.

"It served its purpose," he said. "It kept us going when the only market was the low-price end. But now the costs are climbing and we can't compete against the others. I figure that by next year, times should improve enough to let us discontinue it."

She thought for a moment. "I'll be sorry to see it go. I liked that little car."

"It was a little bastard," he said affectionately. "Made out of leftovers of other cars, but it did have something going for it."

The butler knocked discreetly before he entered the room. "Dinner is served, Madam."

It was after midnight when he looked up from his desk in the small study, his work finished. He began gathering the papers and placing them in his briefcase. He stared down at the briefcase a moment. Then he snapped it shut. There was a finality to the gesture. It was done. A part of the past. There was nothing more to keep him here tomorrow after he returned the papers to the office.

He got to his feet and, turning off the light, left the room. He went silently up the darkened staircase and down the corridor to his room.

He was just about to switch on the light when her voice came from his bed. "Loren! Don't turn on the light!"

He stood there a moment, then closed the door softly. "Why?"

"I've been crying," she said. "And I know I look awful."

He crossed the room to her, his eyes getting accustomed to the dark. She was sitting up, the pillows behind her back. "Crying won't help," he said. "It never does."

"I know. But we've been happy here."

He dragged on a cigarette. She held out her hand. "May I?"

Silently he gave it to her. The tip glowed red, casting a faint light on her face. Her eyes were almost luminous. "Loren?"

"Yes?"

"I'm not going back." Her voice was gentle. "You knew that, didn't you?"

"Yes," he said.

"But I want to be with you."

"Then come back," he said quickly. "Hardeman Manor is big enough. We can—"

"No, Loren," she interrupted. "It won't be the same. Detroit isn't Washington. Here I'm accepted. I'm your daughter-in-law acting as hostess for her widowed father-in-law. There I'm still your son's wife, living with you while her husband lives a few miles down the road. It won't work."

"Then divorce him," he said harshly. "And we can get married."

"No. The one thing I learned about Detroit is that you can get away with murder but not divorce. You still owe the banks twenty million dollars. One open scandal and you lose everything you've spent your whole life in building."

He was silent.

"You know I'm right, Loren," she said. "I would ask you to come with me but I know you must do what you have to do. You build automobiles, Loren. You can't stop or you'll die."

He walked over to the window. The snow had stopped

and the night was clear, the stars sparkling in the dark blue sky. "What are you going to do?"

"Stay here for a while," she said. "Then, maybe move up to New York. Soon the children will be starting school. There are good schools there for them."

"I will miss them," he said.

"They will miss you even more. They've grown to love you very much."

He felt the tears come to his eyes and blinked to hold them back. But now even the stars were blurred. "May I come to visit them?"

"I hope you do. Very often."

Slowly he began to undress. He placed his clothing on a chair and started for the bathroom. She called him and he paused.

"Loren, no pajamas tonight, please. I want to sleep naked with you."

"Can I brush my teeth?" he smiled.

"Yes," she said. "But hurry. I want you inside me."

"Then why wait?" he asked, coming to the bed.

Her legs rose to enfold him, his large, strong hands gripped her buttocks as he entered her. "Oh, God!" she cried, a sudden despair in her voice. "How will I ever live without you?"

Chapter Thirteen

MELANIE WAS WAITING at the kitchen table reading the evening paper when her father came home. He looked over her shoulder at the headlines.

SHOWDOWN DUE AT FORD TODAY
DEARBORN GIVES UAW RIGHT TO
DISTRIBUTE HANDBILLS OUTSIDE
RIVER ROUGE

He began to unbutton the gray blouse of his Ford Security Police uniform, walking to the icebox. He took out a bottle of beer and opened it. Holding the bottle to his mouth he drank until it was half empty, then put it down on the table and belched.

Melanie didn't look up. She began turning the pages to the women's section.

"You can tell your Commie-loving boss to watch tomorrow and see how a real company handles the union," her father said, taking off his blouse. He pulled open his tie and picked up the beer again.

"What do you mean?" She looked up at him.

"You'll find out tomorrow." He smiled secretively. "All I can tell you is that we're ready for those Commie bastards. They're going to wish they never got that okay from the city of Dearborn."

"There's nothing you can do," she said, her eyes going back to the newspaper. "They have the law on their side."

"Ford's got a right to protect its property," he said. He looked at her. "Just because your boss folded up and gave in to the union don't mean that we have to lay down and take it."

"Mr. Hardeman says it's only a question of time before the whole industry is union."

"That's what he thinks," her father answered. "Tomorrow he'll find out different." He finished the beer. "How come you're still dressed?"

"I'm working tonight," she said. "Mr. Hardeman has an executive committee meeting over at the house after dinner. I'm going out there to take notes."

He leered at her. "No wonder he lets you use a company car. You've been doin' a lot of night work lately."

She didn't answer.

"Where's your mother?" he asked suddenly.

"She'll be up in a few minutes," she said. "She's downstairs with Mrs. McManus."

He took another bottle of beer and dropped into the chair opposite her. His voice took on a confidential tone. "You can tell your old man. He knows about those things. What's goin' on between you an' Number One?"

"Nothing," she said.

He opened the bottle. "Nothing? You're too smart a girl to expect your old daddy to believe that." He took a pull at the beer. His voice turned sly. "Like nothing went on between you an' Joe Warren either."

She didn't answer.

"I know all about that," he said. "And I don't blame you for doin' it. If you didn't, there would be a hundred girls jumpin' at the chance."

She felt her face begin to flush. She got out of the chair. "You got nothing but a dirty mind."

He smiled up at her. "There's a guy workin' at Ford with me. He used to be Warren's bodyguard. His name is Mike. Remember him?"

Her face was burning, she didn't move.

"He doesn't know you're my daughter. The names don't mean nothin' to him, there were so many of them. But he remembers picking up a girl one night an' bringin' her to Joe Warren in the hospital. He also remembers what she did." He took some more beer from the bottle. "So don't try playin' Miss Innocent with me an' expect me to believe you ain't doin' at least as much for Number One and maybe more. Girls like you don't get cars and fifty bucks a week just for typin'."

She tried to speak but the words stuck in her throat.

He began to laugh. "I just think you're givin' it away too cheap. Number One's used to shellin' out big dough for his girls. Mike says he was banging his own daughter-in-law an' that he gave her a cool million bucks to get a quiet divorce last year so the shit wouldn't hit the fan."

Abruptly she turned and ran down the hall to her room. She slammed the door shut behind her and began to cry. Through the thin walls she could still hear the sound of his obscenely derisive laughter.

The letter was lying on the library desk when Loren came home. He recognized the handwriting on the envelope, the peculiar wavering underlining of the word "Personal." He picked it up. It was postmarked New York, May 23 P.M.

He picked up the silver letter opener and carefully slit the envelope. It had been more than a year since he had heard from her. Since the time that they had agreed not to see each other again. He had a strange presentiment that he already knew the contents of the letter. He wasn't wrong.

Dear Loren,

A long time ago when you told me that I was not the kind of a woman who could live alone and that someday I would find a man I could love, I did not believe you. If you will remember, I said to you at that time, it was easy for you to talk. You were a man and you have known many women, and perhaps even loved some of them in your own particular fashion. I also said that it would not be so with me, that I did not think I could ever love another man.

I was wrong, as you always knew I would be. On Tuesday next I will be married to Capt. Hugh Scott USN. He commands an aircraft carrier based in Pensacola, Fla., where we will live. The only reason I have for writing this letter is that I wanted you to hear about this from me rather than the newspapers. The children are well and happy and so am I. If you have anything to wish me—wish me—

Love,
Sally

He folded the letter carefully and placed it back in the envelope. For a moment, he thought of picking up the telephone and calling her in New York. But it would not change anything. It was over and done. Slowly he tore the letter into tiny pieces and dropped them one by one into the wastebasket.

Melanie arrived just as he was finishing dinner. He looked up as the butler showed her into the dining room. "Have you had your dinner yet?"

"Yes," she answered. "I came from home."

"Sit down then and have some coffee with me."

The butler held a chair for her and then placed a cup of coffee in front of her. He left the room and she sipped at her coffee silently.

After a while Loren smiled at her. "You're very silent and solemn tonight, Melanie."

"I think my father knows about us."

Loren looked at her. "Knows or suspects? There's a big difference."

"Not to my father," she said. "It's the same thing."

"What if he does?" Loren asked. "There's nothing he can do about it."

"To you maybe," she said. "But he can make my life miserable at home."

"Then why don't you move out and get your own place? He's working now, it's time you used some of the money for yourself."

"I couldn't do that to my mother. You don't know my father. All he cares about is himself. If I weren't there he would drive her crazy."

"I'll give you a raise," he said. "That way you can still give them the same money."

"It's not just the money," she said. "It's him. He's plain mean. And it shows even more since he's gone to work for Bennett at Ford."

"What's that got to do with it?" he asked.

She looked at him. "You know what's going on over there. The whole River Rouge plant is terrorized by Bennett and his gang and my father loves being part of Bennett's storm troopers as they're being called."

"I don't understand it," he said. "Edsel isn't that kind of a man. He wouldn't tolerate it."

"Edsel has nothing to do with it," she said. "My father told me that Bennett has the old man's ear and Edsel Ford is simply ignored."

"The old man will live to regret it," he said. "Someday that whole place will blow up."

"It might come tomorrow," she said.

He looked at her. "What do you mean?"

"You saw this evening's papers?"

He nodded.

"My father says that Bennett is readying a surprise for the union. All of Bennett's goons will be waiting when the union organizers show up."

"There's nothing they can do about it," Loren said. "As long as the union keeps off Ford property."

"What if they go up on the overpass over Miller Road in front of Gate Four?"

"What if they do?" he replied. "It's a public pedestrian bridge. It's always crowded with peddlers and ice cream vendors doing business when the shifts change."

"My father told me that Bennett says it's Ford property because they built it."

He thought for a moment, then nodded. "That could mean trouble." He looked up at her. "Get Richard Frankensteen or one of the Reuther brothers on the phone for me. I don't want to see anyone hurt. It will be a black eye for the whole industry. I'll warn them to keep off the bridge."

She went to the telephone on the sideboard and called a number. After a brief conversation, she put a hand over the mouthpiece and spoke to him. "They're all out at meetings," she said. "And no one knows just what time they will be back."

"Tell them that the first one to come back should call me immediately. It's very important."

She relayed the message and came to the table. She was about to sit down when she changed her mind. Instead she walked to his chair and kissed him.

"That's not very secretarylike," he said with a smile.

"I don't care," she said. "I like you."

He reached up and put a finger on the tip of her nose. "I'll give you a chance to prove how much as soon as the meeting is over."

She took his hand and kissed it, letting her tongue lick the center of his palm. "I can't wait."

"Junior, you sit next to me," said Loren. "Walt, you, Ted, and Scotty sit opposite us."

Silently they took their seats. Melanie took her place at

the foot of the rectangular library table and opened her notebook.

Loren looked at her. "You don't have to take notes, Miss Walker. This is an unofficial meeting."

She closed the book. "Do you wish me to remain, Mr. Hardeman?"

"Please do."

She sank back into her chair as he turned to the others. "You fellows don't have to look so solemn. Nothing terrible is going to happen."

The tension in the room eased slightly. They leaned forward attentively.

"I'll make it simple and brief," Loren said. "What I have to say to you concerns the future management and operations of the company."

He paused for a moment. "I will begin by telling you something I have no doubt that all of you already know. With the repayment of the final installment amounting to two million one hundred thousand dollars for our bank loans today, I have received in return all rights to the stock I own in the company."

"Hear, hear!" Duncan said softly.

Loren smiled at him. "I echo your sentiments. I don't like bankers any more than you do. At the same time I received the resignation of the four directors they had on the board provisionally until the next board meeting."

"Again, hear, hear!" This time the Scotsman couldn't contain himself. He began to clap his hands silently.

A moment later the others joined in.

Loren gestured and they stopped. "Now for my plan."

There was a slight rustling in the chairs. The men settled back, waiting.

"I own ninety percent of the company," Loren said. "My son, ten percent. I am also fifty-nine years old and next year, when I am sixty, I intend to retire from active participation in the affairs of the company."

He paused and the silence around the table deepened. "And so, accordingly, I have made the following disposition of my stock.

"To my grandchildren, Loren Three and Anne Elizabeth, five percent each, a total of ten percent for the two. This stock will be held and voted for them by their father as trustee until such time as they come to maturity. Further provisions have been made in the event of the decease of any of the parties interested in order to protect both the survivors and the company."

He paused and looked at Melanie. "May I have a glass of water and two aspirin, Miss Walker?"

Silently she went to the bar and returned with the water and aspirin. The men did not speak while he took the pills. They were used to seeing him eat aspirin.

He put down the glass of water. "At the same time I have endowed a charitable foundation to be known as the Hardeman Foundation with thirty-nine percent of the stock. It will be the purpose of this foundation to use the funds they so acquire for the good and benefit of the public. The voting rights to the stock of the corporation are held by me in trust for the remainder of my lifetime. Upon my decease, the voting rights will be held by the trustees of the foundation who will be selected from the foremost educators and public-spirited citizens in the country. My son and I will automatically be lifetime trustees of the Foundation."

A curious surprise came into Junior's face. "I do not—"

Loren held up a hand. "Let me finish before you say anything," he said pleasantly.

Junior nodded. He sat back in his chair, the surprise still etched on his face.

"I will still own personally forty-one percent of the stock," Loren continued. "Which will be disposed according to my will after my decease among members of my family, the foundation and certain other people and charitable projects as I may elect."

He picked up the glass of water and sipped from it. "Beginning with the next meeting of the board of directors I shall place a proposal before the board which will, in effect, pass the control of the company from one man, myself or my son, at the moment, into the hands of the five-man executive committee, presently headed by myself and upon my retirement by my son. The head of the committee will have no vote on policy unless there is a tie vote between its members, in which case he will have the right to cast the deciding vote."

He took another sip of the water. "Until my retirement I will remain as a director and chairman of the board of the company, while my son will continue as president and chief operating officer, bound to carry out the policies of the executive committee and the board of directors. Upon my retirement, my son will assume the chairman's duties in addition to carrying on with his own."

He fell silent for a moment, looking down at his hands. Then he looked up again. "There is more, gentlemen, much more to my proposal, but there is no point in my going into it at the present time. Other points cover such items as pension plans and profit-sharing for executives, special insurance and similar side benefits for the employees of the company. Before you leave, Miss Walker will give each of you a folder containing all the details of these proposals as well as those I have spoken about."

He rose to his feet. "I guess that about covers all I have to say at the moment. Thank you, gentlemen."

They rose with him. Quickly Melanie distributed the folders. Within a few minutes, all of them had gone except Junior. He sat in the chair looking at his father.

"May I have a word with you?" he asked.

Discreetly Melanie disappeared from the room.

"Come, have a drink," Loren said.

Junior followed him to the bar. Loren poured himself a Canadian; he looked at his son: "Still drinking cognac?"

"I'll take whiskey," Junior said.

Loren nodded. He poured a good shot into Junior's glass. "Ice?"

Junior nodded.

Loren walked behind the bar and took some ice from the bucket on the shelf. The ice tinkled in the glass he gave Junior. He stayed behind the bar and picked up his own drink. "Cheers," he said. He threw the whiskey down his throat and was reaching for the bottle while Junior was still sipping at his.

Silently he refilled his shot glass. This time he sipped at

it slowly while looking at his son. Junior's face was thin and pale and there were blue circles under his eyes from lack of sleep. He waited for his son to speak.

After a moment, Junior reached into his pocket, took out an envelope and placed it on the bar, without speaking.

Loren looked at it. "What's that?"

"Open it and see," Junior said. "The envelope's not sealed."

Quickly Loren took the paper from the envelope. It was neatly typed on Junior's personal stationery.

To the Chairman of the Board
       and
the Board of Directors of
Bethlehem Motors Company, Inc.
Gentlemen:
   I hereby tender my resignation as president and chief operating officer of Bethlehem Motors Company, Inc. I also tender my resignation as a member of the board of directors of that company as well as officer and/or director of any of its subsidiary companies. All such resignations to be effective immediately.

                           Very truly yours,
                           Loren Hardeman II

Loren looked at his son. "What do you want to do a thing like that for?"

"You know, Father, when you called this meeting tonight," Junior replied, "I thought it was for the purpose of firing me."

Loren looked at him steadily. "What made you think that?"

"Two things," Junior answered. "One, you got your stock back and, with it, complete control of the company. Two, I deserved it. I gave you enough reasons. I wouldn't have blamed you if you did."

"It makes sense except for one thing," Loren said slowly. "You tell me. It seems easy enough for a man to fire an employee, but how does a man go about firing his son from being his son?"

Junior looked at him steadily. "I made war on you where no war existed."

"We did enough damage to each other," Loren said quietly. He began to tear the letter in half. "Long ago when I said all this would someday be yours, I meant it. I haven't changed my mind. You're still my son." He placed the torn halves of the letter back in the envelope and gave it to Junior.

Junior took the envelope, looked at it silently for a moment, then put it in his jacket. He looked up at Loren. He blinked back his tears. "Thank you, Father," he said huskily.

Loren nodded. He didn't speak, for he didn't trust his own voice.

"I'll try not to let you down again," Junior said. "I'll do the best I can."

"That's all anyone can do," Loren said.

They were silent for a moment, then Loren came around the bar and embraced him. They were very still, then Loren stepped back. "You go on home and get some sleep, son. You look like you can use it."

Junior nodded and started for the door. He turned and looked back. "It will be just like old times, won't it, Father?"

Loren smiled. "Just like old times."

Junior returned his smile. "Good night, Father."

"Good night, son." Loren waited until the door closed before he turned back to the bar and poured himself another drink.

Melanie came into the room. "Let me do that for you," she said, taking the glass from his hand. She went behind the bar and put ice cubes in his glass and then gave it back to him. "Everything all right?"

He nodded wearily, tasting his drink. He looked at her. "It's been a long day."

"I'll go upstairs and draw you a hot bath," she said. "It will make you feel better."

She came around the bar and started for the door.

"And don't you go putting all those damn perfumes in

it," he called after her. "You make me smell like a French whore."

She smiled back at him from the doorway. "Stop complaining," she said. "You know you love it."

He came out of the bathroom, the towel wrapped around his middle, his hairy chest and shoulders shining blackly in contrast with the white towel.

"I'm relaxed."

"Do what I tell you," she said. "I know how hard you worked today."

Obediently he crossed to the bed and stretched out on his stomach. Her fingers were strong as they dug into his neck, bit by bit they moved over his shoulders and down onto his back. Slowly the muscles loosened under her hands.

"How does that feel?" she asked.

"Fine," he said. He rolled over on his side. "But I'm getting a hard-on."

"I know," she said, looking at him. "You always do."

"What are you going to do about that?" he laughed.

"It's a muscle just like any other," she grinned mischievously. "It can be handled." She took his penis in her hands and slowly pulled the foreskin down, revealing the reddish purple swollen head. At her touch, his erection came to full stand. Holding his phallus in one hand, she gently stroked his testicles with the other, then slowly began to move her hand up and down.

"You have a beautiful cock," she said, fascinated by the giant strength of him. She bent toward him, her tongue delicately licking him. She pushed his phallus back against his stomach and took one of his testicles in her mouth, then the other. Finally she let her open mouth travel up the length of his penis until she covered its head with her lips.

He sank his fingers into her hair and turned her face up to him. "I want to fuck," he said.

"Yes, yes." She got to her feet and began to undress. Her breasts tumbled free from her brassiere and she pulled off her girdle, revealing her lush, full hips and the heavy black triangle beneath her belly.

He pulled her down on the bed and began to roll over on her.

"No," she said quickly. "You relax. Let me do it for you."

He fell back and she got to her knees over him. Holding his penis in one hand, her other hand balancing herself against his chest, she lowered herself onto him slowly, guiding him into her.

Impatiently he grabbed her buttocks and pulled her toward him. The air spilled from her lungs in a gasp. "Christ! You fill me up!"

Slowly at first, then more rapidly, she began to grind herself against him. His hands reached up and he squeezed her breasts and pulled them toward his face. He took her nipples in his mouth and sucked until they were bright red and swollen.

She pulled back from him and reached down behind her back until she found his testicles with her hand. They were hard and tightly knotted at the base of his shaft. She felt her orgasms approaching and began to shudder as they wracked her body. She felt his testicles swell in her fingers and begin their discharge. A fiery liquid heat began to sear her loins.

"Loren! Loren!" she cried, falling against him in the throes of their mutual orgasm. She clung to him until she stopped the aching shudder and she felt the wet of him flooding back out of her down the sides of her legs onto him.

Slowly she felt him relax inside her, then she rolled off him suddenly. Holding her cupped hand over herself so that she would not spill on the rug, she started for the bathroom. "You wait there," she said. "I'll come back and wash you off. I want you to rest."

"Bring some aspirin with you. My head feels like it's in a vise."

"Okay," she said.

A few minutes later, when she came out, he seemed to be sleeping peacefully, his face turned away from her on the pillow. Silently she knelt on the floor beside the bed and washed him with the warm washcloth, then gently patted him dry.

His hand moved toward her as she started to get to her feet. "You sleep," she said softly. "You need it." She walked back to the chair and picked up her brassiere.

"Melanie!" His voice was hoarse and strange.

"Try to sleep, Loren," she said gently, fastening the brassiere and picking up her girdle.

"No, Melanie!"

Something in his voice made her look at him as she was poised, one foot through her girdle. He was turning toward her. But there was something wrong in the way he was moving. It was almost as if she were watching a slow motion film and everything he was doing took just too much effort.

Finally, he made it almost to a sitting-up position in the bed, his wide, agonized eyes staring at her. The words seemed to come thickly from his lips. "Melanie! I'm sick. Call the doctor!"

Then slowly, as if the words had taken all the strength he had, he began to tumble forward. She leaped to catch him, but his weight proved too much for her and he slipped from her arms and rolled heavily to the floor.

"Loren!" she screamed.

The Detroit evening papers the next day carried banner headlines and pictures of what came to be known as the Battle of River Rouge. Bennett's flying squad descended upon the unsuspecting union organizers in force. Frankensteen and Walter Reuther were in the hospital, the latter with a back broken in three places after being dragged down a flight of thirty-six steps. Several others were also hospitalized, among them a pregnant woman who had been kicked in the stomach. But perhaps what incensed the press even more was that after Bennett's boys had finished with the union people they turned on the reporters and photographers, working them over and breaking cameras. It was reported by them as one of the most disgraceful episodes in the history of American labor relations.

Because of the tremendous news impact of the River

Rouge story across the nation, the story about Loren Hardeman was relegated to the inside pages. There was a small headline in column four of page two of *The New York Times* of May 27th, 1937.

LOREN HARDEMAN ILL

Detroit, May 26—Loren Hardeman I, chairman of the board and founder of Bethlehem Motors, is resting comfortably in a Detroit hospital, doctors report, after an operation for the removal of a benign brain tumor which had been troubling Mr. Hardeman for some years.

═══════════════════════════════ **Chapter Fourteen**

JOHN BANCROFT, vice-president of sales, Bethlehem Motors, swiveled around in his chair as Angelo came into his office. He rose, the salesman's smile broad on his face, his hand outstretched. "Angelo! It's good to see you."

His grip was a salesman's grip. Firm, hearty, impersonally friendly. Angelo returned his smile. "Good to see you, John."

"Sit down," Bancroft said, returning to his seat behind his desk.

Angelo sat down silently and lit a cigarette. He came right to the point. "I got your message. I'm here."

Bancroft looked uncomfortable. "I'm glad you came. We have problems."

"I know that," Angelo said. "What's so special about yours?"

"I'm starting to lose dealers."

"Why?" The surprise was evident in Angelo's voice. "I thought we had more requests for new dealerships than we ever had before."

"We have," Bancroft admitted. "But they're all fringe dealerships. Used-car men trying to upgrade, foreign-car dealers who are not making out too well with their own lines trying to get in on something new. The big problem is that ninety percent of them haven't enough money to back up their sales with an adequate service department. The other ten percent check out all right, but most of those are in areas where we are already well represented."

"That still doesn't add up to losing dealers," Angelo said.

A worried look knitted the salesman's brow. "In the last two months I've been getting letters from our established dealers. Some of them with us ever since the company started. They're beginning to worry about discontinuing the Sundancer. They're afraid the Betsy won't hold their place in the market for them. I've got almost four hundred letters like that." He paused for a deep breath. "But what's even worse, we've gotten cancellation notices from about ninety dealers. Chrysler, Dodge and Plymouth got about half of them, Pontiac and Buick about thirty, American Motors about ten, Mercury four, and Olds one." Despite the air-conditioning, he mopped his brow. "They were all good producers. God only knows if the new ones can match them."

Angelo dragged on the cigarette. After a moment, he spoke. "I don't get it. The Mazda Rotary with the Wankel engine has dealers begging for it from coast to coast and we have trouble. What is it?"

"Most of them are probably the same fringe dealers who are coming to us. They'll take a shot at anything new. Besides Mazda is trying to crack the American market. They're supplying financing for the service departments." He looked across the desk at Angelo. "If we had to do that we'd need another fifty million dollars to spread across the country. That's why Mazda is concentrating only in California and Florida. If they can take off in those markets and build up a demand, they hope they won't have to finance the rest of the country."

Angelo nodded. "And we're locked in. We've got to go

across the country in one shot because we're already there."

"Now you're getting it," Bancroft said.

Angelo put out his cigarette. "What do we do?"

"I can give you my answer from a sales point of view. I can't answer for your production problems."

"Go ahead," said Angelo.

Bancroft's voice was deliberate. "One, don't discontinue the Sundancer. That will keep the dealers from worrying too much. Two, follow the Japanese plan for infiltrating the market by concentrating on limited testing areas and building up demand. If it takes off, we can expand slowly and in two or three years, when we're in solid, drop the Sundancer."

"And if we drop the Sundancer now?"

"My best guess is that we'll lose a net of six hundred more dealers after picking up the new ones."

Angelo got out of his chair and walked thoughtfully to the window. "I need the Sundancer plant to build the Betsy engines."

"I know that," Bancroft said. "But with only about seven hundred dealers left throughout the country we're out of business even before the car is on the market."

Angelo knew what he meant. They had averaged out the dealerships at four new cars a week, counting on at least fifteen hundred dealerships. That was six thousand cars a week, three hundred thousand a year. They broke even at two hundred and twenty thousand units. Seven hundred dealers would only add up to one hundred and forty thousand units and that would be disaster. A one-hundred-and-sixty-million-dollar loss the first year.

He walked back to Bancroft's desk. "Who else have you told about this?"

Bancroft returned his gaze steadily. "Nobody. I just put the figures together and you're the first one I've talked to about it. But Loren Three returns from his honeymoon tomorrow and I have to alert him before the board meeting on Friday."

Angelo nodded. The Friday board meeting was for the

express purpose of reaching a decision about the Sundancer. "I appreciate your telling me, John."

The salesman smiled. "Look, Angelo, you know I believe in the Betsy as much as you do. But I can't make the arithmetic work."

"I understand," Angelo said. "Let me give it some thought. Thank you, John."

He was halfway down the corridor to his own office when the thought struck him. He turned and went back to the sales manager.

Bancroft was on the telephone. He looked up in surprise at Angelo's return. He finished his call and put down the phone.

Angelo said, "Doesn't it seem strange to you that suddenly, in the last two months, you begin to get dealer letters all bearing the same message?"

"I don't know," Bancroft answered. "I never really thought about it. We usually go through something like this at the end of every car year."

"As many letters?"

Bancroft shook his head. "No. Normally we get like twenty to forty or fifty. Usually from dealers who blew their quotas and are looking to squeeze us. All companies go through the same thing."

"Have you read all the letters?"

Bancroft shook his head. "I have to. That's my job."

"Is there any one particular item or thought that seems to be almost the same language common to the letters?"

Bancroft looked thoughtful for a moment. He pressed the intercom on his telephone. "Bring in the file on the last batch of dealer letters."

A moment later his secretary came in with several folders in her hand. She placed them on his desk and left the office. John opened the folders and began glancing through them.

Angelo waited silently as the sales manager skimmed through letter after letter. Almost ten minutes passed before Bancroft looked up, a strange look on his face. He looked down at the letters again, this time picking up a pencil and circling lines in several of the letters in red. A moment later he handed some of them to Angelo. "Just read those lines."

The language was different in each of the letters but the thought was basically the same. They were all concerned that the turbine engine could prove dangerous and might explode at high speeds.

John was still marking letters when Angelo spoke. "It's beginning to make sense."

Bancroft put down his pencil and looked up at him. "What do you mean?"

"Did you ever hear of an outfit called the Independent Automobile Safety Organization?"

"Yeah. It's run by a slimy bastard by the name of Mark Simpson. I threw him out of my office a half a dozen times but he keeps coming back every year."

"What's he looking for?"

"Basically it's a shakedown, I guess." Bancroft reached for a cigarette and lit it. He pushed the pack toward Angelo. "But he's clever about it. He runs this rag which is sent out to a national mailing list; it gives a phony evaluation of cars and makes a great point of its honesty because it doesn't accept advertising."

"What does he do?"

"I'm not quite clear," Bancroft said. "I never got that far into it with him. As near as I can make out, however, he either owns or has interests in some used-car lots across the country. You know the kind. Dealer dumps. Really new cars but with fifty to a hundred miles on them to qualify as used. He intimated that if a hundred Sundancers were made available to him, the car would get a good rating. That's when I threw him out of the office."

"Do you know if any of the companies do business with him?"

"None of them. They don't like him any better than we do."

"Then how does he stay in business?"

"Dealer pressure on the local level," Bancroft answered. "Dealers are always running scared. They figure giving him a few cars won't hurt and besides it helps them make their quota."

"I have a feeling he's the man behind this," said Angelo. "We found out he was the man behind our trouble out West."

"That doesn't make sense," Bancroft said. "Simpson doesn't do anything unless there's something in it for him. What the hell can he gain by keeping the Betsy off the market?"

"That's what I'd like to find out," Angelo answered. "The kind of campaign he's running has got to cost a lot of money. From the looks of it he's getting all around the country."

"Where do you think he's getting it?" Bancroft asked. "He's not the kind of man who puts out on spec."

Angelo looked at him. "I don't know. But whoever he's getting it from doesn't want us to get the Betsy on the road."

"It's not the other companies," Bancroft said. "I know that. They're happy to let us do the pioneering. Do you think it might be the gasoline outfits?"

Angelo shook his head. "No. We've already got arrangements made with all the national gasoline chains. They've agreed to have kerosene pumps at all their stations when we come out on the market."

They both fell silent. Angelo walked to the window. A freight train was pulling from the yards, filled with automobiles, their colors shining brightly in the sun. He watched the train move slowly out of the yard and then went back to Bancroft's desk.

"You get on the phone and talk to every one of those dealers," he said. "Find out if Simpson or anyone connected with him actually spoke to them."

"What good will that do?"

"There has to be something illegal about what he's doing and maybe we can prove it. Slander, libel. I don't know. I'm going to turn that over to the lawyers and let them figure it out." He took a cigarette from the package on Bancroft's desk. "Meanwhile you reassure them that there's absolutely nothing wrong with the car. Tell them about our tests."

"They'll think I'm bullshitting them," John said. "Simpson's line seems to back up the trouble we had when Peerless killed himself; and they read all about that in the papers."

"Then you invite every one of them to come out to our testing grounds at our expense and actually see how the car performs," said Angelo. "That ought to convince them."

"I don't know whether it will convince them," Bancroft said. "But they sure as hell will come. I've never known a dealer yet who turned down an all-expense-paid trip to anywhere, even if it was only across town."

Angelo laughed. "I'll leave that to you. Meanwhile I'll see what I can learn on my end. We're not dead yet."

"I'm beginning to feel better," Bancroft said. "At least we're doing something instead of just being sitting ducks." He rose to his feet. "We still can't afford to ignore any of this."

"I don't intend to," Angelo said. He looked at the sales manager. "I didn't take on this job to destroy this company and I intend to do what's best for it, whether or not it fits into my personal preferences."

Chapter Fifteen

PRINCE IGOR ALEKHINE awoke with the sunlight flooding into the windows of his room overlooking the blue waters of the Mediterranean. He leaped from his bed, smiling, went over to the windows, throwing them wide, and breathed deeply of the sweet morning air. He tugged at the pull cord for the butler to bring his coffee and began to do his morning sit-ups.

Religiously, in front of the window, every morning. Inhale, two, three, four. Exhale, two, three, four. Each time swinging his arms wide. Twenty times. Then the push-ups. Up, two, three, four. Down, two, three, four. Also twenty times.

By then the butler appeared with the coffee and the morning newspapers. The local *Nice Matin* and the *Paris Herald Tribune*. The butler placed the tray on the small table near the window. "Will there be anything else this morning, sir?" he asked as he had a thousand times before.

"Twenty." Igor looked up. He got to his feet, breathing slightly from the exertion. He looked down at his stomach. Flat and hard. Not bad for a man of fifty. He smiled at the butler. "I don't think so, James."

It didn't matter that the butler's name was François. Once they were employed by the prince, they all became James. "Thank you, sir," he said, his face expressionless. He turned to go.

Igor called him back. "Is the princess awake yet?"

"I don't think so, master," the butler answered. "We haven't received her signal in the kitchen as yet."

"Let me know as soon as you hear from her," he said.

"Yes, master." The butler left the room.

Igor walked to the table, and still standing, poured a cup of coffee. He raised the coffee to his lips at the same time flipping open the *Herald Tribune* to the stock market report. His experienced eye glanced down the columns quickly. Automotives, steady. Metals, steady. AT&T, Eastman Kodak, relatively unchanged. Dow Jones Index up, .09. He put the paper back on the table and took his coffee cup to the window and looked out. All was well with the world.

A yacht was heading toward Monte Carlo, the white sails billowing in the wind as it skimmed the calm blue waters. Another power yacht was going by, heading for its berth in Beaulieu sur Mer. It looked like a good day to be out on the water. He would ask Anne when she awakened whether she would like to have lunch aboard the yacht. Until then, he might as well have a swim and work on his tan. She rarely awoke before eleven thirty.

He took the elevator all the way down to the private beach. He came out of the building, his eyes blinking in the sun. He looked back up at the villa.

It loomed five stories tall. It was built of native Pyraneean stone in a group of turretlike buildings into the side of the cliff that descended from the Bas Corniche to the water's edge. Inside the house, the rooms were on different levels, each turret connected to the other by an interior archway. It was a crazy house but he loved it. It was the nearest thing to a castle that he could build on this property.

He walked out on the edge of the small dock and knifed his way into the water. The cold caught his breath deep inside him. He came up sputtering. Damn, it was June and the water was still freezing. He began to swim vigorously and by the time he was back on the dock twenty minutes later, he felt warm and glowing.

He climbed the short stairway to the pool terrace and took a towel from the cabana. Rubbing himself vigorously, he went behind the bar and pressed the intercom switch to the kitchen.

"Yes, master?" The butler's voice echoed hollowly from the box.

"Bring some coffee to the pool, James," he ordered. He flipped off the switch and came out from behind the bar. He went around the side of the small building to the pool. It wasn't until then that he saw her.

A broad smile came to his lips. He liked his niece. "Good morning, Betsy," he said heartily. "You're up early."

Betsy sat up on the *matelas,* her hands holding the straps of her brassiere to her breasts. "Good morning, Uncle Igor," she said.

He laughed. "For all the cover you get from that bikini, you don't have to be so nervous."

She didn't smile, instead fastening the strap.

He turned and looked out at the water. "Another beautiful day on the Riviera." He waved his arms. He turned back to her. "It's hard to believe sometimes with all the trouble there is in the world that here the sun is shining."

She was silent.

He looked at her. It was not like her to be so quiet. "Are you all right?" he asked. Then he remembered. "Weren't you supposed to go sailing this morning?"

"I didn't feel like it," she said shortly.

"Why not?"

She looked at him, her eyes squinting in the sun. "Because I was sick and nauseous all morning."

"You better let me call Dr. Guillemin," he said with quick concern. "I thought that bouillabaisse was a little too spicy last night."

"It's not the bouillabaisse."

"What is it then?" He was puzzled.

"I think I'm pregnant," she said in a matter-of-fact voice.

He stared at her, his dismay showing on his tanned, open face. "How could that be?"

She laughed. "Uncle Igor, for a man who used to be one of the top playboys in the world, you're remarkably naïve. It's really very simple. I brought everything to the Riviera with me except my B.C. pills. I forgot them."

"France is a civilized country," he said stiffly. "You could have gotten them here."

"I didn't," she said. "So forget it."

"Are you sure you're pregnant?"

"I missed two periods," she said plainly. "And I never did that before."

"We better make sure," he said. "I will arrange an appointment with Pierre Guillemin in Cannes this afternoon."

"Don't bother," she said. "I'm leaving for the States this afternoon. Abortions are legal in New York and Max has made all the arrangements. He says I will have the best doctors."

"Max van Ludwige?" he asked in an incredulous voice. "Was it him? But he is supposed to be so happily married. He has a daughter almost your age."

"He is happily married," she said. "But sometimes things like this happen. We were alone on the boat three days while we were sailing to pick up his family."

"What happens if the doctors think it's too late to have an abortion?"

"Then Max will get a divorce and marry me," she said. "After I have the baby, I will give him a divorce and he will remarry his wife."

"You sound very sure of yourself."

"I am sure," she said calmly. "The three of us have it all worked out."

"Three of you?" His voice rose. "Who else is in on this?"

"Rita," she said. Rita was Max's wife. "The only sensible thing to do was tell her about it. Neither of us wanted to hurt her. She was very nice. She understands it was nothing but an accident. That Max really and truly loves her."

The butler appeared with the tray and silver coffee service. "Where will you take your coffee, sir?"

Igor stared at him speechlessly. He pointed to a small table nearby. The butler placed the tray down carefully. Igor finally found his voice. "Get me a cognac, James," he said, and then, as the butler turned away, "better make it a large one!"

Loren III looked at the tall, good-looking Dutchman. Max van Ludwige seemed to be about his own age, but his blond hair and the blue eyes in the deeply tanned face made him look much younger.

"These things are always embarrassing," the Dutchman said in his precise English. "One never knows quite what to say."

"I don't know," Loren said stiffly. "I've never been in a situation like this before."

"We both regret it very much," Van Ludwige said.

Loren was silent. "Where's Betsy now?"

"She'll be down in a moment," Max said. He looked up as the butler came into the living room of the Sutton Place brownstone that his family had owned in New York for many years. "What would you like to drink?" he asked politely.

"Scotch and water," Loren said automatically.

"I'll have a dry martini, straight up," Bobbie said.

Van Ludwige looked at the butler. "My usual Scotch."

The butler nodded and left the room. An awkward silence fell over them. Van Ludwige tried to break it. He looked at Bobbie. "How long is it since I've seen you, Bobbie? Was it at Le Mans in '67?"

She nodded. "I think so. You had two Porsches entered if I remember correctly."

"That's right," he laughed. "But I had bad luck. Neither of them finished." The butler returned with the drinks. After he had gone, Max held his drink in his hand. "I was sorry to hear about Lord Ayres but I am very glad that you are happy once again." He held up his drink. "I hope it is not too late to offer my congratulations?"

"Thank you," Bobbie said. She looked at Loren. "Today is our anniversary."

Loren was surprised. "It is?"

"We're married three months today," she said.

"Let's drink to that," Max said. "To many more happy anniversaries."

They sipped their drinks and the awkward silence returned. Again Max tried to make conversation. "There is a great deal of interest in Europe in your new car. It's a turbine engine, isn't it?"

"Yes," Loren answered.

"Do you expect to have it on the market for the coming year?"

"I don't know," Loren said. "We've been on our honeymoon the past two months. Actually I was supposed to be in Detroit yesterday for a board meeting this week to make some final decisions. But this came along and I put it off."

Max got to his feet as Betsy came through the door. She hesitated a moment, then came toward them. "Hello, Bobbie," she said.

Bobbie looked at her. There were circles of sleeplessness under the young girl's eyes. Impulsively she got to her feet and kissed Betsy's cheek. "Hello, Betsy."

Betsy smiled, a quick smile, then turned to her father who was standing, watching them. She didn't move. "Hello, Daddy."

He made an awkward gesture with his hand. Then she ran into his arms. Oh, Daddy, Daddy! I hope you're not angry with me!"

THE BETSY   281

He shook his head, kissing her. "I'm not angry with you, baby."

"I really made a mess of things, didn't I?"

"It will be all right," he said. "We'll get everything straightened out."

She took a deep breath, regaining her self-control. "At first I was angry with him. But now I'm glad that Uncle Igor telephoned you."

"He did right. He was concerned."

"I know," she said. She turned to Max. "See, I told you my father would understand."

The Dutchman bowed stiffly. "I am most happy for your sake."

Loren turned to face him. "Now that my daughter is here, I assume we can discuss the plans."

"Of course," Max said. He went to the door and closed it. "The servants have long ears."

Loren nodded. He sat down again, Betsy next to him on the large couch. Loren picked up his drink and looked at Max expectantly.

"I've made arrangements to fly to Nassau with Betsy next week. Preparations have been arranged for the granting of an immediate divorce and we will be married. It's as simple as that."

Loren turned to his daughter. "Is that what you want?"

Betsy looked at him, then at Max, then back to her father again. "No," she said in a firm voice.

For a moment there was a stunned silence, then they all began talking at once. "I thought—" Max said.

"What do you mean?" Loren asked.

Betsy glanced at Bobbie. A look of understanding flashed between them. She turned back to the men. "It's a farce," she said. "I don't see why we have to go through with it. Max doesn't want to marry me any more than I want to marry him. He's just being a gentleman. I don't see why we have to put Rita and him through all this just because I've been stupid enough to get pregnant."

"What do you want to do then?" Loren asked.

"What's wrong with just having the baby?"

Loren was suddenly angry. "I won't have any bastards in my family!"

Betsy stared at him. "Don't be so old-fashioned, Daddy. There are plenty of people who are having children who don't want to be married. But this is stupid. Getting married just to have the baby and then getting divorced. Why can't I just go away somewhere quietly and have the baby?"

"Because there have been enough rumors and gossip in the papers already about your being pregnant," Loren said. "There is no quiet place for you to hide."

"Then let the papers have it!" Betsy said. "I don't care."

"Betsy, listen to me," Max said.

She turned to him. "No. I'm not going to put you through all that hassle."

"Betsy, I want to marry you!" Max said.

Betsy stared at him. "What for? You're not in love with me."

"Betsy, suppose you have a son?" Max said.

"Suppose I do?" she retorted.

"Don't you see what that would mean to my family?" he asked. "I have three daughters and no son to carry on the name. My father would be in seventh heaven."

"That's a great reason," Betsy said sarcastically. "And in case I have a girl or a miscarriage, I suppose I'll get a second chance."

"Betsy, you're being foolish!" Max said.

"No, she's not being foolish," Bobbie said suddenly. They all looked at her in surprise. She ignored the men and addressed herself to Betsy. "You're right, and ordinarily I would agree with you and even help you do what you want. But this time you're not being fair."

"I am being fair," Betsy said heatedly. "To Max and Rita. To myself."

"But not to your child," Bobbie said. "I don't have to tell you that Max is a fine man, you already know that. You owe it to your child to know his father. You also owe it to your child not to deny him his heritage."

Betsy was silent. After a moment, she spoke. "At least

you're honest," she said. "You put it exactly where it's at, don't you?"

"I try," Bobbie said. "You made a mistake."

Betsy suddenly understood that Bobbie had known all along why she had acted as she did. Angelo. To show him that she too could do as he did; she realized now she had been stupid.

"Don't make another mistake," Bobbie said quietly.

"Okay, I'll go through with it," Betsy said quickly. Then the tears came to her eyes.

Nothing ever worked out the way you wanted it.

═══════════════════════════ **Chapter Sixteen**

"WE'RE IN TROUBLE," Angelo said. "Big trouble."

"So what else is new?" Rourke asked.

Duncan smiled grimly. "I've spent forty-five years of my life in this business and I've always been in trouble."

"Not like this time," Angelo said seriously. He got to his feet and paced the long length of the living room. He stopped and looked out the windows of the Pontchartrain. Across the street the marquee of Cobo Hall advertised the coming events. The next big attraction was a convention of brassiere manufacturers. He half smiled to himself at the ridiculousness of it. Those men had to have a ball. All they had to think about was tits.

He came back to them. "I wouldn't have brought you both in from the Coast if I weren't concerned."

They nodded attentively without speaking.

"Last week Bancroft told me that we were losing dealers and that we stood a good chance of blowing the dealer network if we dropped the Sundancer." They started to break in but he held up a restraining hand. "We checked it out. It's our friend Simpson again and the IASO. There's been a whole campaign mounted against us, and right now they are so far in front of us, there's nothing we can do to catch up to them."

"What's that guy got against us?" Duncan asked "We've never done anything to him."

"I don't know," Angelo said. "But I'm trying to find out. His money has to come from somewhere. He hasn't the resources to pull off a thing as large as this on his own."

He was silent as he walked to the bar and refilled his drink. He looked at them. They nodded and he made fresh drinks for them. He brought the drinks over and dropped into a chair opposite.

"What's going to happen?" Tony asked.

"It's anybody's guess," Angelo replied. "My own feeling is that the board will cut back the Betsy program at next Friday's meeting and vote to keep the Sundancer."

"But I'm committed to seventy million dollars worth of materials," Rourke said.

"I know that." Angelo looked at him. "But a lot of that would be absorbed if they continue with the Sundancer. That's not the point, however. You have to measure the material loss against the loss of the entire company."

"You sound as if we're already dead," the Scotsman said dourly.

"Not yet," Angelo answered. "I have several ideas. But I don't know how practical they are."

"Try them on us," Rourke said.

Angelo looked at him. "What are the chances of building the Big Betsy engine in our Coast plant instead of the Betsy Minis?"

"No chance," Rourke said flatly. "It would take us another year to retool and even then we would only have the capacity for about fifty thousand units a year at the maximum."

"How many Minis were you planning on?"

"A hundred thousand."

Angelo thought carefully. The Betsy Mini was their answer to the sub-compacts. The Volks, Pinto, Vega, Gremlin. It was styled simply, much like the British minis, which were so successfully copied by the Japanese Honda, but it gave greater power and better performance and was priced competitively at $1,899.

"And how many Silver Sprites?"

"Seven to ten thousand," Rourke answered.

The Betsy Silver Sprite was the sports car of the line, much the same as the Corvette was to the Chevrolet. It was the only car of the line in which all the performance wraps were off. Everything about it was high performance. Axle, heavy-duty suspension, steering, reinforced chassis. The speedometer stopped at 220 miles per hour but in straightaway tests they had the car up to 270.

Angelo reached for a cigarette. "How soon can you get into production?"

Rourke and Duncan looked at each other. Duncan supplied the answer. "If we get the okay now, we could have cars coming off the line in November."

Angelo looked at him. This was the beginning of July. November was five months away. "No sooner?"

Duncan shook his head. "That's pushing it, laddie. We'll be lucky to make it."

Angelo was silent. That left the Betsy JetStar, the mainstay of the entire line. There were two basic models, the smaller of which corresponded to the Nova and Maverick, the other, slightly larger than the Chevelle and Torino, yet priced within the same range. It was for this car the Sundancer factory was needed. It was the only plant with the capability of turning out two hundred thousand units per year or better.

He put down his drink. "That leaves us with only one choice. To go abroad to build our engines."

"Number One isn't going to like it," Duncan said. "He wanted this to be an all-American car."

"He won't have any choice if he wants to get the car on the market," Angelo said. "Even he has to realize you can't market a volume car if your dealer network falls apart."

"It's late in the game to set up a plant somewhere else that would have the capacity we need," Rourke said.

"We have two shots," said Angelo. "Matsuoka in Japan and Waggoner Fabrik in West Germany. Both of them have the industrial capacity and both have expressed interest in licensing the engine from us for their own use."

"If we give them a license," Duncan said, "we're only building our own competition."

"If we're successful we won't be able to hold it back," Angelo said. "Look at what happened with the Wankel. GM here has the rights to it and Toyo Kogyo already has its version on the market." He stubbed his cigarette out in an ashtray and lit another. "It might even work out to our advantage. If they're eager enough we can set up joint venture companies with them."

Rourke nodded. "That could mean a lot of money for us."

"Forget the money part of it," Angelo said. "The important part of the deal is that they must guarantee to deliver a minimum of at least one hundred and fifty thousand engines to us in the next year."

"It's not going to be easy," Rourke said. "Those babies are sharp traders. They'll smell we're in trouble."

"It's up to you to convince them that we're not," Angelo said. He got to his feet. "Tony, you take Japan, Duncan, you have the Germans."

"Okay," Rourke said. "When do we leave?"

"Right now," Angelo answered.

Duncan got to his feet. "I'm getting too old to be running around like that," he grumbled.

Angelo grinned at him. "You know you love it. All those big blond frauleins."

"Laddie, at my age all I can do is look," the Scotsman said. "And if I haven't my glasses on, even that doesn't help much."

Angelo laughed. "You'll make out all right."

Duncan looked at him. "What about the Mini and the Silver Sprite? Do you want us to put them in the works?"

"Not yet," Angelo said. "That will have to hold until after the board meeting on Friday. The decision has to come from them."

The board room was filled with smoke and tension. John Bancroft had made his report simply and without dramatics. But the eventual result was clear to all of them. Without the full dealer network, the Betsy didn't stand a chance.

Angelo cut into the welter of futile conversation. "We'll deal with the problem of Simpson at a later date. That's not the issue before us at the moment. Our problem is how do we do both, get the Betsy on the market, and, at the same time, deliver the Sundancer to the dealers so that we keep them satisfied?"

Silence fell around the table as they turned to look at him. He continued. "We all recognize that if we do not have the Sundancer plant available to us, there's no way we can produce the Betsy JetStar in enough quantities to make the entire venture profitable as well as practical. However there are certain solutions available to us. They are being explored at this very moment.

"Tony Rourke is in Japan talking to the Matsuoka Hevay Industries and John Duncan is in West Germany speaking to Waggoner Fabrik about manufacturing JetStar engines for us. If a satisfactory agreement can be reached with them, it will be possible to produce the JetStar on the third and fourth assembly lines of the Sundancer plant. It would mean an additional investment to get these lines in operative condition again because they have not been in use for many years, but I think the investment will be reasonable in view of our over-all program."

He was silent for a moment, then while a murmur of approval rose around the table, he spoke again. "Of course, you realize, gentlemen, we have no choice, I think, but to delay and reevaluate the Betsy project."

"No, goddamn it!" Number One's fist slammed into the table. "I won't have any part of it! The Betsy is an American car and it will be built right here. All of it. I don't intend to go crawling to goddamn foreigners to help us do what we taught them!"

In contrast with Number One's vehemence, Loren III's voice was calm, almost cool. "You're being most unreasonable, Grandfather. I think Angelo has stated our position very clearly and fairly. We have no choice but to follow that path."

"No fucking foreigners will have anything to do with this car as long as I'm alive!" Number One snapped. "It's my company and my money and I will say what's going to be done with it!"

Loren stared at his grandfather steadily. "You can't do that any more," he said quietly, almost patiently. "The time when a company could be run at the whim of one man who could dictate its life-or-death policy is over. Men like you, Henry Ford and Walter Chrysler belong to another time. You cannot make decisions based solely on your own equity and selfish vanity. There are thirty thousand employees of this company, many of whom have devoted their lives to it, and you have no right to play Russian roulette with their welfare and their future. They have earned as much right to this company as you have and deserve to get every consideration that you expect. We have no choice but to continue with the Sundancer."

"Goddamn it! No!" Number One roared. He held his arms out in front of him. Quickly he undid the buttons of his jacket sleeves, revealing the shirt cuffs beneath. With a pull, he tore the cuff links from them and held them out toward them in his hand. They were gold and shining in his palm.

"Look at these cuff links!" he ordered in an angry voice. "They are models of the first Sundancer I ever built. That was fifty years ago. You talk of living in the past when all you want to do is cling to it!"

He snapped his arm violently, throwing the cuffs links away from him. The heavy links crashed into the casement windows. The fragile glass gave way with a tinkling sound and the cuff links disappeared outside.

He turned back to the silent room. His voice was calm and quiet now. "The Sundancer is dead, gentlemen. This meeting is over."

Silently they filed from the room until only Angelo, Loren III and Number One were left. After a moment, Loren III got to his feet.

He looked down at Number One. "You know I don't intend to let you get away with this. You can ride roughshod over all the others, but not me. I'm going to fight you on this with everything I have in me."

Number One smiled. "You do just that," he said in an almost pleasant voice. "But don't come cryin' to me when you get the shit kicked out of you."

"I don't intend to lose," Loren III said. Now he sounded exactly like his grandfather. "Someone has to care about the responsibilities this company has assumed toward its employees over the years. And there's one thing you seem to forget."

Number One didn't speak.

"Under the law, minority stockholders have some privileges. My sister and I own twenty percent of this company. And Anne has given me her proxy. Neither of us intends to allow you to destroy this company."

"And I own eighty percent," Number One said.

"No," Loren answered calmly. "You vote eighty percent. You own only forty-one percent. There's a big difference." He turned and walked from the room.

Number One watched the door close behind his grandson, then turned to Angelo. "The kid's developing some gumption," he said almost respectfully.

Angelo studied him silently for a moment before he spoke. "He's not entirely wrong. You're going into an S-curve at three hundred miles an hour."

Number One stared at him. "Who the hell's side are you on anyway?"

Angelo didn't answer. The telephone on the table in front of him began to ring. He picked it up.

"I have a call for you from the Bahamas, Mr. Perino," the operator said.

He was puzzled. "Who's calling me?"

There was a click on the line, a moment's silence, then the operator came back on. "Miss Elizabeth Hardeman."

He shot a look at Number One. "Put her on," he told the operator.

"Angelo?" Betsy's voice came on the line.

"Yes." There was a faint hum in the wires like the sound of the surf breaking behind her.

"Angelo." Her voice was strained and tense as if she had

been crying. "This is the last time I'm going to ask you. Will you marry me?"

He tried to make a joke of it. "When?"

"No funnies, Angelo," she said sharply. "I mean it. Right now. Right this minute. This is the last time."

He still tried to keep it light. "I told you, Miss Elizabeth. I'm not the marrying kind."

Abruptly the telephone went dead in his hand. Slowly he put it down. She sounded wild, almost as if she were stoned out of her mind. He looked across the table at Number One.

"That was Betsy," he said, in a wondering voice. "I thought she was in France. What the hell is she doing in the Bahamas?"

Number One shot a strange look at him. "Didn't you know?" he asked. "It was in all the papers."

"I haven't looked at a newspaper in weeks," Angelo said, still bewildered.

"Too bad," Number One said slowly, a note of sadness coming into his voice. "My great-granddaughter is getting married there tonight."

Number One rolled his chair to the door. He opened it and looked back at Angelo still sitting at the table. "I'll see you in the morning."

Angelo lit a cigarette as the door closed and sat there in the empty room. It wasn't until the cigarette almost burned to his fingertips that he dropped it into a tray and left.

He came out of the building into the red-gold rays of the sun setting through the Detroit smog. He looked up at the building behind him. The cracked windowpane of the board room looked down at him with its single eye.

Impulsively, he turned off the path onto the lawn beneath the window, his eyes searching the ground beneath him. He found the first cuff link almost immediately, directly under the window among some pieces of glass. The second took almost fifteen minutes to find. It was lying hidden beneath a privet hedge. He picked it up and stepped over back on the cement walk.

He looked down at the cuff links in his palm. The sun brought out every exquisite detail of the artist's design. The tiny rendition of the Sundancer was so real that it would take only a breath of imagination to give it life and have it go roaring into the evening.

His hand tightened so hard around the small gold cuff links that they were almost cutting into his palm. Slowly he walked down the path to his car.

Book Four
1972

THE WHITE January sun beat down on the salt flats, turning the miles in front of us into sparkling diamonds that would have blinded us if it weren't for the shadowed glass of our crash-helmet visors. The only sounds were the whine of the turbine, the shriek of the wind and the rumble of the giant oversize tires biting into the earth between us. I held the wheel steadily in my hand, aiming the car at the horizon where the white sand met the blue winter sky.

Cindy's voice came into my earphones as calm and as quiet as if we were cruising gently down some country lane. "Red line, sixty-eight thousand rpm; speed, three hundred eleven mph; turbine reactor temperature steady at twelve hundred degrees centigrade."

Radio-control broke in over her voice. Duncan's voice through the earphones had even more of a burr than usual. "Ye're red-lining at sixty-eight thousand, laddie."

"We already have it," I said.

"All systems read normal," he said. "Bring it up to seventy thousand and hold it there for one minute. I'll give you the time. Cindy, you set your clock to check me if radio is lost."

"Wilco," Cindy said. Her hand, holding the chronometer, came into view in front of me.

I opened the throttle. A fraction of a moment later, Duncan came back on. "Start minute. Red line seventy thousand."

Cindy's thumb pressed the button. I caught a brief glimpse of the sweep second hand beginning its trip around the clock. Then her hand disappeared as she drew it back. Her voice was matter of fact.

"Red line, seventy; speed, three twenty-five; temp, twelve hundred; time, fifteen seconds." There was a pause, then she began again. "Red line, seventy; speed, three forty-five; temp, twelve hundred; time, forty-five seconds." A moment later. "Sixty seconds."

Again radio overrode her. "Sixty seconds! Bring it down, laddie. Slowly now."

I was already easing off on the throttle. "Wilco," I said. It wasn't until we were down to under seventy miles an hour and coasting that I dared turn to look at her.

Despite the air-conditioned cockpit, her face was flushed and there was a fine patina of moisture over her upper lip. Her voice was breathless. "Do you know how fast we were going?"

I shook my head. "No."

"Three ninety-one," she said. "I came twice."

I grinned. "I would have come too but I was too busy."

Duncan's voice came dryly through the earphones. "Remember you're on radio. Stop talking dirty."

We laughed. Her hand found mine on the steering wheel. "Hey, baby," she said. "What a car!"

I looked at her. "Imagine what we could do with this at Indy if it were eligible?"

End of track came up about a mile in front of us. I touched the brake pedal. That was all I had to do. The electronic brake pumping system did all the rest.

By the time I got out of the shower and dressed, they were already rolling the Betsy Formula One prototype up the track into its air-conditioned van, ready for its trip back to our own testing grounds.

Duncan turned toward me as I came out of the building, his eyes squinting through the sunlight. "It was a good drive, laddie."

"Thank you," I said. "Everything go A-one right?"

"Perfectly," he said. "The director told me the helicopter shots should be clear as a bell and all the other cameras were working perfectly."

"Good," I said. "We were lucky with the weather."

He nodded. "Well, the TV-commercial people should have no complaints. We've given them everything they asked for."

I looked at him. "Was it any easier in the days before television?" I asked. "When all you had to do to introduce a new car was put it in the showrooms?"

He smiled. "At least we didn't have to waste all our time doing things like this. Imagine the nerve of that director? Saying he wanted more dramatics in my voice while I was talking to you on the radio."

I laughed. "No wonder I thought you were a little hammy."

Cindy came out of the building. She walked toward us, her hair loose and shining in the sun. "Number One's calling you from Palm Beach."

I went back into the building and picked up the telephone. "I was just going to call you," I said. "The Formula One did three ninety-one breezing."

"Who was driving?" His voice was irritated.

"I was."

He was silent. I could feel the explosion building. I held the phone away from my ear. "You stupid son-of-a-bitch!" he shouted. "Vice-presidents don't go around driving test cars. When are you going to give up playing with toys?"

"I'm entitled to a little fun out of the job," I said.

"Not with my money," he snapped. "Why in hell do you think I gave you options on two hundred thousand shares of my stock? Not in order for you to kill yourself and put us out of business."

I didn't answer. The only reason he gave me those options was because he didn't want to return the million dollars I advanced for the deposit on the Washington plant a few years ago.

"You keep out of those fucking cars, do you hear?"

"Yes, sir," I said. "But I have a feeling you'll be happy with the commercials. I'll arrange to have them flown down to you as soon as they're completed."

"I can wait until I see them on television," he said. "We have other problems."

That was the understatement of the year. So far. The year was practically brand new. "Which one are you talking about?"

"My grandson," he said shortly. "We finally heard from him."

"Oh?" Loren III had been peculiarly quiet the last few months. I was wondering when it would break.

"I don't want to talk about it on the phone," Number One said. "You get down here right away."

"But I'm due back in Detroit to give final approval on the new assembly lines."

"Leave that to Duncan," he snapped. "You get your ass down here!"

The phone blacked out in my hand and I put it down. Duncan and Cindy came into the room. "Number One happy with everything?" Duncan asked.

"Not everything. He wants me down there as soon as possible."

Duncan looked at me. "What's wrong?"

"I don't know," I answered. "He didn't want to talk on the phone."

The Scotsman was silent for a moment. "Do you think he found out?"

"Found out?" My head was some other place. "What?"

"The Sundancer project?"

"No, I don't think so," I said. "At least he didn't mention it. Something to do with Loren Three." I looked at Cindy. "Get on the phone and call the airlines. Get me on the quickest connection to Palm Beach." She nodded and went to the telephone as I turned back to Duncan. "You go into Detroit and okay the assembly lines for me. I want everything ready to start on the twentieth."

Cindy covered the phone with her hand. "You're too late for direct flights. The best connection leaves Salt Lake at six tonight; change planes at Chicago to Fort Lauderdale and drive up from there."

"Okay. Confirm it."

"No change in plans?" Duncan asked me. "Lines one and two, Sundancer standard, three and four, JetStar?"

"That's the way they go," I said. "You check with Tony and make sure he has everything ready out there. I want everything to go like clockwork."

"It will," the Scotsman said. "But——"

"But what?" I asked.

"Number One is not going to be happy when he finds out what you've done."

I looked at him. "By the time he presses the starting button, it will be too late for him to do anything about it."

It had all been worked out: 11 A.M. in Florida was 10 A.M. in Detroit and 8 A.M. in Washington. The gold telegraph key was already installed in the library of the Palm Beach house. The cameramen and photographers and news media were all alerted and ready to cover the ceremony. At exactly eleven o'clock, Number One would press the gold key on his desk, starting the assembly lines in Detroit and Washington at exactly the same moment. Fifty-five minutes later the first car should roll off each of the assembly lines and after that, a car every three minutes. On Lincoln's Birthday, less than one month later, every Bethlehem dealer in America would present the new cars.

Cindy put down the phone. "You're confirmed on the flights all the way through."

"Good," I said. "Thanks."

She looked at me. "What do you want me to do? Go back to the test track?"

I shook my head. "No. You go into Detroit. You'll be heading up the test group running checks on production-line cars."

"What about Stanforth?" she asked.

Stanforth was the chief test driver. "He'll stay on the Coast and run the group out there," I said.

"Do I get a raise?" she asked, with a smile.

"What does Stanforth get?"

"Thirty thousand," she said.

"That's what you get," I said.

"He's not going to like it. A woman getting the same salary as him."

"Tough shit," I grinned. "Didn't he ever hear of Women's Lib?"

She was fooling around with her stereo tape player when I came out of the bedroom. "I'm packed," I said.

She looked up at me. "Would you like a farewell fuck before you go to the airport? It'll help you sleep on the plane."

I laughed. "Since when are you worried about my sleeping on planes?"

"Listen to this," she said, turning the "play" switch on the machine.

The roaring sound of a whoosh of air mixed with the peculiar high whine of a turbine came from the far speaker and raced across the room toward me as it traveled through the different speakers. Suddenly her voice came from the center speakers. "Turbine reactor temperature eight hundred degrees centigrade."

Duncan's voice came thin and reedy from the far speakers. "Start on signal. Ten seconds . . . nine . . . eight."

She turned the player off. "How do you like that?"

I stared at her. She never ceased to amaze me. I would have sworn she didn't have the time. "How did you get it?"

She smiled a secret smile. "I had them make duplicates of the computer tape and the camera tapes. All I had to do was mix them."

I was silent.

"Well?" she asked.

I grinned. "Okay. Come back into the bedroom."

"No, there isn't time," she said. "If I have to set up in there, you'll miss your plane. Let's do it here on the floor."

She hit the switch again. The sound came on and she started across the floor toward me on her knees. The whine of the turbine and Duncan's voice came from the speakers.

" 'ven . . . six . . . five . . . four . . .' "

By the time he reached "One and start," she had my fly open and my cock in her mouth.

THE GIANT shepherd guard dogs knew me but not the car, so they followed the car suspiciously up the driveway until I got out, and then came running over, tails wagging and breaking themselves in half to be petted. I scratched their heads before they could knock me down. "Hello, Donner, hello, Blitzen."

The silent call from the sonic whistle pulled them away from me. Number One's man stood on the steps of the house. "Good morning, Mr. Perino."

"Good morning, Donald," I said.

"May I get the luggage from the car?"

"There isn't any," I said. "Just the small bag I have here."

He took it from me and I followed him into the house. "Is Mr. Hardeman awake yet?"

"He's in the breakfast room with Mr. Roberts," he answered.

I continued on through the foyer to the back of the house where the breakfast terrace looked out over the beach and the sea. Number One and Artie were seated at the table. They looked up as I came through the doors.

"Good morning, Number One," I said. "Good morning, Artie."

Artie rose and gave me his reassuring lawyer's handshake. The don't-worry-I'll-take-care-of-everything grip. "Good morning, Angelo."

Number One grumbled. "It took you long enough to get here."

"I was in Fort Lauderdale at one thirty this morning but somehow I had the idea you wouldn't like me to wake the house up." I pulled out a chair, sat down and poured myself a cup of coffee. "It's a lovely morning."

"You won't think it's so lovely after you read this,"

Number One said, throwing a copy of the morning *Miami Herald* over to me.

I picked it up. It was folded to page two. A small banner headline over two columns, circled in heavy red crayon, down in the corner of the page, caught my eye.

LOREN HARDEMAN I SUED FOR CONTROL OF FOUNDATION BY GRANDCHILDREN

Loren Hardeman III and his sister, the Princess Anne Elizabeth Alekhine, trustees of the Hardeman Foundation, petitioned the courts of Michigan to set aside and revoke the trust agreement by which the Foundation gave to their grandfather the voting rights to the stock in Bethlehem Motors Company for his lifetime. Arguing that such an agreement was illegal and invalid and contrary to the public interest which is the principal purpose of the Foundation, they further stated that such voting rights gave Mr. Hardeman control of Bethlehem Motors, which constitutes the only asset of the Foundation, and that his control thereof endangers these assets and as such, imperils the work, welfare and purpose of the Foundation. They were joined in their petition by the Attorney General of the State of Michigan as *amicus curiae* on behalf of the people of the State of Michigan, who further said that in his opinion the loss of and/or the devaluation of the assets of the Foundation would negatively affect those projects for the benefit of the people of the State of Michigan in which the Foundation and the State had joined together. Chief Justice Paul Gitlin took the matter under advisement and set the date of January 17th for a hearing; he gave the Foundation and Mr. Hardeman I until that date to reply to the charges.

I put the paper down and looked at Number One. "Now tell me what it means."

He stared balefully at me. "It means we're fucked!"

"I don't get it," I said. "I thought you told me there

were five trustees. That means there are two more besides
your grandchildren and yourself."

"So what?" he snapped. "I haven't been near them for
years. For that matter neither has Anne. But Loren has
always worked closely with the other two and he has them
in his hip pocket."

"Did you talk to them?" I asked.

"I can't get them on the phone," he said sarcastically.
"They've mysteriously disappeared. Loren's done his job
well."

I turned to Artie. "What are our chances?"

"Do you want a long legal opinion or do you want it
short and sweet?"

"Short and sweet," I said.

"We lose." He looked at me. "I can't say it any shorter
than that."

"Why?" I asked.

"It's a conditional gift. When Mr. Hardeman gave the
Foundation the stock, he either withheld or demanded the
voting rights to that stock as a condition of his giving it to
them. The court would have to rule that it was an in-
complete gift and, since the validity of the Foundation is
not at question here, order Mr. Hardeman to surrender
those voting rights to the Foundation."

"What if the validity of the Foundation is questioned?"
I asked.

"Then the stock would retroactively become once again
the property of Mr. Hardeman. And, of course, he would
then become liable for the income received by the Foundation due to dividends from the stock. A rough calculation
by me determined that approximately one hundred million
dollars was received in that manner since 1937 to date. As-
suming federal and state income taxes averaging sixty-five
percent, that gives us a tax liability to Mr. Hardeman personally of sixty-five million dollars together with interest
thereon at six percent from the year of earned income,
which can very well put his tax liability at over double the
base tax or one hundred thirty million dollars."

I turned back to Number One. "You're right. You are
fucked."

The old man nodded glumly. "That's what I said."

We were silent for a moment. I sipped the coffee. It didn't taste so good right now. Somehow the sparkle had gone out of the morning. I looked down at the newspaper. Something in the story caught my eye. I put my finger on the line and read it aloud.

"—such voting rights gave Mr. Hardeman control of Bethlehem Motors which constitutes the only asset of the Foundation, and that his control thereof endangers these assets." I looked up at Artie. "Don't they have to prove that in order to win?"

"Not really," he said. "Merely the showing of the fact that the entire capital of the company is risked to manufacture and sell a new car would be sufficient for the court. Generally, prudent business sense doesn't permit commitments like that. Part of the capital, yes. All of it, no."

"But if the car is a success, the company will make more money than it ever made in its history," I said.

Artie looked interested. "When will you know that?"

"Six months to a year after the car is on the market."

"Too late to do us any good." He shook his head. "I can't hold them off that long."

"If Loren gets control of the company, the Betsy is dead," I said. "And the company blows a hundred million dollars just like that."

"But they don't lose it all," Artie said. "That's less than half of what I understand you might lose if you can't sell at least two hundred thousand of the new cars."

"I'd feel more positive about selling enough Betsys if we weren't having all that trouble with the dealers," I said.

"That's it!" For the first time Number One's voice had an edge in it.

We stared at him.

"That prick Simpson," he said. "We all knew he didn't have the money to pull off a campaign like that on his own. Someone had to be backing him."

"We checked around," I said. "Nothing turned up."

"Who was doing the checking?" asked Number One.

"Dan Weyman, of course," I said. "That comes under his department."

"Dan Weyman." Number One's voice was sarcastic. "And you took his word for it?"

I didn't speak.

"Weyman is Loren's boy," Number One said.

"You're implying that your grandson is behind that campaign?" Artie asked incredulously. "I can't believe that. Why would he want to destroy the company of which he is president?"

"I'm not saying he is and I'm not saying he's not," Number One answered slyly. "But my grandson's getting more like me every day. And if I were him and I wanted to throw a scare into management, I would do a thing like that. The only thing wrong with it was that we didn't scare."

"If we tie Simpson in to Loren, will that help us in the court?" I asked Artie.

He thought for a moment. "I don't think so. I think that the court would remove Loren as a trustee for violation of his fiduciary responsibilities, but it won't alter their right to vote the stock."

"But if we catch Loren with his pants down, surely they'll switch their votes to Number One," I said.

"If we catch Loren," Number One said, "we won't need the Foundation's votes."

"You got me," I said puzzled.

"I have forty-one percent, right?" he asked.

"Forty," I said. "I just decided to exercise my warrants."

He grinned. "Why now?"

I grinned back at him. "I figured you might need another million in cash with all your problems."

He laughed. "Okay. Forty percent. You got one percent. My granddaughter Anne has ten percent. That's fifty-one percent. I don't need any more than that."

"But how do you know she'll go along with you?" I asked.

"I know my granddaughter," he said. "If she loses her faith in her brother, she'll turn to me. Her husband will see to that. He goes where the money is."

"Then we have only one problem left," I said. "That's to tie Simpson and Loren together."

"That's your problem," Number One said. "You do it and you only have eight days left to do it in."

"How the hell do I go about doing a thing like that?" I asked.

"I don't give a damn!" the old man snapped. "Do anything you have to. It was money that got to Simpson. Money will buy him back."

"What if that doesn't work?" I asked. "What if Loren is really clean?"

The old man stared balefully at me. "Frame him then! This is no child's game that we're playing!"

=== **Chapter Three**

THERE WAS a telephone message in my box at the Ponch when I returned to Detroit that evening. I read it in the elevator going up to my apartment.

PLEASE CALL MRS. HARDEMAN

There was a New York operator and telephone number. I looked at the time at the top of the message. 7:10 P.M. I checked my watch, wondering what Bobbie was doing in New York. It was close to nine o'clock.

The faint sound of the music from the cabaret on the floor above my apartment filtered down through the ceiling as I let myself in. I picked up the telephone at the far end of the living room and looked out the window down at Cobo Hall while I waited for my call to go through.

This week's convention was the morticians. That had to be a fun thing. The operator came back on. "I have Mrs. Hardeman on the line for you."

"Hello, Angelo?" It was not Bobbie's voice. It was Alicia.

I hid my surprise, "Hey there."

She laughed. "Hey there," she said. She hesitated a moment. "I suppose you're wondering why I called?"

"Yes," I said frankly.

"I know you're busy so I won't take up too much of your time."

"Don't go formal with me, Alicia," I said. "We've known each other too long for that."

She laughed again. This time her voice was relaxed. "Sorry," she said. "But since the divorce I'm never quite sure where I stand with people I knew when I was married."

"I knew you before you got married."

"Okay," she said. "I'll still keep it simple. As part of my divorce settlement I received half of Loren's stock in Bethlehem."

"I didn't know that."

"Very few people do," she said. "Loren didn't want to give it any publicity. That's why he has my voting proxy."

"I see." That meant that Loren owned only five percent of the company stock, not ten as we thought.

"I read in the papers about the lawsuit," she said. "I heard Loren and Dan Weyman talk about it many times but I never thought he would really do it." Then her voice went hard. "I don't want them to have control of the company."

"That makes two of us."

"I spoke to my attorney and had him draw a new proxy in favor of Grandfather," she said. "I want you to tell him that for me."

"Why don't you call him? I'm sure that he'll appreciate it."

"No," she said. "His secretary-housekeeper, Mrs. Craddock, reports back to Loren. I don't want him to know anything about it."

I was right and I was wrong. I had figured Number One's man to be the leak. "I'll make sure Number One hears about it."

"I'm sending the proxy to you at the hotel," she said. "Tell Grandfather to vote it any way he sees fit."

"I will," I said. I was curious. "You say Loren and Dan spoke about this many times?"

"Yes. It was nothing new. Every time Loren was angry at Grandfather it would come up. Especially after they learned about the Betsy."

I tried a wild shot. "Did you ever hear them talk about a man named Simpson?"

"Mark Simpson?"

"That's the man," I said.

"He's a friend of Dan Weyman's," she said. "Dan brought him over to the house to talk to Loren several times. They were working on something together. It had to do with automobile safety, I gathered."

Jackpot! I deliberately kept the excitement from my voice. "Would you do me a favor and write a note to me mentioning the times you recalled they met at your house?"

"Of course," she said. There was a curiosity in her voice. "Will that help?"

"It might," I answered cautiously. I looked down at the message slip in my hand. "If I have to reach you again, will you be at this number?"

"No," she answered. "I'm leaving tomorrow night for Gstaad."

"I didn't know you skied."

She laughed. "I'm not going there for the skiing. Betsy's due to have her baby any day now and I want to be with her."

"How is she?"

She laughed again. "She's very calm about the whole thing. Her husband, Max, is more excited about it than she is, but I still can't believe it. I'm going to be a grandmother."

"Grandmothers are getting younger every year. You can thank the younger generation for that. Give Betsy my best."

"I will," she said. "Good-bye, Angelo."

"Good-bye, Alicia." I put down the telephone and walked over to the bar. I broke out a tray of ice cubes, opened a new bottle of Crown Royal and made myself a stiff drink. I needed it.

Number One had been right in his thought that Weyman was covering up. But I wondered whether he really thought that Weyman and Loren were involved with Simpson. It just didn't make sense. Until now.

The music from the cabaret was growing louder. I was annoyed. I went back to the phone and called the assistant manager. "You have to do something about those amplifiers in the cabaret upstairs," I complained. "They're driving me out of my mind."

"You must be mistaken, Mr. Perino," the A.M. said smoothly. "The cabaret is closed tonight. Perhaps one of our guests has the radio on too loud. We'll check into it."

"Please do," I said shortly. I put down the phone and started for the bedroom, the music growing louder. I had enough troubles to manufacture my own headaches without outside help. I opened the bedroom door. The blast of music from the eight speakers almost knocked me down.

Cindy was sitting up in bed, her long hair falling across her naked shoulders and breasts to the sheet over her legs, stoned out of her mind on the sound. She turned to look at me, her head still nodding to the beat. A slow, happy smile came to her lips. "Welcome home, Angelo. Isn't it beautiful?"

"Turn it down!" I shouted above the noise. "What are you trying to do? Break my lease?"

She picked up a remote-control device and aimed it at the tape player across the room. The volume went down to a respectable level. "The latest thing," she said. "I couldn't resist it."

I stared at her. "How did you get in here?"

Her eyes went big and round. "Would you believe there wasn't a vacant hotel room in this whole town when I came in yesterday?"

"That's not answering my question."

She got to her knees on the edge of the bed. "Come over here," she said.

I walked over to her and she put her arms around my

neck and pulled herself up against me. Her lips were warm and soft.

I pulled my mouth away. "That's still not answering my question."

"It wasn't too difficult, darling," she said, her eyes smiling into mine. "I merely told them that I was installing the new sound system you had ordered."

"But that was yesterday," I said. "How come they let you stay all this while?"

"Everybody knows you can't do installations like this in one day," she said innocently. "Besides I was very quiet. Until just now when I heard you come in and go right to the telephone to call another woman." She stuck her hand under the pillow and came up with a telephone message which she thrust into my hand. "Especially her!"

I looked down at it. It was the door copy of the message I had picked up downstairs. When I looked up again, her face was so angry I had to laugh. "You're jealous," I said. "That's not like you. I thought you were too cool for that sort of thing."

"I'm not jealous!" she said heatedly. "But how would you like it if you spent two days in bed waiting for me to come home and when I did, I went right to the phone to call another guy?"

"But I didn't know you were waiting," I laughed.

"That doesn't matter!" she snapped. "I don't think that was very nice. You could have at least looked in the bedroom first!"

"It was business," I said.

"Oh, sure," she said sarcastically.

"It was," I said. "You got the wrong Mrs. Hardeman. This was the first one."

"My God!" she said in a shocked voice. "Don't tell me you've been there too?"

Duncan was waiting in my office when I got to the plant in the morning. Carradine of Engineering and Joe Huff of Design were with him.

I didn't need a second look to know they weren't there

to bring glad tidings. I walked around behind my desk. "Okay, gentlemen," I said. "Hit me with it."

"How do you want it, laddie?" Duncan asked. "One at a time or all at once?"

"One at a time," I said. "This is Monday morning and I'm not in very good shape."

"Okay," he said. "On Friday all work on the production line was stopped. Orders from the president."

"He can't do that. He hasn't the authority. Number One is still chairman of the board and chief operating officer."

"He did it," Duncan said flatly.

"Well go in there and start it again," I said.

"We can't," Duncan said. "We've been barred from the plant. We can't even get into our own offices. This is the only place we could come."

I was silent. Loren wasn't waiting. Maybe he was even a little ahead of himself. "That's one," I said. "What's next?"

"Union troubles," Duncan said. "The UAW said they won't let the assembly line start until all the reclassifications are agreed on. They claim too many jobs are being downgraded."

"I thought we approved a schedule that was satisfactory to them."

"You mean you approved it," Duncan said. "Weyman never passed it on."

Weyman again. He wasn't being very helpful. I was starting to really dislike him. "He's supposed to negotiate only on the basis we give him," I said. "He has no right to alter or withhold our proposals."

"He did," Duncan said. "Of course, he had direct orders from the president."

I looked at him. "Is that all?"

"No," he said. "Did you read *The Wall Street Journal* this morning?"

I shook my head.

"Here, read it," he said, giving me the newspaper.

It was a front-page story. Banner headline across the first two columns.

HUNDRED-FIFTY-MILLION-DOLLAR NEW CAR
OF BETHLEHEM MOTORS ALREADY A DISASTER?

I read on. The story was out of Detroit, dated Friday.

Special to The Wall Street Journal—Informed company sources inside Bethlethem Motors today indicated serious doubts over possible success of their new car, the Betsy, due to be introduced later this year. These doubts came to the surface with the filing of a lawsuit by Loren Hardeman III and his sister, Princess Alekhine, against their grandfather, Loren Hardeman I, and the Hardeman Foundation for what basically amounts to control of the giant motor company.

Company sources further revealed that Mr. Hardeman III began to feel concern over the mounting costs on the project together with progressive reports as to the safety of the car itself, and that he initiated this suit reluctantly after endeavoring to persuade his grandfather to abandon the project in the interest of the public.

There was more but I had read enough. I put the paper down. There was no doubt in my mind as to whom the "informed company sources" were. Weyman. As executive vice-president, he had a pipeline right into the paper. I had the feeling this was only the beginning, there would be more stories like it going to newspapers around the country. If they wanted to kill the Betsy before it reached the market, they couldn't find a better way. A few more stories like this and the public wouldn't buy the car if it were given to them on a silver platter.

"Wait here," I said. Then I went down the hall to Loren's office.

"MR. HARDEMAN's in a meeting," his secretary said holding up a restraining hand as I went to his door.

"Beautiful," I said, brushing past her.

Loren III was behind his desk, Weyman and a man I didn't know were sitting opposite him when I entered.

Loren was the only one who didn't seem surprised. "I've been expecting you," he said.

"I don't doubt that," I said.

The other man and Weyman got to their feet quickly. "We'll be in my office when you're free," Weyman said. They started out.

"You wait," I said to Weyman. "What I have to say concerns you too."

Weyman shot a questioning glance at Loren. Loren nodded and he sank back into his chair. "Wait in my office, Mark," he told the other man.

The man nodded and left. I didn't wait for the door to close behind him. "Is that Mark Simpson?" I asked.

Weyman hesitated. Again Loren nodded. "Yes," Weyman answered.

"I thought so," I said. "The scum's beginning to come to the surface."

They didn't answer.

"I'll get to him later," I said. I moved to the side of Loren's desk where I could look at both of them. "You saw the story in *The Wall Street Journal* this morning?"

"Yes," Loren answered.

"Don't you think you've overreached with that one?" I asked.

"No," he said. "I think it reflects the truth."

"As you see it," I said.

"As I see it," he echoed.

"Have you thought what might happen to the company if you should lose?"

"I won't lose," he said confidently.

"Even if you win," I said, "you lose. A few more stories like that and you'll control a bankrupt company. There won't be a single person left in the world who will buy any car that this company produces."

"What happens to this company won't be any of your concern," said Loren.

"That's where you're wrong," I said. "I am concerned. I happen to be the owner of two hundred thousand shares of stock in this company which I purchased from your grandfather for two million dollars cash."

For the first time surprise showed on Loren's face. "I don't believe it. Grandfather would never sell a share of his stock to an outsider."

"It's easy enough to check," I said. "Why not pick up the telephone and ask him?"

Loren didn't move.

"As a stockholder I have certain rights. If you read the bylaws of the company as carefully as I have you will know what I'm talking about. I have the right to ask indemnification and damages against any officer of the company who interferes with work currently in progress, if that interference leads to losses directly attributable to it."

Loren reached for the telephone. He spoke quickly to Jim Ellison, the company's general counsel. He put down the telephone and looked up at me. "You would have to prove it first," he said.

I smiled. "I'm no lawyer, but that should be a cinch. You halt production on the Betsy now and a hundred and fifty million dollars goes down the drain."

He was silent.

"I'll make it easy for you," I said. "I'll give you the time it takes for me to go from here back to my office. And when I get back there if I don't hear from you that work on the production line has started again and my boys can go about doing their normal jobs without interference, I'm going to hit you and your little prick friend here with a lawsuit requiring you both to come up with the biggest indemnification bond any of you ever heard of. One hundred and fifty million dollars worth."

I started from the office. Halfway to the door I turned back. I looked at Weyman. "And you have exactly one hour to be in my office with the UAW people to straighten out our contract."

I almost smiled at the expression on his face. His devotion to Ex-Lax was a running gag around the plant. He didn't look as if he would need any today.

I turned to Loren. "If I were you," I said almost mildly, "I would go about finding a way to deny or counteract that story in today's paper before it has a chance to catch up to you."

I went back to my office the long way round just in case they needed time to think about it. I passed Weyman's office. On an impulse I went in.

"Is Mr. Simpson here?" I asked the secretary.

"He's just left, Mr. Perino," she said brightly. "He told me to tell Mr. Weyman that he had an important appointment and that he would call him later in the day."

I nodded and went out. The man had all the good instincts of a jackal. He smelled trouble and he was going to be nowhere around when it was happening. I made up my mind to get to him later in the afternoon if things here were under control.

I leaned against the outside door to my office and smoked a whole cigarette before I went inside. I wasn't taking any chances. I wanted them to have all the time they needed.

My secretary looked up at me as I came in the door. "Mr. Perino."

I stopped at her desk. "Yes?"

"I just received a peculiar message for you from Mr. Hardeman's office," she said, a puzzled expression on her face. "I didn't understand it, but he said you would."

"Read it to me," I said.

She looked down at her shorthand notebook. "He said to tell you that everything was arranged the way you wanted it but that he, personally, would come down to say good-bye to you next week."

I smiled. I knew just what he meant. I went into my own office. "Okay, fellows, get back to work. We've already blown four days on this shit."

Duncan looked at me. "How did you get them to back down so quickly?"

I grinned. "I used my Italian charm. I threatened to sing 'O Sole Mio' for them."

We didn't finish the meeting with the UAW representatives until after nine o'clock that night and by then it was too late to go chasing after Simpson. There was a lot more to building a car than just getting it from the drawing board to the assembly line.

It was the first time I had ever been close at hand to a union negotiation and as far as I was concerned, I was willing for it to be the last. But, as little as I liked the son-of-a-bitch, I had to admit that Dan Weyman was good at it.

He was professional and precise. I hadn't realized up to now the number of different classifications that existed within the same assembly-line framework. He did. And knew the exact definition of work responsibilities for each class. Once he got down to it, I was fascinated at the efficiency and subtlety he brought to his work. I only wished that he were on our side, not Loren's, but that did not keep him from doing a good job for the company.

At one point when things got a little sticky, he dug right in and explained it to them in basic terms. "We'll give a little, but so will you have to bend a little." His voice was as calm as if he were lecturing a class at college, which I understand he had done before he went to Ford with the whiz kids. "We're all breaking our asses to keep the Japanese and Germans from walking away with our market. Not only in sales but in manufacturing. It would have been comparatively easy for Bethlehem management to decide to build this car abroad and it would have cost less. You know it and I know it. Last year our average hourly rate of pay was $6.66, substantially higher than

most other companies in the industry. And we lost twenty
million dollars on our automotive division. We had every
justification in the world to go abroad and build the new
car. But we didn't. Because we have a respect for and
obligation to our employees, and to do so would cause a
great deal of hardship among them. Now all we ask is
their cooperation. To increase their productivity together
with our own. You give a little, we give a little. Maybe
between us, we can bring some of the business back home
where it belongs."

I watched the faces of the union representatives while
he made his little speech. I couldn't read much in them,
but they, too, were professional and experienced in their
jobs. From that point on, it took hours. But eventually it
was all done.

After they had gone, I looked at Dan Weyman who was
gathering up his papers. "You did well," I said.

He didn't answer.

"You could have saved all of us a lot of trouble if you
had done it when you were asked in the first place," I
said.

He snapped his attaché case shut. He stared at me for
a moment as if he were about to say something, but then
he turned abruptly and walked out of the office without
speaking.

Cindy met me at the door of my apartment when I let
myself in after ten o'clock. She handed me a message slip.
"Try to tell me that this is business too," she said sarcastically.

I looked down at it. "Am in the piano bar downstairs.
Must see you right away." It was initialed B.H.

I looked up at Cindy. "It probably is."

"Sure," she said. "She called before the message came
up. I would recognize that British accent anywhere. But
she hung up before I could ask who is calling, then the
message came up."

"How long ago was that?" I asked.

"Maybe a half an hour ago."

I thought for a moment. The bar was no place to meet.

Bobbie had to be looking for trouble. "Go down there and tell her to come up," I said. "Then get lost for an hour."

"What do you expect me to do?" she asked.

"Go to a movie, sit in the bar. I don't know," I answered.

A bitchy smile came to her lips as she moved obediently to the door. "Can't I come back upstairs?" she asked. "I'll stay in the bedroom, out of the way. You won't even know I'm around."

"Uh-uh." I shook my head.

"At least then, let me set up a mike," she said. "Maybe that way I can learn something. I was always curious how the British ladies did it."

"I've had a rough day, Cindy," I said wearily. "Now do as I say or I'll belt yuh."

She looked at me for a moment. "Not now," she said. "When I come back." The door closed behind her.

Chapter Five

I HAD the martini, very dry and very cold, in a glass clouded with frost beads waiting on the bar for her when she came in. Silently I put it in her hand.

"You didn't forget, did you, Angelo?" she asked.

I raised my glass to her. "Angelos, like elephants, never forget."

We drank silently. She finished her drink in what seemed like one swallow. I remembered that too. I refilled her glass from the martini pitcher. I still didn't speak.

She crossed the room and looked out at the sparkling lights of Ontario. The blinking sign on the other side of the river went on-off: COME ON OVER!

She turned to me. "You have a good view from here at night."

"When it's clear," I said. "Not so good on smoggy days."

She sipped her drink and turned back to the window. "I'm leaving him," she said. "I made a mistake. I know it now."

I didn't say anything.

She turned to look at me. "Did you hear what I said?"

I nodded. "Yes."

"Don't you have any comment to make?" Her voice was brittle and thin.

"No."

"Nothing?" She laughed. "Not even, I told you so?"

"Nothing."

She turned away again and looked out the window. "The girl that came downstairs. Is she—?" She didn't finish the question.

"We're old friends," I said.

We were silent again. She emptied her glass and held it out to me. I refilled it and gave it back to her.

"Thank you," she said.

I nodded.

"Still don't talk very much, do you?"

"Only when I have something to say."

"Then say something," she said sharply.

I looked at her. "Why?"

She didn't look at me. "Because it's not the way I thought it would be. All he cares about is the company. That's all he lives for. That and the determination he has to avenge his father's death."

"Avenge his father's death?"

"Yes," she answered. "He's a man split in two between his respect for his grandfather because of the old man's accomplishments and his hatred of him for hounding his father to suicide."

"He blames Number One for that?"

She nodded. "He said the old man never got off his father's back, just as he won't get off his."

"I can't believe that."

She turned to me. "I didn't either. Until one night he showed me a letter which he keeps in the wall safe in the house. It was the first time he ever showed it to anyone. Even Alicia never saw it."

"What letter?"

"The letter his father left when he committed suicide," she answered.

"But there was no letter," I said. I remembered the newspaper stories. "The police never found one."

"Loren did," she said. "He was the one who discovered his father's body. He found the letter too. And hid it. Even then he was afraid that if the contents of the letter were revealed, the company would be finished."

"What did it say?"

"I only saw it once but I won't forget it," she said. "It was not addressed to anyone. It was just a note scrawled in his father's handwriting.

" 'I cannot go on any longer. He will not leave me alone. I do not have one day's peace and there is not a day that passes that he does not make impossible demands on me. I have tried for years to get him to leave me alone but now I see that he never will. And I no longer have the strength to fight him. This is the only way out. Believe me. Forgive me.'

"It was signed simply, 'L H II.' "

I didn't speak.

She looked at me. "Loren said it was exactly the way his grandfather treated him. But that he was stronger than his father. He could fight back and would."

I turned away silently to refill my own glass. I took a sip of my drink. "Why didn't he do something about it then?"

"The reason he gave me, and for one other," she said. "He was afraid that his grandfather would not make him president of the company if he did." She took a sip of her drink and held out her empty glass again.

I refilled it and gave it back to her.

"I'm getting smashed," she said. "I've probably been smashed since I came up here. I had two doubles while I was waiting downstairs."

She held her liquor well, her eyes were clear. "You look all right to me."

"I feel it," she said. "I know myself."

I didn't speak.

"You see, even way back then, all he cared about was the company. And nothing's changed. He really doesn't need a wife or even a woman. He doesn't need anyone."

"Then why did he marry you? He could have had you and kept Alicia. It would have saved him a fortune."

She laughed. "But he didn't know that, did he? You knew it and I knew it. But he didn't. I remember you once said he was square." She laughed again. "You don't know how square he really is."

I pulled at my drink silently.

"Do you know every time we make love he asks if I made it before he has his orgasm?" She giggled. "Sometimes I drive him crazy and say no just to make him wait. He goes out of his mind."

"I think you are smashed," I said.

"What's the matter, Angelo?" she asked. "Don't you like to hear me talk about my sex life?"

I looked at her. "If you want the truth, no."

"You're getting very proper, aren't you, Angelo? Like that time out at the test track in Washington and now you won't even talk about it."

I was silent.

"I remember the way it was in San Francisco between us. Do you remember, Angelo? It was beautiful."

"I remember." I also remembered the pain when she left me in the airport. Strange, but there was no hurt now.

She came close to me, so close I could taste the smell of her in my mouth. "It could be like that again."

"No."

She put her drink down and her arms around my neck. Her open mouth seized hungrily on mine, her tongue ravishing my mouth. Nothing.

I held her away from me, my hands gripping her arms. "No."

"Give it a chance, Angelo," she said, her eyes searching mine. "It could be like that again!"

"It won't be, Bobbie. Ever again."

"Why do you keep saying that, Angelo?" she cried. "I love you! I've always loved you!"

This time I brought her to me and kissed her. For a

long time, until her arms fell to her sides and she stepped back, looking up at me, a strangely lonely look in her eyes.

"You would only be making another mistake," I said. "Running from him to me isn't the answer."

Her voice was clear, she wasn't the least bit smashed. "How did you know?"

I took her hand. "I didn't hear the music," I said.

She was silent for a moment, looking down at our hands, then she drew her hand away. "Do you have another martini left in that pitcher?"

I refilled her glass. I watched her drink half of it before she stopped.

"I'll miss you. You do make a good martini."

"I'll give you the recipe," I said. "Straight gin. Lots of ice. No vermouth."

She smiled. "That's a dirty trick."

"It's also a great martini."

"My bags are downstairs. I'm going out to the airport. I'm not going back to him."

I didn't say anything.

"I can make a late plane to Chicago. And leave from there for London in the morning."

"Does he know you're gone?" I asked.

She shook her head. "I'll call him from the airport just before I get on the plane."

"Won't he miss you before then?"

She laughed. "He was locked up in a meeting with Dan, a fellow named Mark Simpson, and a few other gentlemen I never saw before when I left. Rough-looking characters they were too. Not the usual kind of men that have come to the house before. Chances are that he won't go up to bed until the wee small hours." A curious expression came into her eyes. "Now that I think about it, I remember they were talking about you when I passed the doorway."

"Really? Something good I hope?"

"Nothing good," she said seriously. "Apparently you did something today that's gotten Loren very incensed. Did you?"

"I might have," I admitted. "But I work for his grand-father and we don't exactly see eye to eye these days."

"I heard Loren's voice as I went down the hall," she said. " 'I'll play as tough and dirty as the old man anytime and Angelo might as well find that out right now,' he said."

"What else did he say?"

"I didn't hear anything else. By that time I was down the hall and out of earshot." Her eyes were troubled. "I don't like it."

"It's probably just some words out of context that sound much worse than they really are."

She finished her drink and gave it to me. I placed the empty glass on the bar. "You'll be careful?"

I nodded and we started for the door. "You have a coat?" I asked.

"I checked it downstairs."

I held the door open for her. She stepped through and turned to face me. I bent and kissed her cheek. "Good-bye, Bobbie. Good luck."

I could see the hint of tears in her eyes. "Apparently we're always saying good-bye, aren't we, Angelo?"

"Seems like it," I said.

She held back her tears. Her chin came up proudly. "Well, at least we don't have to go through that again, do we?"

"No."

She caught at my lapels and pulled me down to her. Her lips were gentle on mine. "Good-bye, Angelo. Don't think badly of me. Just remember that we did love each other. Once."

I looked into her eyes. The tears were there now. "I'll remember," I said gently.

Then she turned abruptly and walked to the elevator, her back straight and stiff. I stood there until the elevator doors closed behind her. She never looked back. Not even once.

WHEN I CAME OUT of the bathroom after my shower, the waiter had left the breakfast table rolled up against the bed and Cindy was sitting up, eating a Danish, getting crumbs all over the sheet, the stereo blasting.

"Oh, Jesus!" I said, tightening the towel around my waist and pouring myself a cup of coffee. "This early in the morning?"

"It's the Pocono Inaugural Five Hundred last July," she said. "I just got the tapes yesterday."

I swallowed some of the coffee. It was black and hot and tasteless, like all hotel coffee. "You couldn't wait?" I asked sarcastically.

She paid no attention to me, intently following the roar of the motors racing from speaker to speaker. "That's Mark Donohue," she said excitedly. "Hear that other car moving up on him?"

I lit a cigarette without answering. I listened. She was right. There were two roaring engines chasing from speaker to speaker. Now it seemed almost as if they were in the same speaker.

"That's Joe Leonard! Now he's passing him. He's passed him! Mark chickened on the oil slick on the second curve of lap two and Joe sneaked by him. Listen! That's A. J. and Mario right behind them!"

The telephone rang. I picked it up. "Hello," I shouted over the sound of the speakers.

"What's that damn noise?" Number One demanded. "Where the hell are you?"

"Cindy, turn that damn thing off!" I yelled. She picked up the remote. The tape whirred to a stop. I turned back to the phone. "That better?"

"Who is with you?" the old man asked.

"Cindy. My test driver."

"What the hell is she doing?" he asked. "Driving a Formula One around your bedroom?"

I laughed. "Practically."

"It's three days," he said, "I didn't hear from you."

I remembered what Alicia told me about Mrs. Craddock. "I had nothing to report," I said.

"Then what the hell have you been doing?" he snapped. "Driving your test driver around the bed?"

"Why don't you call me later from outside?" I suggested cautiously.

"What for? he retorted. "You know how I hate to go out in this town."

"Security," I said.

He was silent for a moment. I could hear the sound of his breathing in the phone. "Are you talking about Craddock?" he asked.

"Yes."

"I know all about her," he said shortly. "Besides she's out of the house right now doing the marketing. You can talk."

"If you know about her, why do you keep her?"

"She's the best damn secretary and housekeeper I ever had. And, believe me, good housekeepers aren't easy to come by these days." He chuckled. "The way I figure it, the money my grandson pays her makes her job the best in the world and keeps her from blowing it."

"But what good is it if Loren knows everything you're doing?"

He chuckled again. "He only knows what I want him to know. That way everybody's happy. She's not in the house now. See what I mean?"

"Okay," I said. I wondered if any one of us would ever catch up to him. There had to be something to being ninety-four. If there was anything to the old saying that practice makes perfect, being ninety-four was a lot of practice.

He listened quietly while I covered the last two days. When I finished, he was still silent. The line echoed emptily. "Are you there?" I asked.

"I'm here," he said. I heard a deep sigh. "My grandson wants to beat me so bad he can't wait."

It was my turn to be silent.

For the first time I heard resignation in his voice. "When you're young, you're always in a hurry. He should take his time. Monday will come soon enough."

"A lot can happen in six days."

"I told Roberts to turn back the voting trust to the Foundation," he said. "I'm not even coming in for the court hearing."

"Why?" I asked. "Because you know you're going to lose?"

"Don't get impertinent, young man," he snapped, fire coming back into his voice. "No, not because I'm going to lose but because it's the right thing to do. The Foundation is too important to become a football."

I said nothing.

"Besides, that's just the skirmish. The real battle comes at the stockholders' meeting on Tuesday morning. That's where you win or lose. I'll be there for that one." He chuckled ironically. "Of course, my grandson figures that he's got it won or he wouldn't have called the meeting for the day after the hearing."

"He's lost Alicia's votes," I said. "Maybe we can change some others."

"They don't have the same reason that she has. The only chance I see is if we can tie him into Simpson. Even the trustees of the Foundation won't go along with a president who tried to sabotage his own company."

"We've got a beginning," I said. "We already know that he has more than a passing acquaintance with him."

"That's up to you. There's nothing I can do about that down here."

"I'll try," I said. "I remember what you told me before I left."

"Forget that! I was only talking because I was angry. I don't want him framed if he had nothing to do with it."

"Why the sudden change of heart?" I asked. "You develop a conscience in your old age?"

"No, goddamn it!" he roared. "Just don't forget that he

is my grandson and I'm not going to hang him for something he didn't do."

"Then get ready to lose if I can't tie it together," I snapped back at him.

"I won't lose!" he said sharply. "Remember what I said when we started this thing. We would build a new car and by God, that's exactly what we did!"

"Mr. Hardeman's waiting in your office," my secretary told me when I came in.

"Fine. Bring in two cups of coffee."

I opened the door and went into my office. Loren was standing at the window. He turned to me. "Good morning, Loren. You're a week early, aren't you?"

"This isn't a business visit," he said heavily. He walked slowly from the window toward my desk. He looked like a man who hadn't slept all night, weary lines tracing their gray way into his face, his eyes red and pouchy. "My wife left me last night."

My secretary came in with the coffee. We were silent while she placed the cups on the desk and left. I pushed a cup toward him. "You better drink that. You look like you could use it."

He sank into the chair opposite me and reached for the coffee cup. But his hands were shaking so much that some of the coffee spilled over the rim and he returned the cup to its saucer without tasting it. "You're not surprised," he said.

I looked at him. "Should I be? Were you?"

His eyes fell for a moment. "I suppose not," he said in a low voice, almost as if to himself. "I could see it coming for a long time. But there was nothing I could do about it. Detroit wasn't her idea of the world."

I sipped my coffee without speaking. Office coffee was just as bad as hotel coffee, only instant.

He raised his eyes. "You saw her last night?"

"Yes."

"Did she say anything to you?"

"No more than you told me," I answered.

"Damn!" he exploded. He got to his feet and went

back to the window and pounded his fist into his open palm. "Damn!"

I watched him silently, sipping my coffee.

After a moment, he regained his self-control. He turned to me. "Why did she go to you?" he asked in an almost normal voice.

I looked into his eyes. "Because we were friends, I guess. And there was no one else here for her to turn to. I think you put your finger on it. Detroit wasn't her idea of the world. But then, Detroit never tried very hard to make her welcome."

He turned back to the window. "I don't know what to think." After a moment he came back to the desk. "I was jealous of you," he said. "I know she was out in San Francisco almost all the time you were there."

"But that was two years ago. Long before you decided to get married."

"I know," he said. "But when I was told that she stopped off at the Ponch to see you on her way to the airport, I began to think. After all, you're much more her type than I am. I was never very much of a ladies' man."

In spite of myself, I had to smile. "And I am?"

At least he had the grace to look embarrassed. "Come on now, Angelo," he said. "You know what I'm talking about. Stories about you and women have come back here from all over the world."

I laughed. "You have to tell me them sometime. I might discover something about myself."

"Angelo, would you give me a straight answer if I asked you a direct question?" He was in deadly earnest.

"Try me."

"Did you have an affair with my wife?"

"No." I looked right into his eyes, secure in the knowledge I was telling him the truth. Bobbie and I never had an affair after she married him.

He took a deep breath and nodded his head. "Thank you," he said. "Now I can put that away and forget I ever thought about it."

"Okay," I said.

He turned and started out of the office. I called him

back. He stopped in the middle of the room. "Yes, Angelo?"

"Would you give me a straight answer if I asked you a direct question?"

He came back to the desk. "Try me," he said.

"If I could work out a compromise between you and your grandfather, will you give up this stupid fight between you in which one of you will get hurt but only the company will suffer?"

His face settled into grim lines. It was amazing how much he looked like his grandfather. "No."

"Why?"

"Because he's a despot. And I'm not going to let him destroy me as he did my father."

"But that was a long time ago," I said. "He's an old man now and in a wheelchair—"

"He was old then and in a wheelchair!" he interrupted me. "But it didn't stop him then and it won't stop him now!" His eyes grew cold. "Besides you never had to walk into a room and find your father with the top of his head blown off!"

I stared at him. "And you're absolutely sure that your grandfather was to blame?"

"As sure as I'm standing here," he said.

I got to my feet. "I apologize for asking," I said. "Your grandfather would have canned me if he knew I even brought it up. But I had the wrong impression."

"What was that?"

"For a moment there," I said, "I thought you were almost human."

═══════════════════════ **Chapter Seven**

MARION STEVENSON, head of Bethlehem Security, had the faceless look of the FBI agent he used to be. His dark gray suit and characterless tie did nothing to dispel the illusion. He was the kind of man you could overlook in a crowd. He was a medium man in every way except one. He had the palest eyes I ever saw. You could almost see through them to the back of his head.

"You wanted to see me, Mr. Perino?" His voice was as expressionless as the rest of him.

"Yes, Mr. Stevenson. Thank you for coming by." I usually wasn't this formal but I remembered his resentment when I first put the Burns people out at the test track. He had enough J. Edgar left in him to take it as a personal affront. "Please sit down."

"Thank you," he said, equally formal.

The telephone rang. I picked it up. It was Max Evans of the purchasing department. He had a problem.

I covered the mouthpiece while I listened. "Excuse me," I said to Stevenson. "I'll only be a moment." Stevenson nodded and I went back to the phone.

"We've just received a revised estimate from the contractor for the electrostatic connectors for the drivers' seat belts. Up three dollars and forty cents."

"Why?" I asked.

"Additional insulation for lead wires and grounding wires to come up to Underwriters' fire and safety standards."

"Wasn't that covered in our specs?" I asked.

"Yes," he answered. "But Underwriters changed their requirements on us two weeks ago."

There was nothing we could do about it. The driver's seat belt was one of our featured, standard, no-extra-cost safety items. It was connected electrically to a governor on the engine. All belts unfastened, the car would go no more than ten miles per hour. Seat belt fastened, the speed went up to twenty-five miles per hour. Shoulder harness fastened, the governor released completely. But still it was a lot of money. Over a million dollars on three hundred thousand cars.

"Have you checked with other contractors?" I asked.

"Yes," he said. "When we sent out for the original bids. But it's too late now. It would take any one of them at least eight months to get set up for us."

"Then we have no choice," I said.

"Yes, sir," he answered.

"Wait a minute," I said. "This comes under Cost Control. Don't you usually get approvals on things like this from Weyman's office?"

"That's right," he said apologetically. "But as of this morning we were told to secure all approvals on the new cars from you."

"I see." I saw more than that. There were hundreds of items like this every week. If Weyman could unload them on me, I would be so busy shoveling shit that I would have time for nothing else.

"Is it okay to go ahead, Mr. Perino?"

"It's okay, Max," I said. "Send up a purchase order and I'll approve it."

I put down the telephone and turned to my visitor. I took a cigarette and held the pack out to him.

"Gave them up, thank you," he said.

I lit up and leaned back in my chair. I let the smoke drift idly from my mouth while I sat there watching him. After a few moments I noticed he was getting slightly restless.

The telephone rang. I picked it up. "Hold all calls, please." Then I put it down and continued smoking silently.

After about a minute, he made a point of looking at his wristwatch. I ignored it until I had finished the cigarette and ground it thoroughly into the ashtray. "I know you're a busy man, Mr. Stevenson," I said, "but you'll have to bear with me if I seem slow to you this morning. I have a great many things on my mind."

"I understand, Mr. Perino," he said smoothly.

"I have been reading the Table of Organization," I said. "And if I read it correctly, you are responsible directly to the president and executive vice-president."

"That's correct."

"And your responsibilities are all security matters pertaining to the company's business from employee malfeasance to protection of corporate records and industrial secrets."

He nodded. "Yes, sir."

"Let me pose a hypothetical question," I said. "Should you discover a security leak in my office, would you report that to the president?"

"No, sir," he said. "First to the executive vice-president."

"And if you discovered a leak in either of their offices?"

"To the president, if the leak was in the executive vice-president's office, and vice versa."

"And if the leak came from both offices?"

He thought for a moment. "I would then have to assume that the leak was a matter of company policy and approved by them."

I pushed the copy of *The Wall Street Journal* story to him. "Have you seen that story?"

He nodded.

"Would you say that the information contained in that story resulted from a breach of company security?"

"I wouldn't know, sir."

"I call your attention to the phrase, 'informed company sources.' I also call your attention to certain figures quoted in that story. They happen to correspond exactly to the figures in our secret company cost records. There are no more than a dozen executives in the company who are privy to those figures. Suddenly that information appears in a national newspaper and in such a manner as to be potentially harmful to the company. Wouldn't you say that was a serious breach of company security?"

He was getting uncomfortable. "I couldn't say, sir."

"Might I assume then that you feel this matter comes under your classification of approved company policy?"

He was genuinely uncomfortable now. Lawyers and policemen make the worst witnesses. They hate to be questioned. "I can't answer that question, Mr. Perino."

I nodded. "That article happens to be unsigned. Would you know the name of the writer by any chance?"

"Yes, sir," he said.

"Could you tell me?"

"I'm sorry, Mr. Perino," he said. "I've already given my report on that subject to Mr. Weyman."

I paused for a moment. "Do you know of a man named Mark Simpson?"

"Yes, sir."

"What do you know about him?"

"He's head of an outfit called the IASO and publishes a weekly newsletter concerning the automobile industry."

"What else do you know about him?"

"Mr. Weyman has my report on that gentleman," he said. "I'm not allowed to distribute copies of it."

"I see. Is it also against regulations to supply me with a list of the times Mr. Simpson visited this plant and whom he saw on each visit over the past two years?"

"No, sir," he said. I could see he was pleased to find there was something I asked that he could do. "I will have it in your office this afternoon."

"Thank you," I said. "You've been very helpful."

His face flushed. He knew exactly how helpful he had been. Zilch. He got to his feet.

I looked at him. "You have my permission to report this conversation to your superiors if you wish."

"Mr. Perino, if I thought this conversation should be reported to my superiors I would do so with or without your permission," he said stiffly. "I would like to point out that I am in charge of plant security, not plant politics."

I rose to my feet. "Mr. Stevenson, I apologize." I held out my hand.

He hesitated a moment, then took it. "Thank you, Mr. Perino."

I called Weyman the moment he left the office. His voice was almost pleasant when he came on the phone. I think he was expecting a bitch from me about unloading the cost approvals on my office. He didn't get it.

"Number One is bugging me for the report we asked for on Mark Simpson some time ago," I said. "I just spoke to Stevenson in Security and he tells me that he left it with you."

He flustered easily. "I remember seeing it. I'll look around for it and shoot it right over to you."

I put the telephone down knowing damn well I would

never see that report but, at least, I was on record as knowing that he had it.

Early in the afternoon, I received Stevenson's report on Simpson's visits to the plant. There were quite a few of them in the past few years and with the exception of one visit to Bancroft of Sales, all the rest were with Weyman.

I made up my mind to get out of the office and pay Mr. Simpson a visit, but one thing led to another and it was four o'clock before I could leave. I called Cindy at the apartment.

"How would you like to have dinner at the Dearborn Inn?" I asked.

"Fantastic," she said. "I've never been there but I've heard about it. It's right in the middle of Ford country, isn't it?"

"Smack dab in the middle," I laughed. "But don't hold that against it. It's really quite good. I have one stop to make on the way out there, but that shouldn't take long. Be downstairs at the auto entrance in fifteen minutes. I'll pick you up."

"Fifteen minutes on the dot," she said. "I'll be there."

And she was. Even wore a dress for the occasion. I stared as the doorman held the door of the Maserati for her. It was the first time in almost two years that I'd seen her wearing anything but slacks.

"Hey! You're a girl," I said, putting the car into first.

She turned to me with a smile as she finished buckling up. "Man, you're awfully slow. I thought you'd never find out."

The IASO offices were located on Michigan Avenue outside the high-rent district on the way to Dearborn. It was a nondescript two-story building next to a used-car lot. Downstairs was occupied by job printers, with large blacked-out painted windows in what in better days had to be a new-car showroom. Upstairs, over them, the small windows bore the letters IASO in faded blue paint.

I pulled the car into the small off-street parking place in front of the job printers and reserved for their clients and got out. "I won't be long."

She nodded, opening her purse and taking out a cassette. "Mind if I use your tape player?"

By the time I walked away from the car, she had Creedence Clearwater blasting from all four speakers and was leaning back, bathing in the sound, a beatific expression on her face.

There was no separate entrance to the upper story that I could see, so I went into the print shop. The sound of a rolling press hit my ears as I opened the door. There was a beat-up old wooden counter separating the entrance from the rest of the shop. A rusted punch bell sat on top with a sign next to it: RING BELL FOR SERVICE.

I hit the bell but its sound was lost in the roar of the presses. I hit it again.

Several workmen stuck their heads out from behind the machinery to see who was there.

"IASO?" I shouted above the noise, pointing with my hand at the ceiling.

A big man with black hair, his face and hairy arms covered with printer's ink, stepped out from behind the press. He made a sweeping gesture with his arm. "Around the building," he shouted. "There's a staircase in the back alley."

"Thank you," I shouted. I went outside, glad to get away from the hammer of the presses. Cindy saw me and smiled, beginning to roll down the window.

I shook my head and pointed around the building. She nodded and rolled the window back up, leaning into the sound again.

There was a black rusted-steel staircase on the outside of the building off the alley. On the building there was a small sign with an arrow pointing to the steps. IASO. I climbed the steps and went into the building through the faded gray painted steel door.

I entered a deserted reception room. The walls were painted a dull green and were covered with posters: BUCKLE UP FOR SAFETY! SPEED KILLS! And others like it. From somewhere in the back I heard the sound of a bell announcing my arrival.

A moment later a heavy blond girl in a shapeless black

sweater and miniskirt appeared. "What can I do for you?" she asked in a voice equally as bored as the expression on her face.

"Is Mr. Simpson in?"

"Do you have an appointment?"

"No." I shook my head.

"Your name please?"

I told her. There was no change in the bored expression of either her voice or face. "Please have a seat. I'll see if he is available."

She left the reception room and I heard the door lock behind her. I sat down on a wooden bench next to a table, the top of which was covered with the latest issue of the IASO weekly newsletter.

I lit a cigarette and idly glanced through a copy. I learned all about the improvements that GM had built into the new '72 Vega that could not be seen on the outside and the additional performance that could be gotten from the Pinto with the new Boss package, all of which could also be learned from the printed ads and TV commercials of the companies concerned. I got to the last page without having once come across an item that dealt with automobile safety.

I looked for an ashtray in which to stub out my cigarette. There wasn't any, so I got to my feet, opened the door and snapped it out into the alley. Through the thin walls behind me, I could hear the sound of the bell. At the same time, the faint vibration in the floor and the muffled roar of the presses downstairs suddenly stopped. I looked at my watch. Four forty-five. I had been there more than ten minutes.

The blond girl reappeared in the doorway. A surprised expression chased the bored look from her face as she saw me. She looked over my shoulder. "Did anyone just come in?"

"No," I answered. "I just threw out a cigarette."

She looked at me. "Are you waiting for someone else?"

"No," I said. "Still waiting for Mr. Simpson."

"Wasn't his secretary out to see you?"

"No."

"Damn!" she said, a hopeless look coming into her face. "This is the most disorganized place I ever worked in. She was supposed to come out and tell you he was out of town."

I looked at her. "Is he?"

"Mister," she said in a disgusted voice, "the way things are run around here, he might be the next man on the moon for all I know."

She slammed her way back into the inner office and I left. The daylight had almost gone while I was waiting and I stopped to light another cigarette on the steel landing before starting down the steps. I supposed that it had been naïve to expect that Simpson would have seen me under any circumstances. Not after the way he took off from Weyman's office the other day. From beneath the steps I heard the voices of the pressmen leaving their work as I walked down.

The voice came from behind me as I reached the bottom step. "Hey, buddy, got a match?"

"Sure," I said, turning around. From the corner of my eye I caught a glimpse of a large hamlike fist coming at my face.

Instinctively I started to duck. But not fast enough. The fist exploded into my face with all the force of a trip-hammer. I felt myself begin to fall backward, a shower of sparkling lights dancing before my eyes. I shook my head groggily, trying to clear my vision.

Hands grabbed me by the shoulders and began to drag me back into the alley. Even then I didn't suspect that it was anything more than a mugging. I tried to tell them that my wallet was in my back pocket but my lips felt paralyzed and couldn't move.

I felt myself being propped against the building wall. I managed to squint at them through half-shut eyes. There were three of them but I couldn't see their faces. It was too dark.

Then the pain began. Slow. Deliberate. Methodical. And professional. In my ribs, my stomach, my guts, my balls. I slid down the wall slowly and the pain began again on my face. I felt it bursting against my ears, nose and mouth, and I could taste the warm blood pouring back into my mouth as I sank to the ground.

And still I didn't lose consciousness while they put the boot to me. There was a distant nagging thought dragging in the back of my head.

Someone had warned me to be careful. But I couldn't remember who. Somebody had said I would learn they could play rough and dirty. But I couldn't remember who.

I started to pick myself up. I got as far as my knees and was beginning to straighten up when I saw the heavy boot.

There was nothing I could do about it. It caught me under the chin and I felt myself lift into the air and somersault backward into the wall.

I was almost happy to find that night finally had come.

=================================== **Chapter Eight**

IN THE DISTANCE I heard the girl crying. "Angelo! Angelo!" I felt her warm tears spilling on my face. Slowly I fought my way up to her.

In the night her white, frightened face was very close but her features seemed blurred through my puffed and swollen eyes. I felt her arm go under my head and draw me close to her breasts. The tears kept spilling on my face as she held me there, rocking back and forth as she knelt.

"Cindy." My voice was an alien croaking sound that came from my throat. "Help me up."

"Don't move," she whispered. "You're hurt. Let me call an ambulance."

I tried to shake my head but there was too much pain. "No!" I tried to push myself up. "Take me home. My father is a doctor."

"Angelo, please."

"Help me up!"

She responded to the urgency in my voice and put an arm under my shoulders. I almost screamed when I felt

the pressure against my sides as she pulled at me. It
seemed like hours but she finally had me on my feet, my
back supported by the building.

"Don't walk," she said. "Let me bring the car back
here."

I nodded.

"Can you stand?" she asked anxiously.

"Yes," I rasped.

She looked into my face for a moment. I don't know
what she saw there but a moment later she turned and I
could hear her footsteps running down the alley. I didn't
look after her because it hurt too much to turn.

Again time seemed to drag and there was the vacuum
of space churning around in my head. Then I heard the
heavy throat of the Maserati coming toward me, its bright
white headlights cutting up the dark. I blinked with the
pain of it.

She was a shadow coming around the car and opening
the door. She came toward me. "Can you put an arm
around my shoulder?" she asked.

I raised my arm and she slipped under it. I let my weight
rest on her and we made the half mile to the door. She
turned me around and let me slip to the seat back first,
then she picked up my feet and put them in the car.
Quickly she buckled the seat belt around me and let the
seat back down gently until I was almost stretched out.
"You all right?" she asked.

"Yes," I grunted. In the reflected light I could see
bloodstains all over the front of her dress.

She closed the door and came round to the driver's side
and got in. She leaned across me to press down the door
lock.

"I'm sorry," I mumbled. "I ruined your dress."

She didn't answer. Instead she reversed the car out of
the alley and turned back toward Michigan Avenue. "Now,
where do we go?"

Very carefully and very explicitly I gave the directions
to my parents' house. I felt a hole in my mouth with my
tongue where some teeth used to be. I hoped at least they
were caps and not some of the few I had left.

She moved onto the avenue. "Now you rest," she said.

I closed my eyes, then opened them. "How did you find me?"

Her eye stayed on the road. "By five thirty, when you hadn't come back, I got curious. The building was completely dark and I had seen everyone go home. So I went around the back, up the stairs and tried the door. It was locked. I knocked. No answer. Then I heard you moan. I ran down the steps and found you behind the corner of the building." She stopped for a light and looked down at me. "Now, no more talking until I get you home. Rest."

I closed my eyes and sank back into the dark. I opened them again as the car came to a stop in the driveway of the house.

"I'll help you out," she said, opening my door and reaching in for me.

We managed to get my feet out of the car but I couldn't make it any further. Even with her help, the pain wouldn't let me walk. I clung to the car door. "Ring the bell," I said. "Gianno will help me."

She ran up the steps and pressed the doorbell. A moment later the entrance lights came on and Gianno opened the door. All she could manage to say was my name when he was down the steps and picked me up in his arms as if I were still the baby he used to carry around.

"Dottore! Dottore!" he shouted at the top of his lungs as we entered the house. "Angelo, he is hurt!"

My mother was the first one there. She took one look at me and clutched a fist to her mouth. *"Figlio mio!"* she cried. "What have they done to you?"

My father was right behind her. He took one look at me. "Carry him into my office," he said, his face settling into grim lines.

Gianno carried me through the house to the wing that Father used as his office when he saw patients at home. We went into the examination room and Gianno put me gently on the white table.

My father opened a cabinet and took out a syrette and hypodermic. "Call the hospital and have them send an ambulance right away," he told Gianno.

"No hospital," I said.

Gianno hesitated but my father shot a glance at him and he went right to the telephone.

"What happened?" my father asked quietly as he prepared the hypo.

"Three men worked me over," I said, watching him.

I heard my mother gasp. My father turned to her. "Mamma!" he said sternly. "You wait outside."

"But Angelo—" Her voice faltered.

"Angelo will be all right," he said firmly. "I promise you. Now wait outside." He looked past her at Cindy who was standing right behind my mother. "You too, young lady."

My mother took Cindy's arm. "You tell me everything that happened," she said as they left the room.

I looked at the needle in my father's hand. "What's that for?"

"Pain," he said. "I'm going to start cleaning you up and it's going to hurt a lot more than it does now."

"I don't want to go to sleep," I said. "I have to make some calls."

"Who do you want to call?" he asked, casually looking down at me. "Maybe I can help you."

I scarcely felt the prick of the needle in my hip as my father deftly slid down my slacks and hit me with the hypo all in one practiced motion. "First I want to talk to Uncle Jake," I said.

"Uncle Jake?" he asked. I just managed to catch the note of surprise in his voice as the hypo knocked me back into dreamland.

Gianno and I were playing cowboys and Indians in the shrubbery at the side of the house. Right now I was Tom Mix and he was my faithful horse, Tony, and I was firing my six-shooter after the Indians we were chasing through the brush, just as we had seen them in *Riders of the Purple Sage* yesterday at the Saturday children's matinee.

"Whoa, Tony!" I yelled, pulling at his shirt collar as we got to the edge of the driveway. "I think I hear a covered wagon."

I jumped off his back and crouched down in the shrubs. My grandfather's giant black-and-tan Duesenberg came up the driveway. I waited until it had passed us, then I jumped on Gianno's shoulders. "After them!" I shouted. "We have to warn them about the Indians!"

Gianno galloped wildly up the driveway at the side of the car, holding onto my legs so that I would not fall off.

I fired my six-shooter into the air, the caps exploding and making a racket. "Look out, Grandpa!" I yelled. "The Indians are coming!"

Through the windows of the closed tonneau behind the chauffeur, I could see my grandfather. He was sitting on the back seat between two men. Another man was seated on the jump seat in front of them.

The automobile stopped in front of the house. Gianno and I waited for them on the steps as they got out. The two men who were on the back seat with my grandfather waited, leaning against the car as he and the other man came up the steps toward us.

I brandished my six-shooter in the air. "There's Indians in the hills!"

Grandfather stopped in front of us. He was not a tall man, slight, almost small; in fact Gianno, who was five foot eight, towered over him. But it made no difference. No matter who was around my grandfather, he was the big man.

He held out his hand to me. "Give me the gun, Angelo."

I looked in his eyes for signs of displeasure but I could read nothing there. They were dark brown, almost black like his hair, and unfathomable. Silently I handed down my six-shooter.

He took it in his hand and looked at it with distaste. He turned his gaze back to Gianno. "Who gave him this?"

"*Padrone,* its only a toy." Gianno almost bowed but couldn't manage it with me on his shoulders.

"I don't care," my grandfather said in a flat voice. "I thought I said no guns. Not even toy guns. They are a bad thing for children."

This time Gianno managed to bow even with me on him. "*Si, Padrone.*"

Grandfather gave him the six-shooter. "Get rid of it," he said, then held his arms up for me. "Come, Angelo."

I slid from Gianno's shoulders into Grandfather's arms, glad that he wasn't angry with me. Grandfather kissed me as he carried me up the steps into the house. "Guns are dangerous for children to play with," he explained. "Even toy guns."

We walked into the living room where my mother and father were waiting. The moment my mother saw him, she began to cry. Awkwardly, Grandfather shifted me to one arm and put the other around Mother.

"Now, now, Jenny," he said gently. "Don't cry. Sicily is not the end of the world."

"But you're going to be so far from us," she wept.

I began to cry also. "I don't want you to go away, Grandpa!"

"Now, Jenny, see what you did?" my grandfather said reproachfully. "You made him cry." He turned to my father. "*Dottore,* tell your wife to stop. It's not good for Angelo to be upset like that."

My father's eyes weren't exactly clear either, so I took advantage of his momentary hesitation to let out an even greater yell.

"I don't want you to leave me, Grandpa!" I clung to him sobbing fiercely.

This one was so loud that even my mother stopped crying and looked at me. "He's getting hysterical!" she said, reaching for me.

My grandfather brushed her arms away. "I told you," he said triumphantly. "Let his grandpa handle him."

My mother fell silent as my grandfather swung me around in his arms so that he could look into my face. "I'm not leaving you, *Angelo mio,*" he said. "I'm going to Sicily, to Marsala and Trapani where I was born."

I was losing ground but at least he had forgotten about the six-shooter. I tried one more yell. "I'll never see you again!"

Now the tears filled his eyes. He hugged me very tightly. I could hardly breathe. "Of course you will," he said in a choked voice. "In the summer you can come to visit me with your mamma and papa and I will show you the vineyards and the olive groves on the side of Mount Erice where your grandpa grew up."

"Can we play cowboys and Indians there?" I asked, my eyes round.

"No, that's a bad game," he said. "All games are bad where you play at killing people. You be like your father, a doctor, where you can save people, not kill them." He looked at me, not quite sure that I understood him. "Besides there are no Indians in Sicily," he added.

"Only good guys?" I asked.

He knew when he was licked. "There are only good guys in Sicily," he said, giving up and resorting to his ultimate weapon. Bribery. "Besides Grandpa is going to send you a very special present when he gets there."

"What kind of present?" I wanted to know.

"Anything you want. Just tell your grandpa."

I thought for a moment. I remembered the movie Gianno and I had seen the week before. It was with Monte Blue and he played a daredevil race-car driver. "A real race car that I can drive?" I asked tentatively.

"If that's what my Angelo wants, that's what he'll get. I will have a special Bugatti racer built for you!"

I squeezed my arms around his neck. "Thank you, Grandpa." I kissed him.

He turned to my parents. "See," he said triumphantly. "I told you. He's perfectly all right now."

All the while this was going on, the man who had come in with us was watching and kind of smiling to himself. Now my grandfather waved him forward. "Jake, come here."

"This is my son, Dr. John Perino," my grandfather said proudly. "And his wife, Jenny. This is Judge Jacob Weinstein who I told you about."

Judge Weinstein, a brown-haired man of about my father's height and age, shook hands with my parents.

"Don't forget me," I said, holding out my hand.

He turned, smiling, and took my hand. "I don't think I can," he said.

"I made a lifetime contract with Jake to look after

family business affairs while I'm away," Grandfather said.
He put me down. "Now you go and play while your father
and the Judge and me talk a little business."

"Come with me to the kitchen," my mother said quickly. "I just baked some cookies. You can have them with a
glass of milk."

She took my hand and began to lead me to the door. I
pulled her to a stop and looked back. "Will I see you
again before you go away, Grandpa?"

Grandfather caught his breath and I saw his eyes go
misty again. He nodded. "Before I go," he managed to
say.

About an hour later, we stood on the steps in front of
the house and waved good-bye to my grandfather as the
big Duesenberg started down the driveway. I saw him
looking back at me through the rear window and I waved
again to him. He raised his hand and then the car turned
out of sight at the end of the driveway.

We stood there a moment, then I looked up at my
parents. "Those men waiting for Grandpa were wearing
guns under their coats," I said. "I wonder if they know
Grandpa doesn't like guns."

My mother and father stared at each other for a long
moment, then my mother's eyes filled with tears again. My
father picked me up with one arm and put the other
around her. We stood there silently like that on the steps
in front of the house for a long time while my mother hid
her face against my father's chest. I looked at my father.
There were unshed tears in his eyes too. I felt a strange
lump come up in my throat. There were so many things
I did not understand.

But in the time to come I would learn many of them.
Like those two men that waited for Grandfather were
federal agents who were to escort him to New York where
he would board a ship for Italy.

Like Judge Weinstein, or Uncle Jake as I came to know
him, wasn't really a judge at all but an attorney in charge
of all his business affairs.

For many years thereafter, almost until the time I left

for college, Uncle Jake was a once-monthly visitor at our house for Sunday dinners.

Then shortly after I was twenty-one and I was down from MIT in January 1952, I found out how rich a man my grandfather had really been. By that time, my share of his estate had grown under Uncle Jake's prudent management to more than twenty-five million dollars and my parents' share was twice that.

I remember looking at my father and Uncle Jake in complete bewilderment. I knew we were well off. I didn't know we were rich. "What do I do with all that money?" I asked.

"You'd better learn," my father said seriously. "Because some day you're going to have all of it."

"I'd suggest you go to Harvard Business School when you graduate," said Uncle Jake.

"But I'm not interested in business," I said. "I'm interested in automobiles."

"Automobiles are a business too," Uncle Jake said.

"Not my kind," I said. "All they do is cost money."

"Well, at least you can afford that," Uncle Jake smiled.

"I don't need all that," I said.

"Then I suggest you set up an investment trust at the bank and let them manage it," Uncle Jake said.

I looked at him. "Why can't you just keep on with it the way you have?" I asked. "I remember Grandfather said he gave you a lifetime contract. If it's good enough for him, it's good enough for me."

He glanced at my father. "I'm sorry," he said, turning to me. "I can't do it."

"Why?"

He cleared his throat. "Because of certain other business activities of mine which the government says are allied with organized crime, I feel it's wiser to cut you loose rather than chance the possibility of having you and your parents involved in something none of you have anything to do with."

I knew what he was talking about. I read the newspapers too. His name had come up very often in connection with investigations into organized crime. "But can we still call on you if we ever have a problem?" I asked. "A real problem, I mean."

He nodded. "Of course you can. After all, your grandfather did give me a lifetime contract." He got to his feet. "Everything's pretty much set up at the bank, John," he said to my father, "perhaps you and Angelo can come downtown tomorrow. We can have lunch, then go over to the bank, sign a few papers and make it official."

We did that and when I went back to school I got a subscription to *The Wall Street Journal* and for a while religiously checked the market every day against the list of stocks and securities that the bank held for me. But then it got to be a bore and I stopped looking at it entirely, just depending on the bank's quarterly statements to keep me up to date. And most of the time, they wound up in my drawer unopened. After all, how wrong could I go when I started with twenty-five million dollars in blue chips?

Uncle Jake didn't entirely lose his fight with the government, but the following year he gave up his practice and moved to Las Vegas where he had interests in several hotels. We exchanged Christmas cards and once in a while when he came East my parents would see him, but I was always somewhere else. Then just a few years ago I read in the papers that he had sold his interests in Las Vegas and had moved near Phoenix, Arizona, where he embarked on a large program of land development tied to a sport and spa hotel and country club complex called Paradise Springs. I remembered receiving an invitation from him to attend the grand opening of the resort, but that was about the time I had begun working for Number One and I couldn't attend. Mother and Father, however, did go and carried with them my explanation and regrets and good wishes. Mother loved it, and my parents had returned there several times a year since. Father told me that Uncle Jake looked relaxed and content for the first time since he had known him and had gone brown-as-berry native, even to the extent of wearing a white ten-gallon Stetson out on the links for his morning round of golf.

In the time that passed I had learned many things, but

of all of them perhaps the greatest regret was that I never got to see my grandfather again. It took him almost two years to get me the Bugatti that he had promised, but it finally came. And a year later so did the war in Europe and he wrote my parents not to come to visit as he did not want them to take any chances with me. Then we were in the war and for almost two years we heard nothing until the American troops landed in Italy.

But then, it was too late. My grandfather had died of cancer the year before.

Chapter Nine

I OPENED MY EYES to the sunlight streaming into a room filled with flowers. I moved my head slightly. No pain. I grew bold. It hurt like hell. "Damn!" I said.

The nurse who had been sitting in the corner of the room got to her feet. Her uniform rustled as she came to the bed and looked down at me. "You're awake," she said.

I already knew that. "What day is this?"

"Thursday."

"What happened to Wednesday?" I asked.

"You slept," she answered, reaching for the telephone. She dialed a number. I heard the faint crackle of an answering voice. "Will you please page Dr. Perino and tell him that 503 is awake. Thank you.

"Your father is on his rounds but he wanted to be notified the moment you awoke," she explained.

"What time is it?"

"Ten o'clock," she said. "How do you feel?"

"I don't know," I answered. "And I'm afraid to find out."

The door opened and my father came into the room. No Anglo-Saxon bullshit with us, we were Italian. Doctor he might be but he was my father first. We kissed on the lips. "Mother and Cindy are on the way up from the coffee shop," he said.

"Before they get here, how bad is it?"

"You've had worse," he said. "A couple of broken ribs, numerous and heavy body bruises and contusions, but no internal injuries as far as we can determine, mild concussion, you'll have headaches for a while." He paused. "They did make a mess of your face though. Undid all the work you had done in Switzerland. Broken nose in two places, there's a slight crack in your jawbone, not too serious—it will heal practically by itself. I figure you lost about five teeth, mostly caps, and it looks like they shifted your right cheekbone a little, but we can't tell until the swelling goes down. Cuts over the eyes and around the mouth. All in all, not too bad."

"Thank you, Doctor," I said. I reached for his hand and kissed it. Like I said, we were Italian. When I looked up at him there were tears in his eyes.

Then the door opened and Mother and Cindy came in and my father had his hands full for the next ten minutes trying to keep Mother from crying all over me.

Cindy stood there at the foot of the bed, almost shyly watching us. I think it was the first time she had ever seen an Italian family in action. It really was something to see.

Finally, when Mother had kissed practically every part of me, including my feet, she straightened up. "Cindy, come here," she said. "Angelo wants to thank you."

My mother turned back to me. "She's a good girl, your friend. She saved your life and brought you home to us. I thanked her a thousand times. Now, you thank her."

Cindy leaned over me and kissed my cheek chastely. I returned her kiss, equally chaste on her cheek. "Thank you," I said gravely.

"You're very welcome," she said formally.

"Now, that's a good boy, Angelo," my mother said proudly.

Cindy and I had all we could do to keep from breaking up. We didn't dare look at each other.

"Who sent all the flowers?" I asked.

"The story about your mugging was in all the papers,"

Cindy said. "They started arriving yesterday. Number One, Duncan, Rourke, Bancroft. Even Number Three and Weyman sent flowers."

"Angelo has good friends," my mother said proudly.

"Yeah," I said dryly, looking at Cindy.

"Number One called you from Palm Beach," Cindy said. "He said not to worry. He would see you on Monday when he came up here."

Suddenly it all came back to me. Monday was only five days away. I had lost one precious day of time sleeping. I looked up at my father. "How long do I stay in here?"

"I figure over the weekend," he answered. "If everything checks out all right we could let you go Monday or Tuesday."

"If I left the hospital for one day and then came back, would I do any damage?"

My father studied me. "Is it that important?"

"Yes. This was no mugging and you know it. Nobody took my watch or wallet."

He also knew a professional beating when he saw one. You didn't practice in Detroit hospitals for over forty years without learning about that. He was silent.

"There's something I must do," I said. "It's the only chance I have to keep them from taking the company away from Number One."

A strange expression came to my father's face. "You mean old Mr. Hardeman?"

I nodded.

He thought for a moment. "You'll come back within one day?"

"Yes."

"You'll be in agony every minute," he said.

"Give me pills."

"All right." He took a deep breath. "I'll give you one day. I have your word. You'll be back."

"No!" Mother cried. "You mustn't let him! He'll hurt himself!" She started for me, crying. "My baby!"

My father held out his arm to stop her. "Jenny!" he said sternly.

Mother looked at him in surprise. It was a tone that I doubt she had ever heard from him.

"Leave man's work to men!" Father said.

Sicilian women know where it's at. "Yes, John," my mother said meekly. She looked at me but spoke to him. "He'll be careful?"

"He'll be careful," my father said.

I woke up the next time in the cabin of the big, chartered DC-9. The stewardess was looking at me, Gianno standing next to her.

"We'll be landing in Phoenix in fifteen minutes, Mr. Perino," she said.

"Raise me up," I told Gianno.

He bent down beside the stretcher bed and turned the crank, raising the back of the bed until I was in a half-reclining position. "That okay, Angelo?"

"Fine," I said. The afternoon sun was brighter at thirty thousand feet here than it was in Detroit. The seat belt sign went on with a pinging sound.

Gianno bent over me to tighten the straps. That done he checked the floor locks on the bed. Satisfied, he returned to his seat and fastened his belt. The stewardess went forward to the pilot's cabin.

I leaned back with a good feeling. Father really had it all arranged. It had begun that morning when I asked Cindy to check the flights to Phoenix while I put in a call to Uncle Jake.

"Forget it," Father said. "I'll take care of everything."

"But I have to get to Phoenix today."

"You will. You just rest. I'll call Jake and get you to Phoenix today."

"But how are you going to do it?"

"Stop worrying," he smiled. "It's time you learned there are some advantages to being rich."

After he had gone, Cindy came over to the bed. She stood next to Mother who was seated in a chair watching my every motion with an eagle eye. "I think I'll go back to the hotel and get some sleep," she said. "I'm beat."

"I don't want you to go back to the hotel. They know

you were with me and I don't want anything to happen to you."

"Nothing will happen to me," she said.

"That's what I thought."

"Cindy can stay at our house," Mother said quickly. "She can have the guest room she had last night."

I looked at Cindy. She nodded. "I don't want anyone to know where you are." I said.

"Okay," she answered. "I'll tell Duncan to keep it quiet."

"No, you'll tell him nothing. You won't even call him or anybody else for that matter. I don't trust any of the telephones in the plant."

"But I promised to let him know how you are," she said.

"The hospital will give him the information. You just keep out of sight until I give you the word."

"She'll do what you say, Angelo," Mother said. "Won't you, Cindy?"

"Yes," Cindy answered.

"See?" Mother said triumphantly. "I told you she was a good girl. Now don't worry about her. I'll take care of her every minute. Nobody will know where she is."

I could see the beginning of a smile come to Cindy's lips. But it wasn't a funny ha-ha smile. It was the kind of smile you have when you find a friend.

I nodded my head. "Thank you, Mamma."

My father came back into the room. "Well, it's all arranged," he said, obviously pleased with himself. "I spoke to Jake and he'll meet you in his office at five o'clock."

He really did have it arranged. A private ambulance took me from the hospital to the airport where it rolled right onto the field up to the chartered jet. Gianno rode with me and in the plane made sure that the stretcher bed was securely locked into place. Five minutes after we were airborne, he came over to me, a hypo in his hand.

"What's that?" I asked.

"Sleep shot," he said. "The *Dottore* wants you to rest until you get to Phoenix."

"I'll rest," I said.

"The *Dottore* said if you give me trouble I turn the plane back to Detroit."

"Okay," I said wearily. "Hit me."

Father taught him well. I think I was asleep before he got the needle out of my ass.

There was an ambulance waiting on the tarmac when the big plane rolled to a stop. Thirty-five minutes later we pulled into Paradise Springs. I had to say one thing for it. It was a hell of a way to beat the traffic problem.

We were directed to the private entrance to Uncle Jake's office. It was through a screened-in garden facing the golf course.

Uncle Jake was behind his desk in the large, wood-paneled room. Logs crackled in the fireplace, fighting a losing battle against the air-conditioning.

Uncle Jake saw me looking at it, as Gianno cranked up the bed. He got out of his chair and walked toward me, his snow-white Stetson startling against the dark wood walls. "This air-conditioning is so goddamn efficient in here that sometimes I find myself freezing," he said. "And I'm still enough of an Easterner to like a log fire at which to warm my hands."

I smiled at him. "Hello, Uncle Jake." I held out my hand.

He took it. His grip was as strong and friendly as it had always been. "Hello, Angelo." He turned to Gianno. "Good to see you again, Gianno."

Gianno bowed. "Good to see you, *Eccellenza*." He moved to the door and left the office.

Uncle Jake turned back to me when the door had closed. He pulled a chair from in front of the desk and sat down, looking at me. "Do you always travel like this?" he smiled.

"No," I laughed. "Only when I'm too tired to get out of bed."

"Your father told me you really caught it," he said, still smiling. "You should have learned to duck."

"I did," I said. "Right into a kick in the teeth."

The smile left his face. The drooping, heavy lids over his large eyes, the large, curved, Roman nose almost reaching the center of his upper lip above his wide, thin-lipped mouth and pointed, dimpled chin, all combined to give him the dangerous, hooded look of a hunting falcon. "Who did it?" he asked.

"I don't know," I said, deliberately pausing for a moment. "But I can guess."

"Tell me."

I went through the whole story from the beginning. From the very first call I got from Number One almost three years ago. I left nothing out, business or personal, because that's the way I knew he would want it and that's the way it had to be. An hour and a half later I came to the end of my story with the conversation I had with my father that morning.

He was a good listener, interrupting me only a few times to clarify a hazy point. Now he got to his feet and stretched. He was in fantastic shape for a man in his late sixties; physically he looked more like a man in his fifties, and not late fifties at that. "I could use a drink," he said.

"So could I."

"What will be your pleasure?"

"Canadian on the rocks."

He laughed. "Your father said you would ask for that, but all I'm allowed to give you is two ounces of cognac neat."

"Father knows best."

There was a bar hidden in the wall which came out at the touch of a button. He poured cognac into two snifters and gave me one.

"Cheers," I said. The cognac burned its way down my throat. I coughed and winced as the pain ran through my side.

"You're supposed to sip it, not gulp it," he said. He sipped his drink. After a moment he looked down at me. "Okay, now that I've heard your story, exactly what do you want from me?"

"Help," I said simply.

"In what way?"

"There are two things I want you to do. If you can. One is to find out where Simpson got the money to push his campaign against us. If he got it legitimately, good and well, I'll forget about it. But if it came in any way from someone in our company, I want to know it.

"Two, I want that suicide note that Loren Three has in his home safe."

"What good do you expect that to do you?"

"I don't know," I said. "I just have a hunch it may be the key to all of this if I can get it out into the open."

"You're not asking for very much, are you?" Without waiting for me to reply, "A little bit of detective work and a little bit of safecracking, that's all."

I didn't say anything.

"How much time do we have?" he asked.

"Until Monday night," I answered. "I need the information for the stockholders' meeting on Tuesday morning. That's our last chance."

"You know you're asking me to participate in an illegal act with full, prior knowledge," he said. "That's something I've never done. I've been a lawyer all my life and the only thing I've ever done was defend my clients to the best of my ability after they committed the act."

"I know that," I said.

"And you still ask me to do what you want?"

"Yes."

"Why?"

"You're a lawyer, you shouldn't have to ask that question," I said, looking steadily at him. "You made a lifetime contract with my grandfather to handle my business affairs. And this is my business."

He thought for a moment, then he nodded. "You're right. I'll see what can be done. But I'm not promising anything. My contacts in Detroit may not be as good as they used to be."

"That's good enough for me, Uncle Jake," I said. "Thank you."

He looked at his watch. "Time I got you back on the plane. It's after seven and I promised your father you would be on your way by then."

"I'll be all right," I said. But I wasn't. The pain was beginning to dance around inside me.

"Where will you be nine o'clock, Monday night?" Uncle Jake asked.

"Either the hospital or home," I answered. "Depends on what Papa will let me do."

"Okay," he said. "At nine o'clock, Monday night, wherever you are, someone will contact you. They will either have what you want or tell you they haven't."

"Good enough."

He walked to the door and opened it. Gianno was standing just outside. "Okay, Gianno," he said. "Take him back."

"*Si, Eccellenza.*" Gianno took a small metal box from his breast pocket. He tore the wrapper from the disposable syringe and began filling it from a small vial.

"I can understand why your father let you come to see me while you're like this," Uncle Jake said. "But I don't see why you're doing it, what you're getting out of it."

"Money for one thing. That stock could be worth ten million dollars someday."

"That's not it," he said. "You have five times that by now and you never paid attention to it. There has to be another reason."

"Maybe it's because I gave my word to the old man that we would build a new car. And I don't consider the job done until that car comes off the assembly line."

He looked at me. There was approval in his voice. "That's more like it."

Then I had a question to ask him. Something that had been puzzling me. "You said you knew why Papa let me come down here. Why did he?"

"I thought you knew," he said. "It was old Mr. Hardeman who got your father into the hospital as a resident after every one of them had turned him down because he was your grandfather's son."

"Turn on your side a little bit," Gianno said.

Automatically I did as he asked, still looking up at Uncle Jake. I felt the faint jab in my buttock.

Uncle Jake began to smile. "The wheel never stops turning, does it?" Then right in front of my eyes he began to disappear.

That had to be one of the world's greatest shots. I slept all the way from Uncle Jake's office in Phoenix until nine o'clock the next morning when I awoke in my hospital bed in Detroit.

Chapter Ten

BY SATURDAY AFTERNOON in the hospital, I was going cuckoo. The aches and pains had subsided enough so that I could handle them with an abundance of aspirin, and I paced up and down my room like a caged animal. I flipped channels on television and spun the radio dial until it came off in my hand. Finally the nurse fled the room and came back ten minutes later with my father.

He looked at me calmly. "What's the matter?"

"I want out!"

"Okay," he said.

"You can't keep me in here any more," I said, not listening to him. "I've had it!"

"If you'd pay attention instead of running off at the mouth," my father said, "you'd know I said 'Okay.' "

I stared at him. "You mean it?"

"Get dressed," he said. "I'll be back to pick you up in about fifteen minutes. As soon as I finish my rounds."

"What about my bandages?"

"You'll have to keep your ribs taped for a few more weeks, but I'll be able to replace your head and face bandages with a couple of Band-Aids." He smiled. "I'm really very pleased. I just saw your X-rays and lab reports of this morning. You're fine. Now we'll give Mamma's miracle drug, pasta, a chance to do a little work on you."

Of course Mamma cried when I came home. And so did Gianno and my father. I looked over my mother's head at Cindy. Even she stood there, tears welling in her eyes.

I grinned at her. "I see Mamma's been giving you instructions on how to become Italian."

She made a face and turned away. When she turned back, she was fine. "Also spaghetti sauce," she said. "We've been in the kitchen ever since this morning when your father told us he was bringing you home."

I looked at him. "At least you could have told me, Papa."

He smiled. "I wanted to check the reports first just to be sure."

"Gianno, you help him upstairs," my mother said.

"*Si, Signora.*"

"Undress him and get him right into bed," she continued. "I want him to rest until it's time for dinner."

"Mamma, I'm not a baby," I protested. "I can manage myself."

My mother ignored me. "Gianno, don't pay any attention to him," she said firmly. "Go with him."

I started up the steps, Gianno following me.

"And don't let him smoke in bed," my mother added. "He'll set himself on fire."

By the time I got to bed, I knew I wasn't as strong as I thought I was. I was grateful for Gianno's help. I fell right asleep.

Cindy came by before dinner just in time to catch Mother forcing a shot glass full of Fernet Branca down my throat.

I swallowed about half of it, almost gagging at the lousy taste it left in my mouth. I made a face. "That's enough!"

"You'll drink it all," she insisted. "It will do you more good than all those little pills."

I stood there stubbornly, the shot glass in my hand. My mother turned to Cindy.

"You make him finish it," she said. "I have to go down to the kitchen and start the water for the pasta." She went to the door and stopped there. "You make sure that he finishes it before he comes down for dinner."

"Yes, Mrs. Perino," Cindy said obediently. My mother went down the hall and Cindy turned back to me. "You heard your mother," she said with a smile. "Finish it."

"She's something, isn't she? Her trouble is that she really believes it when I tell her that a boy's best friend is his mother."

"I've never met anyone like her," Cindy said with a sound of envy in her voice. "Or like your father either. The money they have doesn't affect them at all. All they care about is each other. And you. They're real people."

"I still won't drink this shit."

"You'll drink it," she said, looking into my eyes. "Just to make her happy."

I swallowed the rest of the Fernet Branca in one gulp. I grimaced, giving her the glass. "Oh, God. It's really awful."

She didn't say anything, still looking into my eyes.

I shook my head in wonder. "My mother's really done a number on you, hasn't she?"

"You don't know how lucky you are," she said seriously. "My family's got more money than yours. Much more. And my mother and father never even seemed to know I was alive."

I looked, surprised. She had never talked about her family before.

"Did you ever hear of Morris Mining?" she asked suddenly.

I nodded. Of course I had. Now I knew why money never seemed to matter to her. It was one of the blue chips. Right up there with Kennecott Copper, Anaconda and the Three M Company. I even owned a thousand shares.

"My father's chairman of the board. My brother's president. He's fifteen years older than me. I was a change-of-life baby and I always had the feeling that they were embarrassed by my arrival. Anyway, they shipped me off to all the best schools as soon as they could. Once I was five years old I wasn't around the house very much."

I thought of my own childhood and how different it had been from hers. She was right. I was lucky. I held up my hands in surrender. "Okay, baby, I'll confess. I love them very much."

"You don't have to tell me," she said. "I know you do.

You came right home when you were hurt. All my life I kept running away when I was hurt."

There was a knock on the open door. Gianno came into the room. *"La Signora* sent me to help you dress and bring you downstairs."

I straightened up in bed, smoothing the covers over my legs and smiling up at Cindy.

She knew what I was thinking. Mother had really done her number.

Dinner was more than an hour away. There was no rush to dress. But good girls don't spend too much time in Italian boys' bedrooms. It's not proper.

At dinner, I found out much to my surprise I was ravenous. Mother had really turned it on for me. The pasta was just the way I like it. *Al dente.* Cooked firm and not soft and mushy. And the sauce had everything in it. Hot sausage, sweet sausage, green peppers browned slightly first in oil, tiny meatballs blended delicately with finely chopped pork, quartered Italian tomatoes cooked into a rich red sauce with just the right touch of oregano and garlic. There was only one fault. As usual it was too sweet. It is very Sicilian to add a lot of sugar.

But I put it away like food was going out of style. I was too hungry to get finicky.

Mother looked at me proudly. "You like the sauce?"

I nodded, my mouth full. "Great!"

"She made it," my mother said. "All by herself."

I looked at Cindy wondering if I could tell her that if Mother gave her another shot at it to go easy on the sugar. Cindy's own words blew that thought to hell.

"Your mother is just being kind," she said. "All I did was to put what she handed me into the pot and stir once in a while."

I should have guessed that. "It's very good anyway," I said.

"A few weeks with me," Mother said, "and I'll make a real Sicilian cook out of her."

The pasta was better than sleeping pills. I found my eyes closing a half hour after dinner, right in the middle of my mother's favorite television show. I went up to sleep.

The next morning was Sunday and the usual routine was that the whole family, including Gianno, went to ten o'clock mass. This Sunday the routine was changed because my mother didn't want to leave me alone in the house.

Gianno went to nine o'clock mass and when he returned, my parents went to the ten o'clock. Much to my surprise when I went looking for Cindy, Gianno told me with a secret, knowing smile lurking in his eyes that she had gone to mass with them.

I went back to my room, mumbling to myself. It was then I knew I was really getting better. I was horny as hell. But Mother was operating in really top form.

I must have dozed off again, for when I opened my eyes, my father was standing over the bed, looking down at me.

He bent and kissed my forehead. "I thought if you were feeling up to it, we'd go down to my office and I'd take the bandages off."

"I'm ready," I said.

I sat, my legs dangling from the examination table, while he snipped carefully at the bandage around my head. Then, as gently as he could, he peeled the adhesive that held my nose bandage and lifted it off. He was just as cautious with the adhesive and bandage on my cheekbone, the side of my chin, and over my left ear.

He picked up a bottle and poured some of the liquid over a wad of cotton. "This is going to sting a bit," he said, "but I want to clean you up."

It was the usual professional understatement. It stung like hell. But he was quick about it. When he finished he peered at me critically.

"It's not too bad," he said judiciously. "When you have some time, you can jump over to Switzerland. Dr. Hans can make it right again without too much trouble."

I got off the table and looked at myself in the mirror over the sink on the wall. A very familiar face looked back at me.

Suddenly I felt good. I was myself again. All the time I

had the other face I had been someone else. Now my eyes didn't look old any more. They belonged to the rest of my face.

"Hello, Angelo," I whispered.

My face whispered back at me. "Hello, Angelo."

"What did you say?" my father asked.

I turned to look at him. "I'm not going back to Dr. Hans," I said. "I think I'll keep this face. It's mine."

I woke up jumpy as a cat Monday morning. And it didn't get any better. Especially after I read the morning newspapers.

It was a page-one story and picture. The photo showed a gutted mass of what used to be a building. The headline above it was simple.

MYSTERIOUS EXPLOSION AND FIRE DESTROYS
MICHIGAN AVENUE PRINT SHOP AND BUILDING

I almost didn't have to read the rest of the story to know what had happened. Shortly after midnight, last night, two violent explosions that shattered windows as far as three blocks away, followed by a flash fire of intense heat, took the Mark S. Printing Company, the IASO, and forty late-model used cars on Simp's used-car lot next door out of circulation permanently. When attempts were made to reach Mr. Mark Simpson, the proprietor of all three businesses, at home, they were informed that Mr. Simpson was away and could not be reached. Police and the fire department arson squads were conducting an investigation into the circumstances surrounding the occurrence. Fortunately there was no one on the premises and no injuries were reported.

That news didn't exactly add to my comfort. I wondered whether Uncle Jake's contacts hadn't gone a little overboard in their enthusiasm. Then I pushed the thought from my mind. If Uncle Jake didn't know what he was doing, then nobody did.

Still the jumpiness didn't leave me. It got worse and worse as the day seemed to drag on. I went upstairs and tried to sleep but my eyes wouldn't stay shut. So I went downstairs again.

I turned to a pro football game on the tube. But my head wasn't into it. I sat there staring at it blindly, smoking cigarette after cigarette. Finally I turned it off in disgust and went back upstairs and stretched out on my bed, my arms on the pillow behind my head, and stared up at the ceiling.

I heard my door open. I didn't look around. My father stood over me. I didn't speak.

"You're in no condition to get yourself all worked up like that," he said.

"I can't help it."

"Let me give you a shot so you can get some sleep," he suggested.

"No."

"Then let me give you a couple of tranquilizers. They'll calm you down."

"Let me alone, Papa."

Silently he turned and started from the room. I sat up in the bed, swinging my feet to the floor. "Papa!"

He turned, his hand on the door.

"I'm sorry, Papa."

He nodded. "That's all right, Angelo," he said and left the room.

I had no appetite for dinner and picked my way through the meal where no one talked. After dinner I went back to my room.

At eight thirty I went downstairs and sat alone in the living room. From the den I could hear the sounds coming from the television set. At eight forty-five, the telephone rang. I dove for it.

It was Donald, Number One's man. "Mr. Perino?"

"Yes," I answered, disappointed that it was not the call I expected.

"Mr. Hardeman asked me to find out if you'll be able to attend the stockholders' and board meetings tomorrow," he said.

"I'll be there," I answered.

"Thank you, I'll inform him," he said. "Good night."

"Wait a minute!" I said quickly. "Can I speak to Mr. Hardeman?"

"I'm sorry, sir," he said, "but Mr. Hardeman is already asleep. We had to make a special stop in Pensacola and have just arrived. Mr. Hardeman was very tired and went right to bed."

"All right, Donald. Thank you," I said, putting down the telephone. I didn't know how the old man did it. He had to be made of ice to be able to sleep at a time like this.

But then what was it that I had read once. General U. S. Grant used to take a nap just before every big battle. He claimed that and whiskey freshened him up for the fight.

Maybe I couldn't sleep but the whiskey didn't seem like a bad idea. I looked at my watch. Five minutes to nine. I started for the bar.

I was on my second shot at exactly nine o'clock when the front doorbell rang. I heard Gianno start for it but I beat him to the door and opened it.

A man stood there in the shadows, his hat pulled down and his coat collar up. I couldn't see his face. "Mr. Angelo Perino?"

"Yes," I answered.

"This is for you," he said, thrusting a large red manila envelope into my hand. "Compliments of the Judge!"

"Thank you," I said. But he had already gone down the steps and into a car which sped down the driveway.

I closed the door and walked slowly back into the living room, untying the flat ribbon that closed the envelope. Inside were two file folders.

I sank into the couch and opened them. The first was the letter I had asked him to get from Loren's safe. I read it quickly. It was almost word for word what Bobbie had told me. I put it back into the file and opened the other one.

This was everything I wanted and more. Names, dates, places, everything. Even photostats of the checks he received as well as his disbursements. Simpson had to be a nut for keeping records. It was either that or he had plans for blackmail at some future date. And from what I knew about him so far, it had to be the latter.

Suddenly I looked up. They were all standing there, watching me anxiously. My father, mother and Cindy. Even Gianno was in the doorway looking on.

"Was it what you wanted?" my father asked.

I broke into a smile. Suddenly the heaviness that was in the air all day was gone. I jumped up, kissed my father, kissed Cindy and began to dance my mother around. "Hey, Papa!" I said, looking over my shoulder at him. "Who says Grandfather isn't watching over us?"

My mother stopped dancing and crossed herself. "He's up there in heaven with the angels," she said solemnly. "Looking after his children."

Chapter Eleven

IT WAS IMPOSSIBLE for me to drive with my ribs still taped, so Cindy dropped me at the administration building at eight thirty in the morning. "Shall I come back for you?" she asked.

I caught my breath. It wasn't that easy getting out of a Maserati with a couple of broken ribs. "No," I said. "You go back to the hotel. I'll grab a cab and pick you up for dinner when I get through."

"Good enough," she smiled. She held out her fist in a thumbs-up gesture.

I grinned and gave it back to her and she spun off down the road. I went into the building and directly to my office. My secretary wasn't in yet, which was just as well. I sat down at her desk, put a sheet of paper in her typewriter and began knocking out a few notes.

I had just finished when she came in at ten to nine. I pulled the last note out of the machine, signed it and stuck it in my inside pocket.

"How are you feeling, Mr. Perino?" she asked. "Better?"

"Much better."

"We were all so shocked when we heard what happened," she said.

"No more than I was." I picked up my attaché case and started for the door. "I'm going to Number One's office."

"Don't forget you have the stockholders' meeting at nine o'clock."

"I won't," I said, as if I needed the reminder.

Number One had not arrived yet. "He'll be a little late," his secretary said. "He had to make one stop before he came in."

I went back to my office, had a cup of coffee and, exactly at nine o'clock, went down to the board room for the meeting. The room was crowded, they were all there. Except Number One.

Loren III rapped a gavel on the table. The conversation in the room stopped. "I have just been informed that my grandfather will be a few minutes late," he said. "While we are waiting for him, I will explain briefly a few procedural changes that have been instituted solely for the meetings today of the stockholders and the directors. These changes have been explained to my grandfather and he is in accord with them."

He paused for a moment, his eyes glancing around the table. I didn't think he recognized me at first glance because his eyes came back for a flash second look, then went on, but I couldn't be sure.

"Both stockholders and directors have been invited to attend both meetings," he said. "At the stockholders' meeting, those directors who are not stockholders will retire from the table to the seats provided for them around the room. Seated at the table with the direct stockholders will also be those trustees of the Hardeman Foundation who will today vote the stock in the company held by the Foundation. I would like to introduce to the general company those trustees of the Foundation present other than myself."

He paused for a moment. "My sister, the Princess Anne Elizabeth Alekhine."

Anne, looking every bit the princess in a chic, tailored

Parisian suit, nodded regally, then sat back in her place
at her brother's right hand.

"I might also add," Loren said, "that my sister will also
vote the stock she holds in the company in her own
name."

He gestured with his hand. "Seated on her right is Dr.
James Randolph, executive director of the Foundation,
and on his right, Professor William Mueller, administrative
director of the Foundation. Stockholders will also be entitled to have legal counsel seated next to them at the
table if they should so desire. Such counsel will not have
the right to address any stockholder directly other than
his own client or clients."

He paused again for a moment. "For the board of
directors' meeting, the exact opposite will hold. That is,
those stockholders who are not directors of the company
will retire from the table so that the directors may proceed
without delay and interference to the business of the company for which the meeting has been called.

"If the nonstockholding directors will now retire from
the table, we will be able to proceed with the stockholders'
meeting as soon as my grandfather arrives."

A shuffling sound rose in the room as the crowd rear-
ranged themselves. When it died down, there were only
five of us left at the table: Loren III, Anne, the two
Foundation trustees and myself.

I sat alone at the opposite end of the table from them.
Loren looked at me but didn't speak. There were a thousand yards of open battlefield between us. A low hum rose
from the other seats around the room. I couldn't help but
feel that we were like gladiators in an ancient Roman
arena.

Silence fell abruptly across the room as the door began
to open. Number One came through first, his arms pushing
the wheelchair over the threshold vigorously. Behind him
came Alicia, a tall, gray-haired, striking woman whom I
did not know, and Artie Roberts.

Number One paused for a second, looking around the
room, then propelled his chair to the table. Artie pulled a
chair away so that the wheelchair would have a place

Number One gestured to the women and they took seats at the table next to him. Artie sat down in the chair directly behind Number One.

Loren III's face was pale as he stared angrily at his grandfather. Anne got to her feet quickly and came down the table toward Number One. Reluctantly, Loren followed her.

Anne stopped at the gray-haired woman and kissed her warmly on the cheek. The surprise was clear in her voice. "Mother! I didn't expect to see you. You should have let us know you were coming!"

Now I knew who the striking lady was. Admiral Hugh Scott's wife. No wonder Loren III was so angry at his grandfather. Bringing to the meeting both his mother and his ex-wife.

Anne greeted Alicia with a peck on the cheek and a "Nice to see you again," pecked Number One on the cheek silently, then made her way back to her seat.

Loren was much more reserved. He kissed his mother's cheek politely, nodded silently to Alicia, ignored his grandfather and went back to his seat.

He picked up the gavel and rapped smartly on the table. "The meeting of the stockholders of the Bethlehem Motors Company, Incorporated, is hereby called to order." He glanced down at his grandfather. "Before we commence the business before this meeting, the chair questions the right and propriety of the seating of Mrs. Scott and the former Mrs. Hardeman at this meeting. It is the contention of the chair that they have no interest, proprietary or otherwise, in this company that would permit their seating, since the chair already holds the proxy of Mrs. Hardeman to vote at its discretion and Mrs. Scott has no interest whatsoever in this company that the chair is aware of."

Artie leaned forward, putting a paper in Alicia's hand and whispering in her ear. She nodded and rose to her feet. "Mr. Chairman!"

"Yes, Mrs. Hardeman," Loren answered formally.

With Artie whispering behind her, Alicia spoke in a thin, clear voice. "I beg to submit, for the consideration of the chair, this notice of revocation by me of the proxy

previously given it and the return to me of the voting
privileges contained therein." She placed the paper on the
table, pushing it toward her former husband, and sat
down.

Loren picked up the paper and looked at it. He turned
and handed it to Dan Weyman, sitting behind him, who
passed it on in turn to the company counsel. Loren began
to speak without waiting. "It seems to me that this revocation is illegal and contrary to a contracted agreement and
is therefore invalid at this meeting."

Artie leaned forward and whispered rapidly into Alicia's
ear. Alicia leaned forward; this time she did not get up.
"This stockholder is willing to agree to an adjournment of
this meeting until the question is settled in court. It would
seem to me that the rights of this stockholder to vote her
own stock are no less valid than the right claimed by the
chair for the Foundation under similar circumstances on
which a judgment has already been rendered and accepted
by all parties concerned."

Loren turned in his chair and whispered to the company
counsel. After a moment, he turned back. He shrugged his
shoulders contemptuously. It was only five percent. He
still held a clear majority, with the inclusion of the
Foundation stock. Fifty-four percent. "The chair will con-
cede the revocation," he said. "But the chair still objects
to the presence of Mrs. Scott."

This time Number One threw a sheet of paper on the
table. "In accordance with the right given to me in the
articles of incorporation of the Hardeman Foundation
whereby I have the right to designate my successor as a
trustee of the Foundation should I retire from that position, I now do so. You will find on that sheet of paper my
formal resignation as trustee of the Foundation and my
designation of Mrs. Sally Scott as my successor trustee."

Loren picked up the paper and handed it to the executive director of the Foundation. The man read it quickly
and nodded. Loren turned back to the table. "The Foundation recognizes Mrs. Scott as trustee and the chair wel-
comes her personally to this table."

Mrs. Scott smiled. "Thank you, Loren."

He nodded. After all, it was no skin off his teeth. He still held four of the five trustee votes. "Now, can we proceed to the business at hand?" he asked sarcastically.

Number One nodded pleasantly. "I guess we can do that, son."

Loren glanced around the table to a chorus of nods until he came to me. I shook my head. He stopped.

"Mr. Chairman," I said.

"Yes, Mr. Perino," he replied.

"Before we come to the proper business of this meeting, would it be at all possible to have a private meeting of only those stockholders who have personal equities in the company, and members, past or present, of the Hardeman family?"

Even Number One looked at me curiously now.

Loren was puzzled. "That's a very strange request, Mr. Perino."

"In view of certain information I have available, Mr. Chairman," I said calmly, "I think it is a reasonable one. Since the information I have concerns members of the Hardeman family personally, I see no point in airing it publicly."

"Would it be possible for the chair to see this so-called information you have so it may better evaluate the propriety of your request?"

"I have no objections," I said, opening my attaché case. I took out the two file folders and separated the originals from the Xerox copies I had made early that morning. I gave them to him.

He looked down at them for several seconds, his face running the gamut of colors from angry red to deathly pale. Finally, he looked up at me with stricken eyes. "I won't be blackmailed!" he said hoarsely. "What I did was for the good of the company!"

"Let me see them," Number One said.

Angrily Loren flung them on the table in front of his grandfather. Number One picked them up and read them. After a few minutes, he looked at me. I saw a tremendous hurting pain in his eyes and I felt sorry for him. It was still his own flesh and blood.

Slowly he looked around the room. "I think we'd better talk this over privately in my office," he said in a weary voice.

And that was the end of the stockholders' meeting.

Chapter Twelve

"I THINK we're entitled to know how you came by this information," Number One asked me in a level voice from behind his desk.

"Last night, at nine o'clock, a man came to my door and asked if I was Angelo Perino. I answered in the affirmative. 'This is for you,' he said, putting the papers in my hand, and he disappeared." It was the truth, not all of it, but enough to answer his question.

"Did you know the man, ever see him before?" he asked.

I shook my head. "No."

"You say this letter is supposedly a suicide note left by my late son?" His voice held a faint tremor.

"Goddamnit, Grandfather!" Loren III suddenly exploded. "You know damn well it is. You recognize his handwriting! Or maybe because he was writing about you you don't want to recognize it?" He took a deep breath. "How Angelo got that letter I don't know, but for all the years since my father died I kept that copy locked away in my safe! So that the world would never find out that you were son-of-a-bitch enough to drive your son to suicide!"

He began to cry. "Oh, God, how I hated you for it! Every time I thought of my father lying there on the cold library floor, his head blown off, his brains staining the carpet, I hated you more. But even then I couldn't believe it. I also remembered when I was little how you used to play with us. But then when you started with the Betsy, it all came back. You were acting to me exactly as you had acted toward my father. But I made up my mind. You weren't going to do to me what you did to him. I would destroy you first!" He sank into a chair and covered his face with his hands.

"Is that what you believe I did to your father?" Number One asked in a quiet voice.

Loren III had regained control of himself. He looked at his grandfather. "What else is there for me to believe? I know what happened to him. I read the letter in which he accused you in everything but name. And I know how you acted toward me."

Number One's voice was still quiet. "Did you ever stop to think that your father might have meant someone else?"

"Who else could it be but you?" Loren charged.

Number One looked across the room at Mrs. Scott. "Truth will out," he said heavily. "If you live long enough it all catches up with you."

She looked at him, then at her son, the same warm compassion in her eyes for the two of them. Finally she spoke. "Your grandfather is telling the truth, Loren," she said. "Your father wasn't writing about him in that note."

"You're only saying that to defend him!" Loren accused. "I've heard the stories about you and him, Mother. And I know how you felt about him. I remember that too when I was a little boy."

"Loren," Mrs. Scott said. "Your—"

"Sally!" Number One said sharply. "Let me tell him!"

Mrs. Scott ignored him. "Loren, your father was a homosexual. For several years he had an affair with a man who worked for him, Joe Warren. Joe Warren was a sick, terrible, perverted man and after his death we thought it was all buried with him. But it wasn't.

"It seemed that Warren had made a careful pictorial record of their relationship and it fell into the hands of an equally unscrupulous man. For years this man bled your father until he could no longer stand it. We were as shocked as you were at the news of his suicide and at a loss to understand it.

"But your father's death did not end the man's greed. He then came to your grandfather. I remember talking to your grandfather at that time. The only good thing about it, he told me, was that the blackmailer came to him and not to you. This way you would never have to learn about your father.

"Your grandfather saw that the blackmailer went to jail and that all the pictures were destroyed. It cost your grandfather a fortune to keep it quiet. And he did it not so much for himself, but to keep you and your sister from hurt. Despite everything that had happened, you see, he still loved his son and wanted to protect your father's memory."

Loren III looked at her, then at his grandfather. "Is that true?"

Number One nodded slowly.

Loren III put his head in his hands. I looked around the room. I was the only outsider. They were all Hardemans, past or present.

The telephone began to ring. Number One ignored it. It continued to ring with demanding persistence. Finally, he picked it up. "Yes?" he snapped impatiently. He listened a moment, then beckoned to Alicia. "It's for you."

Alicia, still dabbing the tears with a handkerchief, crossed the room. Standing next to Loren III's chair, she took the phone from Number One. "Yes," she said into it. "This is Mrs. Alicia Hardeman."

An excited voice crackled into the room from the receiver. "Yes," she said. "Yes, yes. Give them both my love." Slowly she put down the telephone.

She turned to Loren III. "Loren," she said.

He looked up at her with a drawn face. "Yes, Alicia," he said in a dead voice. "I really made a mess of it. In every way I could."

"No, Loren," she said. "That's not what I'm talking about. That was Max on the telephone."

"Max?" he repeated dully.

"Yes!" she said, suddenly excited. "Max. Our daughter's husband. He called from Switzerland. Betsy just had a baby boy! They're both fine!" A sudden awe came into her voice. "My God, Loren, think of it! We're grandparents!"

And suddenly too, they were a family again. All kissing and crying and laughing.

I walked out and down the hall to my office. For a moment there, I was becoming convinced the whole world was Italian.

Half an hour later, my office door opened and Number One rolled his chair inside. He pushed the door shut and sat there looking at me.

I watched him.

After a moment, he spoke. "You fucked up," he said. "You're fired!"

"I know," I said. "I knew that coming in this morning." I took my resignation from my inside pocket and got out of my chair. I walked over and gave it to him.

He opened and read it quickly, then glanced shrewdly at me. "By God, you did know!"

I nodded.

"Do you know why?" he asked.

"I know that too," I said.

"Tell me."

"I wasn't supposed to win," I said. "I know I was supposed to lose."

"That's right," he said in grim agreement. "I lost a son and I didn't want to lose Loren. But if you knew you were supposed to let him win, why didn't you let him?"

"Because there was no way I could do it," I said. "Even if I tried, I couldn't give in to him. It was my track all the way."

"No hard feelings?"

"No hard feelings."

Again he peered up at me. "You didn't do so bad. That stock you own will be worth twelve million dollars when we go public next year."

"Sure," I said. I stuck my hand in my pocket. "I have something of yours." I put the gold Sundancer cuff links in his hand.

He looked down at them. "You fucked me on the Sundancer too," he said. "Why did you change the name of the Betsy Jetstar back to Sundancer?"

"Because it was too good a car for too many years to let it go like that."

He thought for a moment. Then he nodded. "Maybe you're right." Carefully he took the cuff links from his shirt and replaced them with the Sundancers. He dropped the others into his jacket. Then he looked up at me again. "Maybe you're right," he repeated.

I held the door for him while he pushed his chair through, then I let it shut and went back and began to clean out my desk.

Cindy was at the door when I let myself into the apartment. "I plugged in your portable Jacuzzi and filled the tub with your favorite bubble bath."

I kissed the tip of her nose. "I can use it."

She followed me through the apartment into the bathroom and stood there taking my clothes from me while I undressed. "It was on the radio beginning with the noon-time news," she said.

"This is the place. Automobile news travels fast."

I put my hands on the wall to brace myself. Getting down in the tub wasn't going to be easy with my ribs all taped up. "You better help me," I said.

She put an arm under my shoulders and I started to ease myself down into the water.

"You got some calls," she said.

"Anything important?" I asked, my ass just about touching the surface of the water.

"Nope," she said nonchalantly. "Just Iacocca of Ford, Cole of General Motors—"

"You're full of shit," I said, looking up at her.

"I am not!" she said indignantly. She pulled her arm out from behind my shoulders.

I went the rest of the way with a jarring thump. "Oh, Christ!" I yelled.

She was out of the bathroom and back in a moment with a batch of telephone messages for me. "See! I was telling the truth. Also Chrysler, also American Motors. Even one from Fiat in Italy!"

I switched on the Jacuzzi. The water began to churn

and sing its soothing song. I leaned my head back against the wall behind the tub and sighed. It felt good.

"What do you want me to do with these?" she asked, waving the fistful of messages at me.

"Leave them on the table. I'm not that crazy about going back to work in a hurry. It interferes with my being rich."

The doorbell rang.

"Go see who's there," I said.

She left tossing her head and was back in a moment, slightly subdued. "It's Number One to see you."

I looked at her. "Send him in."

"Here?" she asked.

"Where else?" I retorted. "You don't think I can make it out of this tub in less than a half an hour, do you?"

She left the bathroom and came back, pushing him through the door. Then she walked away again.

"Jesus, it's hot in here," he said, looking after her. "Who's the doxie?"

"Cindy." I saw the blank expression on his face. "You know, the test driver."

"I didn't recognize her," he said. "She looks different somehow."

"I think she just discovered dresses," I said.

"For Christ's sake, do you have to keep that damn thing on?" he shouted. "I'm busting my lungs yelling over it."

I flicked off the switch. The sound faded. "That better?"

"Much better." He peered at me. "You look different too."

I smiled. "I got my own face back."

"I was on my way to the airport when I remembered I had something of yours," he said. "So I stopped off to give it to you."

"Yeah?" I couldn't think of anything of mine that he might possibly have.

He stuck his hand in his pocket and came out with a small jewelry box. He opened it and gave it to me.

They were platinum cuff links. The Betsy Silver Sprite. I stared at them. Whoever had made them hadn't missed a single detail of the car. They were beautiful. And I never wear cuff links. I pushed them back toward him. "They're not mine, they're yours."

He didn't take them. "They're ours," he said. "But they're more yours than mine. You keep them!"

He pulled the chair back through the doorway and turned it around. "Young lady!" he yelled. "Help me get out of here!"

Still looking at the tiny Silver Sprites I turned the Jacuzzi back on. They were beautiful. Now I would have to buy some shirts with French cuffs to go with them.

I came out of the tub, wrapping the towel around my waist, still looking at the Silver Sprite cuff links. "Cindy, look at these."

"They're beautiful," she said. She looked at me. "You're beautiful too. You know, I never really liked your other face."

"I didn't either," I said.

"How are you feeling?" She had that familiar, lovely look in her eyes.

"Horny as hell," I said, taking her hand. "Come on into the bedroom and let's fuck."

"Okay," she said.

We walked into the bedroom. I looked around. "Something's different," I said, as she wiggled out of her dress. Then I had it. "Where'd you hide the stereo, under the bed?"

"I threw it out," she said, walking naked into my arms. "Everybody, even a girl, has to grow up sometime."

"Isn't it kind of sudden?" I asked, chewing on the lobe of her ear.

"Not really," she answered. "I'm twenty-four."

"That's pretty old," I said, beginning to work on her neck.

"That's just right," she said. Abruptly she turned her head and looked into my eyes. "Besides you don't really need stereo."

"Sure?" I asked, kissing her lightly on the lips.

She caught my face in her hands. Her eyes were large and dark. "Absolutely sure," she said. "I love you."

I was very still for a moment, then I knew it too. "And I love you."

Then we kissed. She was absolutely right. We didn't need the stereo.

We both heard the music.

HAROLD ROBBINS

25,000 People a Day Buy His Novels.

Are You One of Them?

_____ 81150 THE CARPETBAGGERS $2.50

_____ 81151 THE BETSY $2.50

_____ 81152 THE PIRATE $2.50

_____ 81142 THE DREAM MERCHANTS $2.50

_____ 81153 THE ADVENTURERS $2.50

_____ 81154 WHERE LOVE HAS GONE $2.50

_____ 81155 A STONE FOR DANNY FISHER $2.50

_____ 81156 NEVER LOVE A STRANGER $2.50

_____ 81157 79 PARK AVENUE $2.50

_____ 81158 THE INHERITORS $2.50

Available at bookstores everywhere, or order direct from the publisher.